The Family

The Family

SHADES OF LIGHT AND DARKNESS

APRIL MCKAIG

To order additional copies of this book, contact:
Xlibris
1-888-795-4274
www.Xlibris.com
Orders@Xlibris.com
808918

Dedicated to: My Mom who said I can,
My wife who said you should,
And to God who said you shall.

1

A huge wall of glass faced out over the city, giving the impression to anyone on the street that the occupant was floating in midair. Five o'clock was churning into six, and street traffic was slowly thinning as people rushed home for dinner, arguments, lovemaking, or partying.

The latter was normally the concern of the figure staring through the glass wall, especially on a Friday night. The events of the last few months had changed that. She let her eyes scan the city, taking in the shadows and light. Only one thought was at the center of her mind, of her very being. The Queen. Where was she? Why had all the forces at her disposal not been able to locate even a clue to her whereabouts? Was she even alive after all these months?

Immediately she scolded herself for the doubt that crept in. Of course Regina was alive, likely a prisoner somewhere, but still alive. She was sure of it, had to believe it.

Whoever had taken Regina wouldn't kill her, so she was being used to break down her forces. But what was she enduring after all this time. Sigrid closed off her thoughts, not wanting to let her mind consider the implication. Instead she concentrated on the setting sun. Although the sun was still visible, she could feel the power of the night steadily overtaking its bright sibling.

It was a power that brought her kind to a surging ecstasy. She closed her eyes, trying to savor the sweet smell, taste, and sounds of the coming darkness. Tonight it eluded her, and after a few minutes, she gave up. With each passing day, not even the sacred night could ease the growing tension and fear that was encasing her.

Sigrid Derrick was not a woman who frightened easily, especially after the last ten years. Although not an imposing figure, she could cause others to cower in fear with a mere thought or look. In her high school yearbook, she was described as quiet, intelligent, and with a great business sense who would do great things. If only they had known how dull and hellish her personal life was. She had friends but stayed to herself and never let anyone too close.

Ten years ago that had changed with one chance meeting. A meeting that turned her world upside down and led to her becoming senior vice president of one of the most successful and largest companies in the world.

Fabrick Industries dealt in everything from computers, clothing, art, and even nightclubs. In business, it was one of the top ten companies in the world, and she was one of the most powerful women in the field. At this moment she felt the most powerless.

Her thoughts were interrupted by a soft brushing sound in the far corner of the room. To anyone else it was a sound that would be imperceptible, but to her heightened senses it was as loud as a creaking floor.

Holding her place, she waited for the next sound. It came, the sound of soft steps on the carpet, moving closer to her. Sighing deeply, she let her shoulders slump as if lost in thought. He crept closer, and she could smell the fear and excitement as well as his next movement.

Thinking she was so lost in thought he had the advantage, he rushed her, moving at twice the speed of a normal man. He tried to stop when she turned to face him, eyes red and fangs bared.

Losing his footing on the carpet, he slid down to one knee, his right hand still raised and clutching the silver dagger meant for her heart. Her hand shot out and caught the offending limb and crushed his wrist to powder. With her other hand she seized his throat in a choke hold. He yelled out in pain, dropping the dagger to the ground. He tried to push himself up, ready to use his good hand to destroy the bitch before him. She scooped up the blade and brought it to her face for a closer look.

The handle was made of steel, wood, and leather. The blade itself was a good eight inches and had a delicate and intricate design etched into the silver. He stilled when she sighed and aimed the point of the blade at his eye. Using her foot, she shoved him back to the kneeling position and then dropped the blade down to his heart.

"You must be newborn to think you could sneak up on me and take me out. Terrence must be getting desperate." The man before her was young, probably in his twenties, wearing all black, and had his long red hair in a ponytail.

He tried to man up. "When I fail, another will take my place.' His voice was edged with pain and fear. "You will die. The Master has foreseen it."

"Your Master is full of shit, and it won't be that easy to kill me." She offered him a smile that disappeared just as suddenly when she leaned down within a few inches of his face. "You can still survive this, boy." When she knew she had his full attention, she softly asked, "Where is she?"

Now he smiled. "I wouldn't tell you even if I knew."

"Last chance."

He squeezed out a laugh, and then she snapped his neck, finishing up by plunging the dagger into his heart. As if she was holding something foul, she opened her hands and let the body fall to the floor.

Taking a step away from the body, she released the scream that had been building for weeks.

Ty shoved the door open, gun drawn, and rushed in. He took in the scene and could guess what had happened and why Sigrid had screamed. "You okay?"

"No," she answered sharply and walked over to the bar in the opposite corner. The house wine was waiting, and she filled the glass and drank it down as she was dying of thirst.

Ty holstered his gun and went to the prone body on the floor. He did a quick search of the man's pockets and jacket and found nothing. Standing he moved over to the phone on her desk. He watched her moving around the room like a caged cat and dialed security. After a moment, he simply said "We have a cleanup in the penthouse" then replaced the receiver.

Holding his place, he knew she would speak when ready, but at the moment, her anger and frustration were almost overwhelming her. She calmed her pacing, slowed, and she came to rest at her desk, sitting on the corner facing him.

"What can I do?" he asked.

"We'll be opening soon," she replied. Looking at the casually dressed, tall, muscular man before her, her heart melted. She stood up and moved to stand face-to-face with him. Her eyes reflected exhaustion. "I'm not okay."

He took her in his arms. She was a full foot shorter than his six-foot-four frame, but she was a perfect fit for his arms. "I have to get out of here and do something. I thought work might ease my mind, but if I stay here any longer, I'll go crazy."

Holding her tighter, he felt her relax and cling to him. As one of the few people she truly trusted in the world, he knew that she was in pain to reveal this much of herself. Sigrid was always the strong one, the one you went to for comfort or help. He wanted to take the pain away but could only hold her and offer her the safety of his arms.

"What do you want to do?"

Reluctantly she pulled away from him and instantly regained the cool, controlled pose that was the norm. "Call Patrick," she instructed methodically, her mind working rapidly on the plans. "Tell him we're leaving on business and he is in charge of the club until we return. Then call Garrett. Tell him we're leaving tonight and we'll be there in a day or so. Then get the bikes and our equipment ready."

"By bike?" he interrupted with surprise. "Is that safe? You are a target now as well." He cast a glance at the dead thug on her office floor.

She smiled weakly and took his large, strong hands into her soft, delicate ones. "I know that, Ty, but I need to clear my head, and riding the bike does that. Besides, I'll be safer on the move with you than a plane, train, or car. Garrett will argue but tell him we'll take a safe route and stop at friends on the way to check in."

His dark brown eyes radiated worry, but to argue with her was useless when she was determined. After considering her plan for a moment, he realized she was probably right. "All right. It'll take me about two hours to get everything ready. We can head out around ten."

She walked back into his arms and kissed his cheek. When they pulled away, she whispered, "Thank you, love." She turned and returned to the glass wall. He watched her for another moment and then walked out of the office.

"Hold on, my Queen," she whispered to the night, "I will find you, and soon."

Coming of The Shadows

Ten Years Earlier

By ten after five on a workday, Downtown Atlanta was bumper to bumper. Irate drivers blew their horns, and a few choice obscenities floated on the fall air. The sidewalks lining Peachtree Street SW were filled with pedestrians. Those who lived in Atlanta long enough knew to take a bus, MARTA, or park far enough away to avoid the most congested areas. Then there were those that liked to get in the exercise, especially in the early October crispness.

Justine Reynard enjoyed walking, was only a few blocks from her place of employment, and kept up the brisk pace set by the work crowd. She spotted the familiar awning coming up on her right and with the grace of a dancer worked her way through the awkward sidewalk traffic.

The lettering on the door always made her smile with pride: Cameron Reynard and Associates, CPA. She pushed the door open and strolled into the office.

Nancy Higgins, the elderly white-haired receptionist was heading for the door. "Hello, Justine. He's in the back." She offered a smile and kept on walking, disappearing into the throng outside.

Quietly she walked past the front desk and through the doorway that led to the office hallway. Cameron's office was at the end of the hall, and she found him hunched over his desk, intently working on a ledger. He was a heartbreaker with a six-foot-three football player's frame. It was complemented by thick, curly blond hair, light-brown eyes, a great mind, and winning personality.

Justine was his physical opposite. Five-five, a few pounds overweight, with dark brown hair and ice-blue eyes. When they were out together, people often assumed they were husband and wife, and depending on their mood, they sometimes played along, like children playing dress up.

"Quitting time!" Justine shouted suddenly, ending the peaceful silence of the office.

Cameron dropped his pencil and looked up frowning. When he saw who the interruption was, the frown was replaced with a smile. "Hi, Tine. Must you always make that kind of entrance?"

She skipped over to his desk and kissed his cheek, "Of course I do. Happy early birthday, big brother."

"Thanks, but you didn't come all the way down here just to wish me a happy birthday, did you?" he asked in a serious tone.

Justine looked up at the ceiling, shaking her head, and he, too, looked up. "Nope." Then he followed her gaze down to the top of his desk where a small black box with a red ribbon had appeared. He shook his head. "You know I hate that sleight of hand junk."

"Open it," she ordered firmly but with a grin.

He picked it up and looked at it for a minute. As children, Justine had always ripped right into gifts. Cameron, on the other hand, took his own sweet time, a habit that still annoyed Justine.

"Don't make me help you," she warned impatiently.

Cameron winked at her and opened the box. Inside was a sparkling gold ring with a large onyx stone. A diamond sparkled in each corner of the stone, and the gold initials *CR* curved into one another across the center of the stone. "Oh, Tine," he whispered, "it's fantastic. I love it." He took the ring out of the box and slowly slipped it on his right ring finger. "Perfect fit."

"For the perfect brother," she returned, her face glowing with delight. It had taken her over three weeks to find a man that did this kind of custom work and was pleased to see he truly liked the gift.

Cameron stood up and walked around the desk and hugged her tightly. "Thank you, but you shouldn't have. It is the best gift I've ever gotten. Only one other thing would be more perfect."

Justine laughed. "Oh yeah. What?"

He hesitated, then said, "Dad's having a birthday dinner tomorrow night and I . . ."

"No," she interrupted firmly and pulled away from his embrace. "Forget it, Cam! No way in hell!" she finished, her blue eyes flashing with anger.

Cameron mustered his best calming voice before he spoke again. "Tine, please. You haven't seen him in two years. Do this for me."

"Bet he hasn't changed a bit in two years," she answered defensively. "Cam, if you love me, you won't ask me to do this. His days of cutting me to pieces are over."

Cameron decided to drop it. Justine and their father, Seth Reynard, had always been at odds, especially after their mother's death. On numerous occasions he had tried to patch them together, but it always ended in an argument. Nothing his sister did was ever right, and Seth was always on her about something. The minute she turned seventeen, she was out of the house and making it on her own. Now at twenty-eight years old she was part owner and manager of one of the hottest nightclubs on the East Coast.

Despite her success, Seth Reynard still treated her like the proverbial redheaded stepchild. Even as adults whenever they got together there was always a disagreement usually started by Seth making a comment and nitpicking.

It hurt his heart to see his sister this upset. "I'm sorry. I didn't mean to upset you." He sighed.

Justine took a deep breath and calmed down. "It's okay, I didn't mean to blow up at you. Look at us. Even when he's not here, the old man causes problems."

Cameron nodded agreement and then caught a glance of the wall clock. "Hey, it's not that I want to get rid of you or anything, but aren't you going to be late for the club?"

Justine shook her head. "Nope. We're closed to the public tonight. We have been reserved for a private event."

"Oh," he said in a mixture of mock and real surprise. "Now you're doing private events. Well, aren't you just the queen bee."

Playfully she slapped his arm. "Yes, I am."

Cameron reached to smack her, but she easily sidestepped his aim. "You're getting old, Cam."

He sighed and sat down on the edge of his desk. "Yes, I am, so respect your elders. So who's the event for?"

"Zora has a new show starting tomorrow night at the gallery, some bigshot artist. She wouldn't tell me who, just that she wanted to throw a 'Welcome to Atlanta, Good Luck' reception. She wanted the best place in town and called me."

Cameron nodded. "Wow. Must be a big shot if Zora's going to that kind of expense."

"Atlanta is a very hot spot. We got celebrities, film studios, rappers, you name it, plus the international airport. I don't know who the artist is, just that the clientele is very wealthy. Zora is sparing no expense because of who it is, and that translates to good for me and the club," Justine answered with a shrug.

"Money does make the world go around."

"Thank goodness," she joked and planted a kiss on Cameron's cheek. "I do need to go though and make sure things are ready. Happy birthday, big brother."

He stood up and winked at her. "Thank you, little sister." Putting their arms around one another, he walked her to the door.

Music pulsated in the air of City Lights. Wealthy art patrons drank, danced, and talked business deals and art.

City Lights was a very prestigious upper-class dance club in the high-rise section of Atlanta. It was decorated simply but elegantly. The carpeting and furniture were done in colors of soft blue and burgundy. Mirrors lined the walls around the dance floor and bar. Tables of glass and brass were stationed around the dance floor and glass and brass bar. A few two-seat booths were stationed farther away from the dance floor for those that wanted more privacy and the ability to hear. The dance floor was polished to a shine and strobe and stage lights brought a smoky, mysterious atmosphere to the dancers. Brass lanterns and candleholders offered light throughout, and wait staff dressed in black slacks and burgundy button downs covered the floor.

Justine stood watching the party from the top of the stairs. The entrance to the stairs was located behind the bar and curved around most of the top of the building. Behind her was her office, an extra storeroom, and the apartment she was using. She smiled as she saw her staff scurrying around making sure that no glass or snack tray was empty. They made special efforts to see that all the guests were taken care of, just as Justine had instructed them. "Time to mingle," she said under her breath and descended the stairs.

Walking around the club, she fit in well with the crowd, smiling and speaking casually. She noticed the wealthy blue-blooded crowd, dressed in conservative evening wear. In another corner she saw the upscale modern couples, dressed in their breezy, neutral-colored suits. The group that made up the remainder of the partygoers was the artsy punk crowd, dressed in black, looking morose, and staring at the others with dead, unseeing eyes.

Justine was dressed in a low-cut black jumpsuit and white dress jacket. She didn't fit in with any particular group but could easily associate with them. Bored of socializing, she headed to the bar to people watch. Steve Burke, the bartender for the last four years, smiled as she approached.

"Hello, boss. The usual?"

There was always an empty stool in the farthest corner of the bar, and it was there Justine situated herself. "Please."

He winked and went to the other end of the bar. While Justine waited, she heard a commotion at the door. She was about to investigate when she heard the excited clapping and people moving toward the front door. She caught a glimpse of Zora rushing to the door and assumed that the guest of honor had just arrived. With a subtle signal, Justine let the staff know to be on their toes just as Steve brought her drink. Both watched the crowd and servers as they talked in between orders.

The applause ceased after a few minutes, and the crowd resumed their partying with a little extra zing. Twenty minutes later when the crowd has settled into a dull roar, Zora Oliver buzzed to the bar.

Zora was a tall, thin, fairly attractive woman who had been born wealthy. She was friendly, intelligent, and outgoing with a remarkable business sense. Zora and Justine had met in high school and despite different personalities and upbringings had become friends. They had even shared a dorm room their first two years of college.

"Justine," Zora squealed as she settled on the stool next to the shorter woman. "This party is to die for. You and your staff have done a superb job. I knew I could count on you."

"Thank you, Zora. I'm glad you're enjoying it." She almost had to shout to be heard over the music and chatter.

Zora talked constantly, and Justine had wondered if she talked in her sleep. When they roomed together, she found out the answer to that question was yes. "Have you had a chance to meet our guest of honor? You really must meet her. She is the most interesting woman, and it's a real coup to have her in Atlanta."

"No, I haven't met her," Justine managed to say as Zora took a breath before starting again.

"You know, it really is an honor to have her here. She's a wonderful artist, but that's only the tip of the iceberg with this lady's talent. Thanks to you and this wonderful party, we've shown her that the South can compete with New York, Los Angeles, and any of those big cities."

Justine had known Zora long enough to know when she could get a word in. "I'm glad to help. By the way, you never told me who the guest of honor is."

Zora rolled her eyes and laughed. "Oh, darling, I didn't tell you? Her showing was kept such a secret and she is so fiercely protective of her privacy that I don't think I even told the owner of the gallery. Her name is Regina Derrick. Artist, businesswoman, entrepreneur, you name it, she's got a hand in it."

Justine's interest in artists was rarely stirred, but this was different. Regina Derrick was a well-known name in the business community. She had built her fortune with shrewd business dealings that even awed the deep pockets of Wall Street. Her business savvy was so well known and respected that she had been written up in several prominent financial magazines. Her talents were well known, but as Zora had said, her privacy was paramount to her.

"I would like to meet her," she finally acknowledged.

Zora started to take flight from the bar. "Wonderful. I'll go find her."

Justine lightly grasped Zora's arm. "Whoa, Z. She just got here, let her enjoy the party. I've got to go to the office in a little while, and I imagine Ms. Derrick will need a breather later, so just bring her up there."

"Fantastic idea," she agreed. "You are always thinking on your feet. Ciao." With a wave of her hand she drifted back into the crowd.

Across the room, Regina Derrick watched the conversation. Her entourage of two made sure she was left alone as she watched from the shadows, interest apparent. Ward, her bodyguard, used his massive, muscular form to keep her from view, and Garrett, her assistant and manager, a tall, slender middle-aged man, was the backup. He casually intercepted anyone who came too close and directed their attention elsewhere.

Regina's voice was strong but soothing, almost hypnotizing as she spoke, "Ward, ask her to dance or try to start a conversation. I have to see her more clearly. Meanwhile, I'll find Zora and try to arrange a close-up meeting and find the Reynard woman." The two men nodded their understanding, and all went in different directions.

Justine was making her way back to the staircase when she noticed him. He was over six feet tall, muscular but not muscle bound, dressed in a skin-tight black silk suit. His shoulder-length blond hair shone under the lights, and his face was chiseled, strong but warm and welcoming.

"Excuse me." He smiled as he walked up to her. "Do you work here?"

"I'm the manager as a matter of fact. How can I help you?"

His glittery green eyes locked on hers. "I just wanted to tell you what a beautiful place you have and see if you might honor me with a dance."

"Thank you, no," she answered with ever-so-slight hesitation, dazzled by those green eyes.

He put his hand to his chest and sighed. "Just my luck. The boss gives me a few hours off, I get the chance to meet and possibly dance with the most beautiful woman I've ever seen, and she says no."

Justine returned his smile. His approach was different, and she liked it and his green eyes. "Well, I'm sorry to ruin your night."

He reached out to take her hand. "My name is Ward, and you could never ruin anyone's night."

She reconsidered and accepted his offered hand. When they joined hands, there was a spark, and she followed him out onto the dance floor. As if on cue, a slow song filled the speaker system, and they danced, close but not too close. The mutual attraction was obvious, and they moved in unison, swaying to the music.

"Not only beautiful, but with the grace of an angel," he whispered in her ear.

Justine blushed. "Are you flirting with me?"

"Do you mind if I am?" he asked honestly.

"No, I'm just not used to it. Besides, I don't even know you. You could be an ax murderer for all I know." The aroma of his cologne was washing over her, and she felt a tingle in her toes.

"Nope, not an ax murderer. I just break legs," he stated and watched for her reaction. She tensed and pulled away from him. "Excuse me?"

"I'm Regina Derrick's bodyguard."

She held her ground, still cautious. "Then why aren't you guarding her?"

He smiled and extended his hand to continue the dance. "I'm more of an assistant and bodyguard. She feels comfortable and safe here, so she told me to take a few hours off to enjoy the party."

Justine took his hand, and they began the slow swaying movement to the music. "I'm glad to hear that." He twirled her around and then pulled her in close. She wasn't as relaxed as before, but she was enjoying the way he moved and the feel of his heartbeat.

Regina had settled in a darkened corner where she had a good view of the dance floor. She observed the couple dancing, especially the woman. Garrett approached and brought her out of her daze. "What is it?"

For the first time in his life he heard his mistress stumble with her words. "S-she looks like, b-but that can't be. It's not possible." She looked up at him. "Don't you see it, Garrett?"

Garrett stared at the couple with uncertainty. He closely inspected the woman Ward was dancing with. "Regina, what is it? What's wrong?" he asked, truly concerned now.

"Val," she answered simply.

Suddenly it came to him, and she was right. Taking a second look, he could see the uncanny resemblance and was ashamed he hadn't seen it right away.

As the music died, Justine pulled away from Ward. "I have to go," she apologized.

"Why? The evening is young, and I'm not that bad a dancer," he said, holding her hand. "I don't even know your name."

"I'm sorry, but I have a club to run. I've enjoyed dancing with you, and my friends call me Tine."

"Can I be your friend?"

She felt the tingle of interest again and looked into his eyes. "Yes, but I still have to go."

Tenderly he kissed her hand and bowed. "All right, Tine. Fate brought us together, and hopefully destiny will bring us together again."

She smiled, slipped her hand from his, and disappeared into the crowd.

Regina started to follow her when Zora intercepted. "Regina, I've been looking for you."

Regina stifled her anger and smiled. "Just trying to catch a breather."

Zora patted her arm. "Well, that's what I was worried about. I know a quiet place you can go, and you'll also get to meet the co-owner of this place, Justine Reynard."

Regina's interest turned to Zora. "Wonderful, but I need to talk to Garrett about something. Can you give me a few minutes?"

"Of course, dear. I'll be back in a flash." Zora grinned broadly, showing perfectly bonded teeth, and vanished into the darkness.

Ward joined them, and Regina pulled him back into the solitary corner. "Who is she, Ward?"

"Her name is Tine, and she's the manager here," he informed her. "And excuse me for saying this, my Queen, but the only other time I felt like this was when I met you. She is breathtaking."

Regina offered a forgiving smile. "If she's who I think she is, it's quite understandable. I'm about to meet the Reynard woman. If either of you see this Tine again, follow her. I need to find out more about her." Ward nodded and stepped aside as Regina went in search of Zora.

Justine sat in her office thinking about Ward. She had always been very levelheaded and didn't subscribe to the adage of love at first sight, soul mate, or any of the romance novel's selling points. Ward seemed intelligent, and to be working for Regina Derrick spoke volumes to his character. He should be the kind of man she was looking for, but she remained alone and single for a reason. It was nice to be flirted with, and he was a good dancer. Before she sank deeper into these thoughts, she inhaled deeply and focused on her paperwork. A knock at the door snapped her out of her daydream. "Yes?" she called.

The door opened, and Zora ushered the guest of honor in. Justine was surprised by Regina Derrick. She was nothing like she expected. Before her stood a woman whose beauty men wanted to own and women envied. Short and petite, she had a small, athletic figure with porcelain skin. Her coal black hair was done up in an elegant bun, but it was her eyes that demanded attention, the pupils so dark they were almost black, and they were hypnotic. Her makeup was natural and perfect, as was her short black evening dress. Suddenly Justine felt dizzy. There was a flash in her mind, and she saw herself as a child looking up at a woman who looked like Regina. There was another blonde woman there with ice-blue eyes like hers. Then it was gone, and she was back in her office.

Regina was just as surprised but managed to conceal it. She could not, however, stop from staring. The same-shape face, the coloring, and build, but the clincher was the ice-blue eyes.

"Tine, are you all right?" Zora interrupted, noticing the color drain from her friend's face.

Justine's pallor was replaced with blush red. "Yes, I'm fine." Slowly she stood up. "Please come in."

"Justine Reynard, meet Regina Derrick," Zora replied as they stepped into the office and she shut the door behind them.

"It's very nice to meet you, Ms. Derrick." Justine smiled as she extended her hand to Regina.

"Nice to meet you, Ms. Reynard." Regina smiled warmly and firmly shook Justine's hand. "I hope we're not disturbing you. Zora said I could get a brief respite from the crowd up here, but if you're not well, we can leave."

Justine offered them a seat and drinks and then sat down. "I'm fine. Please excuse me for staring, but when you came in, I could have sworn I'd seen you before."

Regina took a drink of her wine. "Perhaps we met at a gallery. Are you a patron of the arts?"

Zora's quiet spell was at an end. "Patron, hell, she's a painter, but she doesn't like anyone to know it. The canvas behind her desk is one of hers."

Regina looked at the painting Zora pointed to. It was a large oil canvas, done in swirls of purple, red, and black. She was amazed at the depth and feeling the painting summoned. Rising to her feet, Regina moved closer to the painting. It almost seemed as if you could step into the swirls and vanish. "This is beautiful, Ms. Reynard."

Justine blushed. "Thank you, but it was more of a hobby to let off steam, and please call me Justine."

Regina's eyes never left the canvas. "You were very angry when you painted this. Did it help?"

Justine was caught off guard by such an accurate observation and touched by the interest in her work. "I was under a lot of pressure in college. Painting helped, that one in particular."

"I've always told her she should devote more time to it and go pro," Zora interjected.

Regina returned to her seat, a look of respect on her face. "I'd like to see more of your work, Justine. Just from looking at this piece, I'd say you have a natural-born talent."

"Thank you, Ms. Derrick . . ."

"Regina."

"Thank you, Regina," she started again, "but as I said, it was more of a hobby in college. I haven't painted in several years. Now I spend most of my time concentrating on business. That's my real passion."

Regina nodded in understanding. "Very admirable. I can completely agree with that, but if you do enjoy painting, you should make time. I do and find it a great release from the pressure of business."

The phone rang before Justine could say a word. She excused herself, picked it up, and spoke to the caller briefly, then hung up. "I'm sorry, but you'll have to excuse me. I'm needed downstairs. Regina, Zora, please feel free to use my office for as long as you like." She stood up to leave, and Regina reached to stop her.

"Will you be at the premiere tomorrow night? You've given me this wonderful party and made me feel so welcome. I'd really like to see you there and perhaps continue our discussion."

Justine hesitated. "Thank you for asking, Regina, but I'm not sure if I can make it. I'd love to discuss business with you, but you know how busy it keeps you."

Regina stood up and shook Justine's hand. "Again, I do understand, but please try. I think we have a lot in common, and I'd like to discuss art and business with you again. Thank you for the use of your office. I've enjoyed meeting you."

"The pleasure was mine, and I will try to come by the gallery." Justine smiled and then left the office.

A few seconds after the door shut, Regina sat back down. "Zora, do you think she'll come?"

Zora turned in her seat to face the other woman and shrugged. "With Justine you never know. I've known her for twelve years and I couldn't tell you a whole lot about her. We even roomed together in college, but she has always been a very private person and kept things to herself. She had friends and was well liked, but nobody ever got too close. I do know her childhood wasn't pleasant."

"Really?" Regina asked.

Zora tensed slightly. "I don't think it would be appropriate to discuss that, Tine is a dear friend and . . ."

Regina sat forward and stared into Zora's eyes, using her power to pull the information from her. Regina's eyes reflected concern, and her voice was smooth and comforting as she spoke, "It's all right to discuss this with me, Zora. Tell me what you know of her childhood."

Calm immediately settled over Zora, and her body relaxed as she gazed into Regina's eyes. Sleep seemed to be creeping up on her, and she knew that it was okay to tell Regina whatever she wanted to know. Her voice was slow and relaxed. "She's adopted for one thing. I know she and her adoptive father do not get along at all. Her father is Seth Reynard, the famous author. He always treated her like sh . . . badly. She and her adoptive mother were really close, but she died when Tine was twelve. Her mom was a safety buffer between her and the old man, and when she died, it got bad. It bordered on abusive, and when Tine turned seventeen, she left home with a suitcase and about $100 to her name. She took care of herself, working her way through college, making her own career. She worked like a dog, too, and never got any help from her father. Sometimes she worked three part-time jobs to pay for school and carried a full course load. The hard work paid off when she graduated with honors. Her brother was at the graduation, but the old man didn't have the chutzpah to even send a card. Tine is really a remarkable woman."

Regina sat back in her chair and soaked in all the information, committing every detail to memory, and then continued. "Thank you, Zora. I think it's better that you forget we ever had this conversation. The only thing you will remember will be small, incidental things we talked about like the club and the gallery."

"Mmhuh," Zora mumbled in agreement. As suddenly as it had come over her, the sleepiness faded and she became her usual perky self. "You rested up enough?"

Smiling, Regina rose to her feet. "Yes, thank you. I'm ready to get back to this wonderful party you've arranged."

Together they left the quiet office and went back to the party downstairs.

Two hours later, Ward brought the limousine around, and Garret and Regina quickly climbed into the back. He eased the car into traffic and settled into a slow lane as Regina began talking.

"We abort the plan," she ordered firmly.

The only person who could question Regina without losing his life or a limb was Garrett, and he did so now. "Why? Everything is ready."

Regina took a glass from the back seat bar and poured some wine. "Because the Reynard woman is Justine. Tine to her friends."

Ward looked into the rearview and met her eyes. "You mean I was . . ."

"Yes, Ward. Your dancing partner was Justine Reynard."

"So why do we abort the plan?" Garrett argued. "She is still Reynard's daughter, no matter who she resembles, and he is the enemy, Regina."

"His adopted daughter, Garrett," she shot back defensively. "Until I get more information, I don't want her touched. Is that clear?"

With a sigh, he nodded his agreement and remained silent. Satisfied, she continued, "I want a complete file on her in my hands by noon tomorrow."

She leaned back into the soft leather seats, sipping her wine as Garrett used the mobile phone to make the arrangements. When he finished, she handed him a glass of wine. "It's ironic, Garrett. We came here to this town to kill the daughter of our greatest enemy. Now I think we've found one of the lost, and not only that, but my own niece."

Garrett sat silently, hoping she was right and not about to make a deadly mistake.

The next evening, Justine drove to the familiar subdivision on the outskirts of Marietta. She pulled alongside the Reynard home and cut the engine.

The house was a large brick two-story colonial. The yard and hedges were trimmed to perfection. Everything was so perfectly maintained that the house looked like something out of *Better Homes and Gardens*. Seth Reynard wouldn't settle for anything less. He was a perfectionist right down to the way he brushed his teeth. Imperfection was not tolerated in his life or house, and he had little patience for people that did not meet his standards. A shudder passed over Justine as the memories of her childhood in the house came back. The memories of her mother, Cheryl Ann, were sweet, and she liked to dwell there, but slowly Seth would creep in. He was often gone on business, and when he was home, he was short-tempered and critical. Although he was warm and supportive of Cameron, he was strict and uncompromising with her. She remembered hearing an argument between her parents shortly before her mother died. Cheryl Ann had asked Seth why he had adopted her if he was only going to be so cruel to her. The girl was intelligent, well behaved, and did her best to please, yet he acted like he hated her. Seth had not answered, or if he did, she could not hear his reply.

Three months later Cheryl Ann was gone, the victim of a drunk driver. Cameron and his sister had always been close, and he had taken over trying to protect his twelve-year-old sister, but Seth had only gotten worse. Many times he acted like it was her fault his wife was gone, and as result, he became even colder and more unfeeling toward her. Cameron was and always would be his pride and joy. Justine was an unwanted obligation. The children's already close bond became even closer, and it had remained into adulthood.

Justine had been the bride's maid at his wedding and had been the one to hold him while he cried when the marriage broke up. Cameron had denied it, but when Justine talked to his ex-wife, Karen, she revealed that Seth had a hand in the destruction of their marriage. He had not liked Karen or thought her good enough for his son, so that was the end of it. Seth Reynard was the boss, and it was his way or none at all.

Justine had not accepted that view and, when she turned sixteen, had gotten a job, saved up, and gotten the hell away from him. It had been hard, but if Seth had done anything for his daughter, he made her strong and determined. She had gotten a partial scholarship to college and worked two, sometimes three, jobs to cover the rest. A few times when money had been nonexistent, an anonymous envelope would arrive in her mailbox. The smell of Cameron's cologne on the money and envelope had always made her smile, but it was a secret that neither of them ever spoke of.

A man's deep voice interrupted her reverie. "Hi."

Justine jumped and looked at the passenger-side window. Cameron's smiling face had appeared.

"Hi. Happy birthday," she greeted weakly.

"Get out of the car and let's talk," he said firmly and moved around the car to her door.

"Cam, I don't . . ."

"He's not going to see you," he stated and opened the car door. "He's busy in the kitchen. Now come on out."

She grasped his offered hand and got out of the car. He shut the door, and then the two of them leaned against her car. Shaking her head and glancing at the curb, she spoke, "I'm sorry, Cam. I thought I could do this, but I can't."

He scooted beside her and put his arm around her shoulder. "I know, and it's okay. I shouldn't have asked. It was selfish of me. Stay away from him, Tine. I don't like seeing you like this."

Turning to face her, he was surprised to see tears running down her face. He had only seen her cry twice before in his entire life. Once when their mother died and when she was eight and had broken her arm. He reached out and pulled her into his arms and hugged her tightly. He wanted to say something but couldn't muster the necessary words.

The comfort she felt helped her regroup and stop the tears. She pulled away and offered him a soft smile. "I'm okay, but I better get out of here."

"Don't know why you're even here," an angry older man's voice rang out. "You weren't invited."

Cameron and Justine looked up and saw Seth Reynard coming off the porch and charging toward them. He moved well for an old man, and his eyes glared with rage. He was an older, taller version of Cameron minus the warmth and compassion. There was a harsher look about him, and he had a full, neatly trimmed graying beard.

"Dad, I asked her, and there is no need to be rude." Cameron jumped to his sister's defense.

"This is my home, Cameron, and I didn't invite her," Seth argued.

Justine's temper flared, and her case became set in a determined, fiery pose. "I came here to see Cameron, not you. And I was just leaving."

Seth shook his head. "Good. Leave. And don't bother coming back! You left this house of your own free will."

Justine smiled. "That's right. I left to get the hell away from you and your warped ideas, so you don't need to worry about me coming back here." She turned, grabbed the handle, and opened the door.

"Be careful. I love you," Cameron said as she climbed into the driver's seat.

"Me too," she answered as she brought the engine of her Maxima to life. Flooring the gas pedal, she roared down Mountain Creek Road and squealed the tires as she turned the corner out of the neighborhood.

Cameron turned to face his father, anger flashing in his eyes. "That was uncalled for."

Seth walked over to his son. "We need to talk, son. I should have talked to you about this sooner, but I think it will explain a lot."

Cameron looked at him oddly and then followed him back into the house.

After an hour of driving around the city, Justine found herself in the parking lot of the High Museum and Gallery. Cutting the engine, she sighed, trying to decide whether to go in or not. She had found Regina Derrick fascinating and was anxious to speak further with her, but her mood was not the best at the moment.

"Maybe tomorrow night," she said to herself and reached for the ignition.

"Destiny, Tine," a somewhat familiar man's voice sounded out.

Turning, she saw Ward leaning down to the window. "I told you destiny would bring us together again." His face, looming in the window, was so handsome and warm that she couldn't help but smile. "Hi, Ward."

He reached for the handle of her car door. "May I escort you inside?"

Gently, Justine put her hand on his to keep him from opening the door. "I'm afraid I wouldn't be very good company right now. I'm not even sure why I came here, and I was getting ready to leave when you came up."

"Having a bad day, huh?" he asked sympathetically.

"Understated."

Despite her hand on his, he opened the door and kneeled down beside her. "So you're just going to sit here and be depressed in privacy. I don't think so, not while I'm around. You need to be with people and have some fun. Subconsciously you knew that, that's why you drove here. To get your mind off your trouble, that's the best medicine."

The glow from the dome light complemented her features, and she smiled. "Do I call you Dr. Ward now?"

"As long as you call me, I don't care what name you use," he said in earnest as he held out his hand to her.

She felt a flush wash over her and remembered dancing with him the night before. That convinced her to take his hand. "Okay, Doc. Show me some fun."

With a twinkle in his eyes, he helped her out of the car, placed her hand on his arm, and led her inside.

The interior of the High was crowded and brightly lit, made vibrant by the white and gold decorating scheme. Paintings and photographs by renowned artists were displayed carefully and with respect.

They walked down the rose-scented hallway to the main gallery where a large sign announced "The Atlanta High Museum is pleased to present Regina Derrick in a showing of Eternal Seasons."

The mixture of guests was similar to the crowd that had been at the club the previous night, only now all were well dressed in their evening best. Men in tuxedos and the women in long beaded or spangled evening gowns. Justine suddenly realized how underdressed she was in her black and red jumpsuit and felt very uncomfortable.

As if Ward had read her thoughts, he leaned close and whispered, "You look great." Then he proudly led her into the crowd.

He handed her a program and a glass of champagne, then moved through the guests until they were at the first display. Justine's eyes widened and her breath was taken away by the beauty, power, and magnificence of Regina's paintings. As they moved around the room, each painting was better than the last. The collection consisted of abstract and impressionist, an unusual assortment to say the least, yet they all blended. She had been to a few gallery showings before, but never had someone's work taken her by surprise. The emotions that each painting evoked helped her understand that Regina portrayed her feelings on canvas and why she could hone in on the painting in her own office.

"Beautiful, aren't they?" Ward asked as they strolled by various paintings.

She grasped his hand more firmly. "Oh, Ward, that doesn't even begin to describe them. They are breathtaking."

"Thank you, Justine," Regina's silky voice greeted from behind them.

The couple turned around and came face-to-face with Regina and Garrett. Garrett was dressed in a typical tuxedo, and Regina wore a simple white silk jumpsuit, her hair down and curling across her shoulders. "I'm so glad you could make it," Regina greeted with a warm smile.

"Thank you for asking me." Justine blushed.

Regina took a step forward, locked her arm around Justine's, and they began walking, the two men strolling along behind them. "So you're the woman Ward has been talking about all day."

Justine's blush turned brighter, and Ward leaned over her shoulder. "Can you blame me?"

Regina shook her head. "No, I can't." They came to a stop near the refreshment table, and Regina faced her. "I'll let the two of you alone, but I would be pleased if you could join us for dinner after the show."

Ward peeked over Regina's shoulder, his eyes wide and eyebrows up. "Please do."

"I'd love to. Thank you," she said without hesitation.

"Wonderful." Regina beamed. "I must mingle now, so I'll see you later tonight." She took Garrett's arm and walked into the crowded room.

Ward cautiously placed his arm around Justine's waist and was pleased when she allowed it to remain. "I'm glad you're coming tonight. I'd like to spend some time with you and get to know you better."

He smiled when she answered, "Me too." They continued their tour of the exhibits holding hands.

Cameron sat in the study looking at his father, trying to soak in his father's revelation. In his hand he held a glass of whiskey. Not a big drinker, he now took a large swallow, the amber liquid burning a path to his already tight stomach.

Seth sat directly across from his son with his head resting on his hands. "I should have told you sooner, son."

Cameron looked at his father with confusion. "Then why did you adopt her, knowing what her parents were? How did you even manage to swing that?"

Seth stood up and walked across the study to the fireplace. He rolled his glass in his hands and stared into the flames. "When her mother was destroyed," he began in almost a whisper, "she was placed in an orphanage. It was the first time I or anyone had seen one of their children or infants. We were led to believe that they couldn't procreate, and when we found her, I just couldn't bring myself to destroy her. I thought I could keep an eye on her in the orphanage, and if she was one of them, I could take care of her then. I made the mistake of mentioning the case to your mother. Cheryl wanted more children but wasn't able to have any more. She loved you with all her heart and wanted you to have a sibling and another child she could love as much as you. When she saw Justine's picture, that was it. I knew I couldn't argue her out of it, and I loved her so much, son, that I couldn't refuse her. I thought I could make your mother happy and keep an eye on Justine and chart her growth at the same time."

Cameron rose to his feet, arms down by his side and fists clenched. "Wait a minute. You mean you used her in an experiment? A research test case?"

"It was a wonderful opportunity to study their kind. Your mother loved her as if she'd given birth to her, but I could never get close to her. I knew what her parents were, and it might have clouded my research."

For the first time in his life, Cameron despised his father. "You disgust me. She's my sister, and I love her. Justine was only a child, she couldn't help what her parents were. Do you have any idea what you've done to her? How you've abused her?"

His anger threatening to boil over, he moved toward the study door. Seth moved quickly for a man of his age and caught Cameron at the door. "Wait a minute. What if I had been right? You've seen what they do, how they kill. What if she had been one of them? I didn't know if she might hit puberty and change."

Cameron pulled away from his Seth. "But she wasn't, Dad," he shouted.

Seth maneuvered Cameron back into the study. "I know that. As she grew, it became apparent that she was a normal girl, and I wanted her to stay that way."

"By treating her like shit?"

Seth's own voice was becoming loud. "I made some mistakes, but she turned out all right. Suppose I had told her the truth. Justine already thinks I'm a lunatic and a coldhearted killer. What was I going to say? 'Oh, by the way, honey, your real parents were vampires and I staked your mother myself.' Cameron, please understand."

"You drove her away," Cameron continued, but the anger was evaporating. "Did you ever stop to think that by treating her that way she might seek them out?"

Seth answered with assurance and conviction, "No. She doesn't believe in them. She dismisses them as fiction, and they would never think one of my children was actually one of theirs."

Cameron dropped into the seat and looked at the Persian carpet on the floor. "Do you hate her?"

Seth sighed and sat beside Cameron. "No. My line of work has made me a hard man, and maybe I could have done better by my family. I was trained to think with my head, not my heart. I don't hate her, in fact, I'm proud of her. She's a success, and she did it on her own, through hard work and determination. You're my son, and I love you. Justine is my daughter, and although I care for her, I fear her as well. She is one of them, and that will never change. So tell me, Cameron, what would you have me do now?"

Cameron sat silently and thought for a moment. Finally, he looked up into his father's face. "Who were her parents? I want to know the whole story."

La Machion was one of the best restaurants in Atlanta. It was where the society blue bloods and the business tycoons congregated like a second home.

They were escorted to a reserved table stationed in front of the large window overlooking the city that allowed some privacy. During the appetizer and dinner, they conversed on a variety of subjects from Atlanta to music to art. Justine had been a bit nervous at first, but Regina immediately made her feel at ease.

Justine had been surprised at how easy it was to talk to Regina. She was able to lower her defenses and relax when they talked. The two seemed to have so much in common, and after just a few hours, Justine felt as if she had known Regina for years. She and Ward had also talked and gotten to know one another better, but the majority of the conversation was between the two women.

As the waiter cleared away the dishes and took their dessert order from the choices on a silver dessert tray, Regina decided it was time to gauge a reaction.

"I thought your last name sounded familiar last night when we met, and Zora told me who your father is. Seth Reynard, the popular author."

"Yes," Justine answered simply with no emotion.

Regina continued, "I've read some of his books. He's a very intense writer, and I find his work . . . amusing."

Justine looked up, her face betraying tenseness, but she tried to smile. "I've never read anything he's written. I don't care for his kind of work."

Regina sensed the tension increasing and was intrigued. This was a very sensitive topic, and she decided to push a bit further. "You don't like stories of the supernatural? I think they're fascinating. I'm surprised you don't share your father's interest, especially with the way you paint."

It was a struggle for Justine to remain calm and cheerful, but anger radiated from her eyes. Regina was surprised and pleased at the power she felt from Justine.

"Fortunately, he's not my real father, and I find his work and theories on the supernatural ludicrous. I've never shared anything with him."

Regina let it go. She had the information she wanted and needed. "I'm sorry, Tine. I didn't mean to upset you. Please forgive me for prying."

Justine blushed at her reaction and tried to relax. Ward squeezed her hand and offered her a smile. "It's I that owe you an apology for snapping like that. That's a very sensitive subject for me. I apologize."

"It's forgotten." Regina nodded with a smile.

The waiter returned with their dessert and placed the dishes before them, then vanished. After a few moments of silence, the conversation continued. This time it was the quiet, always watching Garrett that began. "How long have you been the manager at the nightclub?"

"Six years. Since opening night. My partner decided I had the best day-to-day business sense, so I became the manager, and he sat back as the silent partner."

Garrett's face registered his surprise. "You're also a co-owner?"

Justine nodded proudly. "Yes. A friend of mine from college and I always dreamed of a business. About a year after graduation, he came into some money and approached me with the idea of a nightclub. I did some research, then scraped together every penny I could beg and borrow and bought in. It's a 45/55 partnership, but I'm good with that."

"It's a beautiful place," Regina complimented. "How long before you recouped your investment? Was it difficult building a clientele?"

Justine was thrilled to finally discuss business with a woman she admired and was considered a true success in the business world. "My partner found a hot location first of all. It was a good part of town, the building only needed minor renovations, and it had great access from downtown. We scouted other clubs, got some ideas, threw in our own, and built from there. We got some friends to help with the renovations and geared the club to the varied taste of our proposed clientele. Our idea was to cater to a wide variety of people and treat every customer as if they were a part of the club. They are the reason you are or aren't a success."

Regina leaned forward, the excitement in Justine's eyes infectious. "So the location and refit were minor, but how long did it take to really get off the ground?"

Justine shrugged modestly. "About six months. We caught a break with good word of mouth, influential customers. Between our contacts and friends we got a lot of free publicity. We were what the people wanted when they wanted it. We were turning a small profit in less than a year."

Now Regina was genuinely impressed. "A lucky break had nothing to do with it. It was good old-fashioned business sense and management." Regina took a sip of wine and leaned back in her chair. "I've been looking for a few new business ventures, and I'm extremely interested in what you've done. I'm only in town for a week, but if possible, I'd like to spend some time with you and learn as much as possible about the nightclub circuit."

Justine's eyes flashed, and she could barely contain her excitement. She squeezed Ward's leg under the table, and he dropped his hand onto hers.

"I'd be happy to show you the ropes, at your convenience. We'll be doing inventory tomorrow morning, if you'd like to come by. It's not very exciting, but I could give you a look from the ground up, so to speak."

"Yes, I'd like that," Regina agreed and raised her wineglass. "I think this will be the beginning of a beautiful and lucrative friendship."

After they finished dessert, Justine and Ward dropped Regina and Garrett off at their hotel; then he took her back to the gallery for her car. They talked, getting to know one another better as soft jazz played in the background. Eventually business came up. "Regina is really impressed with you."

Again, Justine blushed. She had never been comfortable with flattery, and in the last two days she had been overwhelmed by it. "It means a lot to me that she's interested in my ideas."

Glancing to her side, she caught Ward looking at her and then looking away quickly. He nervously licked his lips, a look of hesitance on his face. She reached over and gave his hand a squeeze. "What is it, Doc? Is something wrong?"

"No," he answered more forcefully than he meant to. Catching himself, he smiled sheepishly and tried again. "I'm trying to get up the courage to tell you something."

Turning in her seat, she smiled. "I've always believed that the straightforward approach is the best."

They had reached the High, and he eased the limo into the parking lot and pulled in beside Justine's Maxima. When he cut the engine, he turned to face her. "Okay," he began shyly. "Here it goes. I know we only met last night, and this will probably sound like a line to you, but . . . I think I could fall in love with you."

Justine couldn't mask the surprise at his statement. She started to say something, but he placed his fingers against her lips to silence her. Nodding and smiling at the touch, she waited for him to continue.

"I've never met anyone like you. You're intelligent, beautiful, independent, and you have a great sense of humor. You have a brilliant mind and business sense, not to mention what a wonderful dancer you are. What I'm trying to say is that I'd like to spend a lot more time with you, maybe even the rest of my life. If I'm moving too fast or scaring you or you're not interested, tell me and I'll disappear." He finished with a deep sigh.

Justine's eyes were sparkling. "I don't want you to disappear. We're friends, and I can never have enough friends. I'm not sure what I want, and it is a little scary. Slow down, Doc and let me breathe, okay?"

He smiled softly, leaning closer to her, and after seeing her nod, met her waiting lips with a feathery kiss.

"Besides we don't really know each other that well, and you're only going to be in town for a week."

"Maybe it's time for Regina to get a new assistant," he answered. "Or maybe it's time for you to start a new career. I don't know or care as long as I can be with you and get to know you. We have time, right?"

He scooted next to her and wrapped his arms around her waist, drawing her closer. This time when their lips met there was more passion and wanting. Ward began planting kisses on her neck, and when she leaned her head back to speak, he reached for the zipper on her jumpsuit. Tenderly he began easing the zipper down when her hand intercepted his and she pulled back from him. "No, Ward. Friends to start, remember?"

His head bowed. "I'm sorry. I got a little carried away." Slowly he raised his head, a sly smile on his face and his eyebrows cocked. "You are just so desirable."

"I'm old-fashioned."

It took him a second or two for what those words meant to sink in; then he gently cupped her face in his hands. "Just one more reason to love you. Friends first."

Softly, she kissed his hand. "Thank you." She pulled away from him, sighing. "I'm sorry, but I've got to go. I want to be bright eyed for Regina and the inventory tomorrow morning."

He savored the feel of where her head had rested in his hands and then dropped his hand to hers. "Can you have dinner with me tomorrow night?"

"Yes. Then we can go back to the club and dance the night away."

He winked at her, then got out of the car, walked around it, and opened her door. He took her hand and helped her out, then saw her to her car. "I'll see you about eight?"

He opened her car door, and she slid in behind the wheel. "Okay. See you then, Doc."

Leaning down, he gave her a quick kiss. "Be careful, Tine, and good luck with Regina."

"Thanks." She smiled and shut the door.

She started the engine, and he stepped back. With a final wave, he watched her pull out of the parking space and exit the lot. He watched her car disappear into the Atlanta night and with a smile went back to his own car.

The last of the customers was leaving as Justine arrived at City Lights. Their normal closing time was 3:00 a.m., but on inventory night they shut down at midnight. Justine smiled and spoke to some of the waiters and waitresses as they were leaving, then made her way to the bar. Steve greeted her with her usual drink, a Diet Mountain Dew.

"I'm sorry, Steve," she said as she accepted the glass. "I really did mean to get here sooner."

With a final swipe of the counter, he leaned up against the railing. "No problem, Tine. It was a slow night, and it's nice to see you getting out of this club and having some fun."

Justine mocked surprise. "Are you suggesting that I have no life outside this place?"

"Yes."

They both laughed, and Justine took a drink of her Dew. "Did you have a good time?" Steve asked seriously.

"Great time," she answered dreamily and then winked at him.

Steve blushed. "Uh-huh. Well, I better finish cleaning up, nine-thirty comes awful early."

Justine grabbed the bar towel out of his hand. "Nope. You go home. You've covered enough for tonight. Get some rest and I'll see you in the morning."

"You sure?"

"Yes. Besides, I have a date tomorrow night and will need you to cover again. Now get out of here."

He leaned in and gave her a friendly kiss on the cheek. "It's good to see you get out of here, Tine. There's a whole world out there, and you deserve a piece of it. Good night." He turned and headed for the back. Stopping suddenly, he turned back to her. "I almost forgot. Cameron called three times looking for you. He wants you to call him, no matter how late."

"Thanks." She smiled. "Now go."

After he was gone, she turned to the few remaining cleaners. "Hey gang, as soon as the tables are cleared, load the dishwashers and get out of here. We can finish up tomorrow. Go get some rest."

The announcement was met with approval, and thirty minutes later she was locking up and activating the alarm system. Steve had all the night's receipts in a strongbox, and she grabbed it, turned off the lights, and went upstairs to her office.

Once she settled in to do the bookwork, she picked up the phone and dialed Cameron's number. To her surprise he answered it on the second ring and sounded wide awake, despite the late hour. "You rang?"

"Tine," he responded, his voice edged with relief.

"Why are you still up? It's almost one-thirty in the morning. Isn't there a state law about CPAs being in bed by ten o'clock?"

"I just wanted to make sure you were home safe," he admitted. "I've been trying to reach you all night. I was getting worried."

"I'm fine," she reassured him, feeling like a kid. "I just went out with some friends. What's so urgent?"

Had he reached her earlier, he would have told her the whole story behind her adoption, but he had time to think it over and decided to keep quiet. "There's no emergency, I was just worried after the scene at the house."

"I'm fine, Cam. Just tired."

He hesitated a second. "I'll let you go then. If you need me, call, okay."

Puzzled, she answered, "Okay."

"Love you, sis."

"You too," she said and hung up the phone. She stared at the wall for a minute and then began adding up the receipts.

The inventory was progressing well, with Justine showing Regina the ropes. After Justine had finished the books, she was still wired and finished cleaning the club herself. At 4:00 a.m., she dropped into bed and was asleep almost as soon as her head hit the pillow.

Arising at eight-fifteen, she showered, dressed, and got the paperwork ready for the inventory. By nine-fifteen, Steve showed up, loaded with doughnuts, and scolded her for doing all the cleanup without help. At nine-thirty the other employees arrived, and the inventory had just started when Regina came in.

To Justine's surprise, Regina was dressed casually, in jeans and a pullover, just like the rest of them. After introductions had been made, the inventory continued. Regina had spent some of the time speaking to the employees and looking around, Steve giving her the grand tour. The rest of the time she followed Justine and had helped with the inventory, asking questions and working right alongside them.

The inventory was almost finished by twelve-thirty, and the mood was jovial. As each worker finished, they handed Steve their tally sheets and left. Most of them had to work later and wanted to catch some more sleep.

While Steve totaled up the inventory sheets, Justine and Regina went up to the office. "I have got to give him a raise," Justine stated as she flopped into the chair behind her desk.

Regina plopped on the couch across from her. "Who? Steve?"

"Yeah. He's my right hand. He does more around here than my partner. Maybe it's time I had an assistant manager."

"You have a very impressive business here," Regina complimented. "And your employees. I've never seen a group of people so satisfied and happy with their jobs."

"I've always believed that you should treat people the way you want to be treated. So I give them good pay, benefits, and a nice atmosphere. I don't ask them to do anything I wouldn't. They give me good work in return. When you have staff that enjoy their jobs, the customers sense and feel that, so then you have customer that wants to come back."

"Well, they certainly like you. I lost count of how many times you were referred to as the 'greatest boss.'"

Justine blushed. "Sounds like I need to give raises all around. I appreciate your help with the inventory."

"Well, I certainly wasn't going to stand around while everyone else worked. That's not my style. Besides, how else am I going to learn what makes this place tick?"

Justine laughed and leaned forward on the desk. "I like your style."

Regina smiled. "And I yours." The she leaned forward, becoming serious. "Which brings me to a decision. I would like you to come and work with me."

Justine looked at her in disbelief. "Excuse me?" she asked, not sure her hearing was reliable.

Understanding her reaction, Regina offered an explanation. "I said I want you to come work with me. You're hardworking, intelligent, honest, and have great business and people skills. That combination is rare, and when I find it, I want that person with me."

"Thank you," Justine answered slowly, still in shock. "I'm just a little nightclub manager. What could I possibly add to your corporation?"

"I was the same way when I started my first company. I learned as I went, and some lessons were hard. I could have used a mentor. You are a diamond in the rough and remind me of myself in many ways. I want you to be my assistant. You can learn all the aspects of the company that way. Then when you're ready, you'll move up to director of Entertainment, meaning it will be your job to open clubs like this and keep them up and running. I can't think of anyone more suited to the job. You will get to travel, learn, and earn."

"I thought Ward was your assistant," she questioned.

Regina's smile brightened. "Ward is my assistant, but he has his own duties. I couldn't function without Garrett and Ward. You would be a part of my team and have your own duties. Would working with Ward be a problem?"

"Not at all."

Regina leaned closer. "I didn't think so."

Justine exhaled a deep breath and sat back in her chair, her head reeling. "I don't know what to say, Regina. This is so unexpected and sudden. And exciting."

Regina held up her hand. "Say nothing right now. Just think it over. There will be no hard feeling if you decline. I have gallery obligations but would like to spend the rest of my time in Atlanta getting to know you better and cultivating our relationship."

"I'd like that," Justine answered with sincerity.

"Good. After I leave here, I have to go to New York for a week to finish the gallery circuit. I can fly back then, and you can give me your answer. Is it a plan?" Regina finished.

Justine nodded. "Sounds like one to me. Thank you, Regina."

Standing up, Regina's face was glowing. "I'm famished. Let's get lunch, my treat."

Justine quickly arose. "Now that's a plan."

Together they walked out of the office.

For the next week Justine divided her time between the club, Ward, and Regina. With Steve's help, the club was running smoothly and prosperous as ever during her absences. Her relationship with Ward was still uncertain. She enjoyed his company and liked spending time with him, but there were a few times when he pushed for more and faster. That pressure had caused her to move more toward Regina, and they were becoming very good friends. The woman was amazing—intelligent, polished, but down-to-earth as well—and Justine felt at ease and comfortable with her. For the first time in her life, everything was going well, but so quickly, that she felt dizzy.

That was what she was thinking about as she and Ward ate dinner in her apartment. She had prepared a special meal for their last night together, complete with candles, wine, and music. Ward poured more wine in her glass and looked into her troubled eyes. "What is it, Tine?"

Offering him a weak smile, she said, "There's just so much happening, so many things I'm not sure of. I'm just feeling a little overwhelmed."

Reaching across the table, he took her hand in his and kissed her palm. "I haven't been helping matters by pushing so hard, and I'm sorry." She started to say something, but he shushed her. "Don't deny it. I've never felt this strongly for someone, and I've been trying too hard."

"You don't need to," she blurted out.

"I know that, now. I think our leaving for a while will help. With Regina's offer and our relationship and you running a business and your old man, you need some time for just you."

Justine leaned forward, lightly brushing his lips with hers. "I do care about you, I don't want you to think otherwise. I'm very new to this relationship thing, and it's taking me a while to sort out. I have to go slow, and I don't want to lose your friendship."

He chuckled softly, the candlelight reflecting his clear green eyes. "You aren't going to lose me. I'm stepping back to let you think and make some decisions. I need to think things through as well, so it's not all you. Besides, I don't want to interfere with this decision. Regina never makes these kinds of offers without thorough research, and you have really impressed her. I don't want to be the reason you give up a great opportunity."

Justine emptied her glass and breathed a sigh of relief. "I know I'm not easy to get along with, and I appreciate you being so patient. I don't know why I'm so . . . confused."

He got up from his chair and walked over to her, took her hand into his, and brought her to her feet, then encircled her with his strong arms. "Tine, from what little you've told me about your childhood and everything that's going on, I find it a miracle you're not confused all the time. You are one of the most levelheaded, together people I know. I will be patient with you till the end of time."

Clinging to him, she soaked in the strength and comfort his arms offered. Inhaling deeply, she savored the smell of his cologne and skin.

"Can I call you while I'm away?" he asked, rocking her gently.

"You'd better," she answered with a kiss.

She had seen them off at the airport and then headed for the local shopping mecca. After four hours of power shopping, she came away with a new business clothes wardrobe and assorted executive supplies. Stopping at Angelo's Restaurant, she ordered a takeout plate and then went back to the club. She unpacked her mall purchases then sat down to eat. Now an hour later, she stood on the balcony above the dance floor.

She walked down the steps and around the club, enjoying the peace and quiet of the place. The silence helped keep her thought process clear and on track. She had put six years of blood, sweat, and tears into making the club a success. There was a good memory in every nook and cranny and a few unpleasant ones as well. The club had been her savior. In return for everything she had poured into it, she had received business experience, financial security, and personal stability. Lately, though, she had begun yearning for more, an urge to change, and now she had the opportunity. At twenty-eight she was a successful businesswoman in the local community, but Regina was offering a whole new life, one she had always dreamed of. And it was the chance of a lifetime.

After careful thought and weighing the pros and cons of leaving and risking it all, she decided that she had nothing to lose and everything to gain. Meeting Ward had, for the first time, made her contemplate a relationship with someone other than business. He was everything she thought she wanted in a man, but he was rushing her. After their talk, he had understood that, and now things would slow down. Working with him and getting to know him better would be an extra perk to the job.

Justine had always been friendly and had a lot of acquaintances, but no one was ever allowed too close, until Regina. She had not realized how lonely she had been for someone to talk to and confide in until she met Regina. Her mother had always given her a shoulder and ear until her death, and since then, there had been a void in her life. Regina filled that long, empty void, and with her experience, connections, and tutelage, the world seemed wide open to Justine. The only thing she would miss about Atlanta was Cameron, but even he could understand her urge to move on.

With her decision made, she went upstairs to figure out her share of the club and to call her partner.

Regina had called for a friendly chat three days later, and Justine told her that she would accept the job. Regina had sounded so pleased and excited that Justine knew she had made the right choice. Justine told Regina she needed a week or so to make all the arrangements regarding the club and packing up her things. Regina had told her there was an opening in her apartment building and she would make all the arrangements so all Justine had to do was give the movers her new address and she would be set.

The hard part was going to be telling Cameron, and after many practice runs on an empty barstool, she finally had her speech worked out. Walking into his office, she realized her palms were sweating slightly, but she pressed on.

Cameron was at his desk, deeply involved in his work, as Justine walked over to him.

"Hello, beautiful, want a date?" Payton Robinson, one of the associates, greeted her with a huge grin.

Justine returned his smile. He was a sweet and very married man who liked to flirt, and it had become a game to them every time he hit on her. "No thanks, handsome, but thanks for the ego boost."

Cameron recognized the exchange and looked up. "Tine, what a nice surprise."

Payton gave her a wink and went back to his desk, while she took a seat in front of Cameron's desk. "I thought I'd drop by. I need to talk to you about some things."

Leaning back in his chair, he studied her. "I was wondering why I hadn't heard from you. Is this good or bad?"

"Good," she assured. "Can we go somewhere more private?"

Puzzled, he nodded and stood up, escorting her to the storage room. After he shut the door, he pulled out an old folding chair and motioned for her to sit down.

She declined the chair and leaned against the wall, obviously nervous about something. With that in mind Cameron decided to start the conversation. "I've been very worried about you since the fight with Dad. Other than that night, I haven't heard from you, and we always talk at least once a day."

"I'm fine, Cam, just busy because . . . well . . . I've . . . been offered a job." *There*, she thought to herself, *I've said it.*

She expected to see a little excitement in his face but saw disappointment and hurt. There was no excitement, only an odd coldness. "What kind of job, and where?

"Assistant to the CEO of Derrick Industries. The home office is in New York."

His face tightened, suspicion evident in his voice and body language. "How did that happen? I didn't know you were looking to change jobs."

"The CEO was the mystery guest at the private party last week. We met and hit it off. She was impressed with my business skills and offered me a job." She could no longer hide the hurt in her voice. "What's the problem, Cam? I thought you might be happy for me."

"I am," he said unconvincingly. "It's just so sudden and out of the blue. That's a big job."

Justine masked her disappointment, but her ire was beginning to show. "You're starting to sound like him, Cameron. I've worked hard, and I'm a damned good businesswoman. This is the chance of a lifetime, travel, training, and connections. It's about time somebody noticed my abilities. I've earned this, and I'm not letting it go by."

His head dropped slightly, sounding like the old Cameron as he spoke again. "You are a good businesswoman and do deserve to be noticed. What about the club? You worked hard to make it a success."

"It's taken care of," she announced. "I'm selling part of my share to my partner and the other half to Steve, who will take over as manager and run the place. At least they're happy for me."

Cameron chewed his lower lip and took a few steps toward her. "Sis, I am happy for you. It's just I thought you were happy here in Atlanta."

Smiling cynically, she rolled her eyes. "I was, but it's time for a change. I love you, Cameron, but I will not stay in the same town with him anymore. I have got to live my own life free of his . . . whatever you call it."

Cameron hung his head lower. "I understand, but I'm really going to miss you. You're not just my sister, you're my best friend."

She felt her anger melting away and eased over to him, hugging him tightly. "And you are mine. It's not like I'm leaving forever or moving across country. I'll be a few hours away by plane. I'll stay in touch and visit."

"When are you leaving?" he asked softly.

"In a week."

He pulled away from her, his eyes wide with shock. "So soon?"

"Regina wants to get me started as soon as possible. Would you mind taking me to the airport? I won't be needing my car in New York, and I thought you might want it."

"Your car? You're giving me your car?"

She nodded affirmative. "Yes. You're a CPA, and CPAs don't drive Prius. It's time to step up in the world."

Cameron laughed and pulled her close again. His chest tightened as he realized how much he would miss his sister, and he was in no hurry to release her. Finally, he asked, "When and what time do we leave?"

He drove her to the airport, helped her check her luggage and walked her to the gate. She gave him the car keys and title, and he handed her a small black jeweler's box. In it was a woman's ring, just like the one she had given him, with her initials in gold. Hugging him tightly, she kissed him, and it was then her flight was called. Saying their goodbyes, they hugged again, and then she walked down the passageway to the waiting plane and a new life.

Three Months Later

Rain poured over the city and added a chill to the already-cool February air. The traffic through Atlanta was unusually light for midday, a fact Cameron attributed to the weather.

His father had scarcely said a word since Cameron had picked him up from the airport, and the silence, although expected, was a bit unnerving. Seth Reynard was always quiet and reserved when he returned from his trips, and considering what he did when he was away, it was par for the course.

Cameron could no longer take the tension he felt radiating from the old man. "How was the trip?"

"Successful," he replied and turned his eyes out the window, watching the downpour of rain.

Cameron cut his eyes at his father and for the first time noticed how old and weary his father looked. Every time he came back from a trip, he looked a little older and worn.

"Have you heard from Justine?" Seth questioned as he maintained his stare out the window.

Cameron was so caught off guard by the question he was certain he had imagined it. "Did you just ask about Justine?"

"Yes."

"Uh . . . well," he began, trying to recover from the shock, "I saw her at Christmas and then talked to her about a week ago. We don't talk very often, she's so busy now. But she loves her job, and she said they seemed to be very pleased with her work. She sounded content and happier than I've ever heard her."

Seth slowly nodded. "Good. I'm glad she's happy. I think she's finally safe too."

Cameron's chest tightened, unaccustomed to hearing his father talk like this, especially where Justine was concerned. "What's going on, Dad? What happened on this trip?"

Seth remained quiet, and they drove in silence until the outskirts of Marietta. Ceasing his gazing out the window, he looked at his son, and Cameron was shaken to see the haunted look in his father's eyes. "I staked one that reminded me of your mother. She had family pictures in her house, mementos. It was . . . it just hit me how much some of them are like us. I'm getting old, son. I need help, and I'd like you to come with me full-time."

His first instinct was to resist, but he knew that their work was important. It saved countless lives. He also knew that his father wouldn't ask unless it were necessary. "What about my business, Dad? I can't just close up shop."

Seth smiled weakly. "You'll keep it, son. I'm going to have to slow down, so other than a few weeks every other month or so, things won't change. The investigations I can handle, although you do need to learn more on that. I just need help with the hunts and more physical things."

"I need to think about it, Dad," Cameron answered honestly. He had no qualms about killing them. They weren't human and were murderers. He had done it before when he accompanied his father on a few trips. After seeing the carnage they caused, he was surprised at how easy it had been. That was before he knew the truth about Justine. Now it was different—yet by doing the hunts he would ensure that she remained safe. Sighing, he realized that this would probably keep him up all night.

They pulled into the driveway of the house, and Cameron carried his father's bags into the house. Seth thanked him for the ride and informed him that he had some paperwork to finish up.

"I'd like to help," Cameron offered.

Seth smiled, patted Cameron's shoulder, and led the way to his basement office.

Regina was in an especially good mood as she returned to her office after the business meeting. Derrick Industries had just secured a multimillion-dollar contract, and it was largely due to Justine's diligence in putting the information together.

She was pleased at the instinct and talent Justine had shown in such a short time. In fact, she had to rein in the woman on several occasions for working eighteen-hour days and weekends. The more she watched her young protégé, the more eager she became to expand her natural abilities.

Garrett was standing by her desk, going through a file, as she strolled into her office. He was dressed in a dark blue suit that brought the color of his eyes. His graying moustache and hair were neatly and conservatively trimmed. At the moment he was wearing a very dour expression. "Good news?" he questioned as she came in and sat behind her mahogany desk.

"Yes," she answered, her voice almost melodic. "We got the contract, largely due to Justine's work on the deal."

Raising an eyebrow, he asked, "Where is your protégé?"

Regina heard the tone of his voice and looked at him sternly. "I gave her the rest of the day off. We're going out to dinner tonight to celebrate the deal and her hard work. I can't for the life of me understand why you dislike her so."

Garrett's voice was edged with anger, something that was very rare for the distinguished British gentleman when dealing with Regina. "She is the daughter of one of our worst enemies, and you are playing a very dangerous game by letting her this close."

"She is my niece. My blood."

"And when you tell her this, what if she turns against you? Goes to Reynard?"

Regina's eyes flickered uncertainty for a split second. "It's a chance I'm willing to take. She won't turn on me. I'm sure of it."

"It could destroy us and everything you've built. For your sake, I hope you're right."

Regina felt something else in him, something very troubling. "What, Gar? What's happened?"

Slowly he moved to the front of her desk and slumped into a chair. "Eleanor Curren was killed two days ago. She was staked, decapitated, and then burned."

Regina closed her eyes, willing herself not to cry. Eleanor Curren had been one of her most trusted friends. When her sister had been killed, it was Eleanor who told her the news, then held her and comforted her. "Who?" she asked in a quivering voice.

Garrett hesitated, clenching his teeth. "Seth Reynard."

Regina's eyes opened, glaring red, and her fangs appeared. "I'm going to tear his heart out and eat it while he watches!"

Garrett rushed over to close and lock the door and then shut the window blinds. "Pull it back, Regina!" he ordered firmly. "Now is not the place or time."

Regina bared her teeth and uttered a low, guttural growl. Taking a few deep breaths, she managed to calm herself, and her eyes returned to their normal brown. In another second, her fangs had retracted and the cool, calm composure had returned.

Garrett returned to his seat and watched her for a moment, waiting patiently for the instructions he knew were coming.

"Her family is to be taken care of," she began. "New identities, anything they need."

He nodded his understanding, and she continued, "I want details on what happened. This is becoming too frequent. Call Justine and tell her I've got a meeting and we'll have dinner at my place around eight-thirty. Tonight she finds her past."

She saw the look on his face and added, "If it does go wrong, I'll take care of it myself."

Fidgeting in her chair, Regina arose. "I've got to go out for a while."

Garrett also rose to his feet, concern for his Queen evident. "Are you all right?"

Regina's eyebrows arched, and she smiled. "Of course, Gar. I'm just going to relieve some tension." Kissing his cheek, she turned and walked out of the office.

Regina had succeeded in getting him to follow her. A flash of cash and nervous manner were all that was required as a lure for his type. After a few minutes of walking down the busy streets, she had ventured into one of the seedier parts of New York then decided it was time to give him what he wanted.

She walked a little further until she found a secluded, darkened alley and then cautiously moved down it. Her keen eyesight revealed that it was indeed deserted and secluded. As she continued down the alley, the only sound heard were her heels clicking on the concrete.

Suddenly she was seized from behind and shoved against the cool brick wall. The cold steel of a knife point was leveled at her throat, and with his free hand, he roamed her body looking for anything of value. He was a young man, not more than twenty, with dirty long blond hair, a matching scruffy beard, and bloodshot brown eyes. The odor of alcohol and sweat oozed from his skin, and when he smiled, he revealed yellow teeth. "Keep your mouth shut, bitch, and you may live through this."

Quickly pocketing the bills she had on her, he moved in closer, sniffing her neck. "Nice," he complimented with a leer. Regina could smell and feel his arousal, and she waited until he moved his hand between her legs, clumsily rubbing her thighs. She lifted her head back and closed her eyes, then sighed slightly.

Blondie smiled at the action. "You like that, huh?"

"Not really," she said as she opened her glowing red eyes and smiled, fangs dripping with saliva.

The shock on his face multiplied when she seized his wrist, spun him around, and slammed him against the wall. She squeezed his wrist until he had no choice but to drop the knife. Once it clattered to the ground, she kicked it away then moved closer and began rubbing up against him.

"I . . . didn't mean you no harm, lady," he begged weakly. "I'll give your money back. Just . . . just let me go."

Her free hand repeated his earlier actions, roaming over his body, and she smiled even wider, her fangs almost glistening. "You like hurting women. There have been a lot, and some of them didn't make it out in one piece. I can't let you go. You wanted this so badly, and I don't like to disappoint."

He tried in vain to pull away from her but was only slammed back into the wall. "What are you!" he screamed in her face.

"An Avenger," she snarled and then sank her teeth into the soft flesh of his neck. His struggles only lasted a few seconds; then he relaxed, rapture soaking into his being. She continued to feed as she slipped to the ground. Moaning in pleasure, he turned his head so she could better access his neck. After a hundred years of experience, she knew how to feed quickly and cleanly, and after another few minutes, she released him and stepped away from his almost-lifeless form. Licking the few remaining flecks of blood from her lips, she savored the euphoria of the fresh blood and adrenaline. Taking a deep breath, she stepped back and rummaged through her purse for the can of lighter fluid. That found, she proceeded to empty the contents on Blondie then lit a match and tossed it on his saturated form.

As he burst into flames, too far gone to even make a sound, a pure white mist drifted out of the alley and back uptown.

They had enjoyed a great Italian meal and then adjourned to the living room for drinks and conversation. Justine had spent so much time in Regina's penthouse apartment that she thought of it as a second home, even though her own apartment was on the floor just below this one. The two women had become close friends and enjoyed spending time together away from work as well.

Regina had opened up a whole world of museums, art galleries, and other cultural interests for Justine and was happy to see the childlike fascination that the young woman had.

The furnishings of Regina's apartment reflected her personality. It was done in black lacquer and glass with paintings and statues everywhere. The place could have doubled for a museum with its artwork from around the world. There was a cool, crisp feel about the room, yet it was welcoming. Oddly, though, there was nothing of Regina's, no family pictures or cards or mementos.

They had discussed the deal they had closed today, and Regina kept probing for how Justine had put together such a precise packet of information. Eventually the conversation died down and Regina began to slowly pace, sipping her brandy and wearing a trail in the beige carpet.

Justine sensed something weighing heavily on Regina. In the few months they had worked together, she had developed almost a sixth sense, a sense that also came in handy researching business deals. "Okay, Regina. What is it? Did something go wrong with the contract?"

Regina smiled at her perceptive powers. For a mortal, the girl had highly developed instincts and had developed them much further than expected. She lightly probed Justine's thoughts, finding only trust, confidence, and admiration, almost to the point of hero worship. She decided it was now or never.

"Tine, I consider you not only my assistant but one of my closest friends. A good, trusted friend is a rare thing, especially in the business world, and I value our friendship very, very much. Recently I came into some information that could adversely affect that."

Justine laughed nervously. "Regina, I hope you don't mind me saying this, but you're my best friend. What can be that serious?"

Regina walked over to the couch where Justine was sitting. "It's information that could jeopardize our relationship, and that's the last thing I want, but it's something you need to know."

Justine stood up, her face a study in determination, and at that moment, she looked so much like her mother that Regina wanted to hold her and cry with joy.

"I'm listening."

"I've learned who your real mother is."

Justine's face had fallen. "What?"

Taking a deep breath, Regina said "Follow me" and began to walk across the apartment. They entered the master bedroom, and Regina led her to a painting on the far wall. Casting a final unsure glance at Justine, Regina backed away, letting the young woman get a full view of the portrait that hung there.

Justine was confused by what was expected of her until her attention was drawn to the wall, and then she just stared. She felt like she was looking in a mirror, different, but the resemblance was undeniable. The woman in the portrait looked to be about her age with long, curly brown hair. Her skin was pale porcelain, and she was slender, her face soft and friendly, her blue eyes almost glowing. The woman was dressed in simple white gown, and for a split second, Justine swore that the woman was breathing.

A wave of dizziness and weariness washed over Justine. She closed her eyes for a second to combat it, and when she opened them again, she was no longer in the bedroom but in a forest clearing. She was a child of no more than three, holding the woman's hand as they walked across the clearing toward the nearby woods. The woman spoke in a soft, soothing tone, pointing out a flower here, a butterfly there, each time carefully saying the name of each thing and asking the child to repeat. Every time the child repeated correctly, the woman would lavish her with praise and smiles. Suddenly the woman stopped, turning her head to the side as if she were hearing something on the soft breeze.

Without warning, she shoved the child into the heavy foliage at the outskirts of the forest. Making a motion to stay put, she offered the child a weak smile and then disappeared across the clearing. As the woman reached the opposite end of the clearing, two men appeared, armed with large metal crosses and guns. The woman moved like a cat as she tried to evade them and lure them away from the child, but they were practiced at the hunt and easily outflanked her and moved in. A scream filled the air, a sound that carried on the breeze and drove a spike of fear and dread into the child's heart.

Justine was no longer in the forest. She now found herself back in Regina's bedroom, strong and comforting hands guiding her to the bed. She turned and saw Regina's worried face, and then everything became fuzzy. She reclined against the bedpost and shut her eyes.

Regina sat quietly in the chair stationed at the foot of the bed while Justine got her thoughts in focus. Time seemed to cease, but it was only a few minutes later, while still lying against the post, Justine whispered, "Who is she?"

"My younger sister, Valonia. Now you see why I was taken aback when we first met. She was murdered twenty-five years ago in Austria. She had a three-year-old daughter who disappeared when she was killed. I've spent all these years trying to find that child, but I always seemed to run into dead ends. The men that took her covered their tracks very well. When I first met you, I dismissed it as pure resemblance or longing to see something that wasn't there. As I got to know you, I've became convinced that it might be more than that."

"She died in the clearing," Justine sat up, replying in a trancelike state. "Surrounded by the forest. There were two men with guns and crosses. She shoved me into the bushes to protect me. Then she lured them away, but I could still see."

Horror seized Regina as she realized that the child had watched her mother's death. Her mind reeled at the thought, and she realized Justine had gotten up and was again in front of the portrait, gently touching the woman's face.

"My mother," Justine whispered.

With her own eyes, Regina witnessed the awakening of a long-buried and forgotten past. Justine turned to face her, eyes filled with tears of sorrow and confusion. "She was my mother," she said with conviction.

Regina moved over to her, wanting to hold her but unsure of the reaction she would receive. "And you are my niece." She smiled, crying her own tears.

Justine collapsed into her waiting arms. "Who am I?"

Tenderly, Regina grasped her chin and raised her head until their eyes met. "If you feel up to it and want to, we'll leave tomorrow and find out the whole story and truth from the minute you were taken, but tonight you need to rest." Regina focused her mind, and with a hypnotic suggestion, Justine drifted into a deep slumber. She lifted the young woman in her arms and carried her to the guest room and placed her in bed. After she lay her down, she looked at her and softly touched her face. "You're home now, my heart."

Allowing herself a few more minutes to savor the joy of finding her niece, she turned and went to make their travel arrangements.

4

Helplessly, she watched as the man pinned her mother down. The woman fought them, clawed, kicked, punched, and used every bit of energy she had, but they overtook her. One of the men straddled her and aimed the large piece of wood at her heaving chest.

For a split second, the girl saw her mother look over at her. The child wanted to run to her and stop these men from hurting her, but her mother's voice rang out in her head, "Stay hidden, love." The thought was cut off as the wooden stake was driven into her heart.

Her mother's scream echoed in the air, sending birds aloft and animals into hiding. The child continued to hear the scream even after it stopped. It would be a haunting memory of unknown cause of fear for years. The men leaped back, covering their ears, but keenly watching the woman in case she offered another fight. The last thought the child ever heard from her mother was "Run, my love."

The child's heart threatened to break free of her chest as the tears ran down her face. She didn't want to leave, but the men had begun searching the area and were nearing her hiding place.

One of the men stopped suddenly and stared into the bushes. "Over there." His voice boomed to his partner, and with that, the child broke cover, running as hard as she could for the deeper forest.

Brush, twigs, and branches slapped at her face and body, but she didn't dare slow down. She could hear the voices, grunts, and heavy footsteps closing in behind her, and ran harder. Her heart pounded in her chest, and she ducked under a fallen tree that had come to rest against another tree. Her mind scrambled to think of all her hiding places. She and her mother had spent a good deal of time in the woods playing hide and seek, and she had been a fast learner.

Spotting the nearby rock formation, she decided it was the safest place and made a run for it. She thought of the cool, dark crevices underneath the rocks and could almost feel the safety when she was knocked to the ground.

The fall knocked her breath out, and she landed with a "oomph." Then large, strong hands roughly grabbed her arms and turned her face up and held her down in place.

The man was tall and slender with dark skin and black hair. Sweat rolled down his face, and his black eyes burned with anger. "Hand me one of the damn stakes," he yelled to the other man who came up huffing and puffing beside him.

The other man moved closer, staring down at her, the sun behind him, blocking her from seeing his face, only a shadow. "It's a child," he said in amazement. "Definitely its child. This is the first time I've ever seen one. It's amazing."

The dark-haired man lightened his hold slightly. "So do you want me to stake it or what?"

"I want to examine it first. This is a rare opportunity, and I don't want to waste it. Sedate it," Shadow Man replied, reaching into a large bag. He brought out a small black kit. In less than a minute he had filled a syringe with a murky-yellow fluid and handed it to the dark-haired man.

The child began to struggle, but it was no use against the grown man. As the needle pricked her arm, she screamed.

The scream carried over as Justine sat up in bed. In a flash, Regina was there, holding her trembling body.

"It's all right," Regina soothed as she began rocking the young woman slightly. "It was only a nightmare. You're safe here."

"They killed her, Regina," Justine stated, her breathing becoming more normal. "And they found me and chased me. They kept calling me 'Its child.'"

Regina continued rocking, but she felt her eyes changing with the growing anger and used all her willpower to pull it back. "Tine, it was a memory, a horrible nightmare of a memory. Is this the first time you've ever had these?"

Justine pulled away from Regina and took a deep, calming breath. "I've never been able to remember anything from my childhood before the orphanage. I've had flashes, but never anything that made sense until now. How could I have forgotten that? My mother and her murder."

Regina met her look with compassion. "Sometimes, something so terrible happens that the mind just blanks it out. It's a coping or survival mechanism."

Tentatively, Regina reached out and grasped Justine's hand. When she felt a slight squeeze returned, she continued, "You were a child and that you witnessed . . . what they did . . ." She felt her own emotions threatening to rise up, and this time it was Justine that offered a firm squeeze of her hand. "I hate that you've had to remember all this, but it confirms my suspicions. I believe you are my niece, and after our trip, more things will make sense."

"Trip?" Justine repeated.

Regina stood up but maintained her hold on Justine's hand. "Yes. I mentioned it last night. I thought if you want to, we could start tracking down your past and find out what happened. We both have a lot of unanswered questions, but if you're not up to it or want to wait awhile, or don't want to do it at all, that's fine. It's your decision."

Justine's head was spinning. "I want to know the truth, but what about your business, my job? You can't drop everything." She eased out of the bed.

"Garrett will handle things while we're gone, and besides, you are the most important thing in my life right now, not business."

"What if you're wrong. If I'm not your missing niece?"

"I don't think I'm wrong," Regina started, "but if I am, I'd rather find out now so I can keep searching. At this moment I am certain you're my niece, and verifying that is more important to me than anything."

Justine hung her head slightly. She was not used to being important to anybody; she was the one that could wait, while others came first. To be so accepted and loved so quickly left her feeling unsteady and desperately wishing for it to be true. She managed a smile. "So it would go from Boss Regina to Aunt Regina?"

Regina felt her heart almost stop for an instant, and tears began to fall freely. She had waited to hear those words for twenty-five years, and they were sweeter than she ever imagined or hoped. Her own research had confirmed the woman before her was Valonia's daughter. Now she had to show Justine for herself.

Seeing Regina's tears, Justine took a step back. "I'm sorry. I didn't mean to upset you. I shouldn't have made that assumption, I'm sorry."

Regina smiled warmly and wiped away her tears. "Honey, it's nothing you said or did. Well, actually it is something you said. I am so glad to have you here and have found you after all these years that it was just so . . . overwhelming to hear you call me that."

"If it is true, is it okay to call you that, I mean not in the workplace but privately?"

"Oh yes," Regina said proudly. "Whatever and wherever you feel comfortable with. Why don't you take a bath and get dressed, then you can pack, and I'll have the private jet ready to go in a few hours."

"Private jet. Pack. Yes, okay." Justine stopped after the first step. "May I hug you?"

Regina stepped forward and wrapped the girl in a warm, loving embrace that both held for a minute or so. When they parted, Regina smiled to see the blush on Justine's face. "Shower, pack, check," the young woman said and left for her apartment via the back elevator.

Regina left the bedroom and, as she shut the door, came face-to-face with Ward. "What are you doing here? I didn't call you," she asked, caught off guard by his sudden appearance without being summoned.

"Is she all right? I want to see her," he answered firmly.

Regina looked at him oddly, unaccustomed to such insubordination. "She is fine, Ward, just very confused. We have a plane to catch in a few hours and are in a hurry. You can talk to her when we get back."

She started to walk past him, and he grabbed her arm. "I want to see her now. I love her, Regina, and I want to be with her."

Jerking her arm from his grasp, Regina moved close to him, face-to-face. "Don't ever do that again," she whispered menacingly.

"I'm sorry," he apologized unconvincingly. "But you don't understand."

She backed away from him. "Yes, I do, but you must understand how confused she is right now. She doesn't need more confusion."

Ward made no attempt to hide his anger now. "We love one another, that's not confusing." He turned on his heel and left her apartment, slamming the door as he left.

He went downstairs to her apartment and knocked loudly. After a minute or two, she opened the door wearing only a bathrobe. "Ward?"

"I just spoke to Regina. Are you all right?"

She took his hand and led him into the apartment but stopped in the hallway. "Ward, we need to talk."

He closed the door behind him and drank her in with his eyes. "Are you all right, babe? What can I do?"

She caressed the side of his face and smiled weakly. "I'm okay, it's just so much to take in. My whole life has done a 180."

"What can I do to help," he repeated.

"A hug would be nice."

He took her in his arms and savored the feeling it gave him. He wanted to hold her and protect her forever; then he thought of the argument with Regina. As if she had read his thoughts, Justine met his eyes. "You and Regina do not need to be at odds over this. I care about both of you and have time for both of you, but I can't stand arguing. It reminds me of home, plus it makes me feel as if I've come between you and your work relationship."

Ward lightly brushed her cheek with a kiss. "If we argue, it's not your fault. We argued before you were in the picture."

She pulled away from his arms, face serious. "Regina and I are leaving town for a while to find out the truth about my past. I care for you and I need you, but this is something I have to do on my own. Please understand and be patient and don't blame Regina. She has a lot invested in this as well. She's only trying to help and protect me, just like you."

Nodding hesitantly, he sighed. "You know all you have to do is pick up the phone and I'll be there. I'll be patient and wait. You are important to me, and I know that this is important to you and Regina. Go, find out the truth, and be careful."

"I do love you, Doc." And she sealed it with a long kiss.

The information they needed only took a little over a week to find. As expected, most of the records had been "lost or destroyed." They met resistance at the orphanage, the constable office, and the doctors in Austria. With a simple flex of her mind and greasing of the palms, long-buried files were located. They obtained copies of everything and, as the final confirmation, ventured into the forest around the small town called Aldhelm.

Regina has stayed back and let Justine lead the way straight through the woods and into a small clearing. Justine felt a tightening in her chest, and her breath hitched when she saw the spot where her mother had died. The area was identical to her visions and dreams. The smells of the fauna that surrounded them soaked into her and triggered more flashes of memory. There was a memory of Regina playing with her in the nearby lake as her mother watched. She knew that what Regina told her had been the truth.

Staring over the area, Regina approached from behind and explained that, as per Valonia's wishes, she had been cremated and her ashes spread over their home in Greece. She could hardly tell the child that the ashes had been desecrated with holy water and left to dissolve in the meadow.

Justine nodded, and Regina again retreated, fading into the background but constantly on guard for trouble and protectively watching her niece.

A warm breeze caressed Justine's face, and the sun offered warmth like a blanket. A variety of birds and insects chirped a welcoming greeting, and for a second, she could swear she heard a child's ghostly laughter in the wind. As she walked by a large tree, she was jolted by a flash of memory. In her mind's eye she saw Regina, her mother, and she having a picnic under the shade tree and laughing. Another jolt revealed her lying in her mother's arms while she was told a fairy tale. She felt the sting of tears as more memories came back, after each one, an empty pain stabbing into her heart.

Sensing that the girl had all she could take, Regina moved in. Shortly after, in silence, they returned to the hotel. Regina called the pilot and let her know they would be leaving the next day and watched as Justine studied the files until she drifted off to sleep sitting up.

Now that they were on the plane and airborne, Justine remained in her own silent world. Other than a few words at the hotel, she kept everything bottled up, trying to soak it all in. Regina had understood and given her plenty of space, but now she was becoming concerned.

Leaning forward in her seat, she looked into Justine's eyes. "Tine? Please talk to me."

Justine never took her eyes off the seat in front of her, staying silent a few more minutes. Regina was about to sit back when Justine asked, "How old are you?"

Regina had already prepared her cover story and answered, "Forty-four. Why?"

There was no masking the surprise in Justine's eyes, even though her face was passive. "You don't look it."

Regina smiled. "The women in our family age slowly. You'll appreciate it when you're older."

"How old was my mother?"

"You want the whole story? The things that weren't in the files?" Regina sighed. She dreaded bringing up the pain of Valonia's death, but when Justine nodded yes, she began, "She was fifteen when she got pregnant. She was alone in Austria, and when she called me, I came. She was so young, and as the oldest, I always tried to look out for her. I was angry at her for running away, but she needed me, and my anger vanished." She stopped for a minute and took a breath. "Val never told me who your father was, and whenever I asked, she got very upset, so I let it be. I stayed with her for the next three years. When she went into labor, there wasn't even time to get to a hospital, so I delivered you."

Justine's face softened. "You?"

Regina smiled at the memory. "Yes, me. Guided you out, caught you, and clipped the cord. You were the most beautiful baby, and you've grown into a beautiful woman, like your mother."

Justine blushed; then a shadow crossed her features. "So she ran away, got pregnant, and called for you. Where were you when she was killed?"

Closing her eyes, Regina struggled to maintain control of her anger and grief. "I was in the States, trying to make some business contacts. I was only gone for two weeks. We had been safe for so long, and I knew before we moved to the States we had to have a way to live. I promised you that I'd be back in time for your third birthday. I got back with three days to spare . . . and two days too late to save Val."

The pain Regina was feeling was obvious, and Justine gave her a few minutes before she spoke again. "By safe, you mean, safe from the killers?"

The conversation was interrupted by the pilot's announcement that they were approaching the New York airport and to fasten their seatbelts.

"What was she like?"

Quietly, Regina searched for the right words. Her face glowed as the memories came back. "Val was my best friend and the best mother I've ever seen. She was a loving, compassionate, understanding, and intelligent woman. Oh, she could be stubborn, and though she rarely showed it, she had a fierce temper. She never had hate in her heart for anyone, and she was honest to a fault and loyal to her family and friends. The thing I loved about her the most was her childlike quality. She could look at the sky a thousand times, and each time it was like the first."

Justine was staring at her hands in her lap, pain radiating from her face. Regina lay a comforting hand on hers. "And she loved you more than life itself."

The engines of the plane slowed, and it began its descent. A stewardess quickly secured their glasses and prepared for landing.

"Why did they kill her?" she asked, clenching her teeth.

Regina gave her hand a slight squeeze. "Honey, this is not the place to discuss that. When we get back to the penthouse, okay?"

Justine nodded and reclined her head back against the seat as the plane touched down.

After they had reached the penthouse, Regina went about making phone calls to reestablish her presence and Justine sat at the bar, again studying the files and having a drink.

When Regina returned to the living room, she found Justine pacing and clearly agitated.

"Justine . . . ?" she started but was cut off.

"Seth Reynard killed my mother because he thought she was a vampire? Then he put me in an orphanage and adopted me over a year later. It's bullshit, Regina. This is the kind of crap he writes about."

The time had come. It was now critical to say the right thing. "You have the files, Tine. What more do you want or need to convince you. It's all there in black and white."

"How the hell could he get away with it. My birth certificate was a forgery, the reports were 'lost,' and it was like a giant cover-up. Name of mother was Jane Doe. I . . . can't . . . get my head to wrap around this."

Regina remained silent.

"I mean, I knew he claimed to do this, or this character of his did. That's how he did research on his books. But to really kill innocent people and get away with it. He's nothing more than a mass murderer. How can the authorities condone all this?"

Regina sat down on the couch. "There are those in authority that share your father's beliefs."

"Don't call him that!" Justine growled.

Regina put her hands up in surrender. "I'm sorry, Tine. Seth Reynard is not the only one who does this for a living. There is a whole network of people who do this and those who cover it up."

"They're killing people, claiming they're vampires. How can anybody believe this garbage and go along with it. I know people are crazy, but this is over the edge. He killed my mother because of it."

"Yes, my sister."

Justine stopped pacing and slammed her fist on the bar, causing the glassware to jingle loudly. "Vampires do not exist. They are fictional creatures made up to scare children and moviegoers. Sure, I like a good vampire movie every now and then, but it's fiction, not reality."

"Are they?"

Turning, Justine looked at Regina oddly. "Of course they are. You can't tell me that you believe they exist!"

Regina's voice was calm and soothing as she spoke. "Tine, there are so many things that we don't see or understand because we refuse to be open-minded. Have you ever just stopped and taken a look around you? Can you explain everything you see? And if you can't, do you dismiss it as unreal, fictional? Seth Reynard's job exists because they do."

Justine laughed. "Uh-huh. So you're telling me vampires are real. That my mother, your sister, was one. This is not funny, Regina. I think you've been working too hard."

Regina smiled patiently. "Vampires are not the horrid creatures of the theater who kill innocent people, sleeping in coffins for fear of daylight. They are people who want to live as normal a life as they can, just like everyone else."

Visibly uncomfortable, Justine shifted her feet. "My mother was murdered. I was pretty much kidnapped, and now you're telling me that bloodsucking creatures of the night really exist. Please, Regina, you're making me nervous."

"Tine, I love you, you're my blood. I would never hurt you or try to frighten you, and I will never, ever lie to you. I told you this information might jeopardize our relationship, but you have a right to know."

"What are you trying to tell me, Regina?"

Taking a deep breath, Regina leaned forward. "What would it take to make you believe in them?"

Justine's nerves were frayed, and again she laughed nervously. "Come on, Regina."

Regina's voice was more commanding now. "What would it take to convince you?"

Startled, Justine gave in. "I guess seeing one."

Regina stood up, arms held out as if to say, "Here I am." The she released the change and showed her glowing red eyes before smiling to reveal razor-sharp fangs. She was taken aback by Justine's calm reaction. "Then why am I not one?"

The red glow quickly faded as the fangs retracted. Before her again stood the very normal and beautiful Regina. "We very, very rarely have children. When we do, few are born normal. Most die at birth, but on occasion the child is normal and healthy and does live. You were one of those precious few."

Justine took a step back, shaking her head and laughing softly. "I'm having a nervous breakdown, that's got to be the answer. I'm going to go now, because I need some rest and a reality break, unless you want to bite me or something." She reached down and grabbed her bag and moved for the front door.

Regina remained still, making no advance to stop her. "You're free to come and go as you like. If you don't want to come back, I will accept that, but know that this is your home. You've had a traumatic week, and you need some time to accept everything you've learned. Please just remember that you are not alone any longer. I am your true family, and I will never hurt you. I will always be here if you need me."

Justine looked into Regina's brown eyes and knew that was all true. Her fear melted away, but the anger was growing. "Thank you for everything, Regina. For the truth," she replied and walked out the door.

Ten second later, Ward appeared in the living room. "Protect her," Regina instructed. "Don't let your presence be known. She needs some time alone to accept the truth and everything she's learned. She will need you, us, but we must be patient. Keep me informed."

Ward nodded and left the penthouse.

Two Days Later

Cameron and Seth had just sat down to dinner when the doorbell chimed. "Sit still, son, I'll be back in a minute," Seth said as he got up and walked through the house to the front door. Opening it, he was surprised to see Justine on his doorstep.

"We need to talk," she said firmly as she walked past him, not waiting for an invitation or argument.

He closed the door, unsure of whether the chill was from the cool February air or Justine. "It's good to see you. What brings you back to town?"

When he turned around, the weak smile on his face faded. Justine was standing in the hallway, arms crossed across her chest, her face set and grim. Seth's defensive posture slipped into place, his face hardening as his body stiffened. "Why are you here?"

When Justine spoke, her voice was low and angry. "Because you killed my mother, you bastard. I wanted to see if you had the guts to admit it to my face."

His eyes widened in surprise. Somehow, she had discovered the truth, and now his mind was scrambling to figure out how. "She was a monster. By killing her, I saved you the same fate."

Justine nodded and licked her lips. "And it took you two years that I spent in a hall called an orphanage to decide this?"

"You don't understand my position or the truth about them," he tried to explain.

"I understand that because of your insane belief in mythical creatures, you killed my mother! You took my life away from me!" Justine's voice had raised steadily, and her face reddened.

Cameron appeared with a smile at the sound of her voice, but the smile quickly dissolved when he heard the argument. "What are you doing here, Tine? Why didn't you call?"

"Cameron," she said, trying to remain calm, "this is between Seth and me."

Before Cameron could speak, Seth raised his hand to silence him. "Where did you get all this information?"

Justine laughed and turned around, facing the staircase. She looked up at the ceiling and stomped her foot against the floor. "What does it matter? At least I know the truth."

Seth glanced at the silver cross hanging over the doorway, directly over where Justine had entered the house. He relaxed slightly, knowing she wasn't one of them.

Turning back to face them, she looked directly into Cameron's eyes. "Did you know?"

He looked down at the floor, his silence the answer.

Justine exhaled a shaky breath. Looking around the room, she remembered her youth in this house. The only good memories now were of her adoptive mother. Her eyes settled on the picture of Cheryl Ann hanging in the living room. "Did she know?"

Seth followed her gaze and dropped his head slightly. "Yes, and she loved you as if you were her own."

Justine's face softened, and she smiled sadly. "But she did love me anyway. It was probably her idea to adopt me, and after seven years, I lost her too."

Again, she directed her stare at Cameron, tears welling in her eyes. "I thought we were close, that we had no secrets. You can be proud, Seth, he is truly your son."

"Tine, I never lied to you or kept secrets from you. I only recently found out, right after you were here for Christmas. It didn't make a difference to me and still doesn't. I love you, whether you're my blood sister or adopted sister."

She couldn't mask her disappointment or pain as she spoke. "I wish I could believe you, Cam. I don't know who to believe anymore. My whole life is a lie."

Cameron stepped back as if he had been slapped, her words stinging him more than any blow she could ever deliver. "Tine," he whispered.

Seth now became firm. "He does love you. He never knew any of this until I told him. You can hate me, hell, I deserve it, but Cameron never deceived you."

Her stare became hard as stone. "Have you ever killed anyone, Cameron? One of these supposed monsters?"

"They kill innocent people, Justine. I've seen what they can do," he defended earnestly.

"One of them was my mother." She faced Seth again. "Well, at least I know why you hated me all my life. What I want to know is why didn't you kill me like you did my mother or why you even adopted me?"

"I've never hated you," he disagreed.

Realization suddenly hit her. "You wanted to keep an eye on me, to see if I'd sprout fangs and a cape, that's why."

"You never believed in my work," Seth tried to explain. "I never felt the need to tell you the truth about your mother. Whenever you heard me mention vampires, you thought I was a lunatic. How was I supposed to tell you the real story? You would have never believed me." His anger was showing now in his reddened face.

"You never tried, did you?" she countered.

Taking a few steps closer, he leaned in, his voice soft and enveloping. "You believe now, don't you? You've met one, and they've shown you that they exist. That's how you learned the truth."

Angrily, she pushed past him, headed for the door. "They don't exist, you old fool. The point is, you killed my mother because you're a crazy old man." Yanking the door open, the cool air rushed in, as Cameron moved to stop her. She turned on him and shoved him out of the way, her voice quivering, "I don't ever want to see either of you again."

Seth stepped over to the door as she walked down the sidewalk. "Be careful, Justine," he warned. "They are real, and they are deceivers and murderers."

Justine stopped in the middle of the sidewalk and turned back to look at him. "They they're just like you, aren't they?" Her voice was icy. The words hung in the air as she continued to the waiting rental car.

Both men watched her car vanish and stepped back inside the warm house, quickly shutting the door. "We don't have much time, son," Seth stated grimly.

"What do we do?"

After years of this life, his thoughts came automatically. "Get me on the first flight to New York. I'm going upstairs to pack."

"Why New York?" Cameron asked, picking up the phone.

"That's where she's been, and that's where they contacted her. I'm going to speak to her boss and that man you said she was seeing." He started upstairs then looked back at Cameron. "Write down all the names, numbers, and addresses of the people she's mentioned and given you in New York."

Seth climbed the steps, leaving Cameron alone to make his calls. While on the phone, he decided to get two reservations for the city.

Regina stood up and cheerfully greeted Seth when he arrived for his appointment the next afternoon. She offered him a seat and then offered coffee, which he politely refused. She continued smiling and returned to her desk.

"Now, Mr. Reynard, how may I help you?" she asked in a strong, pleasant voice.

He was practiced in the hunt and watched her closely, trying to appear relaxed. "Thank you for seeing me on such short notice. I needed to speak with you about my daughter, Justine."

Regina nodded and leaned forward. "How is she? She was so upset when I saw her last."

"Could you tell me when that was?" he questioned.

Regina chewed her lip and looked at her desk calendar. "Ah, about a week and a half ago, when she quit."

Surprise registered on his face. "Justine quit? She said she loved this job. Did she give a reason for quitting?"

"I sent her on an assignment to do some marketing research in Austria. She was only there for a week, but when she came back, she was clearly upset. After giving me her reports, she told me she was quitting. I was just as surprised as you. She told me she loved her job and appreciated the chance I'd given her but that something very serious had come up in her personal life and it needed her immediate attention. I told her I was sorry to lose her, and after she collected her severance pay, she just seemed to vanish."

Reynard was puzzled. Who had she found in Austria that knew the truth? "Justine never said what kind of problems?"

Regina shrugged. "No, and it wasn't my place to ask. All I can tell you is she was fine before she left for Austria. I do hope she's all right. Justine was a good assistant, hard worker."

"What about her boyfriend, Ward?" he asked next.

Regina leaned back in her chair. "He's been in Japan for the last month. They kept in touch, but when he reported in day before yesterday, he wanted to know why he hadn't heard from her. He didn't even know, and I had to tell him. I was not happy about being put in that position. He's due back next week. If you'd like to speak to him, I'll be happy to set up an appointment."

"Is there anyone else in town that might know what's going on with my daughter?" he asked, becoming more discouraged by the minute.

Regina smiled sympathetically. "Justine was very well thought of by the associates here, and she had many friends, but no one that she was really close to. In fact, other than business, we didn't socialize that much. She spent some time with Ward, but even he didn't see her a lot of the time. She was a workaholic."

He seemed appeased, if not frustrated, and stood up, a new mystery rising in his mind. "Thank you again, Ms. Derrick. You've been a great help."

Regina also rose to her feet. "I'm glad I could help. When you see Justine, please tell her we wish her the best and to keep in touch."

He reached out, and they exchanged a civilized handshake. "I will. Good day."

She walked him over to the door. "Goodbye, Mr. Reynard. Safe trip."

Seth walked down the hallway, and Regina shut the door with a smile of satisfaction.

The house was still and dark, but she knew it so well she didn't need light. Quickly, Justine made her way downstairs to the basement office of her father. She knew that he and Cameron had left for New York the night before and guessed she had two days at most to do what she was planning. After their confrontation, she had driven far enough down the street to keep out of sight and be able to watch the house. She was rewarded when they left the house, and she followed them to the Hartsfield Atlanta Airport. After they had boarded and the plane took off, she went to the ticket counter and feigned the last daughter who missed the plane and found out they would be back in a day or so.

She drove back to the hotel and made her plans, plans that led her back here tonight, breaking into Seth's house and going for his research material.

As usual the door leading to his office was locked, but with a little patience, she was able to pick the lock and pushed the door open. The interior was pitch-black, and now she did turn on the flashlight she had brought with her. The bright beam revealed a short hallway, its walls covered with various crosses. Gold, silver, wooden, iron, all types and sizes. At the end of the hallway were two steps leading down to the office and a light switch on the wall. She laughed slightly to herself as she closed the door and walked down the hallway, feeling like she was in a B horror movie.

She flipped on the light, and when she saw the den, the feeling was intensified. The far wall where his desk sat was covered with more crosses; in fact, they were all over the walls, as were wooden stakes, swords, and knives made of silver. One wall comprised a line of bookshelves, and she moved toward them. Staring at the spine of the books, she saw that there were no words, only years. After a second, she realized they were diaries. Scanning the volumes, she located the year of her birth and removed it, then seized the following six years. Before she turned, she decided to take the most recent years as well.

Arms loaded, she turned and looked at his desk and saw a medium-sized box filled with discarded paper next to it. She walked over, picked up the box, dumped its contents into the floor, and dropped the diaries in. Looking around the room, her eyes fell on the wall of filing cabinets. Each cabinet drawer was sealed with a small silver cross instead of a normal lock.

Now she began rummaging through the cabinets. She discovered histories of various people, personal facts, descriptions, aliases, contact, means of destruction, and current status. She took a step back and looked at the cabinets, seven in all with four drawers each. It would take her forever to go through them all without knowing what she was looking for. She closed her eyes, thought for a moment, then played a hunch.

Walking along the cabinets, she stopped when she found the drawer marked R. Pulling it open, she searched through the paper-packed files. The hunch paid off when she found a file with her own name on it. Removing it from its place, she opened it and looked at the personal data sheet. Under the name of *Mother*, she found Valonia Fabian. She closed the file, tossed it in the box, and moved back to the *F* drawer. Finding four Fabians, she confiscated them all. After looking through Valonia's file, she got more names and began pulling files. When she was finished, she had at least twenty files in the box.

Beads of perspiration popped out on her face, and she stopped long enough to catch her breath. As she glanced around, she saw the computer on Seth's desk. She lightly smacked her forehead and went to the desk. The desk drawers were locked, but her fury had built up, and after several minutes, she yanked open the top drawer and found the key to the others. The CDs were in the bottom drawer. There were no names only letters of the alphabet, but one did have a label marked *Contacts*. With little thought she grabbed them all and added them to her growing collection.

Rummaging through other drawers, she found and took some books on vampires and legends.

After three hours, she had finished her search and stood in the center of the room looking around. The box was full, almost overflowing, and she felt the urge to set the place on fire but decided against it.

"This was never my home," she whispered to the darkness. She thought of her adopted mother. Cheryl Ann was the only person who tried to make her a part of the family, but her early death had closed that chapter. Cameron, she thought, had tried to do the same, but in the end, he had revealed himself to be just like Seth, a liar and murderer.

With a final, silent goodbye, she picked up the box and left the house for the last time.

Four Days Later

Regina stood on the balcony of the penthouse, looking out over the twinkling New York skyline. She finished the goblet of wine-blood mixture and closed her eyes, trying to read something, anything from Justine.

Ward had called her four days ago when Justine arrived back in town. He had only been able to tell her that Justine had checked into a motel on the other side of the city and had not left since.

Regina hadn't felt this fearful since her sister's murder, and her heart ached for her niece. Garrett had been sympathetic and comforting while at the same time making arrangements for their departure. She had known the risk of telling Justine the truth but had done so anyway. So far it was certain that she had told no one the truth, but Reynard's curiosity had been roused.

Thinking back to their meeting, she smiled slightly, knowing that she had managed to throw off his suspicion and make him look elsewhere. She had so very badly wanted to tear his throat open and gorge on his hated blood, but now was not the time. Her main concern now was for Justine.

Snow began falling again, adding a new coat to the already-white landscape. A sudden gust of cool air made her senses scream with awareness. Dressed only in a silk nightgown and matching robe, the cold that would have frozen mortals invigorated her.

The silence was broken with the shrill ring of her phone. She reached into the robe pocket and retrieved her cell phone. She smiled when she heard Ward's voice and his news: "She's on her way to you."

"Are you sure?" she questioned.

"I've been following her for the last fifteen minutes, and that's where she's headed."

Concern edged into her voice with the next question. "Is she all right?"

Ward hesitated. "She looks really tired, Regina." His voice was full of worry. "She's been locked up in that hotel room for the last three days going over all the things she lifted from Reynard's house. She got pizza one night, but to the best of my knowledge, she hasn't eaten or slept at all. She does have the box with her."

"Thank you, Ward," she said earnestly. "I know this has been hard on you too, and you will be with her soon, you have my word. All I ask is just a little more time."

"All right," he responded curtly and hung up.

She took a deep, cleansing breath and sat down to wait.

Forty minutes later, there was a knock at the penthouse door. Regina waited a few seconds before she answered the door, mentally preparing for her visitor.

When she opened the door, she suppressed the gasp that tried to escape. Justine looked more than a little tired; she was exhausted. Her face was pale and drawn; her normally styled hair was limp and lifeless. The twinkling blue eyes were dull and bloodshot, with black smudge highlights.

Her voice was only a whisper as she spoke, "May I come in?"

Regina's eyes widened as she opened the door further. "Of course."

Justine eased in slowly, almost stumbling and dropping her box, and immediately Regina was there to steady her. She helped her over to the couch and sat down on the opposite end, not wanting to overstep her bounds. "Can I get you something?"

"Something to drink, please," Justine whispered.

Regina flew off the couch and rushed to the bar, grabbing a bottle of mineral water. She fixed a glass with ice and carried it back to the living room.

Justine took the glass and bottle and poured the drink, her hands shaking all the while, then sipped the cool water. She cleared her throat and looked at Regina, who was standing a few steps away. "Did you mean what you said last week? My family? Always being here?"

Regina took a tentative step closer. "With all my heart, Justine."

Justine took another drink, sat the glass down, and leaned forward. "I've never belonged anywhere or to anybody. I was taken from my real mother and put in a home where I was an experiment in progress. Everything I've known in my life has been a lie. I never believed in vampires until a week ago. You may be a vampire, but I've seen you display more loyalty and honesty than I've ever gotten from anybody in my whole life. I want to know who I really am, my true family. All my life, there has been something missing, a hole. When I first met you and got to know you, that hole started closing. If that is what my family is, then that is what I am. I want to know everything about . . . my family, to be a part of a real family. Would you help me? Please?"

Regina felt her entire body relax. This was what she had been waiting for. She, too, was regaining her family. She kneeled down by Justine and lightly placed her hand on Justine's arm. "You are my niece, and I love you with all my being. I will tell you everything, something I have never shared with another person. The entire history. Don't ever be afraid of asking me anything, and you should never fear me. As long as I'm alive, no harm will ever befall you."

Justine was crying, and Regina slid onto the couch and put her arms around the girl's shaking body. "I want you to rest now. When you have your strength back, I'll tell you the whole story if you like."

Justine nodded slightly and within two minutes was asleep in her arms.

Justine woke up late the next afternoon and found herself in Regina's spare bedroom. She sat up slowly and looked around. The room, done in cool blues and earth tones, offered a sense of security. On top of the dresser across the room was a carafe of coffee, a small tray of fruit and pastries, and a vase of freshly cut flowers. Two of her suitcases and her overnight bag had been set outside the bathroom, clean towels lying on top. She smiled slightly, stomach rumbling its emptiness, and she got up to devour the tray of goodies.

An hour and a half later, she came out of the bedroom, running a shaky hand through her shower-damp hair. Taking a deep breath, she proceeded to the living room.

Regina was sitting at her desk, catching up on work, when she sensed the young woman's presence. Laying down the pen, she turned around and smiled. "Feeling better?"

Justine returned the smile as she inched closer. "Much, thanks. What time is it?"

Regina glanced at her watch, "A little before six. Are you sure you got enough rest? You still look tired."

Justine sat down on the couch. "Yes. For now. I am still a bit hungry though."

Regina closed her files and stood up. She was dressed casually in khaki pants and a beige shirt, her hair down and flowing over her shoulders. Justine noticed that she seemed to float as she moved across the room and joined her on the couch.

"How about we order some dinner? What are you in the mood for?"

Justine shrugged. "Just about anything sounds good."

"You've lost about twenty-five pounds since you've been working for me, so why don't we splurge and get pasta?"

Justine laughed. "That's fine, I just have to watch my girlish figure."

Regina went and ordered their dinner and then returned and sat back on the couch. They sat in silence for several moments, each feeling uneasy and unsure of how to proceed now that the truth was out in the open.

Justine finally mustered up the courage and broke the silence. "What is my real name?"

Regina grinned. "Sigrid Megan Fabian. I'd like to add Derrick to that, if it's all right. Fabian is a name known to those that hunt us."

"Sigrid Derrick," she said the name aloud, liking the way it sounded. "Yes, I like that."

"Sigrid Megan is a good, strong Greek name. Your mother never forgot her birthplace."

Remembering the portrait of her mother, she looked at Regina oddly. "She didn't look Greek."

Regina laughed and sat forward. "Our parents had eight children. Your mother and our oldest brother were the only ones with brown hair and blue eyes. Everyone else looked Greek, like me. Some of the village people thought blue eyes were a sign of evil."

"Village? Sign of evil? Where was this and how long ago?"

"The family farm was on the outskirts of a tiny fishing village called Pirkra. It's on the western coast of Greece, not far from what is now known as Patria. As for how long ago . . ." Regina closed her eyes and thought for a moment. "Four hundred and ninety years ago. Just this side of five hundred."

Justine's eyes were wide with disbelief. She handled it the only way she could, with humor. "Well, you don't look a day over three fifty."

Regina snickered. "Thank you. I know it's a shock. I was transformed when I was sixteen, your mother was fourteen, and our brother was seventeen."

"How?"

Regina got up and went to the bar and began fixing them a drink.

Justine noticed that Regina seemed uncomfortable and tried to ease it. "Regina, if you'd rather not talk about this, that's okay."

Regina finished at the bar and returned with their drinks, handing one to Justine. "No, I want to share this with you, it's just been so long, and I've never really told anyone the whole story."

"Relax, Regina." She smiled as assurance. "I've made my decision. I'm not going to run away. I'm here to stay, and you can tell me anything. After finding out that vampires exist, I don't think you could tell me much that would surprise me."

Regina tucked her leg up under her on the couch and muttered, "Don't be too sure." Before Justine asked to explain, she sat back and began the five-hundred-year-old tale.

"Pirkra was a small village at the edge of the Aegean Sea off the gulf of Korthinthiakos. Five miles inland was the most beautiful forest I have ever seen. The trees reached up to the sky, and forest was home to more species of animals than any of today's zoos.

"My parents had built a small farming cottage right between the forest and the nearest village. They kept an herd of sheep, and my father also worked with wood. My father's name was Titus Cadmus. He was the typical Greek, tall, muscular, olive skin, black eyes, and curly black hair. He was seventeen when he met my mother, Zena, she was fourteen. He moved her from Mykinos to Pirkra to live on the Cadmus family lands. The Cadmus clan was respected in Pirkra and the outlying lands. They were hard workers with a reputation for wisdom that led many Cadmus men to become holy men. My grandfather had been one such man.

"Ten months after the marriage, they had their first child, a son named Timon. A year later another son was born, Erasmus, and the following year, Theo, who goes by Terrence now. My father was so happy. Zena had given him three strong, fine sons to carry on the family, although he was a bit wary of Timon because of his blue eyes. He knew mother had been faithful, but it was believed among some of the Greek legends that those born with blue eyes were demons or in cohorts with them. Timon proved himself to be a true Cadmus when he followed the path of a holy man.

"A year after Theo, I was born. My mother named me Megan, and she was thrilled to have a daughter at last."

"Megan?" Justine interrupted. "I was named after you?"

"Yes." Regina smiled and continued, "Next came Solon, Thea, your mother, and then Argus, and the baby of the family, Hesper. Father was thrilled with five sons, and as the years passed, the farm grew. We three girls were always helping Mother with the female chores, cooking, cleaning, and sewing, but I enjoyed exploring and more tomboyish activities. When Father was busy or away from the farm, Erasmus would take me into the woods and teach me how to hunt and fish. I learned rather quickly and became quite good. I never will forget the first time Father found out. I had come in with an eight-point buck, and when he tried to congratulate Erasmus, Erasmus told him the truth. He was outraged at first, then finally had to admit I was as good a hunter as any of his sons, and he was very proud of me. That was probably one of the last times we were all together and happy.

"A month later, Hesper came down with fever and was dead within a week. She was only eight when she died, and we all took it hard. She was such a sweet, loving child. Timon was crushed. He was especially fond of her and had always spent any free time he had reading to her and telling her stories. He was so lost that a few months later he went to the monastery, several hundred miles away, trying to make sense of such a useless death. Father was furious. He was losing his oldest, a good farmhand, but in the end he understood and gave Timon his blessings.

"Six months later we received word that Timon had been killed. He was working with the village children, and a Turk tried to rob him. Only a Turk would never realize that a monk had no drachma, and when he got no bounty, he stabbed my brother.

"Father was devastated. Timon, his firstborn, his favorite. My father was always a friendly, loving man, but he became quiet and withdrawn. He spent more and more time in the fields, and Mother prayed constantly, trying to find answers for the death of her oldest and youngest.

"We children took comfort amongst ourselves. Thea and I stayed close to Erasmus. Solon and Argus, never parting from one another, worked around the farm with Father. Theo stayed to himself. Even as a child he was a loner, showing nothing but contempt for the rest of us, so we stayed away from him. In fact, at times we even feared him.

"Summer was fading into fall, and one day Erasmus decided to go hunting for some meat he could salt and preserve for winter. I begged to go, but Mother refused. His smile was so warm and bright it could melt an ice block. He kissed me on the cheek, promised to tell me all about it. He was never heard from again."

Regina stopped for a minute, memories as fresh and unpleasant as they had been hundreds of years ago. Justine reached out, resting her hand on Regina's. She was about to end the obvious discomfort that the story was causing when there was a knock at the door.

The distraction came at a good time, and Regina went to the door for their dinner. The two women set the table and discussed everyday things then sat down and began to eat. Halfway through the meal, Regina continued.

"Solon, Argus, Theo, and my father searched the forest, but all they ever found was his bow and a few drops of blood. Thea and I were heartbroken. To be killed was bad enough, but he had completely vanished. We knew he had not run away or gotten lost, and as much as we tried to speculate what had happened, nothing made sense. With no body or sure proof he was dead, we were never able to fully accept his being gone. Father withdrew even more, and Mother prayed day and night, ignoring her household duties and leaving the family to us. Thea and I were already close, and we drew even closer, our thoughts never far from Erasmus.

"Solon had a knack at foretelling the weather by nature's signs, and about three months after Erasmus disappeared, he saw that there was a huge storm coming our way. He and Argus helped Father secure the farm while Mother sent Thea, Theo, and I into Pirkra for a few supplies to tide us over. Usually, Thea and I would have gone alone, but since Erasmus vanished, there had been several villagers attacked and killed by what the Elders called 'flying demons,' so Father sent Theo with us.

"We made it to the village, got our supplies, and were on our way home when the storm hit suddenly. It was so fast and fierce that we lost our bearings and stumbled around the countryside. Soaking wet, cold, and scared, we were about to give up when like a beacon, we saw the glow of firelight through the darkness. We followed it and found ourselves by the caverns on the other side of Pirkra, near the ocean. The storm had pushed us two miles farther from home, and it showed no signs of letting up, so we sought refuge in the cavern.

"It was a large cave formed by the rushing sea. It was damp, but as we moved in, we discovered that it was drier toward the back. That is where the fire we had seen was burning. It was a huge fire, and there was no one around. We thought perhaps someone else had gotten lost in the storm, but we never found a trace of them."

"It seemed like the fire had been built just for us. Theo called out for the builder and explored the cave a bit, but it was empty and silent. He was satisfied that we were alone, we sat down beside the fire and enjoyed the shelter and warmth. We still had our supplies from town, so we had some food to tide us over, and we did eat a little, but we were so exhausted. Theo suggested we get some sleep so we would be ready to go home when the storm let up. Thea and I happily agreed and within minutes were curled up together and sound asleep.

"I don't know how long we were sleeping, but suddenly I was awakened. I'm not sure what it was, a clap of thunder, Thea dreaming, or a wolf howling, but something woke me, and I sat straight up. Thea was on one side of me asleep, and Theo was on the opposite side of the cavern. He looked like he had dozed off while standing watch. Then I heard the noise again. It was my name being called very softly.

"I turned toward the front of the cave and saw the shadow of someone standing at the mouth of the cavern. For a split second I was afraid, but then I heard my name again, and it was a familiar voice, and all my fear melted away. I walked to the shadowed figure, and when I got close, I saw it was Erasmus.

"He swept me up in his arms, and we hugged tightly, I almost lost my breath. When I tried to ask him any questions, he shushed me and led me out of the cavern, and I noticed that the storm was over, but a chill was in the air.

"He looked the same, only pale, and his touch was cool. He took my chin in his hand and lifted my face to his. 'I missed you so badly, Megan, that I had to return.' I told him how much I missed him and couldn't stop the tears that began.

"Gently, he wiped my tears away and offered me soothing words. When I finally stopped crying, he said, 'I have something to share with you and Thea, but you must trust me and truly want my gift. If you are afraid, I'll leave now, and you'll never see me again.'

"The thought of him going away again was all I needed to agree with anything. I told him I loved him and trusted him, and he embraced me. As he held me, he nudged my head to the side, revealing my throat. I heard him whisper, 'Take this gift, my child,' and then I felt a combination of pain and pleasure that was overpowering. After that everything is cloudy. I remember flashes, Erasmus leaning over me and feeding a warm, salty fluid in my throat, then he and Thea talking. The next image I remember is of Theo in front of him begging. When I woke up, it was still dark and I was back in the cavern with Erasmus, Thea, and Theo.

"When all three of us awoke, Erasmus began explaining the rules of our new lives. I'm sure you're familiar with the lore, but there are some things that are wrong. We have to hide from the sunlight at first, but over the years we can build up a resistance to it. We do need to feed every day in the beginning, but as time goes by, we can get by with only one meal a week. We do age, but very, very slowly. Then he took us hunting, and there is no way to describe the way everything felt, smelled, and looked after the change. It was overwhelming, but we all adapted quickly.

"Theo and Erasmus began arguing after a few months, and Theo went off on his own. Thea and I stayed with Erasmus for twelve years, until the day we were hunting and got separated from him. By the time we found him, he had been beheaded and a wooden stake driven through his heart. We had lost our beloved brother again and knew that we were in danger from his murderers as well. So we decided to take the money we had been stealing from our victims and leave Greece."

Justine refilled her wineglass. "What about the rest of your family, the Cadmus clan? You let them think you were dead?"

Regina bowed her head. "We did go back and watched them from a distance, but one of the rules is that you can't go back to your old life. Watching what was left with our family . . . we knew we couldn't be a part of that life anymore.

"Thea eagerly came with me, and we ventured to Italy where we adopted new names and lives. She became Vivian Fabian, and I, Risa. We spent two hundred years together, traveling around the world, learning about our powers, building a fortune to help cover our true identities. We eventually went our own ways to discover the world, and we were apart for a little over a hundred years.

"Then I met up with Theo. He was going by Terrence Bakerson at this time, and he was deceitful, cruel, and evil. He would kill for the joy of it and was particularly fond of torturing his victims first. He was like the vampires in the legends. Wearing all black, only living in the night, and he had gained a small following. He swore that he would destroy Thea and I because he didn't want someone being as powerful as him. He said he would hunt us down for sport and then drive stakes through our hearts. I knew he meant it and was frightened. I managed to lose him in France and immediately began searching for Thea.

"I found her in England, posing as an artist. I told her of the encounter, and we decided to stay together for a while. Terrence did track us down, and he made sure we knew he was close, but he never attacked. That was part of his game, to keep us scared and unsteady. Truth be known, I think he feared our combined strength. Anyway we moved around for years, changing names and lives, and we ended up in Switzerland. We lived there for several years, and then Thea, now going by Valonia, decided she wanted to travel again. I enjoyed Switzerland, so I stayed.

"Thirty years later she sent word through others that she needed me in Austria. I went, and I found her pregnant. I stayed with her until a week before her . . . death."

Justine was leaning forward, attentive and focused on every detail Regina shared. When she realized Regina was finished, she asked, "What about Terrence?"

"He's still around," she answered quickly. "He is perhaps a greater enemy than the hunters. He believes in the old ways. Stalking his victims, hiding from sunlight, even wearing all black and a cape. He fashions himself after the vampires you read about or see in the movies. The ironic part is he thinks I'm a traitor to our kind. You have to keep in mind that what I've told you is a very condensed version of our history. To tell you more would take days and probably bore you senseless. I have lived through World War I and II, the Civil War, Invasion by the Turks of Greece, the plague, land wars, and all kinds of disasters and many pleasures. I've met interesting people and a few of our kind along the way. Later, if you want, I can give you more details on our travels, but now I assume you're more concerned with family."

Justine nodded, feeling a little overwhelmed but more curious than ever. "Yes, I am, and I'd like to know more about my mother and Terrence. Is there a feud going on between you and Terrence?"

Regina stood up and stretched her legs. "Let's just say that for him and his kind, a stake through the heart is too kind for the atrocities he has committed."

Justine raised her eyebrows. "You said he believes in the old ways, like the ones in the books. Am I to assume the hunters think you're all like that?"

Regina walked over to the glass doors that looked out over the city. "Yes. Some of the things he's done are more ghastly than the wars in history. What amazes me is that he has so many and such a strong following."

Justine walked over to the bar, refreshed their drinks, and joined Regina at the balcony door. She handed her the glass and leaned against the wall. "How are you different from the stereotype?" she asked bluntly with no sarcasm.

"For one thing, I don't kill unless I have to, as in self-defense. We have followers who are more than willing to donate blood for us, and they are amply rewarded."

Justine couldn't mask her surprise. "You mean you don't attack and fill for food?"

"No." She smiled. "It's very civilized, kind of like a blood bank. There are those that believe in us and want to help us. They seek us out. The only time we attack is if our lives or the lives of our family are in danger. On the rare occasion we do kill, we make sure it's a criminal or someone that is a harm to society. Then, I think, we are justified."

"Even mortals do that, defend their own," Justine reasoned. "You said followers and us. How many are there in your coven?"

"We are not witches, Justine," Regina answered patiently. "But we do have rules, and that means that even though you are my niece, no mortal can ever find out our true numbers. I broke one rule by telling you our true names, but I believe you have that right. Terrence is the only one that uses the word *Coven*. We call ourselves family, because we are."

"Are you recruiting?" Justine asked in a semi-serious tone.

"No," she answered sternly, then turned serious. "That is your decision, just as it was mine and your mother's. If you want the gift, it is your birthright. If not, then you will still be welcome among us. You can continue to work for the company as you did before you knew the truth. I've told you before, that if you want to leave you can. That would break every rule we have, but I would not stop you, only ask that you give me your word of secrecy."

"I would never turn on you, Regina. You're the first person in my life that has been truly honest with me. You are my family, and I won't betray that. I've had enough of that in my life, and it stops now. I give you my word."

Regina reached out and gently touched Justine's cheek, her eyes tearing up. "Thank you, Justine."

"Sigrid," she corrected.

"Are you sure?"

She took Regina's hand. "It's the name my mother gave me. I know the truth now, and since I'm starting a new life, I need a new name. My true name."

"Every two hundred years or so, our kind have been blessed with a child. I'm glad you were born to us."

"One in two hundred years?"

"The legends say that we were granted immortality at the expense of procreation. We believed that until a child was born. Since I came over, I know of only eight children born to us. Four died shortly after birth, the others were taken. Within a five-year span there were four births, including yours. The family thought it was a miracle, unfortunately, three met the same fate you did. One child was killed by a hunter. He killed mother and child. You are the first of those remaining children to be found, and we will never stop searching for the others."

Justine looked at her directly. "No. You came looking for me. When you found out who I was or suspected who I really was, you encouraged the friendship. Were you going to kill me because I was Seth Reynard's daughter?"

Regina turned and walked back to the couch. "No," she said, staring at the coffee table. "Not kill you, turn you. Make you one of us." She turned back to face Justine, her eyes flashing with anger. "Damn it, Jus . . . Sigrid, he killed my sister, your mother, and many other family members. I wanted him to feel the pain I did. I thought by turning his daughter, he would feel that. When I first met you, I was amazed at the resemblance to Val but attributed it to coincidence. Our friendship is genuine. As I got to know you better, I knew you were my niece. I had Garrett do some checking, and when I was proven right, that's when I told you."

Sigrid searched her eyes for the truth. "What about Ward? Was he part of the plan?"

"No," she assured. "I asked him to dance with you at the club, but he fell in love with you on his own. He told me that night that you were breathtaking and that he had never met someone who made him feel the way you did."

"Is he one? A vampire?"

Regina shook her head. "No."

Darkness had settled over the city now, and Regina turned on some lamps stationed around the penthouse. As she returned to the living room, she found Sigrid sitting by the bar, waiting for her.

"I appreciate you telling me the truth about all this," she began. "It's not something I'm used to, so please be patient."

Regina smiled warmly, her eyes alight with love. "Of course."

Justine bent over and picked up the box she had taken from the Reynard house and took it over to Regina, setting it down at her feet. "I visited Seth's library while I was gone."

"I guess that's why he paid me a visit," Regina answered passively.

Sigrid's eyes widened, and the color drained from her face. "Oh, Regina. I'm so sorry. I never thought he would come here. I put you and everyone in danger. I'm sorry."

Regina waved her hand. "It's okay." She soothed and smiled. "I told him you had quit because of family problems and I hadn't seen you in two weeks. He bought it, and I've changed my name and life since he last heard of me."

Sigrid still seemed upset, and following her intuition, Regina took Sigrid's hand and squeezed it reassuringly. "Don't worry, love. It's fine."

"Maybe not," Sigrid said and nudged the box with her foot. "Now it's my turn to say I've got some information you need to know."

Regina glanced at the box and met Sigrid's eyes. "Are you sure you want me to read those? I mean there has to be some very personal things in there. Things you may not want me to read."

Sigrid licked her lips and shuffled her feet. "I don't want you to read those because of certain things in there. Things that concern you, and that's why you have to read them. I think I may have opened Pandora's box, and I'm afraid of what might happen after you've read them."

Concern covered Regina's features, and she looked more carefully into the box and at its contents.

"Thank you for dinner and everything. I think you should be alone when you read those, and I think you should start right way. I'm going to spend some time with Ward and then get some more rest. Call me when you need me."

With that she disappeared into the bedroom, emerged carrying her bags, and left the penthouse, leaving Regina alone and staring at the box.

She found Ward in his apartment, a floor below her own. When he opened the door and saw her, he immediately swept her into his arms and carried her into the apartment.

Once inside, he kissed her passionately and then cupped her face in his hands. "Oh, sweetheart. I've been so worried and have missed you so much. Are you all right?"

She turned his hand and kissed his palm. "Just tired. I missed you too. I wanted you with me, but I had to do this alone."

He led her over to the couch, and they sat down. He draped his arm around her shoulders and savored the feeling as she snuggled against him. "So are you okay with it?"

"You mean the fact that vampires do exist and my mother and family are all vampires. Oh yeah, I'm fine. Things like this happen every day to me."

He looked at her face to see if she was being sarcastic but saw only warmth in her features. "Hell of a note, ain't it?"

She leaned forward and kissed him softly. "What's it like, being with them?"

He took a deep breath and wrapped his other arm around her. "I've been with Regina for ten years, the last six as her bodyguard, and I have been amazed at how much they are like us. They're more confident, more powerful, and a lot more loyal and truthful than mortals. I was a high school dropout, punk kid headed straight to hell when Regina found me. She took me in, took me under her wing. She helped me get my life together, gave me a job, and taught me about responsibility and loyalty. I've never regretted a minute of it, especially now, because I've met you."

She snuggled against him closer, enjoying the safe feeling there. In the last few months, for the first time in her life, she had begun to relax and enjoy the new sense of security she had found with Ward and Regina. She had always been so independent and careful to never reveal her feelings or any type of weakness. But now she had found that she enjoyed having someone to lean on and be the strong one for a change.

Stifling a yawn, she sat up and kissed him. "I hate to, but I've got to go, Doc."

He pulled away slightly and looked at her. "Why? You just got here. I can order dinner and you can tell me what's going on. I want to spend some time with you," he argued.

"I know, honey, but I'm exhausted, and we need to get some rest. When Regina finishes with the information I gave her, I think we may be very busy."

For a moment he looked angry, and then he forced a smile. "Five more minutes and then I'll walk you up, okay?"

She agreed. This was the first time she had caught a glimpse of this side of Ward. It left her unsettled by his tense reaction.

Garrett arrived at the penthouse shortly before eight the next morning. He could sense Regina's anger before he even got off the elevator. As he opened the penthouse door, he took a deep breath, preparing for the stormy atmosphere. He found Regina in the middle of the bedroom floor surrounded by papers and small, thin black books. It was obvious she had spent the whole night looking over these things, and as she looked at him, he saw how weary and haggard she looked. Fear and worry seized him. "You need sleep, Regina," he said softly but firmly.

Her voice radiated anger and weariness. "Garrett, we have some things to do, and they must be done quickly, or more of our family will die."

He eased over to her and kneeled down, glancing over the papers in the floor. "What is it, my Queen? What's happened?"

"I want everything we have on Terrence, and I want to know where he is now. Keep tabs on him at all times, and if any of the families see him or his coven members, they are to contact us at once, then relocate immediately. I know now why so many of our family have been killed."

His face was pale, alarm spreading through his body. "What's going on?"

Her face became hard, eyes burning brilliant red. "Terrence is leading the hunters to our people. He's one of their best informants, and he is the one that led Reynard to Valonia. He led Reynard to her and watched her die."

"Are you certain? Where did you get that information?"

"It's all here," Regina answered as she motioned to the paperwork scattered around her. "In Reynard's personal files and diaries. He really does keep meticulous notes, and that's to our advantage. Just . . . Sigrid brought me Reynard's files on us. He knows Terrence as Terry Baker, mortal."

Garrett stood up, his own anger flowing now. "I'll take care of everything, but you must get some rest, Regina. The family needs you strong and clearheaded, and at the moment you are neither."

Regina stood up slowly, accepting his extended hand as an aid. She turned and offered him a weak smile. "You're the only one who can get away with such disrespect, and you're right."

She walked over to the bed, sat down, and ran a hand through her hair. "I don't want to be disturbed by anyone but you telling me that everything is rolling, All right?"

"Yes. Rest well, my Queen," he answered. With that he turned and left the penthouse.

Sigrid had spent the morning catching up on emails and finishing up on outstanding projects. Once finished, she headed straight to Regina's and arrived promptly at five the next afternoon. The main offices had cleared out quickly, typical for a Friday, so the floor was almost deserted when she reached Regina's open office door.

Garrett was standing beside Regina, who was working diligently at her desk. Ward was seated by the door and smiled as she came in. "Hi, babe," he whispered.

She smiled at him then proceeded to Regina's desk. It was obvious that something important was going on as they whispered and looked over folders. She had expected Regina to call for her sooner and was now convinced that the woman was angry for bringing the information to her. She had been relieved when she finally received the call to meet with her now.

"I can come back later," she said softly as she stood in front of the desk.

Regina looked up and smiled. "No, it's okay, Sigrid, please sit down." Sigrid took the seat in front of Regina's desk. Regina whispered something to Garrett. He nodded and then went over to sit next to Ward.

The tension in the room caused her to shift slightly in the chair, and Regina instantly picked up on it. She offered a warm smile and let her defensive stature fall away. "Don't be nervous. We have a situation brewing here, and it's got me on edge."

Sigrid relaxed slightly. "It has to do with the information I gave you, doesn't it?"

Regina sighed. "You are so very perceptive. You're a lot like us without the trials and tribulations. Your perception is almost like a sixth sense, and now you are in danger like us."

It was Sigrid's turn to look worried. "What kind of danger? Is it because of Terrence, because of what he's doing with the hunters?"

Garrett coughed slightly and cleared his throat. Regina looked at him and nodded, then turned back to Sigrid. "You already put that together? Just from the files?"

Sigrid shrugged. "Not until you told me about Terrence. After that it was easy to figure out Terry Baker and Terrence are one and the same. I never meant to cause you any trouble."

Regina read her thoughts and frowned. "Honey, I'm not angry with you. By bringing this to my attention you have saved countless lives."

Not completely convinced, she cut her eyes at Garrett before resuming her questions. "Then why am I in danger?"

"One, because Reynard will have figured out who stole that information and will be calling all his sources, Terrence included. Terrence will assume that the information is in my hands and that I've found out what he's up too. That will lead to retribution for ruining his plans. Two, if Reynard tells him everything, Terrence will want you dead. You remember the diary stated that Terry insisted mother and child be killed, and Reynard told him you had been. Three, if there is a war, you could be captured and killed, and I can't bear the thought of that. That's why you're leaving town in the morning."

"Leaving town?" Sigrid and Ward said in unison.

Regina shot Ward an angry glance, and Garrett grasped his arm, but Ward shook it off and walked over to Sigrid, placing a protective hand on her shoulder.

"I know it's a shock, and I don't want to do this, but it's the only way to ensure your safety. All of your expenses will be taken care of, and I'll keep in touch. As soon as the dust is settled, you'll be back home."

"You can't just send her away," Ward argued. "If she goes, then I'll go with her as her protector."

Regina gritted her teeth trying to suppress the rage directed at Ward. "You are known to Terrence and his coven. Sending you would be the same as putting a target on her back."

He started to respond when Sigrid grabbed his hand and squeezed it, then stood up. "I don't want to leave, Regina. Do I not get a say in this? This whole situation is my fault, and I want to stay here with you and my family."

Regina rose to her feet and leaned forward on the desk, looking directly into Sigrid's eyes with such intensity that Sigrid felt them burning into her. "Do you want to live, my niece, or are you ready for the grave?"

Sigrid took a half step back. "Is it that serious?" she asked honestly.

Regina sat back down. "If this becomes a war, it could be the end to us all."

Sigrid, too, fell back in her chair, mind reeling. The room was deathly silent, and after several minutes, she looked at Regina, her eyes threatening to release tears. "I swear I never meant to cause you or the family all this trouble. I'll do whatever you ask."

"What!" Ward almost shouted.

Sigrid jumped at his outburst, but again grabbed his hand and squeezed, urging his silence. He complied, but he couldn't keep her from feeling the anger that was radiating from him.

Regina took a deep breath. "Our family, Sigrid. You are a part of this family now, and if I didn't love you, I wouldn't do this. I just found you, and the last thing I want to do is send you away, but your safety is paramount to me." She stopped long enough to catch Sigrid's nod of agreement and continued. "You go home and pack. I'll come over and help in an hour or so, and we'll have dinner."

Slowly, Sigrid rose to her feet, whispered something to Ward, and left the office.

When they were sure she was gone, Regina leaped over the desk and was in Ward's face so fast that he stumbled backward. "How dare you question my decisions and treat her as a possession!" she growled, fangs beginning to extend. "She is confused enough right now. She thinks all of this is her fault, and the truth is, if not for her, Terrence would have continued until we were all dead."

"How dare you use me and this situation to get her closer to you," he growled back.

Garrett had silently eased behind Regina, ready to jump into the fight.

"I never used you to get to her. I asked you to dance with her. The rest, you two did on your own. As for using this situation, I am terrified of losing her, yes. For the last twenty-five tears I have lived with the knowledge that she might be dead. Now that I've found her and she knows the truth, I'll be damned if you or anybody is going to stop me from protecting her."

"You haven't left us alone for a minute since you used me at the club that night. What is it, Regina? Are you jealous? I'm not available to jump in your bed when you're in the mood anymore so . . ." He was cut off when she slapped his face.

Rubbing the stinging red welt she had left on his cheek, he pressed on. "You have interfered from day one, and now you want to send her away from me. I will not stand by and let you destroy what we have." He turned to leave when she grabbed his shoulder and spun him around, clutching his throat and lifting him a foot off the floor. When he glanced his eyes down, he saw she was levitating to maintain the height.

"I am trying to save her life, and you will not interfere with that. She is my niece, my blood, and you couldn't love her any more than I do. I'm sending her away to protect her. She sees that, why can't you? If you truly love her, you'll want her safe." Slowly she lowered to the ground with him and released her hold on his throat.

"What's next to drive us apart?" he asked, rubbing his throat. "Are you going to turn her?"

Regina stepped back and smiled. "I'm beginning to think that you're the jealous one, Ward. Please tell me that I'm wrong and that is not what this is about."

He looked at her harshly and turned, stomping out of the office.

She exhaled and put her hands on her hips, "What's happening to him, Gar?"

"Growing pains?" he suggested.

Ward paced around the room, causing Sigrid to grow nervous as she tried to pack. He had come down to her apartment and been going off since then.

"How can you let her do this to us, Tine? She's sending you away from me." He sighed, with an undercurrent of whining in his voice.

"Sigrid," she corrected patiently as she continued packing. "And she's doing this to protect me, not destroy what we have." She stopped herself before she added, "You're doing a good job of that yourself."

He threw his hands up in the air. "What happened to the strong woman I met in Atlanta? You're letting her run your life, you've even taken a new name, her name."

She stopped what she was doing and looked at him. "Sigrid is my name. The name my mother gave me. Regina told me the truth about who I really am. If you call that running my life, then you're mistaken. I asked for her help and she's given it, but I'm making my own decisions. The woman you met in Atlanta is standing right here, and she's starting to wonder what happened to the wonderful, supportive man she met in Atlanta." Dropping the sweater she was holding, she put her hand on her hip. "Why are you acting like this, Ward? I thought we had something special."

He instantly calmed down and slumped his shoulders as he moved toward her. Hesitantly, she walked into his open arms. "We do," he assured her. "That's why I don't want you to leave. Or if you really want to, let's go together. Both of us can just pack up and disappear."

She pulled away from him. "We can't. She needs you, and I have just gotten my true family. I'm not running away from that. Why can't I love both of you? Why are you making me choose?"

Ward stepped back, his eyes glassy. "So you're choosing her over me. I thought you loved me?"

Before she could answer, he was gone, slamming the door behind him. She watched the door a moment, speechless, then turned back to her suitcase. Staring at the contents neatly packed away led her to make a decision.

Regina, slowly sipping the blood from the goblet, was startled when she heard a soft knock on the door. She rapidly finished the contents of the goblet, stuck it in the soapy water in the sink, and rushed to the door.

Opening the door, she smiled at her visitor. "Sigrid? What are you doing here? I was about to come to your apartment."

"Is this a bad time?"

Regina shook her head. "No. Never for you. Come in." She opened the door wider as more of an invitation.

Once Sigrid was through the threshold, she closed the door and followed her into the living room. Sigrid came to a halt in the middle of the room and turned to face Regina. "I want my birthright."

Regina's eyes bulged, and she stepped back. "Sigrid?" she began unsurely. "Do you know what that entails?"

"Yes," she answered confidently, "I know, and I've thought about this. You told me it was my decision, and I've made it. I want my birthright."

Regina retreated across the room and slumped on the couch. "I know you're upset about leaving, but this is not going to solve anything."

Sigrid shook her head. "It's not that, Regina. I want the life that was stolen from me, and since I'm responsible for all the trouble now, it's time to claim that life and my family."

"You are not responsible," Regina shot back.

"But I am," Sigrid cut in. "You said yourself that I'm in danger and gave me all the reasons, each one concerning me and what I've done. I've just gotten my true family back, and already I've started trouble. My actions endangered you, and I will be there fighting by your side, whether I'm mortal or not. I won't run away from my blood anymore."

Regina sighed, knowing the young woman's mind was made up and that arguing was useless. "You can never go back, Sigrid. This is not like a pair of shoes that you try on and decide you want to take back when they're not comfortable. This is for keeps. You watch people you know and love age and die, while you live on."

Sigrid strode over to the couch and sat down beside her. "What do I have to go back to? A lie? A life that was never my life?"

"Your brother and friends in Atlanta. What about Ward?"

Sigrid squirmed in her seat, clearly uncomfortable. "I only had acquaintances in Atlanta, and Cameron turned out to be just like Seth. This is my home, you're my family. As for Ward, I'm not sure I want that relationship to go any further."

"I guess that's my fault," Regina apologized.

"No," she disagreed. "It's his. He not turning out to be the person I thought he was."

"Sigrid, you're about to step into a very volatile situation. The last time there was a vampire war was three hundred years ago, and it was very, very bloody and horrible beyond description. Do you realize it could lead to your death?"

"I stand a better chance fighting with you than on the run as a mortal. If what you said is true, I'm marked either way. At least this way my odds increase a whole hell of a lot." She got up and went to the bar, grabbed a glass, and filled it with vodka, then took a long, stiff drink.

Regina rose and drifted over to the window facing the city. She had waited for this moment for so long that she was surprised at the doubt that was creeping in now. She wanted Sigrid in her life. For the first time since Val's death and Sigrid's abduction, she was at peace. Yet there was a bitter turmoil raging as well. What Sigrid was asking for was a dream come true and a nightmare. Logically, she had no doubt that Sigrid could handle everything that came with conversion, but surprisingly enough, it was her heart that protested. She loved Sigrid, of that neither one had any doubts. And it was that love that made her hesitate, hesitate to throw her beloved niece into a situation that she could never fully understand as a mortal.

"You'll be immortal, Sigrid. Except for the few things that can kill you, you will see those you love and care for grow old and die while you stay young. You'll be moving constantly, changing identities, always wary of strangers for fear of them being a hunter. It is not a glamourous life or an easy one. As my niece, you will have a lot of responsibility. In the event of my death, you will have to assume control of the company and family. Justine Reynard will vanish off the face of the earth, gone, no more. That's only an inkling of what you're asking for. Do you understand?" She struggled to explain.

Sigrid set the glass on the bar and joined Regina at the window. "I understand that Justine Reynard ceased to exist several weeks ago. She wasn't real, just a made-up cover. I am Sigrid Fabian Derrick. I've always been wary of strangers, and I'm not close to anyone but you. As far as responsibility, nothing will ever happen to you, and in the event that it did, my past work should speak for itself. You sought me out, told me the truth about my past, revealed your secret, and told me to make my own decision. I've done that, and now you're trying to talk me out of it."

"No," Regina corrected gently, "not talk you out of it, make you aware of it." She was losing the battle, running out of arguments.

Sigrid stared at the floor for a moment. Looking back up, she reached out and took Regina's hand and led her across the living room. She continued into the bedroom and stopped in front of the portrait of her mother. Releasing Regina's hand, she kneeled down. She looked up at the portrait and then straight into Regina's brown eyes. "Give me my life back, Regina. Please," she whispered as she turned her head to the side, revealing a willing, slender throat.

Her reluctance dissolved. The look in Sigrid's eyes and the tone in her voice caused her to toss away all the doubt that remained. The girl knew pain and deceit. It had been her whole life, and she had dealt with it and became a stronger person. Regina wanted to ease that pain and prayed that the girl was strong enough to accept and deal with what was about to happen.

Closing her eyes, Regina kneeled down in front of Sigrid, softly placing her hands on Sigrid's shoulders and leaning toward the offered exposed neck. She opened her glowing red eyes and parted her lips, revealing the razor-sharp fangs.

Sigrid remained still, never making a sound as Regina whispered, "Take this gift, your birthright, my child." Then she buried her fangs into the soft flesh. Sigrid jerked slightly, and Regina draped her arms around the girl as a brace.

A wave of euphoria swept over her as she drank the blood and realized Sigrid was still a virgin. In these days and times, it was so rare a find that the sensation caused her to unconsciously roll her eyes back in her head. She was brought back to awareness when Sigrid wrapped her arms around her waist and urged her closer.

Longing had outweighed fear as Sigrid waited for the bite. As she felt the teeth puncture her flesh, fear reasserted itself, joined by pain, and she reflexively jerked.

The pain had vanished, replaced by a falling sensation. She was vaguely aware of Regina's arms holding her and exhaled deeply as weakness enveloped her. She continued to fall, blindly reaching out and finding Regina's waist. Latching on for security against the abyss into which she was falling, she pulled Regina closer. Savoring the feeling of closeness and safety, she moaned and then relaxed as the abyss took her.

The two of them were locked together, breathing in unison and oblivious to everything but the sound of a faintly beating heart. Sigrid arched her back and moaned as she lost consciousness and slumped against Regina's warmth.

Carefully, Regina released her hold on Sigrid's throat, licking her lips for the few remaining drops of pure blood and then scooped the girl up in her arms.

Rising to her feet, she carried her niece over to the bed and lovingly laid her on the bed. She stared down at her, the blood racing through her veins and causing arousal. During the course of her lifetime, she had taken many lovers, mortal and immortal, male and female. From her first meeting, she had been torn between the thoughts of wanting Sigrid to be her niece and hoping there was no relationship between them so she could take the young woman for herself. She had, for a few seconds, entertained thoughts of them as lovers but had quickly scolded herself for such thoughts. It was not uncommon for immortals to take relatives as lovers, but she was strongly against it.

She was brought out of the thoughts by Sigrid's moaning. Reacting quickly, she sat on the side of the bed and took a deep breath. Slowly, she raised her nail to her own throat and made a two-inch slit. Lifting Sigrid's limp body, she positioned her so that her head was resting on her shoulder and her lips fell against the cut in her throat. "Drink, Sigrid," she ordered softly.

She was pulled out of darkness by the sweetest odor she had ever smelled. She heard a slurred, familiar voice say "drink" and then felt softness against her lips. The sweet smell bore into her, and she sighed as a hunger unlike anything she had ever known consumed her.

Her mind spun, desperate to seek out the source of her need. Opening her lips, she was rewarded with nectar that set her soul on fire.

Sigrid stirred immediately, the smell of blood bringing back traces of consciousness. Hungrily, she placed her lips on the cut and began suckling the warm fluid, her tongue darting and lapping at any stray drops that threatened to escape. As she consumed more of the hot, salty sweetness, she felt her strength returning, and her body grew warm and tingly. The hunger was being satiated by the fluid that she lapped up so greedily.

Regina placed a hand behind Sigrid's neck for support and lay her head back for the girl's easier access. When she began to feel weak, she pushed Sigrid away and raised her hand to the cut on her neck.

Sigrid looked at her with glazed, tired eyes, a few smears of red on her mouth. "Rest," Regina instructed. Sigrid obeyed, allowing herself to be guided down to the bed where she quickly drifted off to sleep.

At that moment Regina was looking at the sleeping face of her sister, and she felt a pang of loss for Valonia. Instantly it was replaced by the love she felt for her niece. She stroked Sigrid's face and hair and then leaned down, lightly kissing her forehead.

Sighing, she got up to replenish her own strength and to make a phone call so as not to be disturbed.

She returned ten minutes later just as the transformation was beginning. Setting her goblet down on the nightstand by the bed, Regina sat down on the bed beside Sigrid.

The young woman's body glistened with sweat, her breathing shallow and raspy. Regina scooted closer, watching as her blood dominated what little amount she had left in Sigrid's own body. The girl grunted, tossing her head from side to side, and Regina softly brushed the sweaty strands away from the angelic face.

She turned her head and stared at Valonia's portrait. "Have I done the right thing, Thea? She is your daughter, a part of you, and I find I can refuse her nothing, no matter how much I want to." She continued staring at the picture, imploring it to reply or send her a sign.

A gasp behind her drew her attention back to Sigrid. The color was rapidly fading from Sigrid's face and body, replaced by a glowing alabaster tone. Regina tenderly eased the girl into her arms, cradling her, and ran her hand across Sigrid's shoulder, up her neck, and along her jawline. The skin underneath her fingers had cooled considerably, and she felt Sigrid's jaw tense as the final phase began.

Sigrid's entire body became rigid, her head pushing against Regina's shoulder, jaws clenched as spasms of pain began to rack her body.

Regina held tight, murmuring, soothing, comforting words against Sigrid's ear. When Sigrid's hand shot out into the air, Regina firmly clasped it and brought it back down to rest against Sigrid's chest. Holding her niece closely, she began to rock and hum an old Greek lullaby.

The spasms continued for most of the night. Sigrid's body eventually relaxed and went limp, cradled in the arms of her family.

Ward appeared outside Regina's penthouse shortly after dawn. He was surprised to find Garrett sitting outside the door, scanning the morning paper, but he maintained a stern look and stride as he approached. He stopped in front of Garrett and asked, "Where's Justine? Has she already left town?"

Garrett smiled. "And good morning to you, Ward."

Ward's temper flared. "Dammit, Garrett, where is she?"

"With Regina," he answered simply.

"I want to see her," he stated as he moved for the doorknob.

Despite Garrett's older appearance, he moved like a teenager and blocked the doorway. "Can't let you do that right now, Ward. Regina doesn't want to be disturbed," he said in a friendly but warning tone.

Ward stepped back and glowered in frustration, giving himself a minute to calm down before he spoke again. "Why are the two of you keeping her from me? I thought we were friends, Garrett. I love Justine, and it seems like we're never left alone. It's always Regina this and Regina that."

Garrett leaned against the door, feeling sympathy for his coworker and friend. He was still a young man and had not fully learned what it was to live and be with immortals. "Ward, I know you love her, but you've got to remember that she is Regina's niece. You know yourself how much effort she gave in trying to find Sigrid. It's taken her twenty-five years to find some happiness, and that's a lot of time to catch up on."

"She and I are not immortal like the rest of you. We don't have twenty-five years to wait," he countered and glanced at the door.

Garrett put his hand on Ward's shoulder, the tone of his voice fatherly. "Son, I've known you for ten years. I respect you and your abilities, and I consider you a friend. As a friend, I'd like to give you some advice. You can take it or leave it, it's your choice."

Ward nodded impatiently, and Garrett continued, "Be patient. Right now you're acting like a madman, and that's putting everyone off, even Sigrid. They say that love drives a man insane, and from the way you've been acting lately, you're there, my friend. Cool off, give it time and space. If it's meant to be, it will be."

Ward let the words wash over him. When he looked back into Garrett's eyes, a spark of rationality had reappeared. "She's changing so much, and I don't want to lose her, Garrett."

Garrett smiled again and patted Ward's back. "If you don't get a grip, that's exactly what's going to happen. I'll help you any way I can, but only you can control that possessive temper. I've been there, son, and I know what I'm talking about."

Garrett stepped back as Ward lowered his head and nodded. "Thanks, Garrett. Tell her I'm sorry and to call me when she's ready."

"I will." He watched as Ward disappeared into the awaiting elevator.

Opening her eyes, Sigrid's senses were violently assaulted. Colors were so bright they were blinding. The light flapping of pigeons wings outside the window sounded like the roar of a jet engine to her. So many strong smells attacked her that she thought she might lose consciousness.

Tightly shutting her eyes, she inhaled deeply, steeling herself against the assault. When she felt like she had some control, she opened her eyes again, lying still and taking everything in. This time she was better prepared and allowed the brilliance of everything to wash over her. Slowly turning her head, she was amazed and startled to feel the friction of the sheets against her skin.

At once her eyes fell to the figure beside her. Looking at her aunt's sleeping face, she realized that her emotions as well as her senses were more acute. As her eyes studied Regina's peaceful, beautiful features, she realized that she loved the woman so much it was painful. The feeling frightened her almost to the point that she felt a scream trying to rise from her.

Clenching her teeth, she forced it down and instead felt tears escape her eyes. Her birth mother was dead, but beside her lay her aunt, sister to her mother. A true family member and all hers. Everyone she loved or cared about always left her, and she was petrified the same thing would happen to Regina.

Her eyes traveled over to the portrait on the wall. The conversion had also freed her lost memories, releasing a flood of pain that took her breath away. She again shut her eyes, trying to control the tears, but was unsuccessful. Streams of wetness crackled across her sensitive skin and soaked the pillow beneath her head.

Sensing the turmoil, Regina stirred, and Sigrid froze in place. She wasn't ready to face her aunt just yet. First, she had to deal with the emotions waging a war in her. Regina stilled, knowing what the girl was going through, and wanted to give her space. Sigrid watched Regina sleeping, and after another minute, she eased out of the bed.

Regina awoke and sat up slowly. She glanced over at Sigrid and discovered the other side of the bed empty. Fear engulfed her as she leapt out of bed and called, "Sigrid!"

The fear dissipated when she heard "In here" come from the living room.

Regina hurriedly made her way to the living room and gasped when she saw Sigrid standing at the balcony window, soaking in the sun.

"Sigrid! The sun!" she screamed and rushed forward, seizing the young woman's arm and pulling her into the shaded area of the living room.

Sigrid stared at her in surprise. "What's wrong?" she questioned as Regina closely examined her arms and face.

"Are you burnt?"

"No. Why would I be?"

Certain that Sigrid was all right, she stepped back and breathed a sigh of relief. "Remember I told you that we have to stay out of the sun until we build up a resistance. You shouldn't be able to stand direct sunlight right now. At the very least, you should be burned."

"I've been standing here for over an hour, and I feel fine. In fact, I feel great!" She smiled, wide-eyed, emotion again under control.

"Incredible," Regina marveled. "It's unprecedented." Giving her niece the eye from head to toe, she added, "I wonder what other surprises you have in store for me?"

"How soon can we start finding out?" Sigrid asked with the excitement of a child. Her face glowed with youth and health, and Regina was again amazed at the resemblance to her mother.

"As soon as you like" was the answer.

Sigrid gave her a brief hug and ran back to the bedroom. "I'll be ready in twenty minutes." And she disappeared.

"Kids." Regina smiled and then chuckled as she, too, went to get dressed.

6

The sound of laughter echoed in Sigrid's mind as the motorcycles raced through the night. Ty rode by her side, his eyes constantly scanning for trouble.

Tension melted away as the miles passed beneath her wheels and the night air caressed her face. She felt her body coming alive as the night wrapped around her like a cloak and her memories flared to life with bright clarity.

She smiled as she remembered the look of surprise on Regina's face the day after the conversion. She had easily bent an iron bar in half as if it were nothing more than a twig. Leaping over a six-foot wall had not even caused her to break a sweat, and she ran with the speed of a cheetah without even breathing hard. There had been no aversion to the sun, and her instincts were so well developed that even Regina was awed. The only thing that slowed her down was learning to feed. Regina introduced her to the wine-blood mixture, but it took Sigrid a bit to overcome the mental block that made her hesitate.

During the day, the two women took care of company business, their lives differing very little since Sigrid had been reborn. In the evening and on weekends, Regina trained her in their ways. Although Garrett was friendlier, her romance with Ward had gone cold, but they still maintained a close friendship.

They traveled constantly, and as the months turned into years, Sigrid became Regina's equal in business and powers. As she met other members of the family, she quickly won them over and was so talented with them that Regina appointed her head of family relations. Coordinating family problems, new lives, and sightings of hunters or Terrence's people was a large, time-consuming job, but as Regina expected, Sigrid handled it with skill and ease.

The first three years of her new life were the happiest she had ever known. She had her family, friends, and a true life. Regina watched proudly as she thrived and blossomed into a truly amazing woman. Her own demeanor had changed now that she had Sigrid in her life. It was a welcome change among the family and, although she would never admit it, to Regina herself.

Then the trouble began. Slowly at first, but as the days passed it continued to build.

She was brought out of the memories by Ty pulling close and signaling the turnoff. Nodding, she eased off the clutch and followed his lead.

They turned off the asphalt highway and onto an old, dirt country road. They traveled the deserted roads, passing through woods and pastures for several miles, but never encountering another soul. Thirty minutes later, they arrived at a small two-story wood frame house.

Despite the late hour, the house was lit up, and three occupants quickly came out and proceeded down the steps of the porch to greet their visitors.

Sigrid and Ty dismounted their bikes and smiled at the approaching elderly couple and young man.

The woman was short, chubby, white-haired, and had a kind face that was beaming a smile of welcome. She held out her arms for a hug. "Honey," she said as Sigrid rushed into her arms and hugged her tightly.

Sigrid said nothing for a moment, only savored the feeling of safety that those arms afforded her. Hesitantly, she pulled away. "Evening, Martha."

Her husband, a tall, lanky, white-haired gentleman moved in to give her a hug of his own. She looked into his green eyes, set deeply in a lined farmer's face. "Hello, George," she greeted.

The young man with them moved up, wanting his own chance at a greeting. He was short, muscular Chicano with a brilliant white smile and twinkling brown eyes. "Howdy, Sig."

Sigrid returned his smile. "Howdy, Billy."

Martha gave Ty a kiss on the cheek and then grabbed their hands. "Let's go inside. I know you two are hungry and tired."

Never willing to refuse one of Martha's meals, they followed her inside while Billy took care of their bikes and bags.

"We can't stay long, Martha," Sigrid explained as they sat down at the dinner table.

"You'll have some nourishment, then some sleep and then you can go," Martha instructed from the kitchen. "And don't bother trying to argue with me, young lady."

Sigrid couldn't contain the laugh that escaped her. "Yes, ma'am." Ty smiled as well and nudged her arm.

George ambled in and sat at the head of the table. "Any news yet?"

Ty shook his head. "None, so far. We're going to New York to check in with Garrett." He finished and shot a worried glance at Sigrid.

George picked up on it and stood up. "I'll see if Mother needs any help." Then he vanished into the kitchen.

Five minutes later, Martha and George appeared with several dishes and three bottles of nourishment. When everything was placed on the table, they all sat down for dinner.

After the meal, George volunteered himself and Ty to do the dishes and left the women alone at the table. Staring after them to make sure they were gone, Martha turned back to Sigrid and took her hand into her own. "Are you all right, honey?"

Sigrid shrugged and squeezed Martha's hand. "Just tired."

"You sure?"

Sigrid was quiet for a moment before she spoke. When she did, her voice was little more than a whisper. "She's alive, Martha. I feel it in every inch of my being, and I will find her."

Martha put her arm around Sigrid's shoulder. "I believe you, honey. You would know more than anyone. We will find her, we won't stop until we do."

Sigrid leaned against the woman's shoulder. "I can't lose her. I just found her. We haven't had enough time. I won't lose her."

Martha held her tightly and kissed her forehead. "You won't lose her. The two of you share a special bond, closer than anything I've ever seen before, and I've been around for two hundred years, give or take. As long as you have faith, she will know it and fight whoever is holding her. That I believe with all my being."

"I love you, Martha," Sigrid whispered against her shoulder.

"And I love you," she answered, feeling tears well up in her own eyes. "You need to rest. Leave when you need to, and don't worry about waking us to say goodbye. Just make sure you call and keep us posted. Okay?"

Sigrid sat up and smiled. "Yes, ma'am. Thanks, Martha."

"Anytime, sweetheart," she soothed, her voice strong and comforting.

Ty appeared, as if on cue, and took a stand behind Sigrid, his hand lightly resting on her shoulder.

"You two get some sleep. Take the bedroom downstairs and be careful on your journey."

Martha kissed both of them and shooed them off to the bedroom. She watched until she saw them turn into the room and heard the soft sound of the door shutting. Sighing she finished clearing off the table.

They awoke three hours later, the house still and quiet. A soft breeze whispered through the trees outside the bedroom window and ruffled the curtains. Sigrid rolled over and rested her head on Ty's muscular chest. She ran her hand along the tuft of dark hair that covered his chest and inhaled his scent. She felt him stir slightly and then felt the cool hand brush against the warm flesh of her breast. It had been too long since they had made love, and her yearning came screaming to the forefront with such intensity that she was frightened.

Raising her head, she began delivering light, teasing kisses to his chest and stopped as she teased his nipple with her tongue. He rewarded her by cupping her breast and running dancing fingers across her nipple as his other hand nestled in the small of her back. Letting her hand trail down his toned body, she let it come to rest on his muscled thigh and smiled to herself when she felt his arousal. He grabbed her shoulders and pulled her on top of him, seeking out her lips. Sparks of electricity ignited when their lips met, and they hungrily devoured one another, tongues greedily tasting, as if for the first time.

He broke the kiss and let his mouth travel over her chin, down her throat, and slowly across her chest until he reached his target. Ty smiled as he saw her rigid nipple awaiting his touch and exhaled a warm breath that brought a deep-throated moan from Sigrid. Ever so slightly he ran his tongue across the hardness. Sigrid gasped and arched her back, grabbing his head and urging him to take her breast. Complying, he took the nipple in his mouth, sucking gently. Placing a strong hand against her back, he rolled over, taking position on top of her and buried his face in her breast, ravishing attention from one to the other. He let his hand drift down and come to rest on her thigh. Sigrid released her hold on his hair and let her hand travel down his chiseled body, her touch alternating between soft and firm. When she ran her hands across his buttocks, she was rewarded with a muffled groan from him.

He felt her hand lovingly caress the hardness between his legs and slightly bit her breast in response. He nudged her legs apart with his own and sat up, straddling her, his erection in full view.

"Ty," she encouraged, her voice deep and filled with lust as her body screamed for his touch.

Leaning down, his lips again met hers as he gently entered her. They moved together in rhythm slowly at first, savoring the heat and feel of flesh against flesh. She squeezed his shoulders, urging him to move harder and faster, an urging he happily met. They moved as one, eyes locking as the tension and passion grew. Sigrid felt herself approach the edge of the cliff and saw that Ty was right with her. Digging her nails into his back, she pulled him deeper into her, loudly moaning as he filled her. The speed increased again, and never losing eye contact, they felt the waves crash over them, sharing the sensation as if they were one person, and at that moment, they were.

They remained together as their bodies recovered, and then he tenderly withdrew and lay back beside her. They snuggled together, silent in the afterglow and deep in thought.

"I love you, Ty," Sigrid finally spoke. "I want you with me forever."

He clasped her hand in his, intertwining his fingers with hers, his voice soft but strong and sincere. "I'll never leave you, Sigrid. You are my heart and my life."

She leaned over and lightly kissed him, then reclined her head on his chest. Closing her eyes, she felt herself relax in time to his breathing. He casually began rubbing her back, and she looked up, meeting his eyes. Seeing his passion still burning, she began planting kisses on his stomach before sliding down the length of his body and, with a devilish smile, disappeared under the covers.

"Forever," he swore as she began working her magic under the sheets.

An hour later they were up and getting dressed. They exchanged a final kiss and picked up their things, ready to leave.

Quietly, they eased out of the house, stowed their bags on their bikes, and began pushing them down the dirt driveway.

Martha stood in the upstairs window, watching them as they reached the end of the driveway. The two shadowed figures climbed astride the bikes and brought the engines to life then sped into the dark countryside.

"They gone?" George asked from the bed across the room.

Martha remained by the window. "Yes."

"Is she okay?"

Martha surveyed the landscape in the moonlight. "She's holding up very well, just like Regina would. But the pain and frustration are starting to wear her down. She can't hide that from those that know her best."

George slowly sat up, the bed springs creaking in protest. Slipping off the bed onto the cold wooden floor, he went over and joined his wife of 142 years and wrapped his arms around her waist. Glad for the comforting touch, she rested against him.

"She is like her mother and Regina. Tough and strong, but underneath, she's like a child. Every member of the family is helping in their own way, and Regina will be home in no time," he replied as he rested his chin on her shoulder.

Martha nuzzled the side of his face. "I know." Then she looked up and into his green eyes. "I also know if Regina has been hurt, in any way, Sigrid won't stop until she has Terrence's head on her wall. And, George, I'll be right there to help her hang it."

George leaned in and kissed her forehead. "I don't doubt it, my love. Tomorrow we'll send Billy out to help in the search. Tonight I want to take advantage of that spunk."

Martha smiled and playfully slapped his arm. "Why you dirty old man, you."

George raised his eyebrows. "Heeeheee." He laughed roughly.

Martha blushed. "Oh my."

George scooped her up in his arms, "Oh yes," and carried his mate to the bed.

The first signs of trouble had begun on George and Martha Penshaw's farm six years earlier. They had lived on their farm in West Virginia for ten years and, because of their elderly appearance, aroused no suspicion as vampires.

The Penshaws were two of Regina's favorite and most beloved family members, and she eagerly introduced Sigrid soon after her conversion. Sigrid and Martha had bonded quickly, and their relationship was like a grandmother and granddaughter. Sigrid had fallen in love with the people and their horse farm and had begun spending weekends there when she could. It was during one of these visits that they had spotted a young man dressed in overalls snooping around the farm. They knew instantly he was a vampire, just as foreigners would recognize one of their own countryman. It was all in the walk and the way he carried himself.

The three of them watched his progress from inside the house as he surveyed the area and made notes.

"What should we do?" Martha questioned uneasily.

"Call Regina," Sigrid instructed calmly.

George turned and went into the living room and picked up the cordless phone. He came back into the entrance hall five minutes later and found Martha waiting alone. "Where's Sigrid?"

"Outside," she replied in an unhappy tone. "What did Regina say?"

"Help is on the way. Twenty minutes tops. Regina's coming and will be here as soon as possible. She said to monitor and keep an eye on that guy."

Turning her gaze back out the window, she quickly found him. "Well, he's still out there," she stated and nodded toward the barn.

"I'm going out to help Sigrid," George responded as he started toward the back of the house.

Martha reached out and grabbed his arm to stop him. "You be careful. You're not a young man anymore."

Cocking his eyebrow, he smiled. "That's not what you said last night." Patting her backside, he continued for the door.

Martha went back to the screen door and scanned the property. The man was bold in his wanderings, not even trying to conceal himself or what he was doing. Suddenly he darted behind a dense thatch of foliage and vanished from sight. She scoured the area for Sigrid or George, but both were excellent trackers and knew how to remain undetected.

Martha released control and let her natural instincts kick in, senses heightening. Now she could hear every leaf rustle and every flap of a butterfly's wings. Then she heard a sound in the living room. To mortal ears it would have only been a faint scraping, but to her it was as loud as an explosion. It was the unmistakable sound of a creaking floorboard when tested by weight.

The sound was not the only indicator as Martha picked up on the smell of the intruder. She had picked it up even before the sound in the house. It was a mortal smell, full of hate and fear. A hunter's smell. She remained still as he approached, her fangs dropping and her eyes glowing brightly red.

Her senses screamed now as he came up behind her. She prepared to pounce. But when she turned to face him, she was unexpectedly hit across the head, and she stumbled backward across the floor.

She tried to regain her balance but failed and landed on her knees. She immediately scolded herself for being so out of practice.

"Don't move, you murdering bitch," the man's voice ordered firmly.

When she looked up, she saw the cross he was holding, but it wasn't an ordinary cross. It was a wooden cross mounted on a small crossbow, a silver shaft protruding from the center. The cross arrow was aimed directly at her heart, and his hand was steady with experience.

Freezing in place, her eyes wide, the red vanished and her fangs retracted. She marveled at the ingenuity that the hunters kept using to develop these new deadly weapons. The man holding it was a bald, middle-aged black man, dressed completely in camouflage. His demeanor let her know that he was not a novice at the hunt.

"Who are you? What do you want?" Martha questioned innocently, trying to buy herself some time. It had been years since she had been this frightened. The last time they had fled the hunters was two decades ago in England.

He moved slowly, his arm and aim never faltering. "You know who I am, just as I know what you are."

"I . . . I think you're mistaken," she stammered as she began to rise to her feet.

"Don't move!" he growled and tightened his finger on the trigger.

She fell back into place, silently calling out for help. The fear that had seized her was starting to strangle her, and she couldn't pull her eyes away from his finger on the trigger of the bow.

"We will wipe your kind from the face of the earth." He smiled, grasping the crossbow tighter.

Martha then noticed a smoky haze moving across the room, slipping in and around furniture. She kept her eyes on the hunter but was able to watch the progress of the haze as it moved under the thick coffee table and the table began to inch off the floor.

Afraid he might see, she decided to distract the hunter. "What have I ever done to you? I just want to live my life in peace."

"Life?" He laughed. "What an odd term to use. Especially for one of the undead."

Martha threw a look of disapproval at him. "You've been reading too many books, young man. You don't really know us."

"I know your kind all too well," he answered, "and you're about to become extinct." He finished and prepared to fire. Without hesitation, he pulled the trigger.

There was a muffled pop and whooshing sound as the silver arrow left its cradle and rushed straight for Martha's heart. Wide-eyed, she could only watch and pray that it was over quickly.

Suddenly, the coffee table flew across the room, intercepting the arrow before crashing to the hardwood floor of the living room. The man's surprise held him long enough for the haze to take shape and materialize in the form of Sigrid beside him.

She pounced on him, wrenching the crossbow from his grip and using her free hand to shove him against the wall. The force she used to pin him to the wall caused several pictures to come smashing to the floor, but they were not worth noticing. All her attention was on the squirming mass in front of her. Releasing the crossbow, she let it drop to the floor beside her and moved closer to the hunter.

Her eyes were now glowing brightly red. "You lose," she snarled in a low, guttural voice. The hunter found himself being lifted, one-handed, into the air by the small woman.

Struggling to break free and breathe, he kicked against the wall, bringing more pictures crashing to the floor. Like a magician, he suddenly produced a small gold cross and held it up to Sigrid's face.

She frowned slightly, unsure of what kind of harm the cross would bring her, and when it did nothing, she snatched his wrist with her free hand.

The sounds of his wrist bones breaking was audible all the way across the living room. Wincing in pain, the hunter released his hold on the cross as she released her hold on his crumbled wrist. The cross landed with a thump in her outstretched palm. She looked at it for a moment and then back at him. His shock that the cross had no effect on her covered his face, and sweat trickled down his jowls.

Reverently, she placed the cross on the nearby table and then turned her attention back to the man. He was crying silently, consciousness beginning to fade, and he mouthed a prayer as he met her eyes again.

Snarling, Sigrid tightened her grip on his throat, ready to finish him, when she felt a hand on her shoulder.

Glancing back, she saw the kindly face of Martha. "No, Sigrid. We are not murderers like them," she said in a calming voice.

Sigrid's face softened, her anger dissipating. "Are you okay?"

"Yes, thanks to you." She smiled. Placing her arm on Sigrid's, she began pushing the man downward, his feet coming to rest on the floor. "Restrain him, honey. Regina is on her way, and George may need your help."

Sigrid relaxed her grip on his throat, and he crumpled to the ground, gulping for air and rubbing a very bruised throat. His broken wrist dangled limply at his side. He tried to retreat against the wall but found nowhere else to go.

Sigrid looked down at him, regret trying to pry its way into her. She kneeled and tried to meet his eyes.

"No!" he yelled and tried to look anywhere but at her face. Sigrid grasped his chin in her hand and held his face in place. "Please don't," he begged, afraid he was about to become the hunted.

"I won't hurt you," Sigrid promised and locked on his brown eyes. He stopped fighting almost instantly.

Sigrid reached out with her thoughts. "Sleep. You are very tired, and you just need to sleep," she vocalized her thoughts in a hypnotic tone.

He relaxed even more, and his eyes closed as he slumped against the wall. Sigrid let him slide to the floor, and she did a final probe, making certain he was asleep and not playing possum.

With a sigh, she rose to her feet and backed away from him. She turned to face Martha, her face a portrait of worry. "Did he hurt you? Are you sure you're okay?"

Martha patted Sigrid's cheek. "Fine, honey. What about you?" she asked, searching for some clue to Sigrid's state of mind but finding only concern in her features.

Ignoring her question, Sigrid glanced out the window. "Are you sure you're all right to watch him?"

Martha nodded, now concerned for George, who still had not made an appearance.

"I'm going to check on George," Sigrid replied and to Martha's surprise vanished out the back door in a cloud of smoke.

Regina had arrived an hour after the intruders had been captured, and she had Ward take them to the barn for questioning. She made sure the Penshaws and Sigrid were all right and then began her interrogation. She had wanted Sigrid to accompany her and learn, but the young woman had quietly declined and disappeared from the converging family members.

The last eighteen hours had been long and exhausting. First, she spent six hours questioning the bushman. It was obvious to her that he was one of Terrence's. He repeatedly spouted off Terrence's familiar rhetoric about how Regina was a traitor to their kind and that her family would be destroyed. The brainwashing was so complete that she had garnered very little information. The few pieces she did catch she committed to memory and then left the wiry little man to George. With a smile, George had thanked her and took out his frustrations.

It had taken seven hours to get everything she needed from the hunter. Again, it wasn't much, but every little bit of precious information counted now. She had spent the last two hours erasing his memory of the ordeal and planting different thoughts and memories. She convinced him that the Penshaws were simple farming folk and that the bushman was probably just trying to get even with the elderly couple for firing him a year earlier. After she had his arm taken care of, she convinced him that the crushed wrist was a result of him changing a tire on his car and the jack slipping. As she regained strength, she was filled in on the details of what had happened with the hunter and Sigrid's reaction.

Martha relayed her concern, and Regina agreed, immediately going out to find her niece. She knew where to find the young woman and slowly walked across the pasture, spotting Sigrid in the farthest section from the farmhouse.

Sigrid was leaning against the fence, resting her arms on the wooden planks and watching the horses within. Since the day she had first brought Sigrid here, the girl had become fascinated with the horses.

Sensing the approach of her aunt, Sigrid said with awe, "They are magnificent."

Regina remained silent as she leaned against the fence and assumed the same posture as Sigrid. For as long as she had known them, the Penshaws had an affinity for horses, breeding, racing, and just watching. Martha had told her once that their love of horses had come from their mortal days but declined to supply any more information.

Seven Morgan horses galloped and played across the field. Five females and two males, and all were a cocoa-brown color. As she watched them, Regina couldn't help but think of a ballet, and she felt some of the tension leave her body as she relaxed and watched the show. "They are beautiful," she agreed after a few minutes.

Sigrid's eyes never left the field. "George said the next colt born is mine."

Regina smiled. "That's great, honey. He knows how much you love it here and how much you admire the horses."

Again, they fell into silence. Regina felt herself relaxing to the point of getting sleepy, and she began to understand the attraction of the horses.

"Tired?" Sigrid asked, bringing Regina back to the land of consciousness. "Yes."

"Did you get the information you wanted?"

Regina detected a tone of distaste in the question and sighed. "Some. Terrence trains his followers very well, and he keeps them out of the internal loop, so he wasn't very much help. The hunter is innocent. They're being used by the very things they have sworn to destroy and don't have the slightest idea."

A frown played across Sigrid's face, and Regina knew what the next question was. "Did you?"

Regina shook her head. "No, I didn't. As I said, he's an innocent. If he had hurt any of you, I can't say I wouldn't have killed him, but he's safe and won't be a threat to us."

Sigrid pushed against the fence, turned away from the horses, and laughed sarcastically. "Some vampire I am." Stopping there, she changed subjects. "You need to rest. I'll walk you back."

Regina smiled and fell into step beside her as they started back across the field. Walking in silence, Regina decided to address what had happened at the house. "You did a very ingenious and brave thing yesterday. You saved Martha's life, and I am very thankful and proud of you."

"I'm glad I was here," she answered simply, unconvinced.

Regina sensed the conflict in the woman and continued, "Your powers are unprecedented, and I know it's been hard for you because I can't properly teach you. What you did at the house was a very good thing. Up until now you've only tested and played with your powers. This was the first time you had to really use them, and you did it to protect the family. There's nothing wrong with that."

Sigrid stopped suddenly. "But I enjoyed it, Regina." She cut herself off and bowed her head in shame. When she spoke again, her voice was softer. "That's the problem. That's why I couldn't be with you during the interrogation. I . . ." She stopped, trying to find the right words. "I savored the fear in his eyes, the feel of his bones breaking. I wanted to hurt him."

Regina reached out, grasped Sigrid's shoulder, and pulled her close. "That's normal, sweetheart. As I said, this was your first time to really exert your powers. Yes, you enjoyed it, that's the darkness of the beast. But you overcame that and controlled it. That's what makes us different from Terrence and his people. We rise above our basic instincts. We value life."

Craning her neck to look into Sigrid's face, she was surprised at the conflict she could read on the girl's face. "Sigrid, we try to be civilized and live among mortals, in peace. Every one of us has a dark side, even mortals, and it's a battle to conquer that evil. You did. You beat it."

Sigrid shook her head in disagreement and pulled away from Regina. "I guess Martha didn't tell you she had to stop me."

"Yes, she did," Regina answered nonchalantly. "But I want you to answer me this. If you had been mortal and faced a similar situation, wouldn't you have done the same thing?"

Sigrid looked down at the ground and mumbled, "Probably."

"All right then. The only difference is that you're stronger than a mortal, so you have to use a little more caution. You were angry, and you wanted to hurt him for what he was going to do. Hell, I'm not sure even Martha could have stopped me if I had been in your place. You haven't done anything wrong. What you're feeling is not wrong, sweetheart, please believe me," Regina stated in a cool, reasoning voice.

Sigrid's mood had not changed, and Regina began sensing a more serious problem at the core of Sigrid's thoughts. "Okay, what's this really about?" asked Regina.

Sigrid began walking again, and for a long while they strolled side by side. Sigrid gave her no answer to the question. Finally, Regina accepted that she wouldn't receive an answer and let her thoughts drift over the information she had gotten during the interrogations. She was still walking, deep in thought, when she realized she was alone. Confused, she stopped and turned around, seeing Sigrid had stopped several feet back, her face pale and frightened.

"I'm glad I was here to save Martha. I love her and George and would do anything to protect them. But what if they had attacked you? What if I'm not there when you need me or are in danger?"

Regina's shoulders relaxed as the truth was revealed, and she continued walking until she was standing in front of Sigrid. "Ward is my bodyguard. It's his job to protect me, not yours. In fact, I think it might be a good idea for you to get an associate to help keep an eye on things. You are my niece, not a protector. If anything, I should be worried about your safety."

"You said it yourself. My powers are unprecedented, therefore I can take care of myself and have a duty to use those powers to protect the family, to protect you. I don't want to lose you," she blurted out and then blushed at the admission.

Regina caressed Sigrid's face. "Honey, I've been alive almost five hundred years. I've been in danger on many occasions and even faced death on a few. You may be powerful, but I am no weakling. I have the strength and have learned the lessons many times over." Sigrid started to speak, but Regina rested her fingers against her lips. "Let me finish. I made a promise to you a few years ago, that your family will always be there, and I don't break a promise. I plan to live for another five hundred years with you by my side.

In the event that I was . . ." When she felt Sigrid flinch at the word she was about to use, she changed the direction. "You will never be alone. This is your family, and my life would mean nothing if you were to fall apart on the family and let Terrence move on them." She searched Sigrid's eyes, trying to see if any of this was soaking in.

"I'm sorry," she finally whispered.

"Don't be," Regina scolded and reassured at the same time. "Your concern and love are part of the reason you mean so much to me. It's normal to be worried, especially now with Terrence stepping up his attacks, but don't let it keep you from living. You do that and he's already won."

Sigrid jerked her head up at the statement, grim determination coloring her face as Regina pressed on. "I'm worried about your safety, and I'm dealing with it by trying to keep Terrence from surprising us. Make your fear work for you, not against you."

Sigrid's eyes lit up, and Regina knew that she had managed to reach her. She was convinced when Sigrid smiled slightly and replied, "I'll make it work for me."

Regina could almost hear the wheels of Sigrid's mind working, and she lightly kissed her cheek. Sigrid grabbed her hand, and they continued to the farmhouse.

When the bushman's body was taken care of, Regina did a final check to make sure the hunter's story was in place and then had him taken back to the hotel outside of town. She listened as he made his report that the Penshaws were no more vampires than his own family could be, and he began packing, anxious to get out of the little, boring town.

The next night Regina and company returned to New York, and Regina quickly started using the information she had gotten from the trip. Sigrid stayed out of the way, trying to fade into the background as a plan began forming in her head. Pulling Ward into the idea and getting his approval, she began turning her fear into something constructive. They met secretly and discussed ideas and plans, and it was a week before they had the plan ironclad. Then it was time to take the proposal to Garrett.

Garrett smiled warmly as Sigrid eased into his office. "I haven't seen much of you lately."

Sigrid nodded and returned his smile. "Have you got some free time, Garrett?"

His face reflected curiosity, and he laid his pen down on the desk. "For you? Of course."

She closed the office door behind her and walked across the room to his desk. He motioned for her to take a seat.

Taking a deep breath, she began, "I have an idea I'd like to run past you."

Garrett leaned back in his chair, hands coming together and locking. "Okay. Run away."

Nervously she smiled and plunged right in. "After what happened at the Penshaws, I've been worried about Regina's safety. Ward is capable as are you, but I don't think it's going to be enough." Garrett nodded agreement. Regina had told him of Sigrid's fears after the incident, and he wasn't surprised that the girl was trying to develop some ideas. "We know that Terrence has a group of bodyguards/assassins, and I'd like to form one for Regina's protection."

Garrett pondered the idea. It made sense to add more security for their queen; she was Terrence's number one target. "Are we talking about an army?"

Sigrid shook her head. "No. We need everybody we can get, and forming an army would just deplete our resources. I'm talking about Ward, myself, and five others. All specially trained and totally loyal to no one but Regina."

Garrett liked the way the young woman thought. "Sounds good. A small but lethal unit to keep an eye on her. I like it. Do you have people in mind?"

Sigrid took a deep breath. "That's the part you may not like. We want to choose outsiders, mortals."

Garrett stared at her in disbelief. "You've lost your mind! Outsiders would only add to our problems. There is no way we can recruit mortals that are totally trustworthy. And if we did manage to find some, why would they be willing to give up their lives for an immortal, fictional creature?"

"The volunteers, Garrett," she answered simply.

The volunteers were the mortals who willingly gave their blood donations so the vampires could live without killing innocent people. They also served other functions. Their numbers included doctors, lawyers, law enforcement, and various others. They helped the family anytime they were called upon and always performed above the norm.

"The volunteers?" he repeated.

Sigrid leaned forward, excitement beating down nervousness. "Yes. They are the perfect choice. They know about us and are loyal. We screen all of them very carefully, so we have all the information we need on each and every one. You know yourself that many have asked to help us in more ways, and now we can give a select few the opportunity."

Doubt still tugged at Garrett. "And how do you propose we select those few? Do you realize how many there are?"

"That's where I need your input." She smiled and met his eyes. "You, Ward, and I will draw up a profile of what we need. Everything from skill, intelligence, disposition, occupation, the works. Then we enter the profile into the volunteer computer banks to get a list of possible. We narrow it down from there."

Garrett tapped his finger on the desk. "That's a major undertaking. It's a good idea, but I don't think it can work."

Her face fell and became grim. Her eyes glared at him, and she leaned in closer to him. "I'm going to do this with or without your help. I would prefer your input, but if not, I want your silence and non-interference."

Garrett studied her face for a moment, seeing the determined, unrelenting look in her eyes. He smiled slightly, recognizing the look. "There is no doubt you are Regina's niece."

Sigrid's face relaxed slightly, and she leaned back in her chair as Garrett leaned forward. "Of course I'll help you. Am I to assume that this is to be kept quiet around Regina?"

"I think she has enough on her mind right now. Let us worry about the security end."

"Agreed. We need to get this started as soon as possible. Who knows when Terrence will start the fire blazing. Give me an hour or so to wrap up things here and give Regina a believable excuse for our absence, then I'll meet you and Ward in the private conference room."

They met as arranged and spent the next four hours ironing out the profile of the type of person they needed. Each contributed and offered pros and cons of each decision. When the profile was done, it was so detailed that it took over an hour to enter into the computer.

They had the office building to themselves, and Garrett had concocted a story about a new overseas acquisition to explain their absence to Regina. While they waited for the computer printout, they made their plans about what equipment they would need, a suitable training facility, finances, and strategies.

To their surprise the computer began beeping and printing out in less than two hours. Garrett rushed over and retrieved the report. As he looked over it, he shook his head in surprise. "This is unbelievable. Only twenty out of all those thousands fit the profile." He rejoined them at the table, and Ward and Sigrid gathered around the list.

"I'm glad we were so specific as to what we were looking for," Ward replied as he scanned the list.

"Now we need to pull their files and see if we can narrow it down any more. Then we go to them, and we need to get this done in the shortest amount of time possible," Sigrid stated softly.

"Twelve here in the States," Garrett began, "four in Europe, two in Australia, one in Japan, and one in Milan. That's pretty spread out. Are you sure you can handle it?"

Sigrid cut her eyes at him, and he raised his hand in surrender. "Sorry. Okay, where to first?"

"You two need to get back to Regina. Come up with some cover story for mine and Ward's absence. I'm going to start pulling some of these files and see if I can cull the herd a bit. We can head out in the morning."

Garrett rubbed his moustache. "She'll be thrilled that you are working on some project and not worrying about."

"What about Regina's safety?" Ward asked.

"It's covered. She'll be staying here in town for the next few weeks, and we can cover her here. She'll feel better knowing that you're with Sigrid, keeping her safe."

"I'll text you when I have more details on the team," Sigrid stated.

"Please do. I'll make all the travel arrangements, make sure you have money and everything you need. I'll also have a training facility set up by the time you get back." Garret looked at Sigrid. "Be in my office at six a.m. and I'll have everything ready."

"We'll be there," Ward promised.

"This is a good idea, Sigrid," Garrett acknowledged. "You are becoming quit a force to be reckoned with. I do wish you would get some rest before morning."

Sigrid blushed. "I come from good stock, Garrett, and I'll get some rest, promise."

Ward and Garrett stood up, and the two men started for the door, but Sigrid called out before they left, "Garrett. Please take care of her."

"With my life if need be," Garrett assured her. "You, too, be careful and hurry home."

Without warning, Sigrid walked over to Garrett and kissed his cheek. "We will," she replied and then watched them go on their way.

Grabbing a soda from the office cooler, she went to the computer and started researching.

The sound of a dog howling in the distance was wearing on Cameron's last nerve. He stared at the thing tied to a chair across the room. He and Seth had been led here by one of their informants and found a vampire trying to pass as a bus driver in Newark. With the help of their informant, they had captured the thing and, securing it in the back of their rented Bronco, headed to the nearest isolated location.

Once there, they had restrained the thing, and after administering their tests to prove he was indeed a vampire, they went about questioning him. Several years ago, they would have simply staked him and left. But since Justine's disappearance, they had been questioning their prey, hoping against hope that they would find some lead to her whereabouts.

So far they had not been successful, and Cameron was on the verge of exploding. Rising to his feet, he approached the thing. He was surprised to see it cower slightly, and he could hear the informant's soft giggle from the far corner.

"Where is she? All I want to know is have you seen or heard of Justine Reynard?" he asked patiently and held up her picture again.

The man in the chair looked at the picture and shook his head. "I don't know Justine Reynard."

Cameron licked his lips and leaned closer, studying the vampire's eyes. Before he could ask another question, Seth pushed past him and grabbed the man's collar, yanking him against the chains that held him in place. "All right, you murdering bastard, I want to know where my daughter is. She came to New York over three years ago, and one of you animals contacted her, told her who she was, and she came home long enough to confront me." Seth got right in the man's face, spittle spraying his face as he yelled, "And after she left, she hasn't been seen since. Where is my daughter! If you bastards have hurt her . . ."

Cameron grabbed his father's shoulders and pulled him away. "Easy, Dad," he warned, knowing the old man was not in the best of health.

Since Justine's disappearance, Seth had been consumed with finding her. Hunts had become second for him. His only concern now was finding her and protecting her. He spent night and day following dead ends, and it had taken a toll on his health.

Cameron, too, had been searching. He had sold part of his business to one of his associates, and now he maintained the silent partner's role, dedicating his time to helping his father in the search. His heart ached for his sister, his best friend. He would not allow himself to believe she was dead, but the fact that they had not been able to find even a trace of her was taking a toll on him as well. Terry's people had led them to what they hoped would be several leads on her whereabouts, but so far they had not been rewarded with any information other than "I don't know Justine Reynard."

"He doesn't know anything, Dad," Cameron said in defeat and moved his father to the door of the shack.

Seth's eyes reflected a frightening combination of fear and anger for a few seconds, but then he calmed down, shoulders slumping against his son's hands. "Another dead end," he agreed.

The informant stepped up to them. He was a tall, slender man, dressed in black sweats. His red hair was covered with a black ball cap, and his green eyes twinkled as he grinned at them. "Why don't you let me try," he suggested.

Their captive jerked his head toward them and looked at the informer. He stared at the man with a mixture of pure hate and fear.

Red met his eyes and smile wickedly, unconsciously licking his lips. "Give me ten minutes with him," he said without taking his eyes off the captive. "If he does know anything, I promise, I'll find out."

Cameron watched the exchange between the two, and his brow furrowed in disgust at what Red was implying. "We are not animals, Reggie. We are not like them. Besides, I don't think he knows anything."

Red glanced at Cameron but shrugged his shoulders and eased back. "Fine. I just thought I could help."

"You can," Cameron continued. "Take my father outside, while I finish our business here."

"I'm staying," Seth argued weakly.

"You're going," Cameron corrected firmly. Seth hesitantly agreed and followed Red outside the shack to the awaiting car.

Pulling a stake from his bag, Cameron approached the captive, blocking the look of terror on the man's face from his mind. Reciting a prayer for both of their souls, Cameron rammed the stake into the vampire's chest. The thing screamed like a wounded animal, blood gushing out of his chest in torrents. Cameron stepped back, avoiding most of the spray, and swallowed hard to keep his stomach in place. As he watched the death throes of their prey, he couldn't shake the feeling that something was wrong. The hunts before had been colder, less involved. Now they were talking to their prey, looking them in the eyes, and what he saw there most of the time was not evil but confusion and fear.

As the vampire slumped against his restraints, Cameron lowered his head in silent prayer. He picked up his equipment bag and exited the shack, shivering as the night wind wrapped around him.

He picked up the last part of the conversation with Red and his father as he approached them.

"I don't know why your people can't find out something," Reynard was nagging.

Red looked at him in amusement, but when he saw Cameron approach, it changed to concern. "They are everywhere, Mr. Reynard. Your daughter, if she's still alive, could be anywhere in the world."

7

Sigrid had put in an additional four hours and got the list down to ten. Garrett was waiting for them the next morning with briefcases containing paper files on their targets, credit cards, IDs and travel papers, hotel information and contact information in case of emergency. The plan was simple. Observe, follow, then decide whether to approach or not.

The plan so far had proven effective. While following the man in Japan on their first night, Ward and Sigrid discovered he was a drug dealer on the side and was unacceptable to their needs or the family's. Mr. Milan had given them false information and was, in fact, married with children and was a bit too fond of the bottle, again unacceptable.

They were getting discouraged when they reached Australia and found the first name on their list had been killed in a car accident two days before their arrival. They finally hit pay dirt with Paul Greeson, the second name. He was an ex-soldier and explosive expert and fit their profile perfectly. He had no family, was not a drinker or partaker of drugs, no police record, highly intelligent, honest, physically fit, and a loyal volunteer to the family. He had been called on several times for highly confidential favors for the family and never disappointed.

They watched him for twenty-four hours and then decided it was time to approach him.

The Gator Tooth Pub was on the outskirts of the Australian outback and was frequented by gator hunters, guides, the local alcoholics, and roughnecks. Many years ago it had been a barn that the owner had converted with tables, a bar, a jukebox, and a few pool tables. The floor was covered with grit and straw, and the air smelled of stale smoke and gator guano.

Greeson was a regular, and he always took a table toward the back away from most of the noisy activity. He would normally nurse a mineral water and people watch the entire time. He participated in an occasional pool game and was spoken to by everyone, but he never stayed with anyone too long and preferred his solitude.

His looks warned off strangers, stone-green eyes staring out of a deeply lined and tanned face. He was at least six foot three, lean but muscular with shoulder-length blond hair, and was dressed in typical bushman attire of khakis and heavy boots, a safari hat topping off the outfit. To finish the look, he even had a gator-tooth necklace. A large fatigue bag with his explosive tricks was sitting under the table on the floor right next to his leg, within easy reach.

Ward and Sigrid had managed to move around the pub without drawing too much attention and slowly made their way to the back and Greeson. The few times they were approached, Sigrid had easily discouraged contact with a mere look.

As they moved closer, Greeson looked at them slowly, his face stern with warning. With one look at Sigrid, his face softened. His eyes never left hers except to offer a quick dismissive look at Ward then they fell back on her as she reached the table. He rose to his feet and tipped his hat. "G'day."

Sigrid sensed his enamor and blushed softly. "Good evening, Mr. Greeson." She smiled warmly.

"You know me, but I haven't had the pleasure," he answered and held out a chair for her.

Feeling left out, Ward stayed close but out of the way. He knew Sigrid was well aware of what she was doing, and he was only there for support and safety.

Taking the seat he offered, she sat and motioned for him to do the same. "Allow me to introduce myself. I'm Sigrid Derrick, and this is my associate, Mr. Ward," she explained as Greeson motioned for drinks.

Turning his gaze back on the beauty before him, he smiled sweetly. "S' pleasure, Ms. Derrick."

"Sigrid please." She smiled wider.

"Then you must call me Paul, Sigrid," he insisted, liking the way her name rolled off his tongue.

"All right, Paul," she agreed, enjoying his accent. Hesitating until the barkeep brought over two bottles of mineral water, she began. "Mr. . . . Paul, I understand that you are an expert with . . . shall we say, big bangs and that you are someone the family can rely on."

His face fell slightly, some of the friendliness disappearing. "What family would that be?"

"The Derrick Industries family," she answered bluntly, watching his reactions closely.

Greeson cast a suspicious, wary glance at both of them. "I'm not familiar with that family."

Ward was getting impatient playing these games. "She's Regina's niece," he said lowly and firmly, ignoring the disapproving look she gave him.

Sigrid couldn't help but admire Greeson's innocent ploy. It was very convincing, and he could be very intimidating to those who might choose to push for information or confirmation of the family.

His voice was low but filled with menace. "I don't know any Regina or Derrick Industries family. I think you've got the wrong guy," he snarled and started to stand. He stopped when he caught sight of Sigrid's eyes again, now a glowing dull red.

"Please sit down, Paul." She smiled, revealing a bit of fang.

He complied and looked around the pub to see if anyone else was watching. Looking at her apologetically, he replied, "You do understand why . . ."

Her smile washed away his fear, and he found himself looking into those gorgeous blue eyes again. "Of course, Paul, and I appreciate your caution. I wish we had more friends like you."

Relaxing, he leaned in closer. "What can I do to help you and the family, Sigrid?"

Ward stayed silent, making sure they weren't being watched or that anyone was within listening distance as Sigrid began explaining her proposal. Greeson listened intently, taking in every word until she finished. He studied her again as he considered what she asked and the implications. A minute later he gave her his answer. "I'm honored that you'd ask me to be a part of this, and I will do anything to protect the family and Regina."

His thoughts added, *And you.* Sigrid smiled. "Paul, you do understand that this could be very dangerous, even deadly," she repeated, wanting to make sure he was coming into this with his eyes wide open.

Boldly he reached out and touched her hand, then drew back, afraid he might offend her. Her face reflected no insult taken, and he grinned. "Yes, Sigrid, I understand. Doesn't change my decision. The family needs me. That's all I need to know."

Now she looked at Ward, smiling at their success. He nodded and took another swig from the bottle in his hand. He checked his watch and sat down beside Greeson. "Can you be ready to leave in the morning?" he questioned.

Greeson cut his eyes to catch a quick look at Ward and then turned his full attention back to Sigrid. "I can be ready to leave in an hour."

The next stop was Paris and Mighnon "Silk" Legere. She was a twenty-eight-year-old electronics whiz that worked at one of the Derrick Industries subsidiaries. Her history with the family was long and impressive. At fourteen she had been found on the streets of Paris, starved, exhausted, and almost dead, and it had been a family member that rescued her, giving her a home, education, and love. She was highly intelligent, and her loyalty was beyond question. Her natural skill with electronics and connections with the family had procured for her the current job of chief electronic engineer. Her fiery personality helped her be successful at her chosen profession.

When the threesome arrived, they discovered that the young woman was already being followed by a competitor's thugs. Staying out of the way, they watched as she was approached and offered money, connections, and everything under the sun to sell out her current employer. She politely refused. When they became more insistent, she rudely refused. Now the thugs' plan was to break into her apartment and convince her that it was better to cooperate.

Sigrid had held back, intrigued by the woman's fire, and watched as the events unfolded.

"Idiot," Silk scolded herself as the men pinned her to the floor. She should have been more cautious, especially after the way Groilier was pursuing her and her new toys. She was developing a new super-sensitive, using-artificial-intelligence alarm system, and it would be a real coup for the first company to bring it to the market. Of course she could have gotten some security from the company or, more importantly, the family, but she didn't like to use them that way. Besides, she had convinced herself that she could handle the trouble. She had spent a few years on the street and had learned how to deal with scum like this.

Unfortunately, this scum was well trained and financed, and she was outnumbered. They had boldly knocked at the door, and expecting a delivery from the local market, she hadn't thought twice about opening it.

When she did, she was immediately jumped by four large men and shoved into the apartment. She did manage to claw open one man's face and deliver a breathtaking blow to another's stomach, but a whack across the back of her neck brought her down. Two of the men held her in place as the other two ransacked her apartment looking for the plans to the new system.

She laughed as they became more frustrated. "Do you boneheads honestly think I'd be stupid enough to keep the plans here?"

That question brought a stinging slap across her face that drew blood from her lip. Licking her lip, she glared at the hitter. "Oh yeah. Big man, two against one. You let me up and I'll yank your balls off and shove them down his throat." She motioned at the other one holding her down.

The response was a strong punch to her gut that left her gasping and coughing for air. As she recovered, she realized the other two had joined them and were kneeling beside her smiling.

She was frightened now but wouldn't give them the satisfaction of seeing it. "Can't you find what you want, boys? Too bad. Why don't you drop by later and I'll fix some tea and we can discuss it."

A short, wiry man laughed. "Ah, Mighnon, you have such a wonderful sense of humor." Leaning right into her face, the laugh disappeared. "But if you don't give us what we want, I don't think you'll ever laugh again."

Reflexively, she swallowed the lump in her throat, steely determination on the rise. After everything the family had done for her, she was not about to turn on them. Before she had met them, she would have given them up without a second thought, but that was before they taught her what family and loyalty really meant. Meeting the eyes of the leader, she said flatly, "Tell Groilier to screw himself."

He shook his head on disappointment and pulled the straight razor from his coat pocket. "He thought you might say that."

Seeing the razor, she began struggling against the arms holding her, but they only pinned her down harder. She fell still when the leader slowly ran the blade across her cheek and down her throat. "Such pretty skin," he observed, "it's a shame you don't value it."

She struggled to keep from moving as she felt the bite of the blade on her throat. The men snickered and anxiously awaited the next cut as the blade moved down her throat and stopped at the neckline of her blouse.

All movement ceased when the sound of a woman clearing her throat echoed in the apartment. Every eye, including Silk's, turned toward the front door, surprised to see a small, attractive woman standing a few feet away. She was dressed in black slacks, black sweater, and black leather jacket, all the dark colors making her alabaster skin luminescent. Curly brown hair touched her collar and framed an elegant face with piercing blue eyes that took in the sight with casual disinterest. "Am I interrupting?" she questioned calmly in a deep, smooth voice.

"I am a little busy right now," Silk replied from the floor. "If you leave your name and number . . ."

She was cut off as the blade was laid across her lips. The leader glared at the intruder. "The best thing you can do is to turn around and forget what you saw here."

The woman cocked her head to the side as if considering his advice. A few seconds later she looked back at him and smiled. "I'm sorry, I can't do that." Placing her hands in her coat pockets, she took a step forward. "You see, Ms. Legere and I have some very important business to discuss, so I'm afraid it will be you that's leaving."

Leader laughed and nodded to one of his men. Grinning, a short, greasy brunette stood up and moved toward the woman menacingly. The woman made no move, only raised an eyebrow and watched him with amusement.

Silk was fascinated by the turn of events. She had never seen the woman before and wondered if she was insane or just stupid to take on these thugs. She was a small woman and didn't look very threatening, but there was something about her that seemed dangerous.

Bully moved right up and stopped in front of the newcomer. "You leave now, or I'll help you out."

Smiling, the woman took a step forward and in the blink of an eye had seized the bully's throat and, with a sharp twist, broke his neck in one move. Tossing the lifeless body to the side, she smiled at the remaining men. "Next?"

There was no masking the stunned looks on all their faces as they watched Bully's body thud to the floor. Silk was beginning to understand who the newcomer was and felt a surge of relief.

The leader frowned, not quite comprehending who was defying his authority, and motioned another lamb to eject the intruder. He only got within arm's reach when she coldcocked him, and he dropped to the ground.

Tired of being a bystander, Silk brought her legs up and connected with the head of one of the two remaining men holding her. Both men staggered back and landed on their behinds, and in an instant, she was on her feet and, clenching her free hand, smashed the nose of the leader.

The intruder stood back and watched Silk finish up on the thugs. Watching the way she handled herself, she knew she wanted her on the team.

"Who the hell are you?" Silk asked as she began dragging the living garbage into the hallway outside her apartment. She jumped when an attractive blond man appeared outside the door and took the burden from her. "G'day, love, let me help you with that."

She was beginning to wonder if she had gone from the frying pan into the fire as another dark-haired man joined the blond.

"Ms. Legere, they'll take care of the mess." The other woman smiled and eased over to where Silk was watching the cleanup. "I really do need to discuss some very important business with you."

Silk met the eyes of the woman and immediately felt at ease. "Lady, after the way you just performed, I'd be crazy not to listen to you."

"Sigrid Derrick," she responded, "and I only evened the field some. You took care of the rest."

The name was more than familiar. "I know the Derrick name, but not Sigrid," she said defensively.

"Regina Derrick, the president of Derrick Industries, is my aunt. She's the reason I'm here. Can we sit and talk for a while? I have a proposal for you, and after I'm done, if you're not interested, we'll leave you to resume your . . . party."

Silk watched as the two men with Sigrid vanished with Groilier's thugs. She touched her neck where the blood was drying from the cut she had received. It only took her a split second to think it over. "Have a seat, Ms. Derrick. I'm all ears."

Smiling, Sigrid sat down, crossed her gloved hands on her lap, and began explaining. Three hours later they had another recruit and were on a plan for the United States.

Without the pre-meeting excitement, they had a similar conversation with Nick Chang, a martial arts instructor in Los Angeles. He had been working with the family for the last six years and was eager to become a part of the growing team. Nick and Paul instantly hit it off, and Sigrid was impressed with the easygoing personality of the young man.

A week and a half after they had left on the mission, they returned home, two short of the projected team but with four possibilities located around the Northeast.

Garrett was waiting at the airport when they landed, and once everyone was loaded into the waiting limo, he directed the driver to drive out of the city. He told Sigrid that the company owned a secluded, unused warehouse outside of town and that he had it renovated as a training facility as well as living quarters.

Once there, Sigrid was pleased with how much Garrett had managed to accomplish in the almost two weeks they were gone. The warehouse was more of a state-of-the-art military training area with all the equipment they had discussed and more. The three recruits' eyes sparkled like children on Christmas Day as they moved around the building and found that each had their respective work areas. Leaving them to explore and make themselves at home, Garrett, Ward, and Sigrid headed to the conference room in the back.

"Interesting ensemble," Garrett stated as they sat down at the conference table.

"Interesting and effective," Sigrid said proudly.

"We still have a few more to check out to finish the team," Ward contributed with a yawn.

Sigrid looked around the conference/war room. "This facility is great, Garrett," she complimented. "I don't know how you did all this in just two weeks, but I am impressed."

Garrett bowed his head slightly. "Thank you. I wanted to get this thing under way as soon as you got back."

Sigrid met his eyes. "You feel it too?"

Ward looked at them, dumbfounded and a bit irritated. "Feel what?"

After they exchanged another look, Garrett answered his question. "The feeling that time is of the essence." He turned his gaze back to Sigrid and dropped his eyes.

She instantly knew something was wrong. "What is it, Garrett? Spit it out."

He took a deep breath and sighed, not wanting to be the one to deliver the news. "While you were gone . . . Stanley was murdered."

Sigrid stared at him in disbelief. Stanley Fregata had been one of the first family members she managed to connect to. He was an older man that drove a bus in Newark and was a loner. They had met and hit it off, going to ball games and pool halls. He was not only a friend; she had come to think of him as the fun uncle she always looked forward to being with. The more she got to know him, the more she was touched by his kind and gentle heart. He drove the bus at night, and unlike most drivers, he welcomed the homeless and lost to rest in a safe place. On many nights, you could find several street people curled up in back of the bus, sleeping peacefully, knowing they were safe with him. He always supplied coffee and sandwiches and a friendly word. In the entire time she had known Stanley, Sigrid had never once heard him utter a harsh word or turn anyone away when they asked for help. Knowing he was gone, she felt an emptiness settle into her. "Who?" she asked lowly.

Garrett licked his lips. He and Regina had discussed how the news would be broken to Sigrid. They had decided to tell her the truth, except the fact that a picture of her had been found on the floor of the shack where they found Stanley's body. Garrett had argued that she needed to know everything, but Regina had reminded him how responsible Sigrid felt for all the trouble now. If she knew of the picture, she would assume the full blame for his death. Garrett had agreed and promised never to tell her that one detail. "It was hunters," he answered bluntly.

She looked at her hands on the table, nodding and clenching her teeth. Letting the news soak in, she took a deep breath. "Thanks for telling me."

Garrett eyed her closely. "I'm sorry, Sigrid. Stanley was a good man, and he was very fond of you."

She simply nodded to him, and he decided to press on with business. "We need to get this thing wrapped up. What's your next move?"

"I'm leaving for Chicago in a few hours to check out another candidate," Ward volunteered.

"And I'm going to check one here in the city," Sigrid replied.

Garrett looked at them puzzled. "You're splitting up?"

Sigrid stood up. "I want to speed things up. Ward knows the drill, and I trust his judgment. Hopefully the one I check out will be a winner and we can get training under way within the next twenty-four hours."

Garrett smiled his encouragement. "All right. Go to it and good luck. I'll see you soon."

Tyler Brandt was the volunteer Sigrid went after. He had been connected to the family since he was a teenager, and now at thirty-two, his knowledge about weapons was invaluable to the family. As she observed him, she was first struck by his good looks and the way he carried himself. He was tall, muscular with brown hair and dark brown eyes. He walked with confidence and grace of a panther on the prowl and was aware of everything around him at all times. He was a loner and preferred it that way. According to family records, he had been a troubled youth who had found purpose working with the family. As with Silk, he had been taken in and brought up by them, and his performance record was impeccable.

She found herself having to put aside the personal attraction and concentrate on him during the observation period, and when she was certain he was someone she wanted on the team, she approached him.

The café was small and intimate, and as she walked in, he noticed her instantly. She was dressed in black slacks and a button-down burgundy sweater. As she moved through the dim light of the café toward his table, he couldn't help but admire the confidence and elegance that she exuded. When she got closer, she was hit with his first thought. *I would die for her*, his mind stated calmly, and she found herself blushing and a stirring of desire as she stopped at his table. "Mr. Brandt, may I speak with you for a moment?" she asked softly with a smile.

He studied her for an instant and then stood up, pulling out the chair opposite him for her to take a seat. "The family needs me?"

Sitting, she was shocked and surprised by his frankness. He held no deception or misleading thoughts, just that he knew she was part of the family and that he would die for her.

"I'm Sigrid Derrick," she introduced herself as he returned to his seat. "And you are very perceptive, Mr. Brandt."

"Ty," he stated simply.

"Ty," she repeated and met his brown eyes. His eyes were so brown she wanted to dive into them, but she inconspicuously squelched her desire and resumed a businesslike tone. "Ty, the family has a favor to ask. After you hear my proposal, if you are not interested, that will be the end of that and no one will think less of you."

"Propose away," he replied coolly. As he looked into her blue eyes, he felt himself drawn like a moth to a flame and used every last bit of his self-control to maintain his usual cool façade.

"We are assembling a small team of bodyguards to protect the Queen and the family. There is some trouble brewing, and we want to take extra precautions. Regina, the Queen, will be the priority target if trouble breaks out, and we want to be prepared so that she comes to no harm."

"And you?"

Sigrid raised an eyebrow at him. "Regina, my aunt, would say yes, it's for my protection as well. But I assure you, Ty, I can take care of myself."

He sipped his coffee and sat forward, propping his arms on the table and leaning closer to her. "I bet you can, Ms. Derrick."

Again he had brought a blush to her face, and she cleared her throat to continue. "Sigrid, please. I will be honest with you, Ty. This could be a very dangerous assignment, even life and death. There is a war on the horizon, and I want to take every precaution to protect my family. I would like you to be a part of this team, but I want you to realize how deadly it could be. If you're not interested, as I said before, it will not be held against you."

"Why me?" he asked, not releasing her eyes from his hold.

She, too, leaned closer, her voice soft and friendly. "Because of who you are and the way you've helped the family in the past. You have been involved with us for years, and you hold no prejudice against us. You are part of the family. Your skills are something that we need, and on a personal note, I want the best for my aunt's protection. I think you're it."

He nodded slowly, toying with his coffee cup before he spoke again. "I'd like to share something with you, Sigrid." When she motioned for him to continue, he leaned even closer, his face only inches from hers, his voice low and gentle. "I hit the lowest part in my life when I was fourteen. I was living on the streets and headed for jail or an early grave. I got busted by a cop, who turned out to be a family member. And to this day, I can't tell you what he saw in me or why he wanted to help me, but he did. I was resistant, but he was persistent. He showed me what it meant to be a productive part of society and of a family. For years I was pushed from one home to another, one counselor to another, but no one ever took the time to get to know me. Charley did, and he gave me hope. He took time with me, listened to me, and taught me what it took to be a real man. To me your kind are better than any mortal I've ever met. I helped the family because they helped me and took me in. I love this family like they were my own, and if you need me now, you've got me."

Sigrid scanned his face and felt a stirring deeper than anything she had ever felt with Ward. Reaching out, she touched his arm, both of them jumping with the sudden surge of electricity that sparked between them. "Are you sure?"

He finished his coffee and took a deep breath. "Yep."

Smiling, she asked one last question. "When can you be ready to join us?"

He looked down at his watch and for the first time smiled. A perfect, blinding white smile that caused her heart to flutter at the sight of his dimpled cheeks. "Let's go," he responded and rose to escort her out of the café.

Ward had returned from Chicago with Larry Crane, the final member of their team, a few hours after Sigrid had gotten Ty settled into the warehouse. They only had time to do a quick cleanup before they had to leave for their meeting with Garrett.

They arrived a little after nine that morning and quickly made their way upstairs to the executive offices. He was waiting for them and ushered them in. "Well?" he probed as they sat down.

"Team complete." Ward smiled.

"We're going to begin training this afternoon," Sigrid stated as she handed Garrett the files on the new team members.

Accepting the files, he saw the weariness that was washing over her. "You need rest before you begin any kind of training."

"I'm fine," she dismissed.

He was about to argue when he sensed a presence approaching. "For the record, Sigrid, the deal is complete and will be very lucrative for us."

Shocked, Sigrid recovered when she, too, felt the approaching figure. The office door swung open, and Regina strode in, shut the door, and put her hands on her hips. "Young lady, you've got some explaining to do."

Sigrid's throat locked up. Her mind raced at how Regina could have found out about the team she had assembled; they had been so careful to keep everything under wraps. She scrambled for an excuse but decided to play ignorant. "What did I do?"

Regina moved closer, looking down at her niece, eyes flashing anger. "How dare you get back into town without calling me and letting me know you're home," she scolded. The mock anger fell away, and Regina smiled warmly, opening her arms for a hug.

Relief seeped into Sigrid as she stood and fiercely hugged Regina. "I'm sorry, Reg. We just got back, and I wanted to finish up the details of the merger before I saw you."

Regina released her from the hug but continued to firmly grasp her shoulders. "That's okay, honey, I'm just glad you're back home."

"And with a very lucrative deal," Garrett added from his seat behind the desk.

Regina reached over and patted Ward's in welcome then looked back at her niece. "So the meetings went well?"

Sigrid smiled sheepishly. "We got everything we wanted. The deal is complete except for some side work I'll need to do."

Garrett again jumped into the conversation. "From what I'm told, she was a great negotiator and is the main reason the deal came together like it did."

Regina beamed with pride and gave her another quick hug. "I'm so proud of you. You've become one hell of a businesswoman. I may just leave you to run the company until all this trouble with Terrence is settled."

Sigrid shot Garrett a worried glance, her face falling slightly. "Thanks, Regina, but I prefer being out in the field, at least for now. I may be good at putting deals together, but there's no way I could handle the whole company."

"Don't sell yourself short, sweetheart," Regina disagreed.

"She's good in the field, Regina," Garrett defended.

Sensing she was being outnumbered, Regina gave up. "Okay, okay. It was just an idea."

Sigrid's smile returned. "And I appreciate your confidence in me, but if you want the truth, the only one capable of handling this company other than you is Garrett."

The statement caught him off guard. Flustered, he looked at her with surprise. "Thank you, Sigrid."

It pleased Regina to see them getting along better, and she didn't want to jeopardize it. "I must say that I agree with you on that," she replied casting a loving look at Garrett. "Listen, I'll leave you to finish your work here, but promise you'll come by and see me later. I've missed you."

Sigrid felt her heart swell from the love she had for her aunt and gave her a quick kiss on the cheek. "As soon as I'm done here, I'll be up. We can have breakfast together."

Glowing, Regina gave her a wink and left them alone to conclude their business.

They stayed silent for a few minutes before they were satisfied she was out of hearing range. "Good job," Garrett complimented her.

Sighing with relief, she smiled. "Back at you."

"If you need anything for the team, just let me know. I'll cover your absence with business deals and scouting trips, but we need to have the team ready as soon as possible," he stated firmly, unable to conceal the underlying worry in his voice.

Standing up, Ward moved for the door, followed by Sigrid. "They'll be ready when we need them, you have my word," she assured him.

"Then it's a done deal." He nodded and watched them leave.

As promised, after the meeting she ventured upstairs to Regina's office where she caught the woman busily preparing the table for their breakfast meeting. She was unable to suppress the smile that crossed her lips as she watched Regina hover around, making sure the table was perfect and that everything they needed was within grasp. "You didn't have to go to all this trouble," Sigrid said, startling her aunt.

Regina whirled around and shook her head. "Damn. You're getting so good that I can't even sense you anymore."

Sigrid shrugged. "Sorry."

Gliding over to the door, Regina took her hand and led her to the table. "Don't be. It's a skill that could save your life or someone else's someday."

Both women sat down, and Regina began pouring out a special tea mixture. Sigrid watched her, noticing that, although she was just as beautiful as ever, she looked weary. "You're working too hard," she said as she accepted the teacup.

"Look who's talking," Regina countered. "I haven't seen you in three weeks."

Sigrid didn't want to get into that discussion again, so she changed topics. "So what's been happening with Terrence?"

Regina toyed with her teacup and sighed. "Garrett told you about Stanley?"

Sigrid nodded solemnly, and Regina continued, "We've lost three in the last four weeks. The family is on alert, and so far it's been quiet. Almost too quiet. I think the incident at the Penshaws threw him for a loop. Right about now, he's probably regrouping, doing some recon. I don't know what's worse, the actual trouble or anticipating it."

Sigrid set her cup down and leaned forward, taking Regina's hand in her own. "We'll be ready, Reg, just relax. You will be no good to us if you're exhausted from worry."

Patting her niece's hand, Regina met her eyes. "I seem to recall you getting similar advice not long ago."

Sigrid shrugged. "Good advice should not only be taken but given on occasion."

Frowning, Regina sat back in her seat. "You've been spending too much time with Garrett."

Sigrid smirked and leaned back, crossing her legs. "It's Terrence that I'd like to discuss with you. If you don't mind, I have a suggestion."

Regina clasped her hand together, sighing again. "I'll take any suggestions I can get."

"When Terrence does make his move," Sigrid said, choosing her words carefully, "hold back your response. Downplay your hand."

"Hold back?" Regina asked in surprise.

"If Terrence doesn't know your full strength, you've got an advantage. Right now, you've got him confused. He doesn't know for sure if you have

Reynard's files or even what you will do with the information if you do have it. If he thinks you're still in the dark about his plans and doesn't know how strong your forces actually are, he may become overconfident. When you become overconfident, you make mistakes."

Regina pondered the idea. It was a good point, and if anyone would become overconfident, it would be her brother, and that could be his undoing. "Very good suggestion," she finally stated with a smile. "I had planned on countering with a full-blown retaliation, but you've made an interesting point. Do you have any other suggestions? I think I could use a fresh view on this."

Sigrid took a sip of the tea and allowed the warm, salty fluid to course down her throat. "As a matter of fact, I do have a few ideas."

8

Their training began later that same afternoon. For the next few weeks, the team trained twelve hours a day, and it was similar to army exercises. Each team member took turns teaching the basics of their specialty to the others and then drilled them until it became second nature. It wasn't an easy regiment, but all the team members performed without complaint and excelled with each passing week. Sigrid and Ward had explained how important the mission was and how little time there was to get the team up to optimum levels. And the team rewarded them with their best efforts.

One afternoon three weeks after their training had begun, Sigrid stood on the catwalk over the exercise floor and watched the team as Paul gave a demonstration on building smoke bombs. She couldn't help but feel pride at how well they had come together. There had been no reluctance in the beginning, and blending well, they were now at the point of operating as a well-tuned machine. Paul and Nick's friendship had grown, and the two men were as tight as brothers. They each got along with the others, but both Ty and Silk remained loners. They participated in all the exercises and could be counted on without a doubt. But they liked their solitude and in an odd way had developed a respect for one another because of it. They had all developed a good rapport and camaraderie and had progressed more quickly than Sigrid could have ever hoped.

She could feel a shift in the air as the frequency of Terrence's attacks began picking up. Luckily, they had been prepared and had minimal losses. But Terrence was like a mosquito, nipping here and there, not enough to hurt, but enough to annoy the hell out of you. The time was coming, and she only hoped she had her friends prepared for what they had undertaken.

"Yo, boss," Nick called up to her. "Who gave you a note to get out of class?"

Smiling, she leaped off the catwalk and landed squarely in front of him. "Sorry, Sensei. I just needed some air."

The team sensed her unease and rallied around her. "Com'on, love." Paul grinned. "I'm going to show you how to make a special cocktail, just for our bad buddies."

"Sounds like fun," she responded and followed him to the work area, the others close behind.

The next evening, the team met in the back of the warehouse. Larry had set about converting the area to a garage, and now he spent most of his time tinkering with their motorcycles. After much discussion and deliberation, it had been decided that motorcycles would be the best mode of transportation for the team. Fortunately, all of them except Sigrid had ridden or driven bikes, so she was given a crash course and caught on quickly, spending her free time honing her biking skills.

As they crowded into the garage, their eyes fell on the eight new sleek black Ninja motorcycles that awaited them. Ward and Larry were stooping beside one of the bikes and doing some last-minute tinkering as the others watched in silence.

Finally finished, they stood up and wiped their hands on rags. "Ready?" Ward asked with a gleam in his eye.

The room was flush with anticipation as Sigrid nodded and smiled. Ward nudged Larry, and the younger man promptly climbed onto the bike. He pushed the ignition button and gave it a little gas as the bike came to life. Unlike the usual roar of the motorcycle engine, this one was so quiet they weren't even sure if it had been started. Larry looked over his shoulder and smiled, revving the engine. The only sound heard was a low humming.

"That's bloody quiet, mate," Paul remarked, clearly impressed.

Larry smiled at the compliment. "I fitted all the bikes with one of these mufflers. They won't hear us coming until we're right on top of them."

"We even have a backup silencer, in case something goes wrong with the muffler," Ward added.

Like a kid with a new toy, Nick moved a little closer. "Can we take them out for a test run?"

"The sooner, the better," a new voice said from behind.

Everyone whirled around, poised for action. Only Sigrid remained relaxed as she turned. "Hello, Garrett."

She saw the disappointed look on his face and then saw it was more than that. A sense of dread crept over her as she moved toward him.

"I think you need more training. I could have been one of Terrence's men," Garrett said in a scolding, angry tone.

"You'd be dead if you were," a voice replied from high above them.

Garrett turned around, looked up, and saw Ty positioned on the above catwalk, a high- powered rifle aimed at his heart.

Sigrid moved up beside Garrett, smiling. "I guess you didn't notice the alarm beams that surround the warehouse."

Garrett turned and glanced out the window. Using his heightened senses, he concentrated and then located the faint red laser beam across the window.

"Silk's contribution to our security," Sigrid stated proudly and rested her hand on the woman's shoulder.

"Intruders trigger that, mate," Paul added and motioned to the beeper device on his hip. "The instant anybody comes into range, these little beauties let us know."

Pointing at the entrance and windows, Sigrid continued, "The little boxes over the entrances are Paul's contribution. An explosive little welcome that out beepers can trigger. Lethal to mortal and immortal alike."

"How?" Garrett questioned.

Smiling, Paul stroked the stubble in his chin. "Filled the grenades with pieces of silver that had been soaked in holy water."

"The woods outside are also full of surprises," Ward concluded from the garage.

Taking a final look around the warehouse, Garrett nodded. "Impressive," he admitted grudgingly, the stern, serious look never leaving his face.

"What's happened?" Sigrid asked, knowing the normally stoic Garrett never looked this stern unless there was a problem.

"We've had contact with Terrence. He wants to set up a meeting, and Regina has agreed," he informed them and moved closer to Sigrid, his voice cynical. "It's supposed to be a meeting to discuss a truce."

The atmosphere in the room immediately shifted, becoming tense and expectant. Sigrid looked at each of her team members, and she felt pangs of worry for their safety. The team had been a good idea, and she was proud of what they had accomplished, but she had grown to care about them, and remembering Regina's statements about being in a vampire war as a mortal echoed in her ears.

"Have you got the details?" Ward stepped in when he saw Sigrid hesitate.

Garrett held up his metal briefcase and patted it. "Yes."

Shaking off the hesitation, Sigrid met their eyes. "It's go time," she informed them and, following Garrett, led them to the conference room for the briefing.

They had spent the rest of the day studying the information Garrett provided and Nick had managed to get from the computer. Even Garrett had been impressed with the talent Nick had shown pulling up plans, diagrams, satellite photos and maps of the meeting location. They formulated their plan of action and took it apart at every step, allowing for every possible contingency.

When they had their plan of attack set in stone, Garrett left them to prepare their equipment, letting them know that a truck would be there at five the next morning to load them and their accessories and take them to the airport.

The warehouse became a flurry of activity as they prepared their equipment and completed all their checks. They had finished the last round of preparations shortly before midnight and were primed and ready. Every possible action had been considered and prepared for.

Wearily, they had gone to bed, and within minutes the warehouse was filled with the soft sounds of exhausted snoring. Sigrid was lying in bed, listening to every sound they made, and relaxed when she knew they were all sleeping. Unfortunately, sleep eluded her, and after half an hour, she got up and began walking around the warehouse. She found herself outside their sleeping quarters and watching over them.

As she looked at their sleeping figures, she felt a swell of pride and appreciation. They did everything that was asked of them and more with no complaints or arguments. They had worked hard, and after weeks of work, each doing their assigned jobs, she was amazed at how well they complemented one another and meshed their skills.

She looked at Ty, watching his peaceful face. So mysterious, quiet, and strong, and when he spoke, it was for a reason and usually powerful. There was a mutual attraction between them, but both had put it aside to deal with the job at hand, not an easy task. He had assumed the role of protective father of the team.

Then her gaze fell on Paul. She smiled as she realized his hand was at his mouth and his thumb was propped against his lips. He was so easygoing and relaxed but so very effective at his job. One minute he was joking and acting like a teenager and the next he was in soldier mode and developing a new explosive device. He had become the big brother of the group, and she shivered as she accepted how much she missed Cameron in that role.

Nicky snored softly in the bed next to Paul. Nicky was the clown, and his ability to make you smile even when you didn't want to had endeared him to Sigrid. He constantly smiled and enjoyed getting into mischief, yet he could kill with one hit. She enjoyed watching him practice his arts, reminded of a ballet, as he moved and flowed through his exercises. His stealth and ability to blend into his surroundings had earned him the nickname Shadow. He was the little brother, the one who could always be counted on for fun or in times of trouble.

Moving across the hall, she eased into Silk's room. The woman slept fitfully, tossing and turning, and Sigrid frowned that her sleep was so troubled. She had a tough persona and wore it like a suit of armor, yet in a rarely glimpsed moment, she was so caring and sensitive you would think she was a different person. She held her own with the men, never letting them intimidate or bully her, and was the first one to offer encouragement when they needed it. She was the little sister of the group, able to take care of herself but drawing the watchful eyes of her big brothers to ensure her safety.

She proceeded down the hallway and stopped at the next room. Ward and Larry had become fast friends and stuck together most of the time. Sigrid had been unable to get a good handle on the man, but his expertise with engines and fighting skills had proven that he was a more than capable member of the team. He was quiet and watchful and only seemed relaxed and himself with Ward. Sigrid was curious to learn more about him and planned on spending more one-on-one time with him when this was over.

After a quick check of the warehouse and security systems, she went outside and watched the descending moon. As the moonlight cascaded over her, she again felt the uneasiness trying to pry into her. She tried to attribute it to nerves and pushed it aside, letting her senses focus on all the sounds, smells, and taste of the night air. Taking a few deep breaths, she felt the waning power of the dark and shivered slightly. She was well aware of the soft footsteps approaching from behind her and made no move.

It was a woman's voice that broke the silence. "Is everything all right?"

Sigrid smiled at the slightly accented words and turned around. Silk stood a few feet away, concern on her face. Her fiery red hair cascaded over her shoulders, and in the dim moonlight, she looked very small and childlike. Only the intensity of her brown eyes signaled the potent personality.

Sigrid slowly walked over to her. "Fine. Just thinking, and you should be sleeping. We've got a big day tomorrow."

Silk put her delicate hands on her hips. "Oh, and you don't need rest," she scolded firmly.

"Touché," Sigrid admitted and offered her a warm smile. Silk moved over to her and wrapped her arm around Sigrid's. "Let's walk."

Sigrid complied, and they leisurely strolled around the warehouse, ever cautious of the alarms and traps that covered the compound grounds.

"Are you worried about tomorrow?" Silk quizzed.

Sigrid cringed slightly. "I don't know if worried is the right word."

"You're wor . . . nervous about Regina's safety?" Silk suggested.

Sigrid sighed. "Yes and no." She felt Silk squeeze her arm in support. "I know that we've considered and prepared for everything and that she will be safe. You guys are the best, and I don't doubt that we can protect her. It's just that . . . I'm worried one of you may be hurt."

Silk softly shrugged. "You were very honest about how dangerous this could be, and we knew the risk when we signed on," she reminded her.

Sigrid stopped suddenly and faced Silk, meeting her eyes. "But you are not expendable. None of you are. This team was formed as a working, productive unit, not just a human shield to protect Regina until she could get away. One of the reasons each of you was chosen was because of your survival instincts. I won't sacrifice any of you. I'll give up my life first."

Silk studied Sigrid's face and eyes, surprised by the sincerity she was hearing and seeing. Sigrid was shocked to see a tear come to Silk's eye as she spoke. "You really mean that, don't you? You do really care."

She reached up and grasped Silk's shoulders. "Of course I care. Why does that surprise you so? You are a member of my family, mortal or not. Each of you means just as much to me as any other family member. If any of you were in trouble, I would do the same for you as Regina."

Silk remained silent, and Sigrid probed her thoughts lightly. She was caught off guard at the depth her words had on the young woman. Looking into Silk's eyes, she caught a brief glimpse of herself a few years ago. So unsure of others' true concern and having been hurt so often it was easier to just believe the worst about others and shut yourself off emotionally. Sigrid pulled the woman close and hugged her tightly.

"This team has become more than protection for Regina. It is a family in itself. No one could be more shocked than me that it's happened. I've spent most of my adult life closed off from everyone, not allowing anyone too close. But you and the others are a part of me now and I . . . love you."

Silk tightened her grip on Sigrid and relaxed against the older woman. "Thank you," she whispered after several seconds.

They continued the embrace for a few minutes, its calming effect with that of the night brushing the tension away. Without warning, Silk began snickering. Sigrid broke the embrace and looked at her oddly. "What? I expose my soul to you and you laugh? You French chicks are heartless."

Silk stifled her laughter and blushed. "Yeah, it's the way we're brought up on American TV."

Now Sigrid laughed. "Seriously, what?"

Silk looked down at her feet, shuffling them in the dirt. "It's just that I was supposed to come out here and check on you and cheer you up. Instead you've made me feel like I really matter."

Sigrid's smile returned. "You do matter, to me." She searched Silk's eyes and saw that the young woman had finally been convinced, and she felt relief urging away the concern that had been creeping in earlier. "And you did cheer me up, thank you. Now get upstairs and get some sleep."

Silk raised her eyes and arched an eyebrow. "Yes, Mom. Are you coming?"

"In a while," Sigrid agreed.

With that Silk turned and began walking back to the warehouse. She had only gotten a few feet away when she stopped and looked back at Sigrid, her face somber and determined. "We won't let you down."

Sigrid winked at her. "Nor I you," she assured and motioned the woman on to the building. She watched protectively until Silk vanished inside the building, then resumed her moon watching.

As they drove to the meeting place, Garrett was aware of Regina's nervous fidgeting. If she adjusted the nob on the speaker one more time, he was going to tie her hands down. She had been on edge ever since the call from Terrence. The only relief she had was finding out that Sigrid was on another business trip and hopefully safe. Garrett had been disturbed to watch his beloved queen as she prepared a detailed letter to her niece in the event that the meeting didn't go well. She was always so self-assured that it unnerved him to see her this nervous.

The fidgeting increased as the car eased into the Atlantic View Marina. It seemed to Garrett that she was almost ready to explode as he eased down the deserted boardwalk. He cautiously navigated through the boatyard, keeping his eyes peeled for trouble as they headed for the dry dock area. "Are you all right?" he questioned from the front seat.

She stared out the window, eyes scanning but distracted. "I should have never agreed to this. Not this way. What was I thinking?"

"You don't think he'll stick to the agreement?"

Regina cast him a wary look. "I've never trusted him. We mutually agreed on this place, but he was the one that suggested just the two of us and our bodyguards. No troops or followers, just the four of us. That's what I don't trust. He's being too agreeable, and I know my brother too well, he's never this agreeable. At the very least, we should have brought Ward."

Garrett smiled to himself and met her eyes in the rearview mirror. "Don't worry, my Queen. I assure you precautions have been taken."

Now he had her attention as she met and locked on his eyes. "Precautions? What kind of precautions?"

Garrett broke eye contact and pulled the car to a stop as they reached the center of the dry dock yard. Both of them studied the overcast night and noticed how much darker it seemed. Although their kind could see in the dark, the light fog that was moving in from the bay would hinder even their remarkable sight. Garrett turned and propped his arm on the seat, giving her another smile. "Precautions will be there if and when we need them."

Before she could comment or question, they saw headlights cut through the growing fog bank. A long black torpedo appeared from the haze and rolled to a stop a few feet away, engine to engine with Regina's limo.

There was no movement from either side, both scoping out the other's car. "I'm surprised it's not a hearse," Regina stated sarcastically.

Garret gave her a little wink. "Kick his ass, my Queen." Then he climbed out of the car and took position by the car door.

The driver of the other car did the same. Both men scanned the area, searching for observers or soldiers for the other. Then they regarded one another warily. The other driver was a short, stocky middle-aged man dressed in a chauffeur's uniform. He wasn't Terrence's usual type of thug, but he did look fully capable of defending his master, if need be.

After several tense moments, both men were satisfied that they were alone and the area was secure and, with a nod to each other, turned to open their respective car doors and signaled the okay.

Terrence emerged first, Regina watching as he climbed out of the limo. He was eerily attractive in the fog-shrouded night. Tall, slender, but well muscled, his skin was a light-olive color and his black hair thick and wavy.

His black eyes cautiously scanned the area and finally settled on the other car. As Regina prepared to emerge, she saw that he was wearing his typical outfit—black slacks, black turtleneck covered by a long black duster. His face was finely chiseled, and for the first time, she realized how much he looked like their father. He held his place by the front of his limo, patiently tapping his cane. His gaze immediately fell on her as she eased out of the car.

There was no denying his sister was radiant. The entire Cadmus clan had been an attractive family. As she eased her small, delicate figure out of the limo, he let his eyes roam across her elegant figure. She was slender and athletic with abundant cleavage, but not too much. Her coal black hair was naturally curly and cascaded down her shoulders and back, and the black jumpsuit she wore highlighted her china glass complexion. He found himself sighing, wishing that she wasn't his equal in power. It would have been such a pleasure to own and use her that he had to suppress the lecherous smile that tugged at his mouth.

As she exited the car, Regina felt her nervousness slipping away and being replaced with confidence. Nodding surely to Garrett, she proceeded to the front of their car, noting the sly smile that covered her brother's lips.

He moved forward and met her and stopped when they were a few feet away from one another. "Ravishing as ever, Megan," he greeted warmly.

"Still playing Count Dracula, Theo?" she countered with a sweet smile.

That caused him to chuckle. "Ravishing, but with the tongue and heart of a serpent."

Now Regina uttered a soft, ironic laugh. "Well, you would be the one that knows about serpents."

Terrence brought his hand to his chest feigning pain. "Dear sister, why such insults. I wanted to meet with you to discuss truce and you throw insults."

Regina took a step closer, leaning in and doubtful. "Now why do I find that hard to believe?"

He offered her his sincerest look, but Regina knew him too well and felt the bile rising as he spoke in a voice as smooth as velvet. "We are family, Megan, blood family. This difference between us and our beliefs is a waste of time and life. I've wanted to speak with you for some time, but you know how male pride is. Seeing you now makes me realize that it's been too long in coming."

Defensively, Regina crossed her arms across her chest. "Since when have you cared about our being family? Even in out mortal lives, you didn't care about anyone but yourself. Male pride is something you know nothing about, so why don't you tell me the real reason you contacted me. I'm betting it has something to do with the incident at the Penshaws."

Terrence flinched slightly, realizing that even after all these years, he couldn't fool his sister, but he wanted to try one more time. "There has always been animosity between us, so of course I understand your anger and doubt. What you must understand is that I'm looking out for my people, just as you do." He stopped and looked down at the ground, taking a deep breath before looking back at her and continuing. "The man you killed at the Penshaws was one of my most faithful. He had been with me over a hundred years and was loyal beyond question."

"And the Penshaws are important to me," Regina fired back. Then her face turned hard. "I must admit, you have an interesting way of protecting your people, by using the hunters."

Terrence raised an eyebrow, smiling smugly. "I wondered how long it would take you to bring that up?"

Regina felt her anger, an anger that was as old as they were, trying to consume her and threatening to bring on the change, but she used everything she had to push it back down. When she spoke, her voice was quiet but filled with strength. "You are in cahoots with our worst enemies. You are a traitor to our race and our family. Do your people know how low you've sunk and with whom you are working?"

Terrence threw his head back and laughed. When he finished, he met her eyes again, still smiling. "Of course they do. I am the Master, they are the servants. And they understand that the end justifies the means. My followers will do whatever is necessary to ensure our way of life. If anyone is a traitor to our kind, it is you." Now he stared hard at Regina, his face covered with disgust. "We are predators, superior to the mortals and most of the other puny species on this planet. They are the prey, we are the masters. They are ours to play with, kill, screw, or whatever we want to do with and to them."

He took a step closer, his voice rising a notch, but Regina did not back down. "You," he continued and pointed at her, "you want to live among them as if you are one of them, when we are so much higher than they are. You work in their world, wear their designer clothes, go to the little functions to be seen by hundreds. You buy a bit of blood instead of taking their entire soul. You are the traitor, Megan, and it disgusts me that we have the same blood."

Garrett and the chauffeur sensed the tension on the rise, and both cautiously moved closer to their masters.

Regina shook her head in disbelief. "I disgust you? Now that's amusing." She took a step toward him, stopping only inches from him. "Yes, I live among them, work with them, and get my food supply without taking life. But let's take a look at your life and see how it is so much better. You and your coven hide in basements and abandoned buildings. You stalk and murder innocent people, sleep in coffins, afraid of sunlight. You have no contact with the outside world, and in that sense, you are the living dead. You are not only disgusting in your methods but pathetic as well. You've even resorted to sleeping with the enemy."

"According to my figures, it's been pretty damn effective." He smiled proudly.

Regina could no longer control her anger, and as she released it, a hint of fang appeared against her lips. "You used them to kill Thea while you watched, you bastard. Do your followers know how cold-blooded you really are? Do they know you had your own sister murdered because of jealousy?"

He took a step back and rested his hand on his hip. "I wondered if you were behind the break-in at Reynard's. Are you also responsible for his daughter's disappearance? Seems she vanished without a trace three years ago, and the poor old soul is just consumed with worry. He's not even as effective at staking your people as he used to be."

Regina remained silent. Her only answer was a cold, hate-filled look.

"Okay." Terrence nodded and leaned toward her. "Did you at least fuck her? I mean if you raped her and tortured her to get what you needed, it would certainly redeem you in my eyes. Oh, what a great story it would make for Reynard. Come on, sis, tell me all the violent, sick details." He shrugged and stepped back. "Just don't tell me that you just got what you needed and brainwashed her. I know that's more your style, but please tell me you used and abused Reynard's daughter."

Regina felt the urge to reach out and slap him but instead just sighed. "This is getting us nowhere and a waste of my time," she finished and turned back toward the car.

"Wait!" Terrence took a step after her, begging. "You haven't even heard my proposal of truce yet."

Regina stopped and turned to face him. "Terrence, I'm not interested in your alleged truce. I wouldn't believe you if you offered to let me stake you myself as a sign of good faith."

Terrence looked at her as if she were a child. "I wouldn't do that, silly. My proposal included most of your family remaining intact. Of course they would come under my leadership, seeing as you won't be around anymore."

Terrence's limo door swung open suddenly, and six men carrying automatic weapons emerged and swarmed around Regina. Garrett instantly rushed in front of Regina and, using his body as a shield, ushered her back toward the car.

The six men quickly spread out behind Terrence, pinning Regina and Garrett against the side of the car. They took aim, and Terrence offered a slight nod. One of the men lowered the barrel of the gun and fired a shot at Regina.

Trying to protect his queen, Garret pushed Regina down and to the side, the bullet barely missing her as it tore into his upper thigh. He collapsed beside her, leg on fire. He continued trying to cover Regina from any other shots, but his wound was hindering his efforts. Regina saw the grimace of pain and heard his labored breathing and knew that Terrence had come up with a new kind of bullet.

Glaring at him, she saw Terrence grinning broadly. He walked over to them, followed by two of the gunmen.

Regina and Garrett were more than friends. They were lovers and soul mates. He was a part of her as she was of him. As they both scrambled against the side of the car, she knew that, no matter what, she would never leave him. Bravely, she grabbed his shoulder and using her super strength pulled him to his feet.

"Go!" he whispered to her as he was brought to a slump against the limo.

"Not a chance," she answered.

They were almost standing when Terrence's henchmen stopped their movement a few feet away and took aim at them.

"Tsk, tsk, you silly old fool," Terrence gloated. "Trying to save this bitch's life is probably the dumbest thing you ever did."

"Bastard," Regina growled, the red glow of her eyes nearly blinding. She felt Garrett begin to waver and pulled him close, steadying him.

Terrence clapped his hands together and grinned. "I'm going to enjoy this. Mind you, not as much as I did when Thea was staked, but close. Make it slow," he instructed.

He heard the sounds of rounds being locked in the chambers and waited for the crack of gunfire as he turned to take a few steps away from the scene. Then instead of the expected shots, he heard a whooshing sound.

Whirling around, he was just in time to see two of his gunmen on the ground, slender silver shafts protruding from their chests. Stunned, he glanced at the remaining men. "Fire!" he ordered, baring his own fangs.

He took a step closer and watched as silver shafts appeared from the darkness, striking their hearty targets and dropping the four remaining gunmen into smoldering heaps. His driver was pulling a gun from his jacket and quickly moving to protect his master when they were suddenly surrounded by headlight beams.

Taking advantage of the disorientation, a single motorcycle and rider appeared from the fog and rode into the scene, skidding to a stop between Terrence and Regina.

Six other riders appeared out of the fog. They were all dressed in black leather and wearing heavy, mirrored helmets. He couldn't help but notice they were all armed and ready to fire as well.

Terrence and his bodyguard looked at the forces surrounding them and knew they were now at a disadvantage. His eyes wide and unsure, Terrence took a step backward.

The rider positioned between Regina and Terrence slowly dismounted the bike. Terrence was taken aback by the amount of hatred he felt coming from the figure. It radiated like rays of the sun, and he had never felt anything like it before.

His chauffeur started to make a move when one of the helmeted riders yelled "Don't move!" and raised the gun for emphasis.

"Drop the gun!" another black rider ordered.

The bodyguard looked at Terrence, silently pleading for instructions.

A third black-clad rider took a step forward and released the silver arrow from the crossbow. It zoomed home and hit the chauffeur in the chest. He looked down at the shaft sticking out of his chest, mouth agape in shock and confusion.

"You were warned," the first speaker replied as the chauffeur fell to the pavement and began to smolder, then burn.

"You next?" an accented female voice asked Terrence.

Slowly he dropped the cane and raised his hands in surrender, never taking his eyes off the main rider a few feet away from him.

Regina sensed who was behind the mirrored visor as the leader leaned down to check on them. "Garrett's hurt, I'm all right." She smiled.

The rider caught a quick look at Garrett's leg and motioned for one of the others. In an instant, they were off the bikes and had Garrett up and loaded in the back seat of the limo, Nick and Paul administering first aid. The main rider extended a hand to Regina and helped her to her feet.

"Very impressive, dear sister," Terrence conceded as Regina approached him. "I didn't think you could be this devious, but so much hate from this one." He motioned at the leader, who never left Regina's side. Looking into the mirrored face plate, he questioned, "Do I know you?"

Regina rested her hand on the rider's shoulder as they began releasing the helmet strap. "Meet your niece," she replied as Sigrid's face was unmasked.

Terrence gaped in shock and staggered back a step, visibly shaken by the revelation. His already-pale skin became white, and his hand shook. Regina had never seen him openly show fear, and it was a little unnerving to see now. "This is not possible," he mumbled. "You're supposed to be dead."

"Like my mother, you murdering son-of-a-bitch," Sigrid growled, and releasing her change, she lunged for him.

She moved so quickly that Regina never had the chance to stop her as she knocked him to the ground. The five remaining team members moved in to support their leader, but it was Regina that moved behind Sigrid and wrapped restraining arms around the girl's waist. "No!" she yelled firmly.

Terrence looked into Sigrid's face and had no doubt that she would destroy him if Regina released her hold. He snarled, trying to regain his calm, but he still reeked with the smell of fear. "You'd better destroy me now, little girl, because this won't be over till one of us is dead," he growled with conviction.

Regina felt Sigrid lunge again but kept a hold on her, shocked at the amount of power coming from the girl. Sigrid's body was tense and her breathing rapid as she struggled to pull free of Regina. "I'll dance on your ashes," Regina promised as she finally managed to pull Sigrid away.

"You want war, you'll get it," he spat out and then vanished into a mist and disappeared into the fogbank.

The team stayed ready, eyes peeled in case he decided to try another sneak attack.

Sigrid tore away from Regina and turned to face her, eyes bright red. "Why did you stop me!" she screamed, fangs bared.

Regina grasped for an excuse, shaken by the intensity of her niece's anger and the real reason she had stopped the attack. "Because it wasn't time. When the time comes, you will not be stopped, I promise you that. For now, just trust me," Regina said calmly.

She sighed as she felt some of Sigrid's anger fading. The tension was stepped up when they heard Garrett yell out in pain.

"Gar?" Regina called and rushed to the limo. Inside she found Paul hovering over Garrett with a bloody knife in his hand. Garrett was no longer conscious, and his face was creased in pain.

"What have you done?" Regina demanded as she started for Paul.

This time it was Sigrid that restrained her. "What's up, Paul? How bad was it?"

Paul looked at the angry brunette eyeing him and then turned his attention to Sigrid. "Whatever this bullet is made of was really starting to burn and destroy his leg. I had to cut it out before he lost the leg." Nick nodded agreement as he finished bandaging the man's leg and dropped the bloody silver slug into a ziplock baggy.

Regina looked down, embarrassed that she had almost attacked her saviors. Sigrid patted her shoulder. "Let's get Garrett back to the hotel. He needs more medical treatment than we can give him here."

Regina nodded and stepped into the limo. She offered Paul and Nick a smile as she sat down and propped Garrett's head in her lap. Nick climbed out of the car, as Ward climbed into the front seat. They drove back to the hotel penthouse followed closely by the new security team.

During her lifetime, Regina had always kept a select few loyal doctors to treat mortal and immortal alike. Some were vampires, others not, but they all served to the best of their abilities. She had made arrangements for one such doctor to be on call in the event of an emergency, and he was now bandaging Garrett's leg.

Don Boldway had been administering to the family for the last thirty years, and he was the one called when any of Regina's immediate family needed care. He was one of the most trusted and capable physicians she had ever employed, and as she watched him, she remembered meeting him all those years ago in a small town in Arizona. He was just beginning his practice and had been on his way home when he had come across a fight on the side of the road. The fight involved Regina, Garrett, and a couple of Terrence's coven. This time it was Regina that had been hurt, and while treating her, he discovered their secret. A good Samaritan stop had changed his life, and he never regretted it. He was getting older now, but still efficient. He was balding, short, and slender with a kindly face and strong, soothing voice.

His voice was deep and calming as he finished up the bandaging and began collecting his equipment. "It was much worse than it looked."

Regina flinched at those words and moved closer. "How bad?"

Don smiled. "There won't be any permanent damage, but it will scar and take a while to heal. Whatever the bullet is made of is deadly." He held up the baggy and stared at it. "It was literally burning away the flesh around it. If your man hadn't cut it out when he did, Garrett would have lost his leg."

Again Regina felt a pang of guilt for reacting poorly toward the blond man who had saved her love's life.

Now Don directed his gaze at Garrett. "Stay off your feet for a couple of days and give that leg a chance to heal. When you do get up, I recommend a cane for at least a week or so." He closed his bag and walked over to Regina, holding out the baggie. "My guess is pure silver and soaked in holy water. That would explain the burns around the wound, but I honestly couldn't tell you what caused the other damage."

Regina nodded and smiled with relief. "Thank you, Don."

He patted her shoulder. "Call me if you need me, otherwise I'll be back this evening to check the bandage." Then he took his leave.

Regina sat down on the bed next to Garrett and stroked his hair. "Is it bad?"

Garrett tried to smile but couldn't hide the grimace. "Well, it's more like a tickle."

She hugged him fiercely, exhaling a shaky breath. "Don't ever scare me like that again."

He returned the hug and placed a feathery kiss on her ear. "Sorry, my Queen. That was never my intention. I did tell you that I had taken precautions."

She pulled away from him and met his eyes, her face stern. "Yes, and I'm impressed with what you've put together," she admitted. "I'm also extremely angry at you for letting Sigrid get involved."

Garrett tried to pull himself up, and Regina quickly moved to assist him, helping him prop on the pillow and then drawing the covers up around his chest like a mother hen.

Getting comfortable, he smiled weakly. "You're impressed and angry at the wrong person." He sighed. "I was just the sounding board and moneyman."

Regina sat back in disbelief. "Sigrid?"

"Her gift to you. After the Penshaws, she was worried about your safety. You told her to make it work, and she did."

Regina rolled her eyes. "When will she realize that she is in as much danger as anyone? I can't believe you went along with this. She is not my protector."

Garrett nodded. "No, she is not your protector," he agreed and took her hand into his own. "But she does love you. Stop for a minute and think about the way she was raised. Anyone she's ever cared about or bonded with has been taken away. She was raised in a lie and a mentally abusive home. It's perfectly understandable that she is terrified of losing you too. She's too proud and strong to show that kind of weakness, so she tries to make it productive."

Regina tightened her grip on his hand, knowing that he was right, but still worried for her niece. "But . . ."

"Be patient with her," he interrupted. "You've lived long enough and seen enough to at least sympathize with her feelings. In fact, I'm surprised you don't recognize them. I've seen them in you enough."

Regina glanced at him sideways. "Since when have you become so fond of her?"

Garrett shrugged. "During the last three years, I've been impressed with her business skills and her energy. Over these past few months, I've gotten to really know her, and I like her. She's intelligent, strong-willed, and a lot like the lady I love."

Regina blushed as he continued, "She brought this team together and formed a lethal unit. Believe me, when she first came up with this idea, I was ready to write her off, but then I saw the same look of strength and determination that I've come to love in you. Every one of those people would die for you if she asked them to, and she has. She was very specific about the type of people she wanted on the team and was very honest with them when she recruited them. They willingly agreed to defend you and die for you if need be. They would die for her as well."

Regina took a deep breath and released it slowly, letting his words soak in. Her anger was replaced by calm and admiration. "They were good, weren't they?"

Knowing that he had managed to reach her, he smiled. "Yes, they are. I've watched them train, and they are awesome. Sigrid's gift is that she attracts loyalty. Not by design, but simply by who she is and her actions." He stopped there and stifled a yawn.

Regina stared into space. "That's a rare gift. Not only has she managed to ensure my safety, but her own as well." When she looked back to Garrett to see if he agreed, she found him dozing. She studied his face for a moment, loving him, then lightly kissed his lips and quietly left the bedroom.

Regina silently closed the hall doors and walked into the living room where the team waited patiently. As she approached, she saw the seven of them talking quietly and guarding the perimeter. They still wore their black leather suits, minus the helmets. With their jackets open, she could see that they were fully armed. Each wore a shoulder holster and gun with a case clipped on to their leather pants.

She cleared her throat as she came down the steps into the sunken living room. Instantly, Sigrid and Ward were by her side. "How is he?" The concern very evident in Sigrid's voice.

"He'll be fine, just off his feet for a few days. You and your team saved both of our lives tonight, and I am in your debt." She moved off toward the picture window where Paul and Nick stood watch. "And I owe you two an apology," she admitted. "Had you not taken action, Garrett would have lost his leg. Thank you."

Paul turned red from his toes to the top of his head. "No thanks or apologies needed. I imagine it was bloody frightening to find me hovering over your man with a bloody knife."

Sigrid joined them, her face beaming with pride. "I think it's time for proper introductions."

As she led Regina around the room, she made sure to let her know what their specialties were as they met. Once Regina had met everyone and spoken to them individually for a few minutes, she motioned for all of them to take a seat. She noticed every eye in the room seek out Sigrid before Ward answered, "We'll stand, thanks."

Nodding, she held out the bag and its contents for them to see. "Terrence has a new weapon. It looks like an ordinary bullet, but this one can eat the flesh of a vampire." She held out the bag to Sigrid, and as if by telepathy, Ty appeared by her side and intercepted it.

He examined it closely, holding it up to the light. "Pure silver, custom made, probably cooled in holy water. There is something mixed in with the silver, you can see the irregularities. I need to keep this to run a few tests, if that's okay?"

"Of course," Regina agreed, awed by his expertise. Shaking herself back to the situation at hand, she addressed the team. "I've got to alert the family to what's happened, and then we'll close up shop. Ward, I'll need you."

Ward nodded as Sigrid asked, "Close up shop?"

"Leave town, get new identities and lives," Regina supplied. "Terrence can alert the hunters to my whereabouts and my name now. I had already begun to make arrangements a few days ago. We just have to move before Terrence and the hunters do."

Sigrid slowly looked into space. "I think I can throw a monkey wrench into his plan."

"We have to move quickly. There's no time to formulate a plan," Regina argued.

"Less than twenty-four hours. I can leave now."

Regina looked at her for a moment and didn't need telepathy to know what she had in mind. She knew it would probably be a waste of time, but it was a chance to slow down Terrence. "Okay, but you'll take Ty and Silk with you. And promise me you'll be careful. You'll be going into the lion's den, so to speak."

Sigrid nodded, and Regina continued, "We'll be gone by the time you get back, so go to the Penshaws when you're done. They'll know where we are. And if you have any trouble, call them and I'll be there in the blink of an eye."

Sigrid was surprised at the quick acceptance of the idea but didn't question it. She was also surprised when Ty said, "She'll be safe."

The three of them headed for the door, and Sigrid turned around to look at the remaining team. "Please protect her, my friends," she asked.

"No worries, love." Paul grinned, and with that they took their leave.

At six-thirty in the morning, Atlanta's Hartsfield-Jackson International Airport was lightly populated, but as the day aged, it would become a beehive of activity.

Cameron quickly made his way through the airport to the Fly-By-Night coffee shop on the second level. He had been sleeping soundly when he had gotten the call. After a few minutes on the phone, he had gotten up, showered, and dressed. He was anxious to get there as fast as possible, afraid that the call had been a vivid dream or that he would be too late.

She spotted him the minute he entered the shop and, for the first time in three years, felt a pang of loss for her mortal life. He was dressed in blue jeans and a black, gray, and brown pullover sweater. He had grown a beard and mustache that was lightly peppered with gray, and she saw the few gray hairs mixed in with his curly brown tresses. She noticed that, as he got older, he looked even more like his father. But Sigrid could still see the big brother that had taught her all about football.

When he spotted her, a warm, sincere smile covered his face, and he picked up speed. Rushing over to the table, he swept her into his arms without hesitation. He held her tightly and breathed a sigh of relief. "Tine, I have never been so happy to see someone in my whole life."

Sigrid returned the embrace, feeling tears well up in her eyes. "Me too, big brother." They held on to one another, savoring the embrace and not wanting to be the first to let go. Cameron voiced that thought. "I'm afraid if I let go, you'll disappear again."

Sigrid rubbed his back. "Never again. Unless you want me to."

Now he did release her and pulled back. "I don't ever want to lose you again."

She noticed that a few of the denizens of the coffee shop were beginning to stare. "We better stop this before we get arrested."

The sound of his laugh warmed her heart, and still holding hands, they sat down at the table. His eyes twinkled as he gave her a good going over. "You look fantastic."

She reached across the table and stroked his close-shaven beard. "So do you." He pressed against the warmth of her hand. "The beard's a nice touch." She continued trying to ease the tension between them. Then she turned serious, her voice dropping slightly. "I'm sorry about what I said that night. I was confused and hurt, and I lashed out at anyone in my path. I never wanted to lose you or our relationship."

He reached up and took her hand, squeezing it lightly. "I'm sorry too. If I had seen you before that night, I would have told you everything." His eyes dropped, and he noticed the ring that he had given her so many years ago was still in place on her finger. "You kept the ring."

She glanced at the ring and then back to him. "Of course I did. Cameron, despite what happened, you're still my brother, and I never stopped loving you." She rubbed the ring on his finger. "I see you still wear the one I gave you."

He nodded. "I never take it off." He hesitated slightly, then locked on her eyes. "Where did you go? Did they hurt you? Are you one of them?"

She answered his question with one of her own. "Does it matter?"

His face was a portrait of turmoil. She wanted to take away all the confusion but knew that he would have to deal with it on his own, the same way she had.

"They kill people, Tine," he finally replied. "If they hurt you or forced you . . ."

Her voice and posture became defensive. "I've never killed anyone to feed, Cam, and they are my family. They would never hurt me or force me to do anything."

The turmoil turned to puzzlement. "Then you're not one?"

Sigrid lowered her head and laughed. "Cam, I'm going to tell you the truth. Not what the books say or the hunters believe, but the truth. And I want you to listen with an open mind."

"All right," he agreed.

She cautiously glanced across the room and saw Ty and Silk sitting near the door, watching her protectively.

"There are two factions," she began softly. "One group wants to live in peace among mortals and has for a hundred years. They don't need to kill innocent people because there are those that know of their existence and willingly donate their blood so they can survive without killing. This faction lives in homes, is married, working, does everything that others do."

Cameron listened intently, a shadow of disbelief still on his face. "What about the other faction?"

She sighed deeply. "They are the dangerous ones. They kill for the sport of it and steal from their victims. They are just like the movie vampires, sleeping in coffins, hiding from the sun, the whole deal. Now they have begun recruiting the hunters like Seth to wage war on the other faction. That way there will be no opposition when they spread across the world."

Cameron bit his lip, trying unsuccessfully not to sound condescending. "That's not possible. Dad would never help a vampire."

"Not willingly, no. But one of his informers is, in fact, the leader of the dark faction. I have proof. It was in Reynard's own books."

With those words, he realized who had broken into his father's study. "It was you that robbed Dad's place? We thought they had taken you and used you to find out where his records were. Who did you meet that turned you into a thief and told you all this stuff?"

The defensive posture returned. "I am not a thief. The information I took was about me and my family. I had every right to it, unlike Seth, who prowls around like a tabloid reporter. The person I met was my aunt, the leader of . . . for lack of a better word, the light faction."

Cameron wanted to believe, but Seth's training still tugged at him. "How do I know that this truth isn't just some concoction to turn us against our informants?"

"Check the records, Cam," she replied and leaned closer. "How many were staked in coffins at midnight? How many appeared normal, leading mortal lives?"

He felt a chill go down his spine as he thought about the cases his father had and the ones he staked personally. He had noticed something was off or wrong but had been unable to allow any doubt into his mind.

Sigrid saw his uncertainty. "Cameron, I have never lied to you, and I'm not lying now."

Frowning, he asked, "Who's the informer?"

"Terry Baker," she supplied bluntly.

His burst of laughter caught her off guard, and out of the side of her eye, she saw her two shadows tense for action. When he managed to stifle the giggles, he smiled at her patiently. "You may not be lying, but someone has been telling you some doozies."

Now she was confused. "What are you talking about? Why is that so hard for you to believe?"

"Because I've met Terry Baker," he answered. "Spent time with him. Hell, we've even gone to some ball games together. He turned to us when his sister became a vampire."

"I know," Sigrid stated coldly. "His sister was my mother."

The laughter and smiles stopped. "What?"

"Terry Baker is my uncle. Ask him why he insisted that mother and child be killed. How does he get his information, and why is it so accurate? Why does he insist that one of his people always accompany you on the hunts?"

He looked at her, knowing they were questions he had asked himself. To believe that they had been used like that was too much for him. "No way. You're mistaken, Tine. You leave town for a job then come back angry, knowing the truth about your real mother, and freak out. Next you ransack Dad's house and vanish for three years. You don't call, you don't write. Nothing. Now out of the blue, you reappear with this far-fetched story about how the hunters are being used by bad vampires to wipe out good vampires. You should go to Hollywood, this would make a great movie."

Visibly hurt, Sigrid sat back. "I took a chance coming here because I love you, and I wanted to warn you. Terry Baker knows I'm alive now, and he's going to be coming to you with a lot of tips very soon. One of those tips might be me."

She started to stand when he caught her hand. "I could never hurt you, Tine, no matter what," he said earnestly.

She eased back down in the chair. "Cameron, there is a war breaking out between the two factions. Terry will use the hunters, like you, against my family and friends. One night you may find me on the other end of that stake, believe me, he will not let you stop, no matter what."

"What can I do?" he asked, still torn, but knowing that his true allegiance would always be with his sister.

Taking a deep breath, she smiled. "The best thing you could do is keep the hunters out of it. They will be the ones caught in the middle, and no matter what you think of us, we have no desire to hurt them. I know that not all the hunters will stay out of it, but at least check your sources. If you're willing to trust me, I can help and prove to you everything I've said."

His heart melted as he met her blue eyes. "I do trust you. I always will."

Sigrid felt the sting of tears in her eyes and rubbed them away. Exhaustion from the previous night's activities were beginning to get the better of her, but she continued, "First, you and Seth must be careful. As I said, Terry knows I'm alive now and will demand an explanation. He may even try to involve you in an accident, so be careful and watch what information you give out."

Reaching into her jacket, she retrieved a small, plain white business card with a number scrawled on the back. She inconspicuously slipped it into his hand. "That's my personal phone number. It's not traceable, so don't even try. When you are convinced that this is not some kind of ploy to deceive you or use you, then call me. Until then, there's nothing left to say."

He restrained her from rising by tightly gripping her wrist. "There is a lot more to say, but the only thing that counts is this. I don't care what you are. I love you, Tine."

"I'm your sister, Cam. I would never lie to you or try to deceive you. I love you. Despite what's happened over the last few years, I am still the same person. And if you know me like you always thought you did, you know what's in my heart. I knew what was in yours, that's why I'm here."

He released his hold on her wrist, and she rose to her feet. "When you're sure, call me. Even if you decide to blow all this off, please promise me you'll be careful."

He stood up as well, taking her hand in his and staring down at the ring on her finger. He wanted to say so much, to go back three years and freeze time, but he knew it was impossible, even as she softly said, "I have to go."

He could only nod and release her hand. She stood on her tiptoes and planted another kiss on his cheek and then quickly exited the coffee shop. He continued to watch her until she disappeared into the growing airport traffic.

Seth and Cameron looked at the woman restrained in the chair before them. Later the same day that Cameron had met with Sigrid, Terry had called, reporting a pickup in vampire activity. One such tip had led them to Tampa, Florida, where they met and captured the middle-aged woman who was now their captive. As usual, Terry had sent one of his men to accompany them, and now all three men prepared to drink a toast to a successful capture.

Cameron and Seth watched closely as their guardian gulped down the whiskey they had brought with them. Cameron had indeed told his father of his meeting with Sigrid and everything she had told him. Seth was so overjoyed to hear she was alive, the fact that she was a vampire and all the other information was secondary. Now testing what she had told them, they closely watched as the youthful assistant finished off his drink. In a matter of seconds, he was gagging and clutching at his throat, the holy water in the whiskey accomplishing its mission. Both men stepped back as their associate fell to the concrete floor of the construction house, slowly dissolving from the inside out. A few minutes later, the only thing left was a bloody heap of smoldering goo.

"It's true," Cameron said softly as he kicked at the remains.

Seth stared in shock, the realization that he had been helping the enemy slowly and painfully sinking in. "What have I done?"

Cameron moved closer to him. "Dad," he soothed, "they used us, just like Justine said, and it's time we put a stop to it."

Leaving his father still dazed, he moved over to their prisoner. She was an attractive woman, appearing to be in her early forties, with brown hair and hazel eyes. She tried to cower away from him as he neared her. He stopped, holding his hands out to show they were empty. "I won't hurt you."

Her eyes showed she didn't believe him, and he stooped down, trying to seem less threatening. "Will you answer a question for me?" he asked.

Slowly she nodded.

"What do you do for a living?"

Caught off guard by the question, she only stared at him for a moment. She expected him to torture her and stake her, but this was from left field. Gulping in fear, she spoke in a voice that was little more than a whisper. "I work with mentally challenged adults. I try to help them get along better in society."

Tears stung his eyes as he stood up. He had researched more thoroughly on this case, and he knew the woman was telling the truth. How many other good people had they staked simply because they believed they were murderers? Led on by the one who was really a monster they sought to destroy. For the first time he felt guilt creeping over him and threatening to consume him. Suddenly he felt a strong hand on his shoulder and turned to see his father's pale face. "Let her go, son. She's no danger to anyone."

Her eyes wide and wary, she watched as Cameron eased over and unlocked the chains that held her in place. Fearfully, she sat still, not quite able to grasp what was happening. "Go home . . .," Seth replied softly, "and forgive us."

Now her face softened as she looked at the two men, two men who had finally realized how badly they had been betrayed. "Thank you," she stated and ran from the room.

The two men again turned their attention back to the goo on the floor. "How do we explain this to Terry?" Seth questioned.

Cameron rubbed his beard in thought. "The guy never showed up. When we went to the meeting place to find him, the only thing there was a puddle of gore. There was no sign of him, so we left. End of story."

Seth nodded, a new fire in his eyes as he met Cameron's. "Paybacks are going to be a bitch."

Cameron smiled, glad to see a spark of his father's determination back. "I'll make the call when we get home."

9

Regina had moved operations to Denver, Colorado. The cover story was that she had decided to leave business to pursue painting. But in truth, she still owned everything, just under different subsidiary companies, and the one in Denver was the largest. Exports International was located in the busy downtown business district and occupied a new twelve-story building. The basement of the building had been specifically modified for the security team as a training facility, firing range, gym, and lab.

The trip back from Atlanta had been a quiet one. Sigrid was lost in deep thought. Ty and Silk covered their concern and stayed close by. It had taken a day or so for her mood to change, and that had been helped when Regina received a call from a family member in Florida describing her capture and release by hunters.

While the other members of the team were busy doing their various tasks and activities, Ty summoned Sigrid to the deserted gun room. She walked in and smelled the odor of gunpowder and gun oil permeating the air. Their armory would easily out-fire a gun shop, and all the team members were proficient with the weapons.

"What's with the secrecy?" she asked as Ty moved in and closed the door behind her. Before she could receive an answer, they were interrupted by a muffled buzzing sound. "Sorry." Sigrid blushed as she reached into her jacket and pulled out her cell phone. "Yes," she said coolly.

A smile covered her face as the familiar voice spoke, "Tine?"

"Cam," she replied pleasantly. "Are you all right?"

"Yeah," he hesitated. "Are you busy?"

Sigrid leaned against the cleaning table that was stationed by the wall. "Not for you. You sound funny. Are you sure you're okay?"

"I got an interesting call yesterday," he began, "From Terry Baker. He started quizzing Dad about his sister's death. He wanted to know if Dad had really killed the child."

"And?" she asked.

She could almost hear his smile. "Dad assured him that he had staked the child himself. A three-year-old brunette girl."

Sigrid's eyes widened, and a chuckle escaped her. "Brunette?"

"Yeah." He laughed. "That was pretty much his reaction, but he didn't push it. He said that the vampire activity was picking up and he would keep us supplied with targets." He hesitated again and then continued, "We followed one of his leads, and as usual, he sent someone with us. We decided to test your theory, and . . . you were right." He fell silent waiting for her response, and when none came, he went on. "He called again this morning. He told Dad that he had finally found out what happened to you."

Sigrid frowned. "Cameron, are you sure you're okay?"

Cameron cleared his throat. "What he told us was horrible. He said they had tricked you into leading them to Dad's files, and then when you wanted to leave, they had tortured you for months, then killed you." Sigrid felt a shiver down her spine as he also added, "And then he proceeded to tell us what they had done to you."

"I'm sorry, Cameron," was the only thing she could say, knowing that had she not gone to see him when she did, the hunters would be in this up to their necks, and they would have been urged on by her grieving father and brother.

"He promised to call us as soon as he found out who was responsible for your death and extended his deepest sympathies."

Sigrid sighed. "I didn't expect that plan of action from him. What did Seth say?"

"That he appreciated Terry's help and he couldn't talk right now. Your secret is safe, and your point has been proven. I don't even want to think about what would have happened if you hadn't contacted me when you did." Sigrid could hear the sadness in his voice.

"I am so sorry it had to happen like this, Cameron."

"I know." He sighed. "At least you saved us from making more mistakes. Dad has already talked to the network, and basically, we've decided to take a vacation for a while. Most of the network has agreed as well. Anything Terry gives us will be filtered to you, but I imagine he'll catch on pretty quickly."

Sigrid smiled, her face etched with relief. "Thank you, Cam, and tell Seth that I said the same. The two of you need to be careful. Terry is very smart and very cold-blooded. If you'll let me, I'll help you find a safe place to spend your vacation."

"This is hard for Dad, Tine. He's been doing this all his life because he thought it was the right thing to do, and now the lines have become so muddy. He does love you. I don't think he realized it until you left and were missing. That's why he's trying to be open-minded and help."

Ty watched as her face fell and quiet tears rolled down her cheek. "I . . . don't blame him for my mother. He was used by a very evil man. Tell him that I don't blame him, okay?"

Cameron could hear the emotion in her voice and felt his own tears trying to erupt. For so many years Seth and Justine had been at odds, and now it was this situation that bridged the gap a bit. "I'll tell him," he promised. "You just be careful. I don't want the reports of your death to be true."

"Cam," she said slowly, "don't believe anything you hear. If something does happen, you'll get a call from Regina or Martha. If it doesn't come from them, don't believe it, and if you do get into trouble or even feel nervous, call me."

"I will and same to you. I'll be in touch. I love you."

"I love you too," she responded and heard the line go clear. Taking a deep, cleansing breath, she returned the phone to her jacket pocket and looked up to find Ty watching her every move. "Your brother?"

She nodded.

"Good news?" he questioned.

"Yes, as a matter of fact."

He walked over to her and took her hand. "Want some more?"

Eyeing him suspiciously, she let him lead her to the ammunition cabinet. She waited patiently as he opened the cabinet and then unlocked one of the drawers. He brought out a box of bullets and laid them on the shelf beside the cabinet. Looking at her with a gleam in his eye, he pulled two bullets from the box and held them up to her.

She immediately recognized the silver bullet, but the other one looked like a regular bullet just colored differently.

"The bullet that hurt Garrett was at one time a pure silver blessed cross," Ty informed. "Apparently he had a blessed cross melted down and poured into bullets. I figured we could do the same thing," he said, holding it toward her.

"He's smart and evil," Sigrid observed. "What about the other one?"

Smiling proudly, he dropped it into her hand. "Take a close look."

She took it and held it up under the light on the worktable. Other than the tip it was a typical bullet, but the tip looked different, and she couldn't pinpoint what it was made of. "What is it?" she questioned, examining the tip more closely. Then a look of surprise and excitement appeared on her face. "Wood!?"

He leaned forward, his face lit up like a child's at her pleasure. "I got the idea from a . . . a vampire movie."

Sigrid laughed and held the beauty tightly as she stared into his brown eyes. "Will it work?"

"No reason why it shouldn't, as long as you hit the target in the heart. It's a compact wooden stake and splinters on contact. It should be very fatal."

Sigrid couldn't contain her excitement, and it helped her desire to surface as she leaned forward and lightly kissed him. A bolt of fire shot through her when their lips met, and she pulled away, a bit unsure of what was happening.

His face was no longer without expression. His eyes glowed with desire, and his breathing had increased slightly. They stared at one another for a moment and then mutually embraced, the kiss passionate and full of flame.

The kiss became more intimate as they released long-restrained feelings. They melted into one another, wanting to become one. The mood was broken when the door opened and someone walked into the room.

Ward's eyes widened in disbelief and pain as he watched them pull away from one another and try to reclaim a calm demeanor. "Sorry," he halfheartedly muttered and turned to leave.

"No problem," Ty answered coolly.

Ward stopped and spun around, his look full of anger and hate as it fell on Ty. For a split second, Sigrid thought they might fight, but Ward huffed and exited the room quickly.

Sigrid sighed. "I guess you two don't get along."

"Our problem." He smiled, the dimples making a rare appearance. "I'm sorry if I overstepped my bounds or upset you."

Sigrid smile and brushed another kiss on his lips. "It was upsetting in the most wonderful way, and it's something I'd like to discuss with you later. Right now I think we should get this little wooden beauty upstairs to Regina. I imagine she could use some good news too."

Ty looked into her eyes and knew he wanted to be with her no matter what. He turned to lock the cabinet door and then followed Sigrid upstairs.

Regina leaned against her desk as she listened to Sigrid recount her conversation with Cameron. She was just as surprised about Terrence's tactic as Sigrid, but her brother was nothing if not a master manipulator. She had been so busy with the move of operations that she had not had a real chance to discuss the meeting in Atlanta with Sigrid. She had been filled in on the details of course, but she sensed Sigrid's unrest and her desire not to discuss it, so she had thought it best to wait a few days before trying to address it. After she had heard about Reynard's test, it answered a few questions. "I guess Jean's story about the hunters who released her was accurate. I would have never guessed that it was Reynard who freed her."

Sigrid nodded her agreement and then smiled. "Now the other good news." She held out her hand and waited or Regina. Curiously, Regina, too, held out her hand, palm open, and a small object was dropped into her awaiting grasp.

Regina looked at the bullet in her hand and stared at it. Ty and Sigrid remained silent, looks of expectation on their faces. Bringing it closer, Regina examined it and began pacing around her office.

She came to a sudden stop by a large window behind her desk. The Colorado mountains framed her as she looked even closer at the bullet. "Wood?" she asked softly. As she turned around and faced them, a smile lit up her long, worried face. Directing her gaze at Ty, she exclaimed, "You are a genius!"

He blushed slightly. "Thank you, my Queen, but until we test it, that remains to be seen."

Regina shook her head in disagreement. "You're too modest, Ty. They will work, Sigrid and I both have confidence in your skills and you. The only question I have is, how soon can we begin production?"

Ty had already been thinking about that and shrugged. "If we had a regular ammo factory, it wouldn't take more than a couple of days to change the equipment and begin production."

Regina's smile grew wider. "We do have one, in Nevada. Would you be able to fly down and oversee the start of production? I promise you'll only need to stay until it's up and running to your expectations."

He worriedly glanced over at Sigrid, and his thoughts were so loud that Regina picked up on them without even trying. "He doesn't want to leave her," she repeated to herself. "You are much too valuable to keep in a factory, Ty. If there is someone else that can take care of this . . ."

Sigrid smiled at him and gave him a wink. He turned his gaze back to Regina. "I can be ready to leave in an hour."

Regina clapped her hands together. "Wonderful. You get ready to go, and Garrett will be down shortly to get a list of what you need. I'll make sure that you have the top crew and best equipment."

Ty stood up and started for the office door when Regina called to him, "Ty, for right now, I'd rather this be a need-to-know project and kept between us. Thank you for all your work. I think you may have helped turn the tide in this thing before it's even begun."

He smiled at the praise, nodded, then reached for the doorknob. "Be careful," Sigrid added before he disappeared.

Now it was he that winked and then proceeded down the hall and out of sight.

Regina watched the wistful look on Sigrid's face as he disappeared. "He's very impressive," she baited.

"Yes, he is," Sigrid agreed softly, her voice revealing more than she had meant to, and she quickly resumed her serious posture. She frowned when she sat back down to find Regina smiling knowingly at her. "Okay," she grudgingly admitted, "I'm attracted to him."

Regina laughed and walked around the desk, joining her on the small office couch. "I think the feeling's mutual."

Sigrid shrugged slightly, embarrassed. Her posture suggested that she was uncomfortable talking about it, so Regina decided to change the subject. "I never did thank you properly for what you did with the team and Cameron."

"They're a good group and I think they will be great extra security."

Regina draped her arm over the back of the couch. "They have already proven both things. I appreciate all your work."

"I want you safe," Sigrid said plainly.

"And I am, thanks to you." She again picked up on Sigrid's quiet mood. She was one to keep to herself, but Regina had always been the one person she would open up to. Her niece wasn't exactly brooding, but she had become terribly serious of late. "I know seeing Cameron wasn't easy, and I appreciate your effort and success. Now I think you understand what I meant about being immortal."

Sigrid lowered her head. "Yes, and you were right. Seeing him made me realize some things." From the corner of her eye, she caught Regina shifting uncomfortably. "I don't regret my decision," she assured. "This is my life now, and I wouldn't change a thing."

Gently, Regina took Sigrid's face and lifted it until they were face-to-face. "I love you, sweetheart. I'm proud of everything you've become and accomplished. You are being slammed into a situation that no immortal should have to face, especially this soon, and you're handling it better than some of the veterans. It's just that I worry it may overwhelm you."

Sigrid looked at Regina's features, and her own face softened. "I'm fine."

Regina lowered her head slightly. "You know that if you do feel like it's too much, I'm always here for you."

Sigrid nodded.

"I guess the truth is, I miss spending time with you. You've grown up so quickly, and with this damn war brewing, it seems like we're drifting apart."

"I'm sorry," Sigrid replied. "The last thing I want to do is make you feel like that."

Regina laughed and put her hand on Sigrid's shoulder. "I know. It's just an old lady's insecurities. How about we plan a trip when this is all over? Just the two of us and a nice relaxing vacation."

"I'd like that. I miss seeing you, too, but I don't want to be clingy, so I just do what I always do, ignore the problem."

"It's not a problem," Regina said, "and you are never clingy. Now be thinking about where you'd like to go on that trip."

"With Cameron's help, this trouble may be over more quickly than we think. Terrence really screwed up when he told them about my death. Now they know his true colors."

"Well, his plan would have worked had you not thought ahead and contacted Cameron when you did."

"I know," Sigrid replied. "That's all I've been thinking about."

Regina leaned back on the couch, bringing her hands to rest behind her head, and sighed. "I never thought I'd live to see the day I'd be working with the hunters."

"Times change, as do people," Sigrid offered and then stood up. "And I've got to go."

Grudgingly, Regina sat up. "Why? I was just beginning to relax a bit."

Putting her hands on her hips, Sigrid looked at the woman. "Good, while you relax, let some of us work on this. I want to set up a network for the hunters to contact us, and it needs to be done yesterday."

Regina shook her head. "Okay, but don't work yourself too hard, and promise me we'll have dinner tomorrow night."

"I promise." She smiled and left Regina sitting alone in the office.

Darker Shades

10

Three Months Later

Seth squirmed uneasily as the van sped down the road. Cameron glanced cautiously at his father from the back seat and leaned forward, resting his arms on the seat between them. "How much farther?" he asked, breaking the silence.

"Few miles," the driver answered, seeming a bit wary of their behavior.

As if on cue, the other four men in the van began loading their guns and checking their equipment.

"Still don't know why all this is necessary," Seth grumbled loudly, his face reflecting anger and distrust.

Cameron managed a nervous laugh. "You'll have to excuse my father. We're used to doing this alone, especially this one. This time it's personal."

The driver seemed to relax a bit. "I know, Mr. Reynard," he agreed, "but there are at least six bloodsuckers at this location. That, coupled with the fact that these are the people responsible for your daughter's death, made Terry want to ensure your safety. After what they did to your . . . well, you can see how brutal this group is. Believe me, we are only here as backup, this is your show."

Seth sat back and took a breath, his posture still tense. "Good. I want these bastards all to myself. They'll pay for what they did to my girl."

With his words and Reynard's body language, the suspicion that had been gnawing at the men accompanying them dissipated, and they fell into a comfortable silence.

They arrived at the isolated cabin in the Florida Everglades fifteen minutes later. Terry's men moved with the efficiency of a trained military team. As soon as the van was parked out of sight, the seven men climbed out of the van and began dispersing into the surrounding woods. Once they were all in position, they began easing quietly forward toward the cabin in the nearby clearing. As they moved, they fanned out and finally stopped about seventy-five yards away from the target cabin. Seth and Cameron were well trained, but even they were awed by the way these men moved and more than a little worried. Terry had never sent more than one of his soldiers on a hunt, and now they had a full contingent. The driver gave a signal, and one of the men began creeping even closer toward the cabin. He disappeared into the thick foliage, and the driver motioned to hold position.

While they waited on the recon report, Seth and Cameron prepared their equipment. They had brought the big guns, expecting a full-blown fight, and they exchanged quick glances, each studying the landscape.

It was an odd location for a vampire camp, to say the least. It was located on the west side of the everglades, deep in the forest, and right on the edge of the murky waters. In any other situation the cabin could be considered a wonderful place to hunt or rest, away from the pressures of the everyday world. The cabin was a small single-story log that looked at least fifty years old. There was an old storage shack a few yards to the back that looked newer, only twenty-five years old, and both places seemed deserted. The air was humid and heavy and filled with hundreds of different sounds: frogs, crickets, growls and whistles, all a symphony of nature that seemed to grate on the nerves of the men with them.

They were suddenly aware of the returning man, as he settled next to the driver. "Only four are there. Two in the shack and two in the cabin, one of them is the leader. They have a couple of rifles and a crossbow. They aren't expecting company, so it should be an easy take."

"Any alert devices?" the driver questioned.

Recon shook his head. "Not anymore."

"Good." The driver sighed, then looked at Seth. "It's your call, Mr. Reynard. My opinion is, we won't get a better chance."

"Good or not, I'm not leaving without those bastards' blood on my hands," Seth growled. The assault team smiled, seeing the old man so eager to kill. They watched him as he studied the house again. "How about the three of us hit the cabin, the rest of your men can take the shack."

"Mr. Reynard, it might be wise to take two more men with us," the driver suggested.

Seth clenched his teeth, anger filling his voice. "That animal in there took my daughter from me, the same way I intend to take its life. I can handle the leader, and I'm sure my son can take care of the other one. You are simply backup."

Unwilling to push the point, the driver nodded and turned to his men. He gave them a few hand signals, and they began to maneuver. The four soldiers quickly made their way to the shack and got into attack position. Seth, Cameron, and the driver stowed their gear in their bags and boldly walked up to the front door of the cabin.

Planting smiles on their faces, Seth reached out and knocked on the front door. It was answered by a young brunette man who gave them the once-over and then said, "Yes."

"Excuse me," Seth began in a nonthreatening voice, "but our van broke down a mile or so up the road, and we wondered if you might let us use your phone and call for help. We don't seem to be able to get a signal."

Ty smiled. "Of course, come in," he greeted as he held the door open.

The three men walked into the cabin, and as the driver brought up the rear, he was grabbed from behind and slammed into the wall. Cameron quickly shut the door, so as not to draw the attention of the other watchers, then grabbed his father and pulled him aside from the scene.

The driver struggled to break free of his captures, but Ty and Paul pinned him to the wall, his strength almost too much for the two mortals. Cameron moved forward and quickly slipped the pure silver handcuffs on his squirming wrist, then stepped back again.

"Mr. Reynard, would you like to do your tests now?" Ty called over his shoulder.

Seth brought out a cross and walked over to the pinned man. The silver cuffs were already beginning to burn his wrists, and as Seth got closer, he began to struggle even more. Ty and Paul used everything that had to hold him in place as Seth held up the cross in front of him.

The older man watched in amazement as the driver bared his fangs and his eyes took on a red glow.

Spittle ran down his chin as he growled at Seth, "You have betrayed Terrence, you old fool. He will eat your entrails while you scream for mercy."

"I don't think so," Cameron interrupted. His fury pushed him forward, past Seth, and he drove the stake into the vampire's chest.

The driver opened his mouth, but there was no sound as his heart was pierced. A flow of blood rushed from around the stake, and they all stepped back to avoid the gusher but couldn't escape being splattered as the thing jerked and convulsed in his death dance. After a minute, he crumpled to the floor and lay still, smoldering and clutching the wretched piece of wood in his chest.

"Are you all right?" a woman's voice called from behind them.

Seth and Cameron turned around and saw Sigrid standing nearby. She was dressed in black jeans and a brown shirt covered by a black denim jacket, and Seth's mouth gaped at how beautiful she was. He had never noticed it before, but the woman before him was no longer a little girl who had tried so hard to please him, and he dropped his head slightly in shame.

Cameron smiled at her and stepped forward, hugging her tightly. "We're fine," he answered as they parted.

She let her eyes fall on Seth and smiled warmly. He seemed much smaller and older than she remembered. "Hello, Seth."

She was startled when he reached out and pulled her into an embrace. "Hello, Justine," he said as he hugged her. She shot Cameron a surprised look, and he smiled broadly. For several seconds during the embrace, she felt fear and apprehension as she waited for the stake to pierce her heart. When she realized that Seth was not going to stake her, she relaxed her stiffened body and gently returned the hug.

They pulled apart, and Seth cast his eyes downward. His voice was barely above a whisper as he spoke, "I'm sorry, Justine, for everything. I'm an old fool."

The others stood by, not wanting to eavesdrop, but unable to stop watching the scene. Cameron, especially, was happily surprised to see the exchange.

A million memories flashed through Sigrid's mind as she tried to grasp what was happening. The man who had held her tightly had always been so cold and harsh. She had tried so hard to please him, and her every move had incurred his wrath and criticism. Over the years she had grown to despise him, even hate him. That hate had been magnified when the memories of her mother's death had resurfaced.

Now as she stood looking at this old, tired man, she felt the hate dissipating, manifested by a feeling of weight being lifted from her shoulders. "No," she finally responded, "only misguided."

He closed his eyes and sighed, feeling his own weight lifting.

Before they could continue, Sigrid sensed danger. Her senses immediately heightened, and her body tensed. A stern look covered her face. "Stay here. Something's gone wrong," she instructed and ran out the door.

As she entered the yard, she saw Ward being assisted by Larry, coming out of the shed. A trickle of blood oozed down Ward's face, and he held an old rag to his head, leaning on Larry for support.

"Details!" she called as she approached them.

"Three came inside," Larry began. "We took them out. Fourth waited outside until we were in sight, then he smashed Ward on the head, grabbed Silk, and headed into the swamp. Shadow is pursuing."

Sigrid felt fear rise in her throat. Silk stood no chance against an immortal by herself. "Clean up here. Have Paul check you out, Ward. I'll be back," she replied and ran toward the marsh. Picking up speed, she became only a blur as she vanished into the foliage.

As she moved, her senses were on edge and vibrating with life. She released all her restraints and was inundated with the sounds and smells of the swamp. Although the sun was visible, it had begun a slow descent. Feeling the night approaching, she felt the power surge through her.

Shadow moved with the stealth and grace of a cat. He leaped and dodged the various tree trunks and hanging foliage, never making a sound louder than a whisper. His senses were so sharp he knew the minute Sigrid was running beside him. "They're about a hundred yards away. She's fighting and slowing him down."

Suddenly her form was replaced by smoke that drifted rapidly ahead. "Stay here," he heard in his mind, and he stopped suddenly, never taking his eyes off the mist as it disappeared.

Recon man kept running for several minutes after he heard their pursuers stop. Silk continued to squirm and kick at him, trying to force him to release his hold on her, but he ignored her feeble blows as he tried to find a place to stop.

After a few minutes, he found a small clearing and felt he was a safe distance away and stopped. Silk's thrashing had only made him angrier, and he was going to put a stop to it once and for all.

"You piece of shit," Silk growled as she tried to drive her knee into his crotch.

He laughed and set her on the ground, keeping a firm grip on her shoulders. As she continued to struggle, he picked her up by the shoulders and slammed her into an old swamp oak. The force was so much and so unexpected that she felt all the air driven from her lungs and strained to suck in much-needed oxygen.

Moving up against her, he got right in her face and smiled. The precious air she gasped was now fouled by the smell of decay from his mouth as he spoke. "You are more trouble than you're worth," he whispered, his eyes glowing red.

Silk grinned and tried to hold herself up. "You ain't seen nothing yet."

He moved closer and rubbed against her. "Be nice and tell me what I want to know and you may get out of this in one piece."

Swallowing her fear and disgust, she flashed back a few months to the incident at her apartment with Groilier's men. She had been in trouble then and had been lucky. This time her luck had run out. "Go fang yourself," she quipped.

With one fluid movement, he slapped her face and knocked her to the ground with such power that she bounced when she landed. Stunned, she lay still for a second, tasting the salty blood that now flowed from her busted lip. She shook her head to clear it and was about to move, when he was on top of her, pinning her arms to the marshy ground with his knees.

He ran his fingers across her mouth and then brought the blood-covered digits to his mouth and suckled the blood, making loud, slurping sounds. Withdrawing his fingers, he grinned. "You taste good, mortal. I'll give you one more chance." He let his hands come to rest on her breast and began rubbing harshly. "Who's your informant?"

"You bastard. You let me up and I'll make you think taste good," she yelled as she tried to pull away from his touch.

Laughing, he leaned down and licked the side of her face. "I'm going to fuck you till you scream and then suck you dry. But before I'm done, you'll be begging to tell me anything I want to know."

With her last bit of energy, she struggled against him and screamed, "No!" He ripped her blouse off and baring his fangs moved toward her chest. She continued to fight but closed her eyes and never saw the approaching haze easing around his neck. He was so engrossed in his pleasure that he never noticed the smoke that turned into arms around his throat.

Recon suddenly felt something gripping his neck and pulling him upward. Silk, feeling the change in weight, opened her eyes and saw Sigrid hanging upside down from a tree limb and lifting the man away from her.

Recon was now the one struggling as he tried to break free of the tight grasp. He did break free as he was tossed twenty feet away and came to a crash landing, colliding with an old tree stump.

Sigrid dropped to the ground and took a protective stance in front of Silk. Recon scrambled to his feet and met the eyes of the woman before him. He crouched, studying her and waiting for the chance to pounce.

Sigrid's voice was low and hollow as she spoke. "You want to try me, badass?"

He bared his fangs and leapt at her. She moved forward and intercepted him, delivering a jaw-breaking right hook, using her other hand to seize his head and bring him crashing to ground. Stunned, he stayed still and, before he could fully comprehend what was happening, found himself being hauled up and spun around. Sigrid stopped the spin midair, and keeping a firm hold on his collar, she turned and rammed his body against the nearest swamp oak. She released her hold and stepped away as Recon stared down at the tree branch protruding from his chest. Slowly he threw his head back and let out a long, pain-filled wail that sent the swamp denizens into a hiding frenzy. He convulsed for a second or two then went limp, the remains of his life force puddling at his feet.

Sigrid continued looking at his corpse, and suddenly it burst into flames.

Silk whimpered and tried to scoot away from the scene and the burning hulk before her. The anger and hate radiated from Sigrid in very real waves, and for a few seconds, Silk was terrified of the woman and her power.

Sigrid seemed to sense something and took a deep breath, pushing out the anger as she exhaled. Her fangs retracted, and the red glow was fading as she turned and rushed to Silk's side. She noticed the young woman flinch as she approached and felt guilty that she was the cause of her fear.

Silk now saw only concern and caught a glimmer of hurt as Sigrid kneeled down beside her. "Are you okay?"

She ached all over and slowly sat up, trying to pull the remains of her blouse across her. "Yes, just sore and ashamed."

Sigrid took off her jacket and gently wrapped it around Silk's shoulders. "You have nothing to be ashamed of. I'm sorry I scared you, I was just angry that he hurt you, but you have no reason to be ashamed."

Silk dropped her head. "I failed you and the family."

Sigrid touched her shoulder. "No, you didn't. The only failure would have been to give up."

Silk looked into Sigrid's face and saw no disappointment or disgust, only concern and compassion. She tried to still the tears, but they began falling of their own accord.

"Rest," Sigrid said a hypnotic tone. As Silk responded and dropped forward, Sigrid caught her and gently lifted her into her arms. Making sure she had a comfortable hold, she began the journey back to the cabin.

"Take care of her, please," Sigrid asked as Ty took the unconscious woman from her arms. "I'll be back shortly."

Shadow followed her up to the cabin. "Will you see to the vehicles?" she questioned as they reached the porch. He nodded politely and went to the back of the cabin.

With a deep sigh, she opened the screen door and walked into the cabin. Cameron, Seth, Larry, and Paul stood around the living room and snapped to attention as she entered. Paul looked at her unsure, and she picked up his thoughts.

"She's all right." She sighed and joined them.

Cameron's brow furrowed. "What happened?"

"One almost got away," she answered, then looked at Ward and gingerly touched his injured forehead. "Ae you okay?"

He blushed. "Yeah, just a little hurt male pride. Is Silk okay?"

Cameron moved to her. "What about you? Are you okay?"

"Fine. And Silk will be okay." She smiled weakly. "But we have to leave this place. When Terrence's people don't report in, he will send someone to investigate." Turning to Seth, she locked on his eyes. "Are you ready to disappear?"

He nodded. "Yes. We both need a long, anonymous vacation."

"Good. Terrence will know this was a setup, and it's better to let him think you were killed along with his coven. I know it's going to be hard, but it's your best protection."

"But will you be safe?" he questioned in a fatherly tone.

"Yes, and as soon as it's over, I'll contact you, and you can come home. Remember, no contact with anyone other than me or the two names I gave you. If you need anything, just call. Shadow has your car waiting outside. You better get a move on while we finish up here."

There was silence for a moment, and then Seth touched Sigrid's shoulder. "Thank you, Justine, and please be careful." He brushed a kiss on her cheek and headed out the door.

Cameron pulled her close and hugged her tightly. "You better be careful, sis, or I'll come after you myself."

"Yes, sir," she agreed and pulled away. "Now go, please."

He hesitantly started for the door and then stopped, turning back to her. "Love you, sis."

"You too, Cam." She waved and watched him leave. Moving closer to the front door, she watched as he got behind the wheel of the rented Bronco and slowly drove up the dirt road. She stood there listening until the sound of the engine faded.

She felt Paul moving behind her. "Is everything ready?"

When she turned her head, she saw he was wearing his familiar croc grin. "Aye, love."

"Then let's burn this place down and get out of here."

He nodded agreement, and they set about preparing the cabin to look like a war zone, planting pieces of evidence. Once done, Paul began lighting fuses.

The basement was as dank and musty as the rest of the abandoned apartment building. Terrence and the members of his inner sanctum had been in the building a little less than a week, and other than moving their coffins and a few oil lamps, it remained in the same state of decay.

Dust and debris littered the floor, and huge chunks of plaster occasionally dropped from the rotting ceiling above. In the farthest, darkest corner lay the remains of a few of their dinner victims. Terrence had relieved some of his building frustrations by torturing and terrifying his prey before he dined on them; then he tossed the remainders to his sanctum. Usually after that, there was nothing left but hollow shells that once resembled people.

Mice, rats, and cockroaches left their calling cards everywhere, but even they had sensed the evil in the new tenants and vacated the premises for other burned-out and decaying buildings.

The light from the oil lamps cast an eerie glow across the basement, and the occupants could feel the anger welling up in their master as he paced the length of the basement.

The short, chubby messenger stood by nervously. In the past his master had been in the habit of destroying those who brought him bad news, and this news was beyond the usual bad news. He jumped as the master stopped pacing in front of him.

Terrence's voice was low and full of ice as he spoke. "What about the Reynards?"

The messenger forced himself to steady his voice. "They were also found or rather what was left of them. We found six bodies in the house and one over two miles away. Reynard's equipment was scattered throughout the house." Slowly the messenger held out a closed hand and opened it, revealing a charred ring. "We also found this."

Terrence reached out and snatched the ring from his shaky hand. He dusted off the crust and blew away the remaining dust and ash. It was a man's gold ring, with that looked like a black onyx stone and two diamonds. The *CR* initials were charred but clear. Terrence closed his palm over the ring and nodded. "Cameron would have never taken this off. His beloved sister gave it to him."

He backed away from the messenger, and they noticed his anger subsiding a bit. "It's a shame," he said to no one in particular. "Cameron would have eventually been brought into the coven. He was a mortal with great potential, more open-minded than the old man."

As quickly as it had appeared, the sentiment was gone, and Terrence raced forward, slapping the messenger with enough power to send him soaring across the room. The messenger landed with a thump in the far corner and stayed still. He hung his head in shame as the others watched, glad that they were not in his place.

Terrence whirled around, facing them, his eyes glowing and fangs bared. "Five more of my coven destroyed! We have suffered more losses in the last three months than the last thirty years. Our numbers have been reduced by more than half." He cast a hateful look at the man in the corner. "I can't even afford to kill those that disappoint me now." Focusing his rage back on the men before him, he continued, "Our allies, the hunters, are being destroyed or vanishing at the same rate." He took a step toward a young, slender blond teenager. "I want to know how this is happening!"

The young man did not flinch from his master. "She has someone on the inside. I also can't help but wonder if our allies have turned on us as well. I fear we have a traitor in our midst, my Master," he stated coolly.

Terrence stared at him for a moment then smiled. "I think you may be right, James." He patted the teen's cheek and continued pacing. He admired James's perception and loyalty. The boy had been with him for twenty years and was perhaps his most faithful and favorite servant. He showed proper respect but also maintained a sense of independence and free thinking. Normally Terrence would have beaten it out of him, but on this occasion, he found it alluring. The teen always performed without question and with the best possible results. He had taken him under his wing and was grooming him to be his right hand in their new rule and, when the war was won, his lover.

"May I speak, Master?" one of the other men asked, bringing Terrence out of his dreams. Terrence looked up and saw the tall redhead waiting for an answer.

"Of course, Reggie," he acknowledged.

Reggie took a few steps closer. "It is imperative that the bitch Queen not find out our true losses or remaining numbers. I suggest we step up our attacks, meanwhile trying to find the traitor and see about getting one of our own into her camp."

Terrence thought it over and nodded, pleased at the idea.

Then the messenger spoke up. "Master? I think we may have a candidate for that."

Terrence glanced over his shoulder at the crumpled figure in the corner. His face lightened after a moment, and he eased over to the corner. Gently, he helped the man up. "What do you mean, Oliver?"

The man's shoulders slumped, his fear evident as he spoke. "One of her people has approached us. They want to meet with you."

Terrence smiled and began dusting off Oliver's suit. "Oliver, why didn't you tell me this before?" His voice was fatherly and hypnotizing as he continued. "I do apologize for making you feel the brunt of my anger. Tell me, is this a true opportunity or another setup?"

Oliver began standing straighter, his fear dissolving. He loved this man, would gladly die for him, and now only wanted to ease his master's troubles. The earlier episode faded from his mind. "It's no setup. He approached us a few months ago and indicated that he wasn't happy and might be interested in another way. We've been observing him since then. He sent the go-ahead to our scouts this morning. He wants to help you destroy the Queen."

Terrence frowned. "Why?"

"He has given her many years, and he wants the power, but she refuses him. He wants to gain power and experience the old ways. He says your ways and lifestyle are more to his liking."

Terrence closed his eyes in thought. He picked up on their thoughts and feelings, and that helped him to reach a decision. The coven was loyal, but after so many losses, they were discouraged. They needed a win, and this could provide that.

"Arrange a meeting for tomorrow night. If it is a setup, you had better prevent it, or I'll toss you to the ones below."

Oliver's eyes widened, and he visibly shuddered. The ones below were those who had displeased Terrence so badly that he gave them a punishment worse than death. The creatures he kept no longer resembled human beings; they were more animal like. They could tear a victim apart and devour them before their screams faded. No one was sure what he did to create them, but the threat of being forced into the lair was enough to keep all of them in line.

"It will be secure, my Master," he pledged. And when Terrence waved him away, he quickly exited the basement.

Once he was gone, Terrence returned to the others of the inner sanctum. "I want Regina destroyed. More importantly, I want that creature she calls a niece erased from existence."

James spoke up. "But, Master, Regina is their leader. They will fall without her. What harm can the girl do?"

Terrence stopped in front of James and caressed his face. Suddenly the caress became a viselike grip on his chin. "True, my young friend, but of the two, the girl is much more of a threat. Until they are both gone, we can have no hope of victory."

James stumbled backward when Terrence released him, and he eyed his master with masked anger. Terrence ignored the look and held out his arms to the coven. "Now, my children, we feed."

All thoughts but those of feeding and toying with their prey left as they ventured out into the streets of New York.

Sigrid smiled as she walked into the spare bedroom of her apartment. Silk was sitting in the lounger and staring out the window, gazing at the snow-peaked Colorado mountains.

Since their return from Florida, Sigrid had kept a close watch over Silk, even insisting that she move into the spare bedroom of her apartment. "I brought you a drink," Sigrid announced as she padded across the blue carpet and set the glass on the dresser, next to the lounger.

"You know," Silk said as she sat up, "you don't have to wait on me like I'm an invalid. I'm fine, really."

Sigrid's smile faltered slightly. "I'm sorry. I guess I'm just being overprotective."

For the second time in two days, she realized she had hurt the woman that she considered her best friend. Reaching out, she grasped Sigrid's hand. "I really do appreciate everything, Sigrid, and I'm sorry if I sound hostile. I just need some time, okay?"

"Okay." Sigrid nodded and squeezed her hand in understanding. "By the way, if you're up to it, Regina would like to come in and visit."

Silk paled slightly. "Now?"

Sigrid picked up her anxiety, and her smile became reassuring. "She only wants to make sure you're okay. If you like, I'll tell her to stop by later."

"No." Silk released her hand. "Just give me a few minutes to spruce myself up."

Sigrid gave her a wink and left her to her sprucing.

Fifteen minutes later, there was a knock at the door. Silk sat down on the lounger and took a deep breath, trying to calm her nerves. "Come in," she finally called.

The moment Regina came in, all of Silk's fear and apprehension flew out the window. She was dressed casually in blue dress pants and a silk shirt. Her hair was down and flowing over her shoulders, and her brown eyes twinkled as she glided into the room. She was small in stature, but the room seemed to vibrate with her power.

"How are you feeling, dear?" she questioned in a voice as smooth as satin and full of warmth.

"Fine, my Queen," Silk replied with a nod of respect.

Regina laughed and rolled her eyes. "Please, call me Regina."

Silk blushed and watched as Regina moved over to her and waited. It took her a second to realize what she was waiting for, but then she grinned. "Please, sit down."

With a smile as radiant as the sun, Regina took a seat on the other end of the lounger. "So is Sigrid driving you crazy yet?"

"Of course not," she lied.

Regina cut her eyes in a mock scolding, her tone like a mother's. "Tell me the truth, Silk."

"Well, maybe a little," she grudgingly admitted.

Regina nodded. "I'll speak to her. You must understand that she cares about you very much and it's a new sensation for her. Her childhood was not pleasant, and she never allowed herself to care about anyone or let anyone close. You and the team have brought her out of her shell, and it is such a wonderful change for her. Just between the two of us, she's come to think of you as a sister."

Her statements brought a frown to Silk's face, and the young woman rose from the lounger and walked over to the window. She remained silent for a moment, choosing her words carefully. "Sigrid once told me that none of us are expendable. That mortal or not, we were just as much members of the family as any immortal."

Regina watched her closely. "And that's true."

Silk turned to the head of the lounger, her hands nervously rubbing the chair. "I looked into her eyes and, for the first time in my life, actually believed it. I was taken in and brought up by the family, and I love them, but I've always felt like an outsider. Day before yesterday Sigrid risked her safety and the mission to save my life, and that erased any doubt or concerns. She got so angry when she stopped that guy, that it scared me. I'm not used to someone caring for me that unconditionally."

Regina listened intently, realizing how much alike Sigrid and Silk really were. As Silk continued, she watched the young woman struggle. "In return for her concern and friendship, I blew the biggest chance I had to help the family and her. I failed both of you."

Regina took a breath. "How did you fail?"

Silk chewed her lip and shook her head. "By being captured. I could have endangered the whole mission, not to mention the family and Sigrid."

Regina remained seated. "You were captured," she agreed. "That is a possibility that each of us face, even me. The true test comes in what you do when you are captured. Did you cooperate with this man?"

Silk looked into her brown eyes. "Of course not."

"Did you fight to get away?"

"Yes."

"Did you give him any information? Would you have given him information? Did you accept his offer or a deal?"

"No!" Silk answered, feeling her rage beginning to boil and rise to the surface.

"Did you enjoy what he did? What he was going to do?"

"No! Never!" Silk shot back, feeling tears of anger welling in her eyes.

"What would you have done if Sigrid had not have been there to help you?"

Silk's breath had picked up, and the tears were streaming down her cheeks. "I did and would have fought until he killed me. Had I been able, I would have ripped his fucking heart out." She sank to the floor, sobbing uncontrollably as she released all the pent-up feelings.

Now Regina did move, as she kneeled down in front of the woman and wrapped strong, supportive arms around the crying figure. She held the woman close and gently rocked her, stroking her hair. "You did not fail, child. On the contrary, you showed more spirit and guts than many immortals or mortals I know."

Silk lifted her head and met Regina's eyes. She still looked doubtful, so Regina continued, "You did the exact thing I would have done. He hurt you, and I understand that and will do all in my power to help you. Not because I have to, or feel a duty to, but because I want to. But even I can't help you until you forgive yourself. You have nothing to be ashamed of. You're among people who love you."

Silk reclined her head against Regina's shoulder and released her tears and anger. Regina continued to hold her and offer words of comfort and support.

An hour later, she emerged from the bedroom and found Sigrid and Ty engaged in a rather passionate kiss. Blushing, she cleared her throat loudly.

They parted immediately, and their usual businesslike atmosphere returned. "I was beginning to worry," Sigrid replied as she arose from the couch, her cheeks flushed red.

"She just needed to let off some steam," Regina informed them. Seeing their inquisitive looks, she added, "And she wants to stay."

The couple breathed a sigh of relief. Then Regina looked directly at Sigrid. "Silk needs time alone. She appreciates all you've done, but this is a trip she must make alone."

Hesitantly and a little embarrassed, Sigrid nodded, fully understanding Regina's wish. At once Regina's smile returned. "Ty, I need to speak with my niece privately."

Ty stood up. "Of course. We have a few hours before we meet with the hunters again. I'll wait downstairs." Then with a look at Sigrid, he left the two women alone.

Regina moved across the room and sat down on the couch. "Meeting with the hunters?"

Sigrid joined her on the couch. "Yes. We have another setup for Terrence's people."

"I'm very proud of you," she began. "You have handled this situation with Terrence beautifully. Again, you've risked your life for one of our own. Although I fear for your safety, you repeatedly prove your abilities." She cut her eyes at Sigrid. "According to Silk, you have a new ability you neglected to tell me about."

Sigrid hunched her shoulders. "I'm sorry. It's just that . . . I'm not exactly sure what I did?"

Regina made no movement or sound.

Sigrid gathered her thoughts and explained, "I simply pictured him on fire and he burst into flames."

Regina leaned in and rested her hand on Sigrid's. "What were you thinking, feeling?"

"Hatred," she answered softly. "He was hurting someone I care about. It's like the anger I felt at Martha's, but this time there was no fear, just hatred."

"Can you control this?"

Sigrid shrugged her shoulders. "I don't know. This is the first and only time it's ever happened. Truth is, after it was over, it scared me as much as it did Silk."

Regina sighed with frustration. "You display powers beyond my grasp, and I am powerless to help you understand them."

Sigrid reached out to her aunt and pulled her close, hugging her. "The skills I have are because of your training and teachings. I will come to grips with everything as long as you are there to advise me."

Regina pulled back, studying the young woman's face. "I do love you so. You remind me so much of your mother that I feel like she's still with us at times." Deciding to change subjects before they both got emotional, she next asked, "Did the Reynards get settled?"

"Yes. The ball's in Terrence's court now. His numbers are rapidly dwindling, so I suspect all this will come to a head very soon."

"We've allowed for every contingency, and your team has been invaluable. I will never be able to repay you for that gift. Everything has gone as planned, with the exception of the incident at the cabin."

Sigrid's voice reflected confidence. "You don't have to repay me for anything. It was something that did and still does give me as much pleasure as putting it together for you. Don't worry about Terrence. Before long he will be nothing but a bad memory." She glanced at her watch and stared at the time. "I've got to get going. We reduce his numbers by five tonight."

Regina saw her hesitate and throw a quick look at Silk's door.

"I'll keep an eye on her for you," Regina volunteered. "You just come back to me in one piece. Promise?"

"Promise." With that she left the apartment.

For the next few weeks, everyone was kept busy by Terrence's frequent attacks, but without the hunters' help, they lacked much accuracy, and his numbers continued to slide.

Ty's new wooden bullet had proven successful and was immediately supplied to the entire family for self-preservation.

Garrett and Regina coordinated all the movements of Terrence's coven and kept the team supplied with information and locations. The team handled any skirmishes that involved multiple numbers of the coven members, always leaving two behind to protect Regina. Silk had quickly regained her momentum with Regina's help and was back out with the team in less than a week. Sigrid continued to keep an eye on her and couldn't help but notice the glow that was now covering the young woman's face. With the constant pressure of running the company and working with the team, as well as dealing with the hunters' network, she could never find time to question Silk about her new attitude.

Ward had assumed control of the team and worked to keep them in shape. Sigrid always accompanied them on their missions, realizing that they needed at least one immortal on their side when dealing with the enemy.

The family was a flurry of activity, and as time went by, they noticed how much less Terrence called on the hunters, guessing that he had figured out the turn of his allies and deciding to deal with the family on his own.

Then as suddenly as his attacks had started, they stopped, and everything fell quiet. Everyone remained alert and ready, expecting anything. After three weeks of no interactions with the coven, Terrence made his move.

The team had been called to the basement conference room by Garrett. They sat patiently and quietly, awaiting his appearance and assuming they had a new mission.

He strode into the room, briefcase in hand, and they knew this was more than the usual meeting. Laying his briefcase on the table, he rested his hands on it and looked at each of them.

"Terrence has called for another meeting, and Regina has agreed."

They all sat up straighter as he proceeded to lay out the details. "The meeting is scheduled for Thursday night at a gravel quarry in Virginia. Both sides have agreed to only one bodyguard, and since we know how true to his word Terrence is, we will be ready."

He opened the briefcase and began handing Sigrid stacks of papers and maps. She assigned them accordingly.

"What you have in your hands is everything we've been able to get on the meeting place, and knowing your skills, I'm sure you can find more," he replied and directed the last part to Shadow.

Garrett allowed them a few minutes to study the information before he began pacing around the table, all eyes following him. "I don't need to remind you how important this meeting is. Terrence has lost the majority of his coven. That makes him desperate and dangerous. He will either offer up a surrender and stall for time to rebuild his forces or try to kill our Queen.

We know the chances for a surrender, so prepare for the other alternative." He stopped at the head of the table and leaned against it, staring at each of them for a moment. "Last time we had the element of surprise. This time we don't have that luxury, and any mistakes could cost us everything. We have three days to prepare, my friends, and this must be a flawless operation."

"It will be," Sigrid and Ward replied in unison for all of them.

Garrett smiled and, with a few final instructions, left them to their planning.

The team left for Virginia the following morning. Garrett had prepared their training accommodations, and after they arrived and set up, they began a rigorous training regime. They spent the next two days training harder than they ever had. They meticulously studied the maps and layouts, double- and triple-checked their equipment, and by Thursday, they were functioning as one person, even to the point of finishing one another's sentences. Sigrid was confident that they would be ready to handle anything that arose, until Thursday morning. From the time she got up, it had been one thing after another, all minor problems that reared up, but still annoying.

The topper had been an unexpected meeting with a client in Virginia that had demanded her attention and called her away from the team's training. With the problem solved, she now hurried back to the warehouse, checking her watch and cursing as she drove beyond the speed limit. The meeting with the hunters had lasted until five-fifteen, and after leaving the meeting, she had been delayed by a wreck that stalled traffic for much longer than she had to waste. As she tore into the parking spot outside the warehouse, she now only had twenty minutes to get dressed, go over last-minute details, and leave. She had hoped for a bit of quiet time to focus her mind and thoughts, but that was a luxury she didn't have.

It was six-o-five when she walked into the ready room and was surprised to see the others relaxing, each one taking advantage of the time to meditate and think. "Why aren't you ready?" she asked, her voice as tense as her posture.

Paul stood up and smiled. "Relax. Garrett called and said the meeting had been moved up to nine o'clock. We leave at seven thirty instead of six thirty."

Sigrid's eyes scanned the room, the look on her face becoming more alarmed by the minute. "Where's Larry and Ward?"

"Said there was something they had to do for Garrett. Said they would be back by seven," Shadow stated as he turned and watched his leader become more agitated.

Sigrid's eyes darted to and fro as the thoughts came fast and furious; then she turned and left the ready room. Ty caught up with her in the gun room. He watched as she picked up her guns of choice and ammo and knew she was not happy.

"What's wrong?" he questioned, his own feeling of unease applying itself.

Sigrid jammed the .44 into her shoulder holster. "It doesn't feel right. Who took the call from Garrett?"

"Ward," he answered.

"A mysterious call from Garrett that sends them away on the night of an important mission? Something's not right, Ty."

He nodded agreement. For some time he had begun to be suspicious of Ward and Larry and had kept an eye on them, but it had revealed nothing. He had been hesitant to mention it to Sigrid and dismissed it as jealousy. When the call had come, Ward had been so casual and cool that he had believed what the man said, even though his sixth sense said otherwise. The other team members also picked up the undercurrent but said nothing and waited for her return. Now Ty silently cursed himself for not taking action. Seeing Sigrid reacting like this told him that his suspicions were shared. "I'll call Garrett," he volunteered and left the gun room.

Sigrid smiled her thanks and finished loading her guns. She quickly moved to the dressing room and was in her black leather ensemble in a matter of minutes. She was just zipping up the leather jacket when she heard Ty call her name.

Fully armed and ready to go, she ran out to the work area. Ty slammed down the phone with such anger, it smashed into several pieces. "They already left. Fifteen minutes ago."

Sigrid's eyes widened. "They weren't supposed to leave until a quarter of seven."

"They did," he said plainly.

Sigrid looked down at her watch, and it read six-fifteen. Both jerked their heads toward the clock on the wall over the work area and saw six-fifteen.

Dawning came crashing over Sigrid, and she bared her teeth. "It's a setup." Not wasting another precious second, she turned and ran to the front of the warehouse where their motorcycles were stationed.

Ty hit the garage door button as she kicked the starter. Giving the bike full throttle, she had to duck to miss the still rising door as she roared off into the darkness.

Hearing the commotion, the other team members had already begun assembling, unsure of what was happening, but knowing it wasn't good. Ty barked a few short commands, and ten minutes later, they roared out of the garage.

The night was inky black, and a soft breeze caressed the hills of Virginia. As Sigrid rode closer to the meeting place, she felt the transformation coming on, and by the time she reached the gates of the quarry, it was complete. As she topped the hill, she saw a scene that made her blood run cold.

There were two cars at the bottom of the quarry, parked hood to hood. Garrett was fighting off three men that were stabbing him with silver spikes, while Regina was holding off four of Terrence's men and the bastard himself.

Sigrid turned off the head lamp of the bike and aimed downhill.

Regina's eyes darted from side to side, trying to keep the coven members in sight at all times. She could hear Garrett holding his own behind her, but they were badly outnumbered. She kept expecting Sigrid's team to appear at any moment, but so far there was no sign of them, and that made her terror grow. Her thoughts kept playing on Terrence killing off the team before the meeting, and worry for their safety consumed her.

The meeting had begun like before, down to the men clambering out of the limo and attacking them. Terrence was nothing if not predictable, and she had expected their own aces in the hole to show up, but Terrence had not seemed concerned. That was her first sign of trouble. Now they moved around her like sharks. She knew it was trouble.

"Six on two, Theo," Regina called. "You never did play fair."

He took a step forward and sneered at her. "Neither did you when you turned my hunters against me. It took me years to cultivate that relationship, and what I want to know is how you did it."

Regina smiled. "I made them a better offer."

From the side of her eye, she saw one of his men lunge at her, a flash of silver in the air. She spun around and, lifting her leg in a sidekick, drove the wooden high heel of her shoe into his chest. He clutched her foot, and she slipped out of the shoe, hopping back a step as he fell to the ground. Terrence moved in like a bolt of lightning and seized her shoulders. Regina realized her error instantly, but Terrence had the advantage as he lifted her up, took three long strides to the nearest limo, and slammed her down on the hood. The metal groaned and dented as she hit. Before she could recover, he pulled her up and slammed her down again.

Mustering all her energy, she lifted her leg and caught him between the legs. His face cringed in pain and, releasing the hold on her arms, staggered back from her. "Bitch," he wheezed.

Sensing their master's pain, the others moved in again but were stopped when the motorcycle appeared from the darkness and skidded to a stop beside Regina's limo.

The rider leapt off the bike and grabbed the nearest thug. Holding him in a chokehold, the man tried to plunge the spike in his hand back at her to attain release. She seized his wrist, twisted it, and drove the man's own spike into his chest. A spray of blood shot out across the scene, and the others stopped their circling, drawing back toward their master.

Terrence and his men held still, watching the newcomer warily. Regina rose from the car hood and patted the shoulder of the barrier in front of her, relief filling her being.

Terrence tapped his cane on his palm and grinned. "Welcome to the party, niece."

She took off the helmet and tossed it aside, the gravel popping and crackling as it carried down the incline. "My invitation was late," she replied coldly.

The tone of her voice seemed to throw him for a split second. Even Regina felt a chill travel down her spine.

Sensing the danger now, Terrence's thugs left Garrett and returned to their master. Sigrid and Terrence began to circle one another. Her eyes never left his as she eased closer, the sound of his voice and the crunching gravel under her boots the only thing she concentrated on. She showed no sign of noticing that he was maneuvering her away from Regina and Garrett; her full attention was on him.

"I've got business with my sister," he stated lowly. "When that is finished, I'll be more than happy to deal with you." He turned his back on her and faced Regina.

Sigrid leapt in the air, flipping and landing squarely between him and Regina. Snarling, she moved toward him again. "You'll deal with me now, you murdering bastard."

Terrence threw back his head and laughed. "Stupid girl." He grinned as his henchmen surrounded Regina and Garrett, separating her from them. One of the thugs lunged at Regina, aiming a wooded stake at her chest. Another moved toward Garrett, silver spike poised and ready to go. At the same time, they heard a cling as Terrence pulled on the tip of his cane and withdrew the silver sword that was hidden within.

Regina leapt at the henchmen, easily grasping his neck and snapping it in one swift move. Thrown off by the action, he could do nothing as she ripped the stake from his hand and rammed it into his heart. Garrett was just as successful in his fight, and Sigrid turned back to face Terrence.

He miscalculated her sudden movement, expecting her to help her aunt with the others, and plunged the sword through her left shoulder, just above the left breast, instead of her heart. The miscalculation showed on his face as he released the sword and stumbled backward.

Sigrid's scream pierced the air and was heard by the team as they topped the hill of the quarry. Regina's scream of anguish followed it.

The coven ceased their attack and withdrew to stand beside Terrence. They watched as Sigrid looked down at the protrusion from her chest.

Time seemed to stop, then began again and moved in slow motion as she grasped the handle of the sword and with her right hand yanked it out, flinching at every inch that cleared the skin. Once free, she stared at the bloody blade in disbelief and then dropped it to the ground.

They all sensed a building energy, and no one moved. Blood poured from the wound as Sigrid threw her head back and screamed again. The scream was more anger than pain, and the air reverberated with the feeling of a coming storm.

Both Regina and Terrence were startled when she lowered her head. She had transformed into a creature that, in all their years, neither had seen before. The red glow of her eyes was blinding, and her fangs had doubled and elongated, catching the moonlight like shiny razors. Her face was contorted and seemed to stretch, almost like a wolf in appearance. Baring her fangs, a line of spittle trailed down her chin, and she seemed to swell in size.

As the team roared to a stop by Regina's car, Sigrid leapt on Terrence, her strength doubling his. They tumbled to the ground with a loud thud, Terrence's face showing true fear as he struggled to get control of the situation. She raised her hand, which now closely resembled a claw and raked it across his face. Now it was his turn to scream as she left jagged, deep tears in his face. He raised his arms, not wanting to win now, just survive, and tried to ward off her blows, but only succeeded in having his arms torn open as she continued to wail on him.

Ty appeared behind Regina and pulled her back from the scene, as Silk, Paul, and Shadow used the shock of the coven to their advantage and quickly dispatched them. Garrett moved in and took out one on his own, feeling the same rage as the team. In a matter of seconds, the ground around the cars was littered with bleeding, dead, and smoldering bodies. Once they were done, they joined Regina and Ty, each of them awed by the power and ferocity of the attack they were witnessing.

Sigrid continued to claw and tear at Terrence, and although he managed to land a few defending blows, he was no match for the creature that had him pinned to the gravel. She shook him like a rag doll as she took a few more swipes at him; then the blows began to lack as much power. Her injuries were serious and beginning to catch up with her as her strength started to dissipate.

Terrence sensed her weakening strength and knew that his own injuries were severe. Using his last bit of energy, he changed into a mist and vanished from beneath her, disappearing into the night.

Sigrid continued to kneel in the gravel, her head and arms hanging in exhaustion. Regina and Ty rushed to her, approaching cautiously in case she didn't recognize them. The young woman made no move, and Regina carefully moved behind her and rested her hands on her waist. Instantly Regina realized she had reverted back to her normal self, whatever power that had engulfed her was gone now. Fully wrapping her arms around her waist, she felt Sigrid lean against her slightly. "It's all right, honey. We'll get you help," she said soothingly, trying to remain calm.

Sigrid weakly struggled to catch her breath and, with every gasp, lost more blood. She glanced up at Regina and tried to speak but could only muster a whispered groan. A few drops of blood oozed from Sigrid's mouth; then her eyes rolled back, and she slumped against Regina, unconscious.

Regina caught her weight and looked at Ty, the fear plainly radiating in her voice. "Ty?"

He was instantly by her side and helping lift the limp form into her arms. He motioned to the other team members, whose concern was just as tangible as Regina's. "It's all right, my Queen," he said, trying to convince himself as well as her.

Never releasing her hold on her niece, she was led to the car and guided into the back seat. Settling in while Paul administered first aid, the car tore out of the quarry and into the darkness, racing for help.

Regina stood by impatiently as the doctor finished his exam and bandaged Sigrid's wound. The young woman had not regained consciousness, only moaned as Don packed the wound.

When he was done, he walked over to the bathroom and washed his hands. Regina met him as he came out of the bathroom, drying his hands on the towel. "Is she okay? Will she live?" Regina pressed.

Don sighed. "I'm not sure. The blade was silver of course, and it splintered some on impact. I had to remove several slivers of silver from the wound, and I can't tell if there are any in the wound itself. The blade went completely through her shoulder, and had it been three inches more to the left it would have pierced her heart. There are no major organs injured or severed that I can tell, but her makeup has some oddities, things I've never seen before. The slivers of silver made the injury worse, and I may have to go in and check to see if there are any in the wound itself. I removed everything I could, but I honestly don't know if she will live. I will continue to do everything I can, and if she gets worse, I'll go in and check for more silver, but as it stands now, I can't give you a solid answer. I'm sorry, Regina."

"What can I do?" she asked in a voice that lacked her usual power.

Don rested his hands on her shoulders. "Make her comfortable. I'll stay here and do everything I can," he answered, unable to hide the defeat in his tone.

Regina went over to the bed and sat down softly next to Sigrid, ever conscious of not jostling the girl's wound. She looked down at the woman and felt a scream wanting to escape. Sigrid looked so small and helpless lying in the queen-sized bed. Her breathing was shallow and her face so pale that Regina felt like each breath might be her last. Lovingly, she reached out to brush some loose hair from the girl's forehead and was surprised to find her skin hot. Her eyebrows bunching in confusion, she rested her hand on Sigrid's cheek and felt the heat there as well. Regina's eyes and mind were drawn away by the growing red stain that covered the white gauze on her shoulder. In seconds it was saturated and trickling down onto the bed.

Almost as soon as it happened, Don was there changing the bandages, his own face creased with worry.

"She needs strength to fight. She's losing too much blood," Regina stated, looking at Don for agreement.

"Couldn't hurt. In fact, you might want to call in some donors. I think I need to go into that shoulder and check for silver slivers," he answered.

Encouraged but fearful, she brought her nail to her wrist and opened a slit, then eased the bleeding wrist to Sigrid's lips. Gathering up dirty bandages, Don quickly left them alone, giving them their privacy as Regina coaxed Sigrid to take nourishment.

Thirty minutes later, there were four donors in the apartment and four more on the way as Don began the delicate procedure to examine her wound for more damage. Indeed, there were more silver pieces in the wound, and one was lying by her heart. With skilled precision, Don removed every last piece and stitched the wound closed. He packed it with gauze and continued to work as the donors did their work.

Sigrid regained consciousness an hour later, Regina sitting by her side with Silk and Ty hovering nearby. Ty had informed Regina of the events leading up to the showdown and saw the flicker of anger in her eyes.

Sigrid stirred slowly, groaning as she moved her shoulder slightly. Opening her eyes took another great effort, as did her first word when she saw them beside her. "Betrayed."

Regina leaned down close. "Who?"

Sigrid looked over Regina's shoulder and saw Ty. She offered him a weak nod.

Knowing what she meant, he spoke aloud the thoughts they all had but not voiced until now. "Ward."

Regina took a deep breath. A flurry of feelings washed across her face in the blink of an eye, the final one being anguish. Sigrid felt the same, and a tear escaped her eye. "Sorry," she wheezed.

Realizing that she was broadcasting her feelings, Regina looked down at her niece's face and gently wiped the tear from her cheek. "Dear heart, you have nothing to be sorry for."

"He's going to be the one that's sorry," Silk mumbled under her breath.

Surprised, Regina looked up and was shocked at the amount of fury in the redhead. Casting a glance at Ty, she saw he echoed the sentiment.

"Use it," a voice whispered.

All attention focused back on Sigrid. The two women leaned closer to her. "What, sweetheart?"

With great effort, she repeated, "Use it."

Confused, the two women exchanged looks. Ty stepped in closer. "She means to use it to our advantage."

A small smile from the exhausted woman was their indication that he was right.

Silk's eyes lit up as an idea hit her. She eased off the bed and went to the far side of the room and began rummaging in her bag of tricks.

"If he has the guts to show his face again . . ." Ty stated.

Before another word could be spoken, they heard the sounds of an argument outside the bedroom. The door flew open, and Ward strode in, pushing past Paul and Ty.

"What's going on? I heard . . ." His booming voice was cut off when he saw Sigrid and Regina. The surprise on his face was unmistakable when he saw Regina alive and well.

"What happened?" he questioned as he rushed to Sigrid's side and kneeled down by the bed. Watching the scene, Regina saw that the young woman had lapsed into unconsciousness again, and she forcibly swallowed her anger.

"She's dying," she said in a wavering voice. "Terrence attacked her. It was her he was after, not me."

Ward's eyes teared up as he looked at Sigrid. He brushed his hand across her forehead and turned to glare at Don. "Can't you do something? You can't just let her die."

Don followed Regina's lead. "No. I've done all I can. Whatever Terrence used on that sword was meant to kill, whether it hit the heart or not."

"Where were you?" Ty interrupted.

"After Garrett told us about the time change, he asked Larry and I to check on another lead. It was a setup. When we got there, some of Terrence's people were waiting. We barely made it back."

Ty's eyes roamed over Ward, and other than a bit of dirt and grime here and there, he showed no signs of a life-threatening battle.

Regina had already asked Garrett about the mysterious call. She knew he didn't make it because he had been with her all day, never out of sight. She wanted to leap on Ward and tear his heart out, but she squelched those feelings. Mustering up her most desperate and shaky tone, she spoke softly to him, "You must find him, Ward. He has taken my life from me. You loved her, too, at one time. Do you not want vengeance?"

He looked at Sigrid another minute and then to Regina. "I still love her." He turned and glared at Ty, then stood up. He looked into Regina's eyes, and for a moment, she thought she saw true regret in his eyes. "I will find him, Regina. I swear."

Silk moved up behind him, her eyes watery and red. "Find that bastard," she sobbed and hugged him tightly, patting his shoulder. He held her for a second and pulled away. With a final look at the injured woman, he exited the bedroom and called for Larry. He never noticed that Regina followed him. The two men left the apartment, and Shadow instantly appeared by Regina's side.

"Follow him. I want to know where he goes and who he meets," she instructed.

Silk joined them and held out a small black box to Shadow. "This will help."

Regina looked at her and smiled. She realized now that the hug had been an excuse to plant a tracking device on Ward, and she smiled her thanks at the girl's ingenuity. "Be careful," they said in unison as he disappeared into the night. Once he was gone, they went back to Sigrid.

Shortly before dawn, Regina was awakened from a fitful nap by the sound of a struggle. Her first thought as the dream fugue wore off was that Terrence had found them, but as she opened her eyes and jumped up, she saw Don, Ty, and Silk gathered around the bed and restraining a thrashing Sigrid.

Fully awake now, she sprinted across the room to her niece's bedside. Sigrid was stiff and shaking violently. Her eyes were rolled back, and her teeth were locked down on the leather strap Don had provided. They struggled to keep her still and from reinjuring the shoulder wound, but it was a losing battle.

"Seizure!" Don called as Regina moved in beside him and latched on to Sigrid's waist. Even with their combined efforts, it took everything they had to hold her down. Blood began oozing from the bandage on her chest, but they could do nothing now except ride out the convulsion. Don had explained earlier that any type of medication or treatment he would normally use on an immortal could prove fatal to Sigrid in her current condition.

Regina's heart ached as she watched the scene. Unable to do anything, she could only flinch each time Sigrid groaned or screamed, feeling as if she had been punched in the heart. The spasms that racked Sigrid's body during her conversion were minor to what she was enduring now, and with each thrash, Regina made a mental note to take it out of Ward's flesh. Seeing the straining faces of Silk and Ty, she knew they were having similar thoughts.

After what seemed like an eternity, the seizure stopped. Sigrid's eyes fell shut, and her body went completely limp. Exchanging worried glances, Regina called her name, "Sigrid." They detected no sign of life, and Regina grabbed Sigrid's arms firmly. "Wake up, young lady, now!"

Don checked her pulse and sat back. "It's all right, Regina." He smiled reassuringly. "She's still with us."

A shared sigh arose from them, and they hesitantly released their hold on the small form. Instantly Don moved in to redress the wound and check for new injuries from the convulsion. "Before you ask, I don't know what caused it," he addressed Regina, as he skillfully cleaned the wound. "But despite the episode and her busting the stitches open, she seems to be holding her own."

Regina's face lit up. "You mean she's going to be okay?"

"She's holding on," he emphasized. "It's too early to be certain, but she seems to be slowly stabilizing. I think the feeding helped some."

"Then she'll have more," Regina stated firmly as she started to sit down. But Silk rested her hand on Regina's wrist.

"It's my turn. You're weak enough already. Let Ty and I do something." Ty moved up beside her in confirmation.

Regina looked at each of them, signs of weariness creasing their faces, but she knew that these two would never leave Sigrid; they would drop in place first. Smiling her appreciation, she answered, "All right."

Silk went first, and after Regina showed her what to do, Don stayed close by to make sure the woman didn't give too much. Regina hovered nearby like a watchful mother.

Several hours later, Sigrid awoke. The room was quiet, except for the soft sound of snoring. As the veil of fog cleared her eyes, she squinted against the brightness for a few seconds until her eyes could stand the new sensation. She slowly gazed around the room and recognized it was her room at the training facility. With each move she felt pains and aches shooting through her body and slowed down her movements even more to avoid as much pain as possible. Her eyes lit on Don asleep in the couch across the room. She was then aware of a presence beside her. Turning her head, she found Silk lying by her side, her hand resting on Sigrid's.

As she continued to scan, her eyes fell on Ty. He stood by the foot of the bed, right in front of the door, a silent, unwavering protector. He seemed to sense a change in the room and turned his head toward her.

She saw him relax slightly, and relief consumed his features. His smile warmed her as he came to her side and, kneeling down, wrapped his hand over hers. They knew one another well enough that there was no need for words. They spoke with their eyes and actions. She saw the worry and relief in his face, felt his anguish for not being able to prevent her pain, and saw the anger at their betrayer deep within his brown eyes.

As she looked into those eyes, she could feel some of the pain fading, and she realized that she loved this man with every inch of her being. When she had met Ward, she thought she had been in love. Now with Ty, she knew what love really was. Ward had been infatuation, a dawning of feelings she had denied. Ty helped her overcome that hesitation, and those feelings came to full bloom.

He looked into her blue eyes, and his thoughts echoed the same thing as at their first meeting: "I would die for her." He wanted to lift her up and carry her away from the pain that tore at her now, but he could only stay by her side and offer her all his strength and love. Reading his thoughts, she weakly squeezed his hand in agreement. He could see in her eyes that the feelings were mutual, and he slowly leaned down and delivered a light brushing kiss on her lips. With the little strength she had left, she tried to return the kiss but couldn't convey all her feelings into the weakened touch.

Understanding, he leaned back, smiling like a little boy being granted his fondest wish. Both became aware of Regina's stirring, and with a final look, he pulled away and returned to his sentry post.

Regina was in the chair beside the bed, her head dangling down as she dozed lightly. The sunlight poured through the blinds and cascaded over Regina. Sigrid felt her breath hitch in her chest at her aunt's radiant beauty. For a split second she could see her mother in that face, and then she felt the pain of her mother's death reemerging. She thought of how the legends told what horrid, ugly creatures vampires were. Looking at her aunt, she saw none of that, but a flash of memory from the previous night shattered that thought. Terrence made the legends real, and with that thought more flashes of the attack began. Before they could overwhelm her, she closed her eyes and fought the memories into submission.

With a sigh, she opened her eyes again. One image was still in her mind's grasp: the startling revelation she had learned during the attack on Terrence. She forcibly pushed it aside as Regina began to open her eyes.

Surprised at herself for falling asleep in the first place, she was certain she was still dreaming when she opened her eyes and found Sigrid awake and watching her. Sigrid's greeting, "Good morning," made her realize that it was not a dream, and she almost flew onto the bed.

Afraid she might hurt the young woman, she let her hands hover over her for a second before letting one hand come to rest on the restrained left arm as the other brushed hair from Sigrid's face. "Honey?" she asked, almost fearful of a reply.

"You look tired," Sigrid stated softly.

Regina smiled. "Are you in pain? Can I get you something?"

Sigrid threw a glance at the window where the sunlight streamed into the bedroom. "It's kind of bright in here."

Regina was up and shutting the blinds a second later, struck by the oddity of the statement. Sigrid had always loved the morning sun, even rising before dawn on many occasions to watch the sunrise and enjoy the first hour or so of the new day. All of a sudden, the sunlight was obviously uncomfortable for her. Regina quickly dismissed it as a side effect of her injury and returned to her niece.

"Thanks."

Their short conversation, although softly spoken, had caused Don and Silk to stir from their naps. Don gave her a quick check and then began changing the bandage on her chest. As he checked the wound, he noticed Regina's shocked reaction when she saw the jagged tear and flesh. "It will probably leave a nasty scar," he began as he continued his work, "and it may take a while to heal, but it will heal. As far as I can tell, there's no permanent damage." He finished the job and looked into Sigrid's eyes. "That feels all right?"

Sigrid could only muster half a nod. "Fine."

He studied her carefully. "The wound itself, any pain?"

"A little," she understated.

"Describe it," he ordered gently.

"Burning. Sharp, and feels like it's shooting through my entire body."

"Can you move your fingers?"

It took some effort, but Sigrid managed a slight wiggle of her fingers.

Don laid his hand across her forehead. "You still have a bit of fever. I'm going to let you get a little stronger before I try to bring it down." He stood up, hands on his hips. "You are a very lucky woman, Sigrid. I had doubts about your survival when they brought you to me. You seem to be stabilizing and on your way to a slow recovery. You need rest, a lot of it, and nourishment." He turned and looked at each of his exhausted companions. "That goes for the rest of you too."

No one made a move, and with a deep sigh he decided to lead the way. He began gathering up his equipment and the bag that he had used for the dirty bandages and sheets. "I'll be back in a few hours to check on you and change the dressing. The bleeding has almost stopped, but there's still some drainage. If I'm needed, I'll be in the room across the hall." With a final look at his patient, he left the room.

Silk, still sitting on the bed beside Sigrid, moved to leave but stopped when Sigrid touched her hand. "Thank you," she said sincerely, her eyes and voice filled with emotion.

Silk winked. "That's what family is for. I'll be back in a little while." Accepting Sigrid's nod as an okay, she too went to get some rest.

Ty's reluctance to leave was evident. "Please," Sigrid asked, "get some rest, for me."

He looked at her doubtfully for a second and then looked at Regina, who smiled in agreement.

"For you," he pledged and left her side, closing the door behind him.

Once alone, Regina sat on the bed beside Sigrid and held her good hand, relaxing in comfortable silence. After several minutes, tears began running down Regina's face as the events of the last twenty-four hours caught up with her, and she broke the silence. "I thought I had lost you last night, dear heart."

The defensive sense of humor jumped into place. "You know you can't get rid of me that easily."

Sigrid knew instantly it was the wrong thing to say when Regina's tears began falling freely, her body shaking with the intensity of the emotion. "I'm sorry, bad joke," Sigrid offered with regret.

Regina sniffed the tears to a stop and wiped her eyes. "I realized last night how much you mean to me. I . . . don't think I could live without you in my life. I've done it once, and I don't ever want to feel that alone again."

Sigrid felt her own tears welling up, but in her weakened state, she couldn't spare the energy to release them. The one question that she wanted to ask, the one that had been revealed last night, would wait. Now she focused her strength on the current conversation. "I'm not going anywhere," she reassured. "You know how stubborn I am."

A small, ironic laugh escaped Regina. "Yes, I do. That and your sixth sense saved my life last night and almost cost you yours."

"I'm in no more of a hurry to lose you than you are to lose me," she said bluntly. Then another thought jumped up. "Ward," she said, remembering his treachery. She tried to sit up, and a wall of agony crushed down on her.

A red-hot pain ripped through her shoulder and chest, and she fell back into bed, gasping.

Regina immediately placed comforting hands on her arms. "Stay still, young lady," she scolded firmly. She gently stroked Sigrid's arm until the girl's breathing slowed back to normal. "Don't worry about Ward," she continued. "That's being taken care of."

Clenching her teeth against the pain in her chest and concentrating on Regina's touch, she finally relaxed against the bed. "I should have seen it sooner," she mumbled.

"Oh no, you don't," Regina corrected.

"What?"

Regina raised an eyebrow. "You have a tendency to take the blame for everything bad that happens, and I won't let you do it this time."

"But—"

"No buts. He fooled all of us," Regina admitted. "We've been so caught up in this thing with Terrence that we didn't see what was happening under our noses." She was interrupted by a knock at the door. "Come."

The door opened, and Shadow eased in. Seeing Sigrid awake and alert brought a smile to his face. "Hey, boss."

Sigrid returned his smile. "Hey, Shadow."

He stared at her for a moment, face unreadable. Then he turned to Regina's expectant look and gave her a slight nod. She smiled back at him, and then he took his leave.

Sigrid looked at the closed door and then at Regina. "What was that?"

Regina brought her hand up and brushed it against Sigrid's still-warm cheek. "Just tidying up some business."

Sigrid let her eyes drop down to the bandage on her chest. She felt so weary, the pain and exertion taking its toll. "I'm really tired now, and I know you have things to do, but will you do a couple of things for me?"

Regina leaned in closer "Of course."

Looking back up at her, Sigrid replied, "Please get some rest."

Regina sighed and nodded agreement. "Okay. Next?"

"I know you're angry right now, but try to control it. I don't want to lose you."

Taking a deep breath, Regina smiled warmly. "You won't. I'm taking your advice. I'm using it to my advantage."

Sigrid frowned, unsure of what she meant, but she trusted the woman implicitly. "What amazes me," Regina continued, "is that even seriously injured, you think on your feet." Sigrid blushed as Regina leaned down and kissed her forehead. "I'll be back in a while."

"Take your time," she said, her eyes beginning to droop.

By the time Regina shut the bedroom door, she was sound asleep.

Her exhaustion evident, Regina slumped down on the sofa in the ready room. She smiled as Garrett took a place next to her and draped his arm around her. Shadow waited patiently across the room until she motioned for him. He ambled over and took a seat across from her. "How is she?" he asked before Regina could ask for his report.

"She's tough," Regina answered with admiration. "Don says she should be okay."

Relieved at the news, he leaned forward and pulled a small black notebook from his jacket. "He and Larry are in a trashy little hotel about a hundred miles out," he began. "He'll be calling soon and telling you that he's got a lead and wants to follow it up before the team is involved. He contacted Terrence's people about an hour after he left here, and they have a meeting set up for day after tomorrow."

"Fantastic, Shadow," she praised. "Can you get a location and time?"

Shadow smiled broadly. "Oh yes, my Queen. Silk's bugging devices are state-of-the-art and in place. I'll be able to tell what he had for breakfast. He was instructed to stay put until they call him tonight with the meeting information. Your order, my Queen?"

Regina looked at Garrett, reading his thoughts and allowing him to read hers. After several moments of silence, they both broke into smiles. "Good plan," he acknowledged.

She stood up and went over to Shadow. He instantly rose to his feet, and she wrapped her arm around his shoulder. Paul had been standing guard outside Sigrid's room and was motioned over to join them. "I know you're tired, my friends," she said sympathetically. As if on cue, Ty and Silk entered the room and joined the growing cluster in the center. Once everyone was there, she continued, "I want all of you to catch a nap and try to get some rest. We have one chance to finish this, and I need each and every one of you for that to happen. We have until tonight to get rested and have the team ready to go. Are you up to it?"

The fire and determination she saw in their eyes and posture caused pride and love to flare in her heart. She had never met a group more diverse and yet more able to function as one than this team. Only Sigrid had been able to choose what the people for her team needed to be successful, and each one of these individuals exuded success.

"We will be ready," they said in unison, the power and conviction in their voices sending a chill down her spine.

She gave them a few last-minute instructions and then sent them to the sleeping quarters.

Once they were alone, she fed on the love and strength that Garrett's company offered, and they began planning.

Sigrid slept through the day and wasn't awakened till after eight that evening. Had Don not been changing the bandage and causing the wound to hurt, she probably would have slept a few more hours.

"Good evening," Don said in his best Dracula voice as she opened her eyes.

He was such a sweet and gentle soul who could make you smile when you least wanted to. She liked the man who was as skilled a doctor as anyone she had ever met and grinned at his greeting. "Evening, Don. How am I doing?"

He tossed the dirty bandages into the trash and sat in the chair by the bed. "The good news is that the bleeding and drainage have stopped. I know that healing is normally rapid in you immortals, but this is a serious wound, unlike anything I have seen before. It almost destroyed you, and to be honest, I'm surprised it didn't."

Sigrid flinched at his bluntness. She appreciated it, but she also realized how close to dying she had really come.

"Had it been three inches to the left, you would be dead," he pushed on. "I want you to rest in bed for at least another forty-eight to seventy-two hours. No matter how good you think you feel, you have to take it easy. I'll be staying with you for a few days to make sure that you're out of danger, but if you feel anything, you tell me. I don't care if it's only a small ache, a wave of dizziness, anything unusual, you let me know. Understand?"

Sigrid felt like a child being reprimanded and didn't care for it at all. She was about to tell Don her exact thoughts when Garrett appeared from the shadows. "She will, Don," he answered for her and gave her a quick, knowing wink.

Don sighed, knowing from past experience that family members were perhaps the most stubborn and worst patients. "I'll check in later," he replied as he picked up his bag and left the room.

Garrett eased over and handed her a wine goblet. "For strength," he said simply. He watched in surprise as she accepted it and downed the contents rapidly. "More?" he asked.

She held out the goblet. "Please."

He quickly retrieved the cup and was back in a matter of seconds with another full cup. After she accepted it, she downed it just as rapidly. She licked the last few drops from her lips, and he took the cup from her hand, setting it on the table by the bed.

The drink seemed to energize her, and he saw the familiar twinkle in her eye as she spoke. "Can you sit and talk with me awhile?"

He nodded and pulled the chair closer to the side of the bed. As he took a seat, she noticed his bruised face. "How badly did they hurt you?"

He reached up and touched the bruised flesh around his mouth. "They just hurt my pride. Their main concern was Regina. Thank you for being there last night. They would have killed both of us if you hadn't shown up. I think I need to spend some time training with your team. I'm not as capable as I used to be."

She tried to scoot up into a sitting position, and Garrett jumped up and helped pull her up and settle against the pillows. She winced with every move, but he aided her with slow, patient movements, and after a few minutes, she was situated in a comfortable reclining position. Certain she was settled, he returned to his seat.

She took a few deep breaths to push away the burning in her chest before she spoke again. "We would have been there sooner if it hadn't been for Ward."

He noticed the disgust in her voice when she said the name. He decided to broach the subject with her just as Regina had done the night before. "You know," he started slowly, "that I had nothing to do with his betrayal. I would die before I betrayed her."

She held her head sideways and watched him closely. "How long have you been with her?"

It was not the expected question or statement, but he answered, "Fifty-two years."

Sigrid's surprise was obvious. "You're an immortal?"

He grinned and nodded. "Yes. It was her gift to me about thirty years ago. She wanted me to accept all of it, but I refused."

"Why?"

He shrugged. "I only want to be with her until I'm destroyed. I have no interest in the powers. I only want to serve her and be with her."

"You love her," Sigrid stated more than asked.

For the first time since she had met him, he blushed. "With all that I am."

Satisfied and touched by his comment, she smiled at him. "I know you had nothing to do with Ward's betrayal. It makes me happy to know that someone loves Regina that much, and it's pretty obvious she loves you the same way."

His blush turned deeper, and they sat in silence for a few minutes. "Did you know my mother?" she asked out of the blue.

He looked up at the ceiling as if searching his memory. A lightness appeared on his face, and he looked back at her. "I met her once. She was all Regina ever talked about. Then when you were born, every other word out of her mouth was about you. We met in Austria about six months before you were born. I was in the States setting up Regina's business and finances, but she needed me to come to Austria to take care of some things."

His gaze now seemed to look beyond the haze of the present and into the clear past. His eyes were turned in her direction, but he was not seeing her; he was in the memory. "Valonia was a beautiful woman inside and out. She seemed so frail and innocent, but she was as tough as granite on the inside. Her voice was thickly European and as soft and melodious as a love song. Her eyes were like sparkling sapphires and her skin so light it seemed to glow in the sunshine. She could have owned any man's heart, and had I not loved Regina, she would have had mine."

He took a breath as he finished and saw Sigrid had closed her eyes, seeing the memory with him.

She took a few more seconds to savor the description then opened her eyes. "I would have liked you for a father, Garrett."

He smiled sincerely, touched by her statement. "And I would have been delighted to have you as a daughter."

"Did you know my father?"

He was aware that she knew the situation involving Valonia's refusal to name him, but he answered her. "No. It was never discussed."

"Did you ever have children? In your mortal life? I could see you as a parent," she said, prying more than she meant too.

Her ability to jump topics almost made him dizzy. "I almost was," he answered, then hesitated, shifting uncomfortably in his seat.

Sigrid's eyes widened as his thought reverberated in her head. "You and Regina?"

He licked his lips nervously. "I shouldn't talk about it."

"I'm sorry, Garrett." She sighed. "I didn't mean to pry. I respect your privacy."

"It's not that." He stumbled over the words. "It's just that we . . . I . . . we never discussed it with anyone."

"Anything we say in this room stays in this room," she assured him, "If you want to talk, I want to listen. But I don't want you to betray a trust or relive a bad memory."

He considered her words and sensed her concern more than curiosity. "I've never talked about it to anyone. Probably the only person Regina ever confided in was Martha, and that's if she even talked to her about it."

Sigrid remained silent, letting him wrestle with the decision. Once he decided, he took another few minutes to gather his thoughts. "We've been lovers off and on since we first met," he began slowly. "A few years after your abduction and your mother . . . was killed . . . we conceived a child. Regina was ecstatic, as was I. I pampered her and waited on her hand and foot. It drove her crazy, but she relished the attention. We planned everything for the child. The name, the kind of education he would have, everything. We even had the nursery all ready for the big day. It was the happiest she had been since Val's death and your abduction. She was seven months along when there was an altercation with a hunter. She went into premature labor, and the baby died a few minutes after he was born." Garrett stopped and took a deep breath, trying to control the feelings that had been bottled up for so long.

"Regina was crushed. I tried to be strong for her, even though my own heart ached. Our child's death, on top of Valonia's death and your disappearance, left her in a very dark place. For a while I thought I was going to lose her. She spent a lot of time alone, brooding. She wouldn't let anyone even try to help her. After a few months, she seemed to pull out of the depression, and she turned her efforts to finding you and the other lost children. We've never spoken of our son since. You're the first and only person I've ever told this to."

He stood up and walked over to the window, struggling to maintain his cool British demeanor. She stayed quiet, allowing him time to deal with his revelation. Only after she sensed that he was more himself did she speak. "I am so sorry, Garrett. I should have stayed out of it."

When he turned to her, she saw the dampness still on his cheeks and felt even worse. "Don't be sorry." He smiled. "Actually, it feels . . . it's a relief to be able to talk to someone. Thank you for caring."

Sigrid decided it was time for a topic change. "Does Regina still search for the lost?"

"Yes," he answered, happy to change the subject. "It's a very delicate matter though. We have to search without drawing any attention from the hunters or Terrence. Because of that, it's a very time-consuming operation."

Now it was her turn to look uncomfortable. Garrett thought she might be in pain and leaned over to check but was waved away. "Garrett, I think . . . I know where two of the . . . lost children are."

She was prepared for a dismissal or argument but not the reaction she got. "You mean Silk and Ty?"

Shocked, she could only nod.

"After you chose them for the team, my own suspicion was aroused. I've been running a check on them ever since."

The surprise was wearing off but not the confusion. "Does Regina know?"

"Of course, she gave me the go-ahead after she found out about the team. Unfortunately, with all the trouble from Terrence, the last few months, I haven't had a chance to finish the investigation and confirm it."

"Are they? Am I right?"

He directed his gaze back to her, and his eyes creased with a smile. "I believe so. Both are orphans, with no trace of blood family. Both learned to take care of themselves and eventually found their way to the family. Their descriptions fit some of the children described in the hunter's reports. I've still got some of our people working on it, but yes, I believe there is a very good chance that they are two of the lost. The fact that they fit every part of the profile you outlined and that you were drawn to them helps convince me."

"Why?"

"It's the same as when you are around other vampires. You can sense it. You told me yourself that, with Silk and Ty, you felt as if you knew them, that they were kindred spirits."

Sigrid nodded. "Yes, I guess so. Does Regina agree?"

Garrett cleared his throat. "Yes, even more so now that she knows Silk much better."

It took a moment for the statement to ring in. Her eyes showed a bit more alertness, and she cocked her head sideways. "Silk and Regina?"

Garrett instantly realized his error and bit his lip nervously, not eager to go any further with the slip.

"Garrett?" she called waiting for an explanation or conformation.

"I'm sorry. I thought you knew. They . . . got together after the incident in Florida. Does it . . . bother you? That they are lovers?"

"No," she answered, still unsure of how she felt. "I'm just surprised." Now she understood what had caused Silk's change, the glow on her face and the constant smile. Her young friend had found love. "Does it bother you? I mean, you do love her. It can't be easy to sit back and watch her be with others."

"A long time ago it did bother me, but not anymore," he assured her. "Over the years, she's had a couple of lovers. I love her and understand that, even though she loves me, she can love others as well. She's over four hundred years old. It's only natural that she meet and love more than one person during all that time, but she always comes back to me. The last one was Ward, and she always remains friends with them, as do I."

"Is that where she's gone tonight?" Sigrid questioned.

The way her mind shifted track so quickly kept throwing him. He leaned forward in his chair. "Yes. Shadow got a lead, and she took the team to follow it."

Her mood became dark and serious, and she lowered her voice to an almost-hushed whisper. "Are they going to finish it?"

He nodded and sighed. "She hopes to. You hurt Terrence last night, and he's weak and vulnerable. She thinks this is their best shot, and truth be told, nothing or nobody could stop her or the team. They're doing it for you."

"And Ward?"

"The team wants him. As badly as Regina wanted to settle it herself, she wouldn't deny them their request," he answered honestly.

Sigrid closed her eyes and pushed all the breath out in a long sigh. "And it's my fault. The war, the lives lost, the betrayal." She looked up at the ceiling, wincing as the muscles in her chest protested the movement. "Regina spent years looking for me, and when she succeeds, I turn her world upside down. All the effort, time, and energy, and it reaped trouble. Was it worth it? I don't think so."

Garrett was sitting by her side in the blink of an eye, his voice strong. "Then you're the only one who thinks that. Yes, all those things happened, but believe me they would have happened had you not been here. Terrence would have continued using the hunter's network until all of us were wiped out. If anything, you are responsible for bringing the family together. I've seen you with the family members and volunteers. You have a rare gift with people. You enable them to be the best and do the best they can, even when they don't know they have it in them."

"Garrett . . ."

"I'm not done," he scolded her for the interruption. Chastised, she snapped her mouth shut. "The Regina you know now is not the same person she was six years ago before she found you. That Regina was hardened by all the lost loved ones and pain. She worked constantly, always on the move, never staying in one place too long. It was almost as if she were lost. She sought out death and never knew or allowed herself any peace. For a brief period of time, I was afraid she would become like Terrence. Then she met you. You gave her the peace that she had sought for so long, and, my dear, whether you believe it or not, you gave her back her life. She risked everything to tell you the truth, and that included her love for you that kept her from crawling into blackness forever. Was it worth it, from where I sit? Hell, yes."

She laughed to herself and leaned in, meeting him and planting a kiss on his forehead. "You British sure do get temperamental, don't you?"

A smile appeared on his face. "Only when we're passionate about something."

"Why did we wait so long to talk like this?"

His eyebrow raised cynically. "The occasion never arose."

"Well, let's make sure it's not another six years before the opportunity arises again. I like talking to you. When we first met, you were a bit intimidating, but now I know you're just a gruff old teddy bear," she chided with a wink.

"Teddy bear?" he huffed. "Well, I don't know if I like that description, but I have enjoyed spending time with you."

She tried to stifle a yawn unsuccessfully. "I'm sorry. I guess I'm more tired than I realized."

He took his cue and stood up. "You must take it easy, as Don said. You get some sleep, and I'll let you know as soon as I hear from Regina or the team."

"Thanks, Garrett. For everything," she replied, her eyes beginning to droop with exhaustion.

He blew her a kiss and watched as she drifted off to sleep. He realized that he had gained a new friend tonight, and he couldn't suppress the smile that curled his lips. They had spent so much time together, but it wasn't until the last few months that he had come to know her, not as just Regina's niece, but as Sigrid Derrick. He reached over and flipped off the light and eased out of the bedroom. He dreaded the next few hours of anxious waiting as he paced, staring at the telephone and trying to will it to ring with Regina's call.

11

The lower east side of Chicago was home to, among other things, several abandoned warehouses. A lot of businesses had folded during the last few years of financial insecurity, and the only reminder of their creators' dreams were empty shells that now housed junkies and the homeless. A cool breeze caressed the buildings, and the metal offered a groaning chorus as it brought several loose pieces crashing to the cement. A few dim fires speckled the warehouse row, but there were no signs of life, not outside anyway.

The building that Larry and Ward now occupied had at one time been a machine and tool manufacturing. Remnants of its previous tenants still lie scattered in the grim-filled corners, and the odor of alcohol and urine floated on the dank air. As if they had sensed that the building was no longer a safe place to be, the tenants had cleared out shortly before the two men arrived, leaving many usable items in their haste to depart.

The building was a two-story brick with the floor space the size of almost two football fields. All the machinery had been sold off to pay the creditors months ago, but as with any move, a few items still littered the floor. Bolts and metal shavings were scattered about, and the faint trace of oil and grease could be detected just under the fouler odors.

As they paced around the floor, their boots scraped against the dust, grime, and rat droppings that now covered the concrete floor. They stayed in the center of the room, pacing in tight circles and waiting. The only light, other than moonlight, was from the few battery-powered lamps they had stationed around the perimeter of the first floor.

Larry kicked at an old bolt that was lying on the floor while Ward nervously watched the shadows. "Where the hell are they?" he mumbled. His voice was edged with anger and slight shaking from the chill in the air.

Larry kicked the bolt into the shadows. "Chill out, man. They're only a few minutes late."

Ward glared at Larry's casual and calm demeanor. Frustrated, he jammed his hands into his jacket pockets.

The sound of rolling metal caused both of them to glance down as the bolt reappeared from the shadows. When they jerked their heads up to look around, they found themselves surrounded by ten members of Terrence's inner sanctum. The group looked passively at the two men before them, their faces set and stern.

"You're late," Ward grumbled as James came forward.

"After the fiasco the other night, we had to be certain you weren't followed," he replied sarcastically.

Ward yanked his hands out of his pockets and leaned toward James. "There wouldn't have been a problem if your people had gotten to the intersection on time and caused more of a delay."

"Enough!" Reggie called firmly. He scanned the room again before making a motion to one of the others. Oscar ran to the large steel delivery door and threw it open.

The darkness was pierced by two bright headlight beams as the black Rolls Royce eased into the center of the room and came to a stop. The windows were black glass, and Ward strained to see the occupant as the coven surrounded the car.

The rear right window opened with a squeak, and the silhouette of Terrence appeared in its place. His voice was deep and powerful as he asked, "Was he followed?"

"No, Master," James answered.

"What is the deal?" Ward called out loudly, his voice and posture full of anger. "I told you I wasn't followed. I risked everything coming to you, and you keep jerking me around."

Terrence leaned closer to the window. The lamplight wasn't very bright, but it adequately illuminated the ragged red claw marks that crossed his face.

Ward took a step back, his anger vanishing and fear taking its place. The wound looked as if it had just happened. The side of his face now resembled ground beef, and letting his eyes fall down, Ward saw that Terrence's arms were by his side, hands lain on his lap, useless.

"Attractive, isn't it?" Terrence said grimly. "Compliments of your foul-up the other night."

"I'm . . . I'm sorry, Master," Ward stammered, his voice devoid of any strength. "I did all I was supposed to. The emergency meeting, changing the clocks, even setting up the phone call. There was no other way I could delay them without revealing myself."

He noticed that Terrence had a twitch in his left eye above the scratched mess of his face. "It's true that my forces failed on their part and they have been dealt with, but now you understand my uneasiness."

Ward nodded. "Yes, Master, as I told your people, Regina doesn't suspect me. She's too consumed with worry to think clearly. I told her I was heading to Wisconsin to check out a lead. She and the team are so distraught over Sigrid that they can't concentrate on anything else, so they've asked me to find you, for vengeance."

Terrence's eyes seemed to lighten. "What is the . . ." He hesitated as if the next word left a foul taste in his mouth. "The girl's condition? Is she dead?"

"When I called this afternoon, Garrett told me she was fading fast and they didn't think she would make it through the night. He said Regina and the team haven't left her side and won't," Ward supplied proudly.

"Good," Terrence responded, his mind working. "That will be to our advantage. They will be so grief-stricken that Regina's guard will be down. Her need for revenge will outweigh her logic."

As Terrence gloated in his plans, Ward's mind flashed on Sigrid and their time together, his feelings for her, and his still-present love for her. He swallowed hard to suppress his feelings before they got the better of him. When he turned his attention back to Terrence, he was surprised to find him watching him.

"You loved her?" he asked bluntly.

"Yes," Ward admitted, "a long time ago."

Terrence's smile, more like a snarl in the remains of his face, sent chills down Ward's spine. "Then, my dear Ward, your betrayal is complete. Now to finish it."

Larry moved in and stood beside Ward. "How?"

"Tomorrow afternoon, you will make a phone call," Terrence began, his black eyes twinkling as the wheels of his mind turned. "You will tell Regina that you have found my lair and that I am badly injured. When she and her precious team arrive, we will be waiting." He opened his mouth to continue, but instead of words, he emitted a scream. Ward saw him jerk, as a piece of his jacket exploded. He felt the wind of the next bullet rush past him as it hit home in Terrence's neck.

The warehouse was suddenly full of smoke as a canister fell from the ceiling and the air was filled with high-pitched buzzing. The coven that had gathered around the car were now twirling around the floor in a bizarre dance as the wooden bullets hit their marks. One by one they fell to the floor and began dissolving, becoming one with the dust and rate droppings.

The Rolls squealed its tires as it leaped across the floor and aimed for the doorway. The rear window where Terrence had been was now closed and the bullets ricocheted harmlessly off the bulletproof glass. Nicks and dents appeared magically in the sides as it sped out of the doorway and into the night.

Watching as the coven fell, the master left, and the smoke disguised the area, Ward and Larry did the only thing they could; they dove for the ground, scrambling for cover.

Although it seemed like the buzzing and smoke continued for an eternity, it was over in a matter of minutes. Ward tried to cough quietly as the smoke assaulted his lungs, and he groped around trying to find Larry.

The warehouse fell silent and was as quiet as a crypt. Cautiously Ward lifted his head and as the smoke cleared saw that none of Terrence's men had survived the attack. Their bodies littered the floor and left a gleaming sheen on the concrete. He turned his head to the side and saw Larry lying a few feet away. He began to crawl over to his friend but stopped dead when he saw the glistening bullet hole in his forehead.

"My, but haven't we been busy," a familiar female voice rang out, breaking the silence.

He lay still for a minute, breathing heavily, and he licked his lips nervously. Slowly, he rolled over and found Regina standing at his feet. Squinting against the slight haze still in the air, he saw the rest of the team close by, watching and armed to the teeth.

"Eighteen years," she said lowly, pain radiating from her face and words. "Eighteen years and you throw it away. For what? Immortality? Did you think Terrence would have given you that? He knew if you could betray me, you could betray him."

Ward laughed nervously and sat up. "Regina, you've got it all wrong. I was trying to infiltrate his coven. Just let me explain, please."

Regina brought her finger to her lips and made a shushing motion. "I heard your explanation." She propped her hands on her hips and looked at him with disappointment. "Sigrid loved you. I took you off the street, gave you an education, a job, a life. You were my right hand, my friend, my lover. I gave you everything and trusted you with the most important thing in my life, my niece."

Ward attempted to stand up but was kicked back into place by Shadow's booted foot. He glared at Shadow and gritted his teeth but stayed still. "Yeah, you gave me everything. I busted my ass for you, and the one thing I wanted, that I earned, you denied me. I gave you my life, my blood, and my love. Then suddenly you find your long-lost niece. You give her to me, then take her away before she could give me what I wanted. You even gave her the gift. Her, the girl raised by your worst enemy. Me, the one that served you loyally, I wasn't worthy of the gift."

Regina cocked her head sideways as if she hadn't heard correctly. "Deserving? Worthy? That's what all of this is about? Jealousy? You betrayed all of us, the family and the woman you loved, because you craved immortality?"

His silence was her answer. He glared at her, and she saw in his eyes something that she had never seen before. How cold and calculating he really was. She sighed deeply. Her anger was gone and replaced by something else. The team noticed the difference in her voice when she spoke, no longer as sure and determined as before. "This family," she said, motioning to the team, "this group that you helped bring together has served me loyally and never asked for anything in return. Until now."

She took a few steps back and looked at Ward, a tear running down her face. "My children," she said softly, "he's yours." With that she turned her back on him and began a slow, steady walk into the shadows.

"Regina?" he called as she disappeared and he understood what was about to happen. "Regina!" he repeated with desperation.

The team moved in, and he began sliding and scrambling to get away, but found himself bumping into their legs as they surrounded him. "Regina, please!" he begged as he ran out of room.

She continued walking and, when she was surrounded by the darkness, covered her ears, trying to block out his cries and then screams.

Don had been surprised the next morning when he found Sigrid healing faster than expected. He theorized that the heavy intake of nourishment had helped the healing process and, after some badgering from his patient, gave her the okay to travel. Garrett hurriedly packed their things, and the three of them were on the company jet that evening. They arrived in Denver and, once Sigrid was settled, waited anxiously for news from Regina.

She had called the next night and only told Garrett that it was finished. The tone of her voice had worried him greatly. It was the voice of someone who had lost hope and only knew despair in its wake.

He was waiting at the airport when her plane touched down and was surprised when he saw the exhaustion on Regina and the team's faces as they disembarked. He greeted them warmly and, before they could even ask, assured them that Sigrid was much better. Then he ushered them to the awaiting limos. Once the team was loaded and on its way, he escorted a very quiet and sedate Regina to another waiting limo.

Once inside, he gave the driver a few instructions and raised the partition, sitting back in the seat next to Regina.

The car proceeded into the afternoon traffic, and they rode in silence for a long while, Garrett watching Regina as she stared out the window, focusing on nothing. "Jealousy," she finally whispered. "He did it because of jealousy."

She turned to face him. "I trusted him, loved him. He gave us up because Terrence promised him immortality. It's not a gift, it's a fucking curse."

He put his arm around her and drew her close. "It wasn't jealousy," he soothed. "Ward was dedicated but very easy to sway. When he got angry, he did stupid things. When push came to shove, he decided to take the easy way out. Until this started, Ward had never had to deal with the true nature of our kind. He envied the power, and that's what he wanted. Power, without your restrictions. Had you given him immortality, he would have left soon after. Jealousy. No, it was envy. Even Sigrid sensed his true face, that's why they didn't last."

Regina looked up at him. "I thought I was the reason they didn't last, and how do you know so much about Ward's feelings?"

He smiled slightly. "You were too involved. I was able to stand back and see things more clearly. Why do you think I urged you to keep him close and on a short leash? Why do you think he went after Sigrid with such gusto? He wanted the power that he could get from you. If you wouldn't give it to him, he hoped to get it through Sigrid."

She sighed and leaned back against him, savoring the warmth and soft scent of his aftershave. "Then why do I feel like someone has torn my heart out."

He patted her arm. "Because, my love, for the first time in your life you have everything you've ever wanted. And for the first time you were betrayed by someone you trusted with your life and who could have taken it all away."

"How can I ever trust anyone again?"

Garrett gently but firmly grasped her chin and lifted it until their eyes met. "If you think that way, then Ward and Terrence succeeded in part of their mission and the family is lost."

Regina's eyes widened in fear. "No! No, Garrett, this family will not fall apart."

He released her chin. "Then pull yourself together. We need you strong and sure headed. You've brought us through the war, now lead us into peace. As for whom to trust, follow your instincts. Ward was a mistake, and we all make mistakes from time to time. I hate to break this to you, but you're not perfect. You have made and will make mistakes. The secret is to learn from them and go on."

She lowered her head, letting his words sink in. She knew he was right; it was just that she had been so hurt that she had lost sight of the bigger picture. As always, he was her steadying force, her touchstone.

When she brought her eyes back up, he saw that her face was less troubled and slowly regaining its regal, elegant glow. She kissed his cheek. "Thank you, Gar. You force me to look into the mirror and deal with the reflection. You are my soul mate, and I do love you so."

"Glad to be of service, my Queen." He smiled.

"Drop the 'my Queen' shit and hold me," she said with a smile and snuggled against him.

He planted soft kisses on her head and began trailing down her neck. "You want some good news?"

"Please."

"Our sources tell us that Terrence has left the country and he was very, very badly hurt."

"But not dead." She sighed deeply.

"No," he agreed, "but close to it. When they found the limo he was in, the rear interior was covered with blood, so the shots did hit."

"Ty and Silk." Regina supplied the names of the shooters.

"Our intelligence reports that his numbers have been reduced to one-fourth of their original count. From everything we've heard and seen, I don't think he's going to be bothering anybody for quite a while."

"I hope so."

"The other news concerns our inquiries about the lost."

Regina immediately sat up and faced him. "What is it?"

Garrett hesitated for a second, savoring her look of anticipation; then he smiled slyly. "They are. Ty and Silk are both lost children. Silk's family were the Gaultairs from France. Her mother was mortal, and the only thing we know about her father is that he was an immortal. Ty has a cousin left. His family were the Checklovs."

"The Checklovs?" Regina gasped in surprise. "As in the European royal family?"

He nodded. "His mother was Ulia."

Regina shook her head, still shocked. "I remember when Ulia told me she was pregnant. Then I began to get reports of hunters in the area and told her to seek a safe place until her child was born. She vanished several months later. I remember when the reports of her and the child's death came in." She remained silent, remembering another in a long line of painful moments in her life. "Are you sure about them? Both of them?"

"It's confirmed," he assured her.

"Does Sigrid know?"

He laughed ironically. "I think she always has. They were the only two that matched the team profile perfectly. When they met, she was drawn to them, and well, you see how the three of them are together."

Regina glanced out the window. "Her powers," she began cautiously, "are so amazing and so frightening at the same time. Of all the immortals I've met over the centuries, none of them has had her capabilities, not even me."

"You taught her well," he acknowledged. "But I sense a restlessness in her. I think she's ready to leave the nest. I see the way she and Ty look at one another, and I think she's anxious to pursue that."

"I know," she replied with despair and melancholy. "It seems like I just found her and now it's time to let go. I don't know what hurts more, losing her or letting her go."

He leaned forward and kissed her. "Ah, my delicate, sensitive flower."

She felt her passion growing and returned his kiss. "Did you say something about servicing me earlier?" she asked, her eyebrow raised.

Slowly, he eased her down on the seat, his lips never leaving her flesh, and he let his hands roam along her slim, muscular body.

They made love at a leisurely pace, savoring the time, peace, and gentle motion of the moving car.

Paul, Silk and Shadow headed straight for their quarters when they returned to the office building, exhausted and ready to catch up on some much-needed rest. Ty quickly cleaned up and went up to Sigrid's apartment.

He let himself in, not wanting to disturb her if she was resting, but he stopped as he cleared the door. He was surprised to find her up and standing on the balcony, looking at the surrounding mountains.

Easing in, he held his place in the living room and watched her. She was dressed in a flowing blue robe, and her hair ruffled with the cool breeze sweeping down from the mountain peaks. The sun cast a glow around her, and although her eyes were covered by dark glasses, he could sense the peace she felt.

Watching her made his chest tighten, his heart beating so ferociously that he feared it might rip through his shirt. The love he felt for her was so strong that it hurt and frightened him, threatening to take his breath away.

When she sensed him there, she turned around and offered a bright smile. He took a step and leapt across the table and couch that blocked his way to her. He landed in front of her and took her into his arms. He held her snugly, conscious of her shoulder wound. "Are you all right?"

She clung to him, feeling whole in his arms. "Yes. Just a bit sore. Are you all right?"

"I am now." He grinned and leaned down to kiss her, a kiss that lasted for several minutes and almost ignited the curtains on the balcony window.

They pulled apart, breathing heavily, and Sigrid laughed softly. "I guess you missed me as much as I missed you."

His eyes twinkled. "More than you know. I have been so worried about you."

"You're here now. That's the best thing to help in my recovery." She noticed how tired he looked and gently clasped his face between her hands. "You look exhausted. You should go to bed."

He savored the feeling of her touch and rubbed his face against her hands, sparks of electricity bringing him wide awake. "Is that an offer?"

She looked into his eyes for a second and then kissed him.

He swept her into his arms, noticing how light she was, and carried her into the bedroom. They continued kissing as they arrived in the room, and he set her down on the carpeted floor next to the bed. She watched his every move, her eyes mesmerized by him. He reached for her robe and then hesitated. "Are you sure? Your shoulder, is it okay? I don't want to hurt you."

She let her hands fall and untie the robe for him. It dropped away, and he felt like he might cry when he saw her beautiful body and the bandage that covered the wound. "Not being with you is more painful than this," she said and lightly touched the bandage, "Don't worry, I'll manage."

He stepped forward and took her in his arms.

As they came together, he was incredibly gentle and attentive, and she discovered, much to her pleasure, that he was infinitely patient. They learned more about one another, and although her injury prevented her from getting as physical as she wanted, she knew that there would be time for that later. At times she became so swept up in passion that her shoulder sent out sparks of pain as a warning. It was at these times that Ty slowed them down, letting her catch her breath as he continued to lavish attention on her.

Two hours later, they lay in one another's arms, wonderfully exhausted. "That was . . ."—she searched for the right word—"fantastic."

He smiled slightly. "I want to be with you forever." He sighed drowsily.

"And I want you with me," she agreed.

He rolled onto his side and propped on his elbow, fingers brushing against her shoulder, his tone serious. "I mean it, Sigrid. I don't want to just be another lover to you."

She leaned in and kissed his forehead. "There haven't been any others."

"I'm serious," he replied, not appreciating her candor. He rolled onto his back and stared at the ceiling, locking his hands and resting them on his stomach.

Slowly, she eased onto her side, laying her head on his chest and meeting his eyes. "So am I."

He looked down at her. After a few seconds, she could literally see the light bulb going off in his head. "You mean . . . you're a virgin?"

"Was," she answered seductively and kissed his muscular chest.

He continued watching her, surprised and uncertain of a response.

She sensed his trepidation. "I never met the right person . . . until now."

"But I thought you and . . ." He stopped before he said the name and caught a look of tension on her face. "I mean . . . you never . . . but . . ."

She smiled as he stammered over his words. It was the first time she had ever seen him caught off guard, and she liked the childlike quality it brought out in him. "You mean you couldn't tell it was my first time?"

He shook his head. "Well . . . I thought you were just being careful because of your shoulder."

"That too." She grinned.

He ran his hand across her back, a new light in his eyes. "I've never met anyone like you. So strong and sure yet so innocent and naive."

"I hope I'm not that innocent and naive." She pouted.

The love she saw in his eyes and heard in his voice made her heart flutter. "Oh no. You were incredible. In fact, I think I'm going to have to work on my stamina before you fully recover, or I may be in trouble."

Smiling, she snuggled against his chest. They fell into silence, enjoying the closeness of one another. He noticed her fidgeting slightly after several minutes and stroked her hair. "You okay?"

She remained silent for a few seconds before saying, "There's something I need to tell you."

She began moving to sit up, and he helped her until she was in a sitting position beside him, looking down into his face. She pulled the covers up to her chest. "I'm not sure how to tell you or how you'll react."

His brow creased as he sat up and leaned against the headboard. "You know me. Just say it."

She exhaled nervously. "You know the stories about the lost children?"

He nodded positively.

"There were three unaccounted for," she began cautiously. "Regina and Garrett have continued to search for them, even after all these years, and after checking the records, Garrett has found out that you . . . are . . . one of those three. So is Silk. He's certain, there's no question."

He leaned his head back and stared at the wall. "So what does that mean? How does it change things? I've been with the family for a long time. Does this make me legitimate and not an adopted child?"

"You were never an adopted child," she said firmly. "It just means that you can now find out who you really are, know who your true family was, and claim your birthright."

"Immortality?" he questioned.

"Among other things, yes."

He concentrated on her eyes. "If I were not one of the lost and asked you for immortality, would you grant me the request?"

"If you wished it," she answered sincerely, "yes, I would. I love you, Ty, and I don't want to lose you. If granting you that would keep you by my side, yes, I'd give you immortality. If denying you that would keep you with me, then I would." She leaned in closer, resting her hand on his thigh. "Don't you see? It makes no difference to me. I love you, who you are."

He scooped her into his arms and brought her to rest on his lap, holding her securely. "Then why should it make a difference to me? Whether I'm Tyler Brandt or some family heir, I'm still me, and I want to be with you and the family I know and love."

She kissed him fully then smiled warmly. "Until six years ago, my entire life was a lie. Regina found me and told me the truth, and I swore from then on that I would never lie to anyone. I thought you had a right to know the truth. That's why I told you. That's the only reason. If you have any questions about your family, Garrett has all the information we have on them. No matter what you decide, know that I love you."

He shrugged. "You think I'm going to run off in search of my roots now?"

She seemed to shrink a little. "That's what I did. I wouldn't blame you if you did, but I'd hope that you'd come back to me. I want you with me."

He eased down on the bed, cradling her with him as they settled. "That was never in question. My place on this earth is by your side."

She snuggled closer and closed her eyes, crying silent tears of happiness.

Sensing a presence, Sigrid opened her eyes. The sun was beginning its downward descent, and she realized they had been asleep only a few hours. Glancing over at Tyler, she found him sleeping deeply and snoring softly.

Gently, she lifted his arm and slid out of bed. He fidgeted when he realized she was gone but was so exhausted that he rolled onto his side and fell deeper into sleep.

She watched him as she pulled on her robe and felt the urge to resume their passionate lovemaking but knew there would be plenty of time for that after both of them were back to full speed. She was tying the robe together when the bedroom door opened and Regina's head popped in.

Regina's eyes scanned the scene, and her cheeks flushed red. Embarrassed, she cast an apologizing look at Sigrid and quickly retreated from the room.

Smiling, Sigrid tiptoed out of the bedroom, quietly shutting the door behind her. As she stepped into the living room, she squinted against the bright light pouring through the windows. Regina noticed instantly how uncomfortable the light was for her niece and drew the blinds closed.

"Thanks." Sigrid smiled as she met her aunt and hugged her tightly.

Regina held the embrace. "It's so good to see you up and around. How are you feeling?"

Sigrid pulled away, her face slightly flushed. "Wonderful."

Regina's already-red cheeks became redder. "Uh, well, sorry about the interruption. I should have knocked. It's just that Don told me he ordered you to get plenty of rest, and I didn't want to bother you and . . ."

Sigrid smile became broader, her own blush coloring her face. "It's okay, Reg. You didn't interrupt anything."

Regina decided to drop it and took Sigrid's hand and led her over to the couch. Both women took a seat, turned, and faced one another. "I just wanted to check on you and let you know what happened."

Sigrid held her hand up, her face suddenly grim. "I don't want to know, ever. Garrett told me that the mission was a success, and that's all I care to know. The only thing I care about is knowing that you and the team are home in one piece."

Regina let her eyes drop to the floor. "As you wish. We'll never speak of it again. I only wish we could have finished all of it."

Garrett had also told her that Terrence had gotten away but was not in very good shape. Taking a deep breath, Sigrid let it out with a sigh. "Thank you, Reg. For everything."

Regina reached across the couch and took her hand. "I can't tell you how relieved I am to see you up and feeling better. In more ways than one," she added with a giggle.

Sigrid shrugged. "I love him, Regina."

Regina watched her. She knew of her niece's choice and had been just as surprised as Ty when she learned that the girl had never had a lover before. "I know, honey," she acknowledged, knowing that it was truly love by the way the girl glowed when she thought of the man in the next room. "I'm glad that you've found someone, and I know that he'll be good to you. Have you told him about his past? Who he is?"

Sigrid nodded. "You know how I am about keeping secrets. I told him the basics today."

"Has he made any decisions yet?"

"He's going to stay with me. Other than that, he hasn't said. I think we may take a trip later to find out about his family. Kind of like you did with me." She stood up and walked into the kitchen. "Have you told Silk yet?"

"No," she answered as she watched Sigrid fix the drinks. The young girl that she had met in Atlanta was now a grown woman who was starting a life of her own. She thought back to what Garrett had said in the car, about her wanting to leave the nest, and for the first time she saw the same thing he saw. Realizing that Sigrid was waiting for an answer, she shook off the thought. "We're having dinner tonight and I'm going to tell her then." Garrett had informed her about his slip to Sigrid about her new relationship. "I should have told you about Silk and me, I'm sorry."

"It's none of my business," she replied casually as she continued puttering around the kitchen.

"I promised you, no secrets," Regina disagreed. "It's just when we did . . . get together, all of the things with Terrence seemed to explode, and there was never a chance."

Sigrid stopped her preparations. "Regina, don't worry about it. Two people I care about found one another. It seems to me that you both are happy, and that is the only thing that concerns me."

Deciding to accept Sigrid's blessing, she fell silent.

Sigrid returned to the living room and handed Regina a glass. Then she settled back onto the couch, drawing her legs up under her, and quickly downed the contents of her glass. She refilled the glass with the bottle she had brought over and then set it down on the coffee table.

As Regina watched her empty a second glass of the red fluid, she couldn't help but worry. Garrett had warned her about Sigrid's unquenchable thirst. Don attributed it to her injury, and there was no denying that the large intake had helped in her healing, but something about it nagged at Regina.

"You look tired," Sigrid stated softly and again joined hands with Regina.

"I guess I am," Regina mumbled, trying to mask her surprise at the warmth of Sigrid's hand now.

Sigrid never took her eyes off the woman as she smiled. "Surprising, isn't it?"

Regina's eyes widened, embarrassed that she had been caught. "Uh . . . I'm sorry, Sigrid. I was just caught off guard."

The time had come, Sigrid thought to herself. Taking a deep breath and steeling herself, she said, "So was I. How long have you known, Regina?"

Genuine confusion covered her face. "Known what?"

Sigrid's expression never changed as she calmly answered, "That Terrence is my father."

Regina choked on the bit of fluid that was in her throat. She found that her throat refused to swallow, and after a few coughs, she managed to push the fluid down. Her mouth fell open, and all the color drained from her face.

"That's why you didn't let me kill him that first night, isn't it?"

"No," Regina whispered, quickly trying to regain some control. "I only suspected at that time."

Sigrid sat quietly for a few minutes, letting Regina collect her thoughts and composure. "How?" Regina asked simply.

"When I attacked him, it flashed through his mind," she answered. "A lot of things make sense now."

"What things?"

Sigrid laughed sarcastically. "My powers, for one thing. You've told me that my powers are unprecedented, and now I know why. I'm a mutation, a freak."

"No!" Regina almost screamed as she leapt from the couch. "You are not a mutation or freak."

Sigrid remained seated and calm as she spoke. "I'm the product of a brother and sister, both immortals. I was brought over by you, my aunt. I have three doses of the most powerful blood among immortals running through my veins. I have powers that no one else has, not you, not Terrence or my mother. What else would you call me?"

Regina kneeled at her feet and cocked her head sideways. "My niece. Nothing more and nothing less."

Sigrid reached out to Regina and, grasping her shoulders, pulled her back on the couch. "I'm not angry, Reg." Sigrid smiled as Regina sat back beside her. "Just curious. Something happened when I got hurt. A transformation of some sort."

Concern appeared on Regina's face. "Transformation? I don't . . . understand. Are you in pain? Is that why your thirst has increased? Why your skin is warm to the touch? What have you kept from me?"

Sigrid shrugged. "I can't explain what's happened, and neither can Don. I only know that I'm not the same person I was a week ago. I think that's why Terrence wanted me dead. He knew that his child would be different. Stronger."

The concern was still clear in Regina's posture. "I wondered when I read Reynard's diary why Terrence insisted that the child be destroyed. It was the one point he was adamant about."

"So you didn't know then?" Sigrid asked innocently.

Regina shook her head. "No. My suspicion became aroused at the first confrontation with him at the boatyard. His reaction to you was . . ." Regina grasped for the right word. "Extreme. He was afraid when he saw you."

Sigrid smiled. "Afraid, huh?"

A sly smile played across Regina's lips as she remembered how much she had savored his fear. "Yeah, terrified. More so than I've ever seen him. Well, up until last week." Regina's smile faded as she thought about how badly Sigrid had been hurt. "I didn't know for sure he was your father until the other night, when you were hurt. Before you arrived, I had confronted him with my suspicions." She finished with a sigh.

"Tell me," Sigrid prodded.

Regina took a drink and swallowed slowly. "No," she stalled. "Now is not the time. You're still recovering from an almost-fatal wound. I planned on telling you the whole truth when you were fully healed. We'll discuss it then."

Regina stood up and started to move away from the couch. In a flash Sigrid was up and blocking the way. "No secrets, Reg, remember? I have to know the truth," she stated as she held her ground.

Regina looked down at the floor, tired, flustered, and angry. She inhaled deeply, trying to suppress her feelings, and when she looked up and met Sigrid's eyes, her voice was icy. "You already have enough hate in your heart for him. I'm afraid that any more will cause the person I know and love to disappear forever. Please let's discuss this later. I'm tired."

Sigrid stood firm, her eyes never faltering. "He raped her, didn't he?"

Silently Regina cursed herself for letting her feelings rise so close to the surface. With Sigrid's heightened senses, it was easy for her to pick up on the emotions and thoughts. She took a step back, only wanting to leave now and collect herself. "I have to go."

"Tell me!" Sigrid ordered loudly.

She took another step back, her anger now clearly visible as her eyes took on a deadly glint. "Dammit, Sigrid, why do you persist? I told you we would discuss it later. Can't you just let it go?"

Sigrid maintained her position. Regina felt chills down her spine as she noticed the look on Sigrid's face. For the first time she could see Terrence in that lovely face, and it made her heart ache. "Yes!" she admitted, almost yelling. "Yes, he raped her. He followed her and captured her. Then he raped her over and over, trying to break her spirit, but before he could kill her, she escaped and went into hiding. When she realized she was pregnant, she sent for me. She never told me he had captured her and tortured her, because she knew I would not stop until I had destroyed him or he me. Her secrecy about the father had us fearing the worst, and while all of us urged her to dispose of the thing inside her, she held strong. She was convinced that the child she was carrying was created for a special purpose. There, now you know the truth." She stopped, instantly regretting what she'd said. Her breath hitched in her chest, and her own tears welled up in her eyes.

Sigrid's face radiated hurt and disappointment. Regina started to reach out to her but stopped when the woman screamed. A scream that was a mixture of pain and rage. She ran across the living room to the patio. Tearing through the blinds and slamming the glass door open, she took two steps and launched herself off the balcony. She fell a few feet before she transformed into a cloud of smoke and vanished on the cool breeze.

"Sigrid!" Regina called as she rushed to the railing. "Forgive me!" she wailed as Ty emerged from the bedroom and ran to the balcony.

Confused, he looked around, trying to locate his life. "Sigrid?" he called as he buttoned his jeans.

Regina slid down the railing to the floor, tears streaming down her face. Alarmed, Ty bent down and looked at her. "What happened? Where's Sigrid?"

"Gone," she sobbed. "My fault."

He frowned, afraid. "What do you mean gone? What happened?"

Regina never answered, only continued looking at the clouds floating in the pale blue sky.

The sound of the horse's hooves resembled thunder as they raced across the grassy meadow. The rider flowed with the horse's movements, savoring the touch of the breeze and feeling of power from the horse's long strides.

After a few more minutes of riding, the rider urged the horse to pick up speed and head for the large plank fence that surrounded the meadow. She bent down close to the mane and neck, whispering words of encouragement.

With the grace and fluidity of a dancer, they soared over the fence, never missing a beat. When they had cleared the fence, the rider pulled in the reins and the horse slowed, barely breathing hard. The rider scratched the mare's neck and offered words of praise and thanks. The horse whinnied softly in appreciation. She gave the horse a few minutes to calm down before pulling the reins to the side to head back to the barn. From the corner of her eye, she spotted someone standing further up the fence, watching them. Firmly nudging the horse, they began a gallop to the observer.

Martha smiled as the horse came to a halt. "You are a natural-born horsewoman, dear."

Sigrid dismounted the horse with a grimace, her shoulder still tender. "Thanks. She's so beautiful and graceful." Sigrid grinned as she pulled a carrot from her pocket. The horse instantly hoofed the ground in anticipation of the treat and greedily accepted it from Sigrid's hand.

"Regina called again," Martha said as Sigrid lovingly stroked the horse's neck. "She wanted to know if I had seen you or heard from you."

Sigrid continued her stroking. "What did you say?"

Martha sighed. "I told her no. I promised I would call her if I did."

"Thanks," she said as she let the horse's reins drop to the ground and leaned up against the fence.

Martha leaned against the other side. "You know I love you, sweetheart, and this is your home. You're welcome here anytime and always, but it's not right to let Regina worry about you. She loves you."

"I know," Sigrid grudgingly agreed. She turned her eyes up at the sky and shaded them against the sunglasses she already wore. Her sensitivity to the sun had died down a bit, but she still felt uncomfortable.

Reading her body language, Martha motioned toward a large shade tree a few yards away. "Let's get out of this hot sun."

Billy, their farmhand, rode up suddenly and flashed them his gap-toothed grin. "I'll take her in, Sig, and give her a good rubdown."

"Thanks, Billy." She winked.

Like the expert he was, he leaned over, retrieved the reins, and began a slow trot back to the barnyard.

Martha was already sitting under the shade tree and softly patted the grass beside her. "Nobody can ever accuse you of having a dull life," she remarked as Sigrid sat beside her.

Sigrid laughed. "No, I guess not."

Martha patted Sigrid's arm. "I know that, after everything you've been through, the last thing you needed was to find out that Terrence is your father. I also know that you are angry and hurt about what Regina said. But, honey, you're going to have to deal with this. I know you, and you've never run away from anything. Don't start now."

"I know," Sigrid agreed, toying with a blade of grass. "I just keep wondering if everything I've done is a mistake. I was a mistake, so how can I be sure my life and decisions haven't been as well?"

Martha turned and gave Sigrid a scolding look. "Yes, you've made mistakes. I've made mistakes. Regina's made mistakes. Everyone makes them. You, however, were not a mistake."

Sigrid's expression remained stoic as Martha continued, "I'm going to be honest with you. I've known Regina for at least seventy years, and I knew your mother as well. When we discovered Val was pregnant and we couldn't get her to discuss the father or any of the details, we suspected the worst. Regina was not alone in urging her to abort the child."

Realization struck Sigrid like a rock, and she turned her full attention to Martha, her eyes radiating an even deeper hurt with the new admission.

"You have to understand, honey. We didn't know what was happening. We were worried for and about her. Yet, Val, after her initial shock, realized what a miracle it was." Martha leaned in closer, taking Sigrid's hands into her own. "Immortals don't procreate, or so the legends say, yet there she was, a very pregnant vampire. She told us that she was certain that this child, her child, was created for a very special reason, and she convinced us as well. When you were born, you were the most welcomed and loved child any family could ever want. When I looked at your sweet face, I knew that we had been mistaken and that Val was absolutely right."

"You were there?" Sigrid asked, some of the hurt disappearing.

Martha nodded. "Yes, honey, I was there. Regina and I stayed with Val until she had you. I stayed until you were about three months old, and then I had to come home and take care of my own family."

"Why didn't you ever tell me?"

Martha shrugged. "It never came up. I couldn't have loved your mother any more than if she was my own. Same goes for Regina. They are my daughters, just as you are my most precious gift from them. If it had been Silk or Regina in the same situation as Val, don't you think you would have reacted the same way?"

She thought it over and knew that she would and hesitantly nodded. "Yes."

"Your man, Ty, and the family you brought together, how do you feel about them? Are they a mistake?"

"No. I love him and the others," she answered, aghast that the suggestion was even thought of.

"If you could go back in time, would you change any of it, knowing what you do now? Would you try to change all these mistakes you think you may have made?"

Sigrid considered the last six years. True, they had been full of peril and excitement, but they had also been the most fulfilling of her entire existence. "I would have ducked sooner at the quarry," she announced firmly.

Martha laughed. Sigrid's sense of humor signaled an upswing to the girl's mood. "That would be a good thing to change."

Sigrid loved to hear Martha's laugh. It was comforting, but she still had her doubts, and as her shoulders slumped, she still felt uncertainty. "You know what Terrence is, how evil he is. That is a part of me."

Martha shook her head, another soft laugh on her lips. "Only if you let it. You've been among us for over six years and have dealt with more family members than most of us can even name. Of all the terms I've heard used to describe you by the family, evil was never one of them."

"But some of the family will have doubts now," Sigrid argued.

Martha radiated confidence as she spoke. "No, they won't, because no one ever need know. I know how you feel about the truth, and there is no reason to lie. You just don't have to tell anybody. There may be five of us that know the truth, and it's a given that we will respect your privacy and keep quiet."

"Can you accept me?" Sigrid asked softly.

Martha placed a soft kiss on her forehead. "I accepted you the minute you were born and again when you returned to us. In my mind, nothing has changed. You are my granddaughter, and I love you."

Sigrid closed her eyes and sighed, relishing the loving hands and comforting words she heard. "Thank you," she whispered and lightly kissed Martha's hand.

Now Martha pulled her into a hug, swaying slightly as she tried to relay all her love and acceptance in the single action. When she felt Sigrid relax against her, she knew that she had succeeded. Pulling away, she brushed a few loose strands of hair from Sigrid's face. "Are you ready to go home now? I know Regina's going nuts, and I imagine Ty is searching the entire country for you."

Sigrid's smiled warmed her heart, but she felt the need to urge a warning of caution. "Remember," she began seriously, "that of all the emotions, hate is the most powerful and destructive. I know you hate him, and you have every reason to. But if you let that hate consume you and take over, you will truly become Terrence's daughter, and Val will cease to exist, as well as Sigrid."

Sigrid soaked in the advice and felt a chill as she remembered similar words from Regina. The anger she had felt had slowly been dissolving since she arrived at the Penshaws, and although there was still an ember remaining, she knew that she could control it. She had spent the last few days gathering her thoughts and dealing with festering emotions. While riding Thunder, she had felt more like herself, and that had helped her reach a lot of decisions. Talking to Martha had only confirmed them. "Sigrid and Val aren't going anywhere except back home," she assured Martha.

Martha's face lit up. "Wonderful news. Let's get you packed."

Sigrid jumped to her feet, and Martha braced against the tree, pulling herself out of the sitting position. Sigrid tried to hide the smirk that covered her face, but Martha saw and shot her a stern look. "Well, don't just stand there, give an old lady a hand."

Sigrid held out her right hand, and Martha firmly grasped it. With a slight pull, Martha was brought to her feet as if she weighed no more than a leaf.

"Thank you," Martha replied as she dusted off her dress.

"No problem," Sigrid said, trying to stifle the laugh that was building.

Martha raised her eyebrow. "Whelp," she mumbled under her breath in mock anger. "Let's see how well you move when you're my age." She marched off toward the farmhouse still mumbling.

Sigrid's laughter could no longer be contained, and she released a hearty chuckle. The sound was music to the older woman's ears, and she slowed her step as Sigrid ran to catch up.

Their conversation was casual and relaxing as they reached the house but stopped as Billy came rushing out of the house toward them. Both women saw the look on his face and the portable phone in his hand and ran to meet him.

He extended the phone in his hand out to Sigrid. "I know you said no calls, but it's Cameron."

Her face fell as she took the phone. "Cam, what's wrong?"

Martha watched silently as Sigrid listened, her posture becoming tense and her face grim. "I'm on my way, Cam," she responded and clicked off the phone.

"Honey?" Martha questioned. "Is he okay?"

Sigrid took a deep breath and faced Martha. "Seth's dying. He had a heart attack, and he's asking for me."

Martha rested her hand on Sigrid's shoulder. "What can I do?"

Sigrid licked her lips and began walking toward the house, climbing steps two at a time. She cut off emotions, letting instinct kick in. When she did speak, her voice was cool and professional. "I need you to make some calls for me. I need the fastest transportation to Florida I can get. Then call Regina, let her know the situation and that I'll be home when I can."

Martha nodded and followed Sigrid into the house.

Four hours later, when she eased into the Miami hospital room, her senses were assaulted with the sounds of life-preserving machinery and the smell of death.

The lights were low, but she had no problem making out Cameron sitting next to the bed, holding his father's hand. Silently, she moved closer and was able to see Seth and the machinery that kept him clinging to life.

He was so small and pale, not at all like the man she remembered. To her surprise, she found her emotions emerging and betraying her. The grief and loss were trying to settle in, and she realized that, despite all the things in their past together, she did care about him.

Swallowing the lump that had risen in her throat, she moved over to the bed. "Cam?" she called softly.

He turned and, when he saw her, smiled weakly. He, too, was pale and looked very tired, and as he stood up, knees cracking from the action, he went to her.

She held her arms open for him and embraced him tightly as he walked into the welcome. He clung to her like a man clinging to a life preserver, and she felt like a mother trying to take away the pain of a child. She loved her brother and only wanted to make everything better and take his pain away. "What happened?"

He took a deep breath before withdrawing from the security of her arms. "Heart attack," he answered simply. He took hold of her hand and guided her to the foot of Seth's bed. "We were on our way back home from lunch, and he said he had a really bad case of heartburn, then he just slumped over. I drove straight here. Luckily, we were only a few miles away. The doctor said it was a massive heart attack and that his heart is damaged. They didn't expect him to live this long."

"We'll get a second opinion. I'll have the best doctors in the country here in a few hours," she argued, unwilling to accept defeat this easily.

Cameron pulled her close, his arm around her shoulders. "I've already had a second and third opinion. There's nothing we can do. The damage is too bad."

She clenched her teeth, trying to grasp at any other options, but nothing useful came. "It's okay," Cameron soothed, sensing her struggle. "It's his time. I don't want to lose him, but I don't want to see him hooked up to machines for years either, and I know he doesn't want that."

"Has he been conscious?"

Cameron nodded. "He's in and out. Mostly, he's been asking for you."

Sigrid patted his shoulder and went to Seth's side. She gently took his hand and leaned close to his face. "Seth?" she called softly.

He took a small breath but did not wake. Cameron moved to the other side of the bed and took his father's other hand. "Dad?" he said in a low voice. "Dad, Justine is here."

Seth's eyes fluttered slightly and then opened. It took him a few seconds to focus, but when he did, he looked at each of them and squeezed their hands in recognition. He opened his mouth, and Sigrid was shaken to hear his voice. His once-strong, commanding voice was now wispy and barely audible. "You came."

She smiled at him, brushing her hand across his forehead. "Of course I came. We've made our peace, Dad."

Slowly he looked over at Cameron. "My children. Both of you are my children."

Cameron began to tear up. "Save your strength, Dad."

Seth half smiled. "No time, son." The he turned his head a bit, his gaze falling back on Sigrid. "I need you to answer a question."

"Anything," she replied.

He looked into her eyes and saw that, although his body was failing, his mind was still clear and sharp. "If I asked you for it, would you do it?"

Cameron seemed confused by the question, but Sigrid understood completely. Ty had asked her the same question only a few days earlier.

As she looked at him, she could see his fear and the knowledge that he was dying in his eyes. Regina's words about seeing those you know and love dying while you live on rang in her ears. The man, whom she had despised growing up, who was critical, unsympathetic, and cold, had made her the strong, sensible woman she was when Regina found her. When his crimes were compared against Terrence's, they were insignificant. No matter their past, this man was her father, and she did love him. She answered him with a question, "Do you want that?" knowing already what his answer would be.

Seth smiled and squeezed her hand. "No. Just wanted to know if I had the option."

She could feel his life force ebbing away, and his fear seemed to go with it. "I didn't do right by either of you"—he sighed—"but I do love you both."

"And we love you, Dad," Cameron added.

Sigrid and Cameron joined hands, completing the triangle. "Rest, Dad," Sigrid soothed as Seth's eyes began to close. "Be with Mother and be happy."

"Tell her . . . you said hello," he whispered and, with a final shallow breath, closed his eyes.

The heart monitor emitted a high-pitched whine, and in a matter of seconds the hospital personnel began to rush in.

Sigrid firmly pulled Cameron back to allow them to do their jobs. They stood against the wall, watching as the doctors and nurses checked Seth and tried to resuscitate him, all of them knowing it was useless.

After several minutes, the doctor called the time and whispered something to the nurse; then he walked over to them. "I'm sorry. There was nothing we could do," he stated coolly and with little emotion or sincerity. Then he began explaining what needed to be done as Cameron's tears flowed.

Mustering her professional manner, Sigrid told the doctor they would discuss things later; right now, they needed some time. The doctor started to argue but was silenced and agreeable after one look from her. He left them alone, deciding it could wait, and he stepped aside as she led Cameron out of the room.

Sigrid sat on the deck of the beach house watching the sun sink into the sea. A soft breeze enveloped her and ruffled her hair as her mind replayed the events of the last three days.

The night Seth died, Sigrid had been surprised to meet Cameron's girlfriend, who had rushed to his side the instant she found out about Seth. Her name was Katie Conner, a thirty-seven-year-old financial counselor, with shoulder-length blonde hair and ocean blue eyes. Sigrid had immediately seen what the attraction was. They were like two pieces of a puzzle and meant for each other, even down to the same offbeat sense of humor.

She liked Katie right away and was glad to have help with Cameron, who was completely devastated by his father's death. Sigrid had always thought he was the strong, stoic one, but she learned he was more tenderhearted than she ever suspected. And she was the strong one in this instance. He was unable to make any arrangements, so Katie and Sigrid took care of everything and the next evening began the painful process at the funeral home.

The two women took turns keeping an eye on Cameron. The night before the funeral, when Sigrid had greeted and smiled and consoled until she felt like she might run screaming from the place, she had glanced at the approaching figure and smiled with relief.

Ty was dressed in a dark gray suit and slowly made his way across the room to her. "I thought you might need some help," he greeted in in a deep, loving voice.

She walked into his arms and tightly clung to him. "I am so sorry. I shouldn't have just run away like that," she whispered against his chest.

"No apologies needed," he replied and held her tighter. After a minute or so, she released her grip and stepped away, but retained her hold on his strong hand.

"How are you doing?" he questioned.

Sigrid smiled, but he could see the distress underneath. "Just tired and grieving."

He squeezed her hand and urged her closer. "If you need anything . . ."

"All I want or need," she interrupted, "is you."

It was his turn to smile. He directed his look across the room and motioned toward Cameron, who was standing a few feet away. "How's he doing?"

Sigrid let her eyes fall on her brother, her voice tinged with sadness. "Holding up. But he's taking it very hard. Come say hello," she said and, clasping his hand, led the way.

Sigrid admired the way Katie kept him moving and a safe distance from the casket. Cameron's eyes were bloodshot and radiated exhaustion, but he managed a weak smile as she shook Ty's hand. "Thanks for coming, Ty. Justine needs some support, and I haven't been much help."

Ty returned his smile. "I'm sure you're doing fine." He moved closer, speaking lowly so as not to be heard by other mourners. "The entire family sends their deepest sympathy and wants you to know that if there is anything you need or that we can do, we are at your disposal."

Cameron nodded and patted Ty's shoulder. "I appreciate that. If it weren't for the family and Regina, I don't think my family would have reunited and made peace." He cast a look at Sigrid, who smiled warmly at him. Then he introduced Katie to Ty.

Back on the beach, Sigrid jumped when she felt Cameron's hand on her shoulder. She had been so deeply in thought that she had blocked out her surroundings, and she silently scolded herself for it.

"I'm sorry. I didn't mean to startle you," Cameron apologized as he knelt beside her. "To be honest, I didn't think I could."

Sigrid chuckled and leaned over, planting a kiss on his chin. "What's up?"

Cameron held his hand out, and as she took it, he pulled her to her feet. "Let's take a walk on the beach."

They walked down the steps of the deck and started a slow, leisurely walk along the sandy turf. Only the last glimmer of the vanishing sun and the evening stars lit their way, but Sigrid could see more clearly at dusk than others did in sunlight.

They took it easy, in no hurry to reach a certain destination, holding hands and watching as the surfers on the beach were replaced by the lovers.

"I like Katie," she finally said, breaking their comfortable silence.

"She likes you too," he replied softly.

"Cam," she began anew, not anxious to say what she had to, "I'm going to have to head back home day after tomorrow."

Cameron released her hand and draped his arm around her shoulder. "I know, you've got a business to run. It's been good having you with me again. It makes me realize how much I miss you."

"I'm not going to disappear. You'll see me again, hopefully more often than in the past."

"Tine, when Dad asked you if you would grant his request, you answered him with a question. Would you have done it if he asked?"

They continued walking, Cameron waiting patiently as she considered her answer. After several minutes, she answered simply, "No."

He stopped and turned to face her. "May I ask why not?"

Sigrid also came to a stop and sat down in the sand, gazing at the incoming surf as she spoke. "He spent his entire life seeking and destroying vampires, except for the last few years of course. Then when he was dying, he sought to become what he detested? No, he was frightened, and he was checking his options. As afraid as he was of dying, he didn't want to trade that for the curse of immortality."

"Curse?" he repeated, surprised by her choice of words.

Sigrid laughed cynically. "What do you call never aging while you watch your friends and loved ones grow old and die?"

Cameron eased down on the sand beside her. "I never thought of it like that."

Sigrid sighed. "Neither did I, until I saw you in the airport that day. I managed to push it aside and not think about it again until I saw Dad in the hospital."

"I like to hear you call him that. He did too."

She leaned against his broad shoulder. "Despite everything, I realize now that I did love him. He may not have been the best father in the world but I could have had much worse," she admitted, her thoughts flashing on Terrence again.

"What about your brush with death?" he asked out of the blue.

Sigrid sat up, angling her head to look at him as if she hadn't heard him correctly. "What?"

His nostrils flared with anger. "Don't play innocent with me. You didn't even have the decency to call me, Tine."

"How did you find out?"

"Regina called me about a week ago. As she put it, after you were out of danger, when I insisted on speaking with you, she said you were on a recuperative trip. Why didn't you call me? Dammit, haven't I lost enough family already?"

"That's why I didn't call," she argued sympathetically. "I wanted to wait until I was okay. All my life you have been the peacekeeper, the soother of hurt feelings, and the compassion giver. Forgive me if I wanted to spare you any more of my pain."

Cameron's ire evaporated. "You forgot something, Tine. You're my sister, and I love you. Your pain is my pain. Blood or not, we are connected. Immortal or not, we are family. I bullied Ty into telling me a few of the details, and I would have liked to have had a little bit of vengeance too. That bastard almost killed you, and I may just stake him myself."

Fear reared up in her. "No, Cameron," she warned. "He has been taken care of for now. The whole reason for you and Dad moving was to keep you safe. If he were to find out that you're alive . . . he . . . well, I want you safe. I want Katie safe."

Seeing the fear in his sister's eyes, he decided to drop it. "Okay. But I can't promise anything if he tried to hurt you again."

Calming, she smiled at him and conceded. "I'm sorry I didn't call. You had a right to know."

"That's okay," he answered cavalierly. "I'll try to remember to let you know when Katie and I set a date."

Sigrid punched him in the arm. "It's that serious?"

His face glowed. "I love her."

Now she smiled genuinely. "You better call me."

They resumed their silence for a minute as the mood turned somber. "What will you do now, Cam? The war is over. Terrence has left the country. Dad is gone, and you've met a wonderful woman."

He had obviously been thinking it over and readily answered, "First, I need to take Dad's ashes back to Atlanta and bury them next to Mom. Then I'll settle the estate and come back here. I like Florida, and I want to be with Katie. Then I guess I'll find a job so I don't become a beach bum."

Sigrid nodded. "You and Katie could start your own business."

He sighed. "Yeah, but I'm kinda tired of the CPA biz. It would be a letdown after the last few years."

"I can't imagine why?"

"You know"—he hesitated—"you are in Dad's will too. You should have some say . . ."

"No," she cut him off. "I trust you, and so did he. I took my inheritance when I broke into his study. I don't deserve anything."

He started to argue, but she held up her hand. "End of discussion. If you need my help or need an attorney, I'll be happy to have someone . . ."

"No," he interrupted this time, "I can handle it. Thanks though." He decided to try to broach the will once more. "You should have all of Dad's research and information. It needs to be somewhere safe."

She shrugged and took a deep breath of sea air. "Yes. I would like that, if you're okay with it?"

Cameron leaned over and nudged her shoulder. "Of course, I am. Let's go back to the beach house, get dressed up, and go out to dinner."

It was the first time he had shown any interest in food or going out in public since Seth's death, and Sigrid was elated at the change. Cutting her eyes at him, she asked, "Who's paying?"

He stood up and offered her a hand. "Well, you're the corporate bigwig. I'm an unemployed vampire hunter."

Sigrid took his hand and was lifted to her feet; then they began chasing one another down the beach, children once again briefly.

Ty had used the company jet to fly down to Florida, and now they were in the air jetting back toward Denver. She seemed relaxed in the quiet private cabin, and she and Ty had a lot to discuss. She told him about the argument with Regina and her true father. Then she explained where she had disappeared and the things that she had learned and decided.

He listened patiently and with understanding as she bared her soul to him. When she ran out of words, tears streaming down her face, she sought the comfort of his arms, and he happily complied.

They remained together for nearly an hour, never speaking, only holding one another and thinking about their own private worries.

"We'll be arriving in Denver in an hour and a half. Per your instructions, no one is aware of our arrival," a cold voice filtered into their silence through the loudspeaker.

Ty lightly kissed her head. "You have lived a dozen lives, but never one that you want. It may start out that way, but something or someone always changes your course. What do you want to do? Where do you want to go?"

Sigrid looked up at him and smiled. "Would you believe that's all I've been thinking about for the last few days?"

"Reached any decisions?"

Sigrid batted her eyes and slowly ran her hand up his thigh. "One. It's something that I'd like to know a lot more about, especially now that I'm more . . . able."

"Good decision, boss," he agreed and began nuzzling her neck.

Regina quickly pulled a robe on as she rushed to the front door. She had left strict instruction that she was not to be disturbed and she was going to lower the boom on the intruder. That thought faded when she opened the door and saw Sigrid's smiling face.

"Oh, honey, you're home," she cried, her ire vanishing as she reached out to her niece.

Sigrid walked into her aunt's arms and returned the hug. "I'm sorry if I woke you or interrupted anything."

Regina hushed her. "You're home now. That's all that's important."

They pulled apart and Regina led Sigrid into the apartment and to the couch. Once she had Sigrid seated, she floated into the kitchen to prepare them drinks. When she returned, she handed a glass to Sigrid and took her seat on the couch. "I am truly sorry about Seth," she offered as she settled in.

"Thanks," Sigrid nodded. "And I'm sorry about reacting the way I did to our . . . discussion."

Regina waved her hand, the motion causing a long black curl to fall across her face. "You have nothing to be sorry for. Considering the circumstances, I'd say your reaction was underscored."

"Well," she sighed, "it's in the past. I will not allow Terrence to influence or affect my life. I've got plans of my own.

Regina immediately changed the subject, not yet ready to accept that the girl was ready to fly away to her own life. "How's Cameron? Is your shoulder all right? Is there anything you need?"

Sigrid raised her hand. "Whoa, Reg. Take a breath every now and then."

"Okay," Regina agreed and took a drink from her glass as Sigrid did the same.

"Cam was shaky at first," she began, "but he's better now. He's met a wonderful woman, and she was a rock for him during and after the funeral. I really like her. She's strong, intelligent, and witty. She's his perfect match."

Regina leaned back on the couch, listening intently as Sigrid continued. "Cameron is giving me all of Seth's research and work. He wants it somewhere safe and that's with us." Regina nodded and let her continue. "As for me, my shoulder's much better. It just seems to be taking forever to heal." She stopped and took a long drink, then stared at the half-empty glass. "Seth asked me if I would give him immortality before he died?" She could see the surprise on Regina's face. "Of course, I knew he wouldn't have taken it, but it did make me realize a lot about him. It hurt to watch him just fade away, but when he was gone, that pain was joined by a peace. Blood or not, Seth Reynard was my father."

Regina remained silent, offering herself as a shoulder and steadying force as Sigrid dealt with these new feelings. After a moment, Sigrid looked up, a slight blush in her face. "You weren't alone when I came knocking this morning."

Regina smiled at Sigrid's embarrassment. "Silk joined us last night."

Sigrid's eyes lit up. She was torn between excitement and the feeling that she had intruded.

"Is she all right? Why didn't you tell me? I'll go and we can talk later."

She started to get up, but Regina grasped her wrist. "Now it's your turn to slow down. Why don't we see if she's awake?" She saw Sigrid hesitate and tugged at her arm. "Come on, she's family and will be delighted to see you home."

Sigrid allowed Regina to pull her up from the couch, and the two women went to the bedroom door. Quietly, Regina opened the door and they eased into the darkened room.

Silk was lying across the bed, her hair cascading over the pillow and still damp with perspiration from the change. The blue satin sheets on the bed were rumpled and strewn about, and Sigrid would easily guess what they had been doing before the change. A single sheet covered the dozing young woman and outlined her small, well-proportioned body.

Sigrid noticed the radiant glow of Silk's skin and how it made her reddish-brown hair even more fiery. As Regina approached the bed and took a seat beside the young woman, Sigrid stayed back in the shadows.

Silk instantly began to stir as Regina brushed her hand down her shoulder to her arm, and she opened her eyes.

"Good morning, sweetheart," Regina greeted in a smooth voice. "How are you feeling?"

Silk reached up and ran her hand through Regina's hair, coming to settle on her cheek, "Wonderful."

Regina's satisfaction was evident in her smile. "Good. You need to build up your strength so we can begin your training."

"My strength is fine," Silk purred as she slowly sat up. She let the sheet fall away and slightly thrust her breast forward. "Care to try me?"

Regina's eyes widened with surprise and embarrassment as Sigrid cleared her throat softly.

Silk flushed and grabbed the sheet, pulling it close.

"Good morning," Sigrid greeted as she eased over to the bed, her own cheeks a bit red.

"Sig!" Silk squealed and scooted into a kneeling position. "You're home!"

The shared embarrassment was gone, when Sigrid reached the bedside and Silk rose up, embracing her tightly, still managing to keep the sheet secure around her.

"Welcome, my sister," Sigrid whispered before they pulled apart.

"Can you help with my training?" she asked like an excited little sister.

Sigrid gave her a broader smile and wink. "I think it can be arranged, if Regina agrees. Right now, do what Regina says and get some rest. I've got to unpack and take care of some things, so I'll check on you later."

"I'm glad you're home. I missed you." Silk grinned.

"Me too," she admitted and turned toward the door. Regina rose to her feet and caught up with her. "We need to discuss a few things, Reg," Sigrid said lowly as she grasped the door handle.

Deep in her heart, Regina knew what was on Sigrid's mind. Between the conversation with Garrett and Martha, she knew that it was time to let go. She wanted to put Sigrid off but knew that it would serve no purpose other than her own selfish one. "We'll have dinner tomorrow night, just the two of us."

Sigrid lightly kissed Regina's cheek. "It's a date. It will also give us a chance to discuss that vacation we wanted to plan."

She stared at the door for a few seconds after Sigrid had gone, her feelings a jumble. Her ears picked up the throaty breathing of her roommate, and only one emotion seemed important then. Turning on her heel, she found Silk had tossed away the sheet again and was lying back in the bed invitingly.

Raising an eyebrow, she let her eyes scan the beauty's form and smiled. "Little minx," she called and leapt across the room, landing at Silk's waiting feet.

The Present

Garrett was waiting in the conference room when Sigrid and Ty arrived in town. They came up through the back entrance, and when Garrett saw their appearance, he was glad they had. Both were rumpled and covered with road dust and exhaust fumes. Their hair was sweaty and ruffled out of control. Dark smudges of grease and dirt dotted their faces, and to anyone who didn't know, they looked like street trash or low-class bikers. Even through the dirt and grim, Garrett could sense Sigrid's power and unease.

"I'm amazed that with all the modes of transportation available in this day and age, you insist on riding the equivalent of a dust buster," he greeted in mock seriousness.

Sigrid ignored his attempt at a joke. "Sorry we're late. Any news yet?"

His face turned grim. "Not a peep. We did find out that Terrence was here in the States for a few days, but that was about a month ago. Since then it's been quiet."

"Why was he here? What did he do? Who did he see?" she pushed.

"We don't know," he answered. "He was here and gone before we knew it had even happened. We don't know why or even if Regina was with him."

Sigrid took a deep breath and slowly released it. "She was with him. I sense . . . it's so faint . . . but I know it's her."

Garrett watched her. It was known throughout the family that Sigrid and Regina shared a special bond, and he believed her now with more faith than his own feelings.

"It was a . . ." She closed her eyes, searching for when the sensation had begun. "Thursday."

Garrett nodded, amazed at the accuracy of her feelings. "Yes, that's what the reports say."

"She's here in the States, Gar. We have to get every available person on it. I want reports every twelve hours."

"I'm on it," he agreed and moved toward the phone.

"I'll get things rolling, Garrett," Ty volunteered. He motioned toward Sigrid, then moved to phone.

Garrett nodded at the hint. He moved over to Sigrid. "I need a drink and hate to drink alone," he smiled. She knew what they were up to but went along anyway and followed as Garrett led her out of the conference room. Once they were gone, Ty sat down and began making the necessary phone calls.

Garrett sat the glass down in front of Sigrid and took a seat across from her. "You're exhausted," he stated as he played with the glass.

"I'm fine," she answered shortly.

Garrett watched her a moment and then decided to try another approach. "Did you ever stop to think that if you were weak because of exhaustion, you'll be no good to Regina."

She jerked her head up and met his eyes. Knowing that it worked, he watched as her face became haunted. "What do I do, Garrett? I can't sleep or eat. She's on my mind every minute of every day. I'm so afraid of what he's done to her . . . if she's okay after all this time." She flinched as she mentally scolded herself for such thoughts. "I know we have the entire family searching, but so far we haven't been able to find a trace of her."

He laid his hand on hers. "You think this is a one-woman war, and you are trying to carry all the weight and responsibility by yourself. The family wants her back as much as you do and are doing everything they can to help, but you need to let them handle some of this. You're killing yourself and we can't afford to lose you too."

Her head hung down, pain encasing her features. She knew he was right. She was so tired that she had almost wiped out on the bike a few hours outside of town. She thought of Regina trying to explain how much responsibility she would have if anything were to ever happen to her, and she guessed she'd taken it too literally.

Garrett saw the dawning and continued. "Get some rest, Sigrid. When we find her, and we will," he stressed, "she would need you at your full strength, for her and to take care of Terrence."

"You're right," she agreed and promptly downed the glass's contents, feeling the road dust cut by the life-giving fluid. "I do need to check on a few things first, then I'll get some rest."

"She's upstairs," he supplied to her unasked question.

Sigrid chewed nervously on her bottom lip. "How is she?"

Garrett shrugged. "Well, Don says physically she's healed and fine. She has a few scars but nothing serious."

"And mentally?"

"She blames herself for the abduction and, I think, Paul's death. She stays in her room, never goes out, won't see anyone. She only tolerates me for the little food she takes and information on the search. I'm afraid we might lose her."

Sigrid shook her head. "No we won't. I haven't done right by her, and that's going to change now." Her face set with determination, she left her seat and headed upstairs.

Upstairs, as Sigrid and Garrett talked, Silk curled into a fetal position, unable to escape the memories that haunted her almost continuously for the last few months. Eyes open, eyes closed, it made no difference what she did—she could not escape the horror of that night. Her entire body began shaking as the events replayed again, like a bad movie that never stops.

The three of them, Regina, Paul, and herself had been on a mini vacation and had gone out on their last night in town for a quiet late dinner.

Fall had descended on Chicago early, and the air held a nip that was only felt by Paul as he pulled his leather jacket closer. The evening had been so clear and bright as they left the small Italian restaurant, that they decided to walk the six blocks to their hotel. The week before, they had stopped in New York to visit with Sigrid and Ty and were still on a natural high from that visit. They became so engrossed in their conversation that they didn't notice the black van until it was too late.

It had been following them since they left the restaurant, and as they walked into a more secluded area, it made its move. Pulling up and screeching to a halt, the three quickly found themselves surrounded by ten figures dressed in black and armed with guns and silver shafts. Instantly they fell into a fighting triangle stance.

A tall, muscular black man took a step forward and smiled, revealing pearly white fangs. "We bring you greetings from Terrence, Regina."

"You can tell Terrence to go to bloody hell, where he belongs," Paul growled, reaching for his ever present .44.

"You'll be going there before he does," the man replied and then laughed when Paul produced his gun and aimed it at the nearest enemy.

His laughter stopped when the shot rang out. The man standing directly in front of Paul clutched his chest as the wooden slug ripped through his heart, dropping him to the ground.

Before Paul could get off another shot, a hand shot out, seized his wrist, and promptly twisted it, breaking it with a snap and causing the gun to fall from his mangled hand.

Silk leaped forward, delivering an equally bone crushing kick to the man holding Paul. Releasing Paul, he staggered back. Paul looked at his friend, silently thanking her, when suddenly she was hit from the side by a truck disguised as a man.

As she went down, she saw Regina skillfully fighting the black man and a tall Amazonian woman. Using her powers and training, Silk hit the concrete with a thud but immediately bounced back onto her feet. She threw a punch at the approaching henchmen and whirled around in time to see Paul fall to the ground as his arm was yanked from its socket.

Paul let out a scream of pain but continued to fight as he was seized by the ankles. Her attention was pulled away when she felt a searing pain run through her stomach. She glanced down and saw a broken table leg protruding from her abdomen.

Silk turned around and met the grinning face of a young, brunette boy. A grimace of pain streaked her face as she pulled the wood from her stomach. She held it up for him to see and smiled. "You missed." Then she rammed it into his chest.

He fell to his knees, eyes wide and staring at the growth from his heart. As he tumbled forward, she turned her back on him and saw Regina, half conscious being dragged to the van.

Like a cat, she leapt at the woman helping drag Regina and wrestled her to the ground. The Amazon fought to get free and stabbed out at Silk with a silver spike. Silk easily dodged the weapon and delivered a strong right cross to the blonde's face. The blonde fell backward and Silk shoved her aside, scrambling to reach Regina.

She blindly delivered blows, knocking attackers out of her path; her only goal was to save Regina. She staggered to the van and stretched out her hand to Regina, who weakly grasped it.

The large man, yanked Regina from her grasp a she wailed, "No!" She was hit from behind and knocked into the side of the van. Regina was thrown into the van and still she continued to fight her captors even as the van door slid shut, cutting her off from the still raging Silk.

Silk spun around the next man that moved toward her and continued to deliver blows to the remaining attackers. Dizzy and exhausted, she turned and found herself face-to-face with the Amazon, who rammed a silver spike into her already bleeding stomach. She felt another stab her leg and then her arm as she was finally brought down. The Amazon straddled her and raised the gleaming silver spike into the air.

"Hurry it up, we've got to go," a man's voice called as the sound of sirens could be heard in the distance.

The Amazon met her eyes, and Silk noticed that her eyes weren't glowing with hatred like the others. As she lay expecting to feel the spike puncture her heart, it was instead plunged into her shoulder, just above her heart. The Amazon jumped off her and raced to the van, slipping in the front passenger seat as the van tore off into the night.

She lay still, pain engulfing her, and she felt consciousness beginning to fade. She turned her head and saw what was left of Paul a few feet away. His bloody torso was stretched out on the sidewalk; his arms, legs, and head strewn about the roadway. She felt the hot sting of tears and heard the approaching footsteps then the world went black.

The police called it a brutal mugging of a young couple. One of the responding officers was a family member, and he quickly made a call. Silk was rushed to the hospital where another family member, the night ER nurse, was waiting with a family doctor. Once they had taken her in and began treatment, the nurse called Garrett.

The fact that the kidnapping had even taken place was a simple matter of calling in favors and greasing palms. Garrett used all the families' influence to keep it out of the papers and off the television. Once Silk was stable, he had her moved to a private care facility run by family friends. The search for Regina began immediately, only slowing long enough for Paul's funeral. As Silk recuperated, she became consumed with guilt and fear, causing her to shut herself off from the world. It was her own private hell that she resided in now, curled into a ball and crying uncontrollably, her heart dying piece by piece.

An hour later, Sigrid knocked on the apartment door once and then ventured in. The apartment was dark and unkempt. Sigrid let her eyes adjust and she moved farther into the place. She found Silk dressed in an old bathrobe, sitting in the darkness and facing a curtained window.

Silk's head moved slightly when she sensed the new presence; her voice was low and raw. "I don't want any visitors."

"Tough," Sigrid replied firmly.

Silk ignored Sigrid's tone and continued to stare at the curtains. "Is there any news?"

Sigrid took a few steps closer. "What do you care?" she shot back.

This did catch the redhead's attention. She moved slowly as she turned around and looked at Sigrid's shadowy figure. She craned her head to the side, certain she hadn't heard correctly, "What?"

Sigrid stood her ground, bringing her hands to rest on her hips. "I said, what do you care?" She repeated, making no attempt to hide the contempt in her voice.

Shocked, Silk sat up a little straighter and for the first time in months showed some emotion. "How dare you! Of course I care."

Sigrid took another step. "Why? Because it's your fault?"

She leapt to her feet and stared at Sigrid. "My fault?"

Sigrid shuffled her feet and nodded. "Well, Paul got ripped to shreds and Regina is still missing, but you're alive and well. You stay in here all the time and make no attempt at trying to find her. Sounds kinda fishy to me. What'd you do? Make a deal, maybe like Ward did. Or maybe you just went down on them in exchange for your life."

Silk's eyes pulsed with a red glow, her breath ragged and hard. "You bitch!" she screamed and then charged at Sigrid.

Sigrid smiled to herself and sidestepped the attack. Silk stopped just short of hitting the wall and spun around.

Sigrid continued the provocation. "You did make a deal, didn't you? Was it good for you? Did you enjoy sitting back and watching while they tore Paul apart and took your lover away?"

A scream of rage erupted from Silk and she made another charge. This time, Sigrid allowed the tackle to succeed. Silk hit her with the force of a linebacker and carried her a few feet back before bringing her to the ground with a crash. She straddled the older woman and pinned her to the floor with her knees. She was so angry she never noticed that Sigrid offered no resistance as she slapped her across the face twice.

Leaving red marks on Sigrid's cheeks, Silk stopped and stared down at her captive. "How dare you!" she growled, spittle glistening on her fangs. "I fought them! I never let up! I wish I could have saved Paul. I would have gladly died in his place. I would let you rip my heart out now, if it would bring Regina back home." Her body began to sag a little as the anger began to dissipate. "I wish they had killed me, because without her, I don't want to live."

The red in her eyes was gone now, her own dark brown saturated with tears. She released her grip on Sigrid's wrist. But remained sitting astride her, her breathing slowing. "I can't bear to think of what he's doing . . . to her. I wish they had killed me," she repeated.

"Is that what you're trying to do? Sit here and waste away?" Sigrid asked, feeling her own anger and fear rising at the thought of losing her friend as well. "I should have been here to help you and I know that now. I have been so consumed with finding her that I ignored you, one of the most important people in my life. I need you now, Silk. I haven't been there for you, but I need you now. Please forgive me and help me find her. Help us find her. Regina would be ashamed of both of us. Me, for letting you go through this alone, and you, for sitting on your ass. We both know that she would move heaven and earth if the situation were reversed."

Silk finally slid off Sigrid and leaned against the nearby couch. She brought her knees up to her chest and hugged them tightly. "I thought you blamed me. I thought that's why you never came back."

Sigrid sat up and scooted in front of her. "No, honey, never. I was so lost and angry that I closed everyone off." She cupped the woman's face in her hand. "Even the ones I love most. Forgive me, please?"

Silk continued to look at the floor. Sigrid urged her face up. "Wherever Regina is, she can sense our faith and strength, that's why I know she's still alive. I can feel her, the same way she can feel me, keeping the faith."

Still Silk remained quiet. Frustrated, Sigrid leaned in, getting right in her face. "You can hate me, but not yourself. She needs you, Silk. Hate me later, but for now, please help me."

Silk's shoulders slumped, tears coursing down her face. "I don't hate you. I could never hate you," she said with heartfelt sincerity. "I want her back and I want to help, but I am so afraid. I'm not as strong as you and Regina."

Sigrid hesitated. She was relieved that Silk didn't hate her, but that could change in the next few minutes. Up until now, her plan was working. The question was, would the next bit of information pull Silk out of her self-hatred and fear, or plunge her deeper. For the first time, Sigrid realized what Regina had gone through when she revealed the truth about her own identity.

Sigrid took a deep breath. "Oh, yes, you are. The blood in our family is strong."

Silk cut her eyes at Sigrid. "You mean because Regina turned both of us?"

"No."

"Our families are related?" She tried again.

Sigrid shook her head, no.

Confusion and uncertainty with a hint of fear crossed Silk's face as she weakly asked, "Did Valonia have two children?"

Sigrid's eyes never wavered or left Silk's. "No. Terrence did."

Silk's eyes widened and her breathing quickened once again. "You . . . You're joking, right?"

Sigrid smiled. "All my life I've wanted a sister. When I was little, deep inside, I knew I had a sister. Of course, I thought it was wishful thinking, but now I know it's true. I love Cameron. He's my brother, but he's my adopted brother. In my heart of hearts, I always wanted a blood sibling, preferably a sister."

"Terrence is my father?" she whispered in disbelief.

Sigrid took another deep breath, staying close to Silk. "He fell in lust with a mortal woman. When he discovered she was pregnant, he tried to kill her, just like my mother, only he didn't succeed and she escaped. When she sought help from her family and the authorities, they thought her insane and she was put into a hospital. Six months later you were born. She died giving birth to you, so you were adopted by the family you know as your own." Sigrid stopped there, refraining from telling her how serious her real mother's insanity had been and that there had been repeated abortion and suicide attempts.

Silk blinked, trying to soak it all in. Her mouth was agape, and she rocked slightly to and fro as it sank in. Then a new look of shock crossed her face. "Then Regina's my . . . aunt? My lover is my aunt?" She covered her eyes with her hand. "Does she know?"

Sigrid could pass no judgment and shrugged. "No. I didn't find out about this until after the two of you were involved. I found out a few months after Seth died, and I should have confessed it to you both the minute I found out. Me, the one who is so big on truth and no secrets. I haven't known for very long, and I thought we would have plenty of time."

Silk looked into Sigrid's blue eyes. This woman was her best friend and mentor, and she loved her. She knew she should be angry with her for keeping the secret, but couldn't find it in her heart, not now. "You're my sister," she stated.

Sigrid bowed her head slightly. "Disappointed?" she asked unsurely.

"Never," Silk cried and wrapped her arms around the older woman.

Sigrid returned the fierce hug, letting out a slow sigh of relief. In her wildest dream she had only hoped that Silk would be this happy and now she had her wish and was finally able to acknowledge her sister. "I am so sorry that I had to tell you like this. It's not at all the way I wanted to. I know all of this is new and a shock. When it does start to settle in, it may be hard to accept and deal with. I know, I've been there. But I promise, you won't go through it alone. I haven't done right by you the last few months and that will never happen again. I promise."

Silk hugged her tighter, her body shaking as a new batch of tears came. "All this time I've wasted. I should have been helping you, the family. You are not the only one at fault here. I should have fought back and helped you whether you wanted it or not. I'm sorry too, Sig."

Sigrid patted her back and they released one another. "We have both been so consumed with worry and self-hatred, that we wanted the same thing, but went in different directions. I say it stops now. How about you?"

Silk smiled for the first time. "I'm in. So what now, sis?"

The word soared through Sigrid like a warm summer breeze. It was a similar sensation to what Regina had felt upon hearing Sigrid call her aunt for the first time. She lightly kissed Silk's forehead. "As team members we were a pretty amazing force. As sisters, there will be no stopping us." When Silk smiled her agreement, she continued. "First, we need to get some rest. We've got a lead and we need to be up and ready to kick ass when we find her. And we will."

"Sigrid?" Silk asked shyly. "Do you think Ty would mind if you stayed here? I . . . don't want to be alone."

"No problem," she smiled. "Just let me make a few phone calls and then we'll crash."

Now Silk planted a kiss on her sister's cheek and rose to her feet, vanishing into the next room, allowing Sigrid some privacy.

First, she called Garrett to tell him everything was fine. She asked him to relay a message to Ty and to keep her posted on their progress. When she was done, she had only one more call to make.

She dialed the number from memory and drummed her fingers on the desk anxiously as it rang. On the fourth ring, she heard the warm, familiar voice answer. "Cam," she began, "I need your help."

Sigrid had learned the truth of Silk's parentage when she returned to Florida a few months after the death of Seth Reynard. She and Regina had indeed gone on their vacation as planned and, after they had returned from two weeks in Switzerland, she received a call from Cameron. He asked her to meet him in Atlanta and help him settle the remainder of Seth's estate. She left the next day and found him waiting for her at the airport. He was doing well as was his relationship with Katie and, on the drive to the family home, they talked about general things.

She couldn't help but feel off when she saw the large yellow and brown for sale sign posted in front of the house. He was selling it and, despite her protests, splitting the profits fifty-fifty. He told her that Seth had plainly stated in the will that he knew she probably didn't need the money, but he wanted to provide for her now to make up for the past when he didn't.

Walking into the house caused a flood of nostalgia to wash over her, and it was quickly joined by grief. They walked through the house and he told her she was welcome to any of the furnishings she wanted. He planned to take a few things and give the rest to local shelters. They finally found themselves descending to the basement office, and she couldn't shake the guilty feeling that had edged its way in.

Sensing her turmoil, he took her hand and squeezed it for reassurance. As they walked into the office, she was surprised to find all the books, files, and other records boxed up and waiting in the center of the room. She was glad that he had given her a heads-up, and she had brought Ty, Paul, and Shadow with a rented van to take all the items back to the private plane.

"He stated in his will that he wanted you to have all his records on the vampires," he said after several seconds of silence. "He knew that he no longer needed them and hoped that maybe you could use them to do some good and counter all the evil he did with them."

She frowned, understanding how much guilt Seth had carried around with him, and it made her heart ache for him. She stared at the boxes, speechless. All his work, his life was packed away neatly in cardboard boxes, and he had left it to her, knowing it would be safe. She was so wrapped up in thought that she didn't notice her team members enter the basement, and Cameron disappearing for a second and then coming back to her side, carrying a small black book.

"Dad found this shortly after we learned the truth about Terry. He didn't really have time to study it, but I have."

Sigrid pulled her attention away from the cartons and looked at Cameron. "What is it?"

"A diary," he answered simply.

"A diary?" she repeated. "Whose? Terrence's?"

Cameron shook his head. "No. His mistress. If this diary is right, you may still be in danger."

Sigrid's surprise was apparent. "Why?" The three men behind her stopped moving the boxes and waited to see if they were needed or if there was a new threat.

"Because he has a child."

Sigrid felt fear grip her throat as she mumbled, "A child?"

"Yeah," he answered, misunderstanding her reaction. "Born about twenty-eight years ago in Paris. He appeared as an angel to the woman, and they were lovers for about four months. She eventually went insane and had to be locked away, but she did have the child."

She relaxed slightly, knowing her secret was still safe, but now wondering about the new wrinkle in the game. "Male or female? Did the child live? What about the mother?"

He shrugged. "I think you need to read this. There's enough information in here for you to find out everything you need." He held the diary out to her.

She cautiously took it, then clutched it tightly to her chest. "Thank you, Cameron."

"Just find them before they can start trouble for you, okay?"

"Okay," she agreed.

Ty, Paul, and Shadow began moving the boxes out to the van, while Sigrid and Cameron went through the house once more.

Reading the diary was a heartbreaking ordeal. The young girl was from a poor, very religious family, and she thought she had been chosen for a special purpose when the angel appeared to her. She knew it was a sin to consort with him, but he had been so convincing and earnest that she had, indeed, taken him as a lover. As the days went by, she realized that there was an evil to him; and when she confronted him, he admitted he was an angel, from hell.

Frightened, she ran from her home and family trying to escape. She would catch glimpses of him now and again, and when her family found her, she was just entering insanity. He didn't resurface until she found out she was pregnant. She prayed to the church to let her abort the demon growing in her belly. Dismissing her as quite unbalanced, they convinced her family that whoever had raped her had also caused her breakdown, and that to protect her and the child, she needed to be committed to an asylum. Her parents, grieving and embarrassed by the stain of insanity on their family, agreed and signed away all their rights to her, never seeing her again. She resided in the hospital for the next few months, sometimes accepting the child within her and at other times, screaming about the demon that appeared outside her barred window. She died during childbirth, that determined by the last entry of the diary, as she went into labor and begged God's forgiveness for her sins.

By the time Sigrid was done reading, she felt a new level of hatred for Terrence and cursed him under her breath. Then she took Ty into her confidence and together, they began investigating the new threat to the family.

It had been easier that either of them expected and within two months, they knew the identity of Terrence's other child. Sigrid was surprised and pleased at the information, but together they decided to wait until everything had settled down before they revealed it to Regina and Silk. Feelings were still running high where Terrence was concerned, and Sigrid didn't want to burden either one of them at the moment. Little did she know it would be close to a year before the truth was revealed.

Regina had called the meeting, stressing its importance and insisting that everyone be present. Paul, Shadow, Silk, and Garrett had already taken their seats at the circular conference table, when Ty and Sigrid ambled in. Both were smiling and slightly flushed, and the group couldn't help but emit a few giggles as the couple took their seats. They exchanged pleasantries and discussed ordinary things, ignoring the innuendo.

Now that Terrence and the hunters were out of the picture, the family was experiencing its first true peace in years.

When Regina strode into the room, they fell silent. She was dressed professionally in a gray skirt and jacket highlighted by a blood-red silk blouse. She had taken to wearing her hair down and flowing, and it took years off her. Her eyes sparkled and she seemed to glow as she set her file down on the table and sat down, delivering a bright smile to each of them. "Good afternoon, my friends, and thank you for coming."

Garrett busily worked over his papers as the others watched Regina intently. "I've reached some important decisions the last few weeks, decisions that, as my inner sanctum, will affect you."

There was a slight shifting of positions throughout the room and the tension seemed to rise just a notch.

Regina felt their unease and smiled wider. "There is no need to worry. This group was brought together in a time of war and now that we have peace, it only stands to reason that some things will change."

The room was silent. Garrett quickly glanced up and then went back to work as Regina continued. "In all my years, I have never met a finer group of people, and I'm proud to call you all friends and family." Opening her arms for emphasis, she said, "You have given me over a year of your lives and words can't begin to express my gratitude to each and every one of you."

Paul piped up, grinning. "No gratitude needed, love. Everything we did was because we wanted to."

Silk, Ty, and Shadow nodded their agreement and looked at Sigrid with admiration and love in their eyes.

Regina watched the action knowing that, although she was their queen, it was Sigrid whom they truly followed. She felt no jealousy, only pride as she watched her niece look at the team with all the love of a mother for her children.

The seven years since their first meeting seemed like only yesterday to her. The young woman before her was so very much like her mother and grandfather—strong, loyal, loving, and giving. In the last seven years, Sigrid had been through more than most mortals or immortals should ever have to endure and had survived and grown. As Regina looked at her, she realized that she was no longer their true queen; it was Sigrid.

Smiling to herself, she remembered the meeting and blushed as she saw the others staring at her, waiting for her to continue. "You have my gratitude, whether you want it or not," she joked.

The laughter that followed seemed to lighten the mood in the room. It stopped abruptly when she made her next statement. "Export International will cease operations in six months, and I will be going on an extended vacation."

There was stunned silence. They had known something was up with all the private meetings that Regina, Sigrid, and Garrett had been in constantly for the last week. This was from left field, and they were unsure of what to say or how to react.

Regina plunged ahead, trying to soothe their fears. "This doesn't mean I'm throwing you out on the streets. It simply means that we are all exhausted and need a breather. I'm tired of the corporate world and want to move on to something new. I wanted you to be the first to know of my decision and to explain your options."

"We stay with you," Paul interrupted defensively. "That's our option. We came together to protect you and the family. I, for one, don't want to give up either, unless you don't want me."

Regina and Sigrid smiled proudly. "Not want an old croc hunter like you around? Please," Sigrid said with a wink.

"Of course you're welcome to stay, Paul," Regina beamed. "That is one of the options. If you wish to stay by my side, I'd like nothing better."

Paul sat back, his choice made.

"But," Regina went on, "some of you may wish to resume your own lives, and I will not stand in your way or try to deter you. I am in your debt. You have saved my life on numerous occasions, and I want to repay that. If you choose to leave, I offer anything you need to get you on your way."

Sigrid knew that Shadow longed to return to California and reopen his martial arts school. He had been dating one of the secretaries at the company and although he wanted to remain available to the family when they needed him, he was anxious to start his own family. Sigrid had relayed that desire to Regina, and she subtly directed this option to him.

"The other option is a branch company in Chicago. It's a small, growing, and lucrative business we call Fabrick Industries. Garrett will assume the role of CEO, and Sigrid will be senior vice president in charge of entertainment. And she will be based in New York. If you desire, you can stay with her or work in one of the companies. No one has to decide right now. You have plenty of time to decide, and if you have other ideas or suggestions, I'm willing to listen. The time has come, as it does in all families, to leave the nest."

When no one said or asked anything, Regina thanked them for their time and adjourned the meeting.

The next evening Regina and Sigrid met for a late dinner at a small Greek restaurant on the outskirts of the city. At first they simply discussed the plans for shutting down and selling off the company. As they finished their meal and waited on dessert, their talk became more hushed and specific.

"Any options chosen yet," Sigrid questioned as the waiter refilled their wine glasses and vanished.

"Yes," Regina answered happily. "Shadow will be leaving in a few weeks for California. Paul and Silk will be staying with me. Paul as my bodyguard and Silk as my . . . uh . . . companion and assistant."

Sigrid nodded, pleased. "Good. I know you'll be safe with them."

"Safe," she laughed. "Sweetheart, Terrence is gone. The hunters have slacked off. For our kind, these are the safest times we've ever experienced."

Sigrid shrugged slightly and twirled her fork against her napkin. *Always the worrier*, Regina thought to herself. Sigrid had spent her entire life in some type of turmoil, and she knew the girl would never completely relax. But maybe as time passed, she could enjoy life more fully.

"What about Ty?" Regina prodded, changing the subject, hoping to get Sigrid's mind on more pleasant things.

"He wants to stay with me. We were thinking about maybe taking a month off and touring Europe," she smiled.

"That sounds like fun," Regina agreed. Then she noticed that Sigrid raised her head, started to speak, and then lower her head again. "What?"

Caught, Sigrid met her eyes. "I need . . . I need to ask you a special favor," she said hesitantly.

"Anything," Regina promised.

Glancing around the room, Sigrid made sure no one was listening or watching them. "Ty wants his birthright. As badly as I want to give it to him, Don says it's not possible."

Regina was seized with fear. "Why not? What have you kept from me, young lady?"

"The transformation altered me, that much you know. But it also changed my blood chemistry. Don has been checking and double checking ever since I got hurt. He says my blood has properties he's never seen before and because he can't be sure of what it might do to others, he advises against me bringing anyone over. I want you to give Ty his birthright."

Regina sighed, "I can't believe you kept this from me."

"There's nothing you could do, so why worry you with it," she answered calmly.

Shaking her head, Regina stared at the girl. No matter what the situation or how much Sigrid grew, in some ways she still remained shut off from others. Her first instinct was to launch into all the reasons she should have been told but decided it would do no good, and she didn't want to ruin their dinner. "What does Ty say? Is he okay with it?"

"He understands. We've discussed it thoroughly and we both agree that if I can't be the one, there is no one we'd rather take care of it than you. If you choose not to, he says he will remain mortal."

"Of course, I'll do it," she said louder than she meant to. Casting a quick look around the room, she lowered her head and her voice. "I just wish you had told me about this with Don."

Sigrid reached across the table and touched Regina's hand. "Can I be there when you bring him over, please."

Regina grasped her hand. "Of course, sweetheart. That was never in question."

A week later, Tyler Brandt was given his birthright and brought over. Sigrid stood by nervously watching in silence like a protective mother as Regina buried her fangs in his neck. The feeding and exchanging of blood was mechanical, neither Ty nor Regina showing any emotion, only performing the act. When the exchange was done, Regina excused herself and let Sigrid take over, leaving them alone to begin their new life.

The six months flew by and by the end of April, the inner sanctum disbanded and went their own ways. Garrett had left a month earlier to get the Chicago office up and running. Regina had expected to feel hesitant with a sense of loss as they all departed. Instead, she felt joy and was almost giddy with excitement.

Sigrid, on the other hand, felt excitement with an undercurrent of dread. She wanted to be on her own and knew the sanctum would be together again, but still she felt as if she were losing another family.

Regina had thrown them a lavish going-away party, and they all noticed how quiet Sigrid was at the end of the evening. When they exchanged hugs, she seemed to cling longer and harder to each of them.

Regina had understood and did all she could to alleviate some of the woman's uncertainty and had succeeded to a point. A week before her departure, Sigrid had begun acting more like herself. Shadow leaving several months prior had helped her learn to deal with the feelings.

When Shadow left, they all went with him to the airport to see him off. Regina presented him with the deed to the building that housed his martial arts school. "If you gotta work, be the boss," she instructed him with a smile.

Sigrid presented him with a black leather jacket emblazoned with his name and the yin and yang sign. In the pocket was a picture and when he looked at it, he saw the newly redecorated studio of his school.

He thanked them, blushing at all the attention and hugging everyone fiercely. He made each of them promise that they would stop by and visit him when they were in LA. After they said their final goodbyes, they watched him board the plane to California.

Now months later, the remaining sanctum ventured to the airport and prepared to go off in various directions.

Sigrid and Ty were off to Europe for a month, before spending a couple of weeks in Florida and then returning to Chicago.

Silk, Paul, and Regina were heading to Australia and then to all points around the globe. Paul and Ty left to check their bags, and Silk went to verify their reservations. Although it was an awkward way of leaving the two women alone, Sigrid and Regina appreciated the time. Leading Sigrid to a quiet corner, she found a place for them to sit out of the way.

"I'm going to miss you," Regina stated as she handed Sigrid a small black box. "Something to remember me by."

Sigrid hesitantly took the box. "I could never forget you," she groaned with a smile. For a brief instant, she flashed on her departure from Atlanta when Cameron had presented her with a box similar to this one.

Slowly she opened it and found a glittering gold nugget necklace with a small gold and diamond heart pendant. Carefully she removed it from the box and held it closer, for a better look. "Oh, Regina," she gasped, "it's beautiful."

"I'm glad you like it," she smiled proudly and helped her put it on.

"I love it," she gushed and hugged Regina tightly. "Thank you."

"That is my heart," Regina whispered in her ear. "As long as you possess it, I'll always be with you." They held one another for moment and then pulled apart as Regina continued. "We share a bond so strong, that even though the miles separate us, we will always be together."

"I agree." Sigrid smiled and she produced a small red box.

With a skeptical look, Regina accepted it. When she opened it, she found a woman's gold ring with a black onyx heart-shaped stone and single diamond in the center. "Now it's complete," Sigrid said as Regina admired the ring.

"Thank you, honey," she replied leaning forward and planting a kiss on her niece's cheek. Sigrid felt dampness on her skin and was surprised to see Regina crying.

"We're checked in, love, and the plane is boarding," Paul beamed as he approached them.

Regina slid the ring on her finger and wiped away the tears. Both women stood up and regained their composure.

Paul's face fell slightly. "Sorry, didn't mean to interrupt."

Sigrid waved her hand. "It's okay, Paul." Then she grabbed him and gave him a big bear hug. "I'm gonna miss you, you old croc hunter."

Paul laughed. "Yeah, life's going to be bloody dull from here on out."

"Take care of yourself and her," she added quietly in his ear.

"Count on it," he promised her.

Silk and Ty had rejoined them and after a very tearful goodbye, Paul, Silk, and Regina walked down the passageway leading to their plane.

Sigrid and Ty, their arms tight around each other, watched as the plane taxied down the runway and flew into the sky. Twenty minutes later, they boarded their own plane.

Sigrid lie in bed unconsciously toying with her gold necklace. The room was dark and silent except for Silk's soft snoring.

Quietly, she eased out of bed and went to the kitchen for a drink. She silently scolded herself for sleeping a full twenty-four hours. Not realizing how exhausted she was, once she had lain down, sleep had overpowered her. Although she would never admit it aloud, she did feel better than she had in a long while, but she still hated losing so much time.

She filled the glass with blood and ventured over to the balcony of the penthouse. Chicago was winding up for a full night of parties and crime, and as she looked out the window, she felt her senses come alive as the night crept in. Smiling, she remembered the dreams of her sleep.

During the two years before Regina's abduction, she and Ty had kept busy. Not only with the clubs, but she spent as much time as she could with Cameron and his new family as well. Cameron and Katie now had a daughter to join the Reynard clan, and she was her aunt Justine's pride and joy. Cameron had followed in his father's path and was now a successful writer, even owning his own successful supernatural bookstore.

When they returned to New York, they started with one small club. With Sigrid's touch, it had turned into three large and very prosperous clubs. She seemed to thrive as she put the clubs together, and Ty loved to sit back and watch her, her face aglow as she worked.

They were constantly scouting other clubs and taking notes. Disco, punk, rap, and grunge had all come and gone and come again. The people seemed younger and wilder, the drugs more predominant and stronger. Instead of bending to the current style, she modeled the clubs her way and apparently, there had been a large number of people waiting for the change.

She and Ty divided their time among all three clubs, but their favorite was a rooftop club in Manhattan. Sigrid decided to locate her offices in their Manhattan skyscraper and spent most of her time there. Garrett gave her free rein; other than monthly meetings and conference calls, they stayed in their respective cities.

Regina and her entourage managed to visit every six months or so, and it was after one of these visits, that she had been abducted.

A shiver seized Sigrid as she remembered the panicked phone call. It had been shortly after midnight before Garrett had been able to call.

Ty had taken her out for dinner and dancing to celebrate their third anniversary and they had just returned to the penthouse, ready to finish the evening with lovemaking, when the phone rang.

Ty huffed and answered it while Sigrid ventured into the bathroom to undress. She had just stepped out of her dress when he came into the bedroom, his face pale and grim. "Honey?" he called softly.

She stopped when she heard the tone of his voice. Fear crawled over her as she slowly turned to face him and saw his expression. "What's happened?"

"That was Garrett," he began. "There's been trouble in Chicago."

Sigrid's breathing quickened and she struggled to maintain her composure. The only sign that she was failing was her shaky voice. "What kind of trouble?"

He shifted his weight from one side to the other, trying to think of the most gentle way to deliver the news. "There's a jet waiting for us at Newark International." He hesitated slightly then continued. "Regina was abducted tonight. Silk is badly hurt and Paul . . . is dead."

She was frozen in place. She didn't move at all, not speaking or even breathing. He was about to take a step forward when she became animated again and without a word began to dress and then pack a bag. Following her lead, Ty packed a small bag and forty minutes later they were on a jet bound for Chicago.

Once they were airborne, she asked him for the details, and Ty gave her what little he knew. She listened patiently, staring out the window and toying with the necklace she had received from Regina. "If he hurts her, I'll eat his heart," she growled as her eyes glowed red.

Ty felt his own anger building, but he was also startled by the fury in her voice and posture. He knew who she meant but still asked, "Who?"

"Terrence," she answered through clenched fangs.

A voice brought Sigrid out of her daze as she continued to face the window.

"Sigrid, are you all right?" Silk softly asked as she approached. She was unnerved when Sigrid turned around to face her and she saw the red glow of her sister's eyes.

Instantly, Sigrid was aware of the change and closed her eyes, willing it back. "Sorry," she mumbled in a tense voice.

After a few seconds, she opened her eyes and they were again their normal shade of blue. "Just remembering some unpleasant things," she explained.

Silk, displaying strength that had been absent for the last few months, continued toward Sigrid and wrapped her arms around her. Sigrid was stiff for a split second and then relaxed into the embrace. Silk ran her hands through her sister's short hair, her voice comforting. "Why do you always have to be the strong one, Sigrid? You're the one that we come to for reassurance or comfort, but you always close us out when you're hurting. Have you ever gone to anyone in your time of need? Has anyone ever known when you needed the comforting?"

Sigrid's voice quavered, "Regina."

Silk pulled her in tighter, placing a kiss on her head, "Let go, Sig. For once, just be the one that needs reassurance. I promise I won't let you fall."

She knew she had succeeded when she felt Sigrid's body begin to quake as long-held tears finally emerged.

Several hours later, the sisters ventured downstairs to Garrett's office. Garrett and Ty juggled incoming calls and intelligence reports, with Ty marking each sighting of Terrence or his people on a large wall map of the country. Both looked up and smiled when they saw the two women, rested and more like their old selves.

"Feel better?" Ty asked as he kissed Sigrid hello.

"Much," she smiled. "Now you need to rest." She looked at Garrett. "That goes for you too."

Garrett raised an eyebrow at her and went back to his phone call. Ty shrugged and wrapped his arm around her. "I will." He saw the cynical look and ducked his head in surrender, dropping his arms to his side. "I promise."

"Any news yet?" Silk questioned, as she began scanning the map.

"No," Ty answered. "We've stepped up the search and if she's in the States, we'll find her."

Sigrid eased over to Garrett's desk and sat on the corner of it, watching his work. He looked up at her and then cut his eyes to Silk, who was helping Ty mark the map. "You were successful?"

"Yeah," Sigrid agreed and then licked her lips nervously. "Uh . . . Garrett, there's something I need to tell you. It's something that you should have known a while ago."

Garrett's face darkened, "What?"

She hummed and hawed for a second and then forged ahead. "Terrence fathered two children," she said bluntly and laid the diary on his desk, inconspicuously covering the papers he was working on. "It's all in there. I've already double checked and verified everything."

Garrett eyes were wide in surprise and anger. "How long have you known this? How could you keep something of this magnitude to yourself? This child could be a danger to us, and we need to be prepared."

"I don't think so," she sighed.

Garrett sat forward, leaning closer to her. "You have discovered the child's identity?"

Sigrid smiled and motioned over her shoulder to Silk.

"Silk?" he gasped lowly. "That's not possible."

"It is," she finished as Silk and Ty approached them.

Garrett stared at the redhead, not even trying to conceal his shock and anger at the new situation.

Ty put his hand on Sigrid's shoulder. "You told him?"

Silk's insecurity and unease were apparent as Garrett continued staring. Sigrid reached back and put a bracing hand on her arm. "Garrett," she scolded mildly, "It's not polite to stare."

Snapping out of his trance, he rose to his feet directing his glare at Sigrid, his face contorted with anger. "How dare you! You bloody little . . ." He stopped there when Ty moved closer, ready to defend his mate if one more word was uttered.

Swallowing his words, he clenched his teeth and continued. "You should have notified us the minute you got this information. You have no idea how this might affect things. And Regina. I can't believe you kept this from us. You had no right—"

Now it was Sigrid who moved in to defend herself. Her face was stoic and harsh and Garrett was forced a step back when he saw Terrence clearly etched in the young woman's features. "Right?" she repeated in a low, grave voice. "I think you forget to whom you're speaking. I have every right, and you'll not address me like that again. I am an adult and an immortal, and I will do what I think is right for this family. Neither you nor anybody else will dictate my actions."

An icy cold seemed to float over the room. Ty and Silk were just as taken aback as Garrett by the stance Sigrid assumed. Concerned, Ty moved closer to her and gently touched her waist. The action seemed to lull her into a calmer state and her features softened slightly. Once again, she was the Sigrid they all knew and respected.

As the haze of anger faded, Sigrid took a calming breath. Of course she understood Garrett's anger, but she couldn't understand why her own anger had flared so quickly, especially at the gentle British man. "It was a judgment call," she began more softly. "And it was wrong. I understand that I should have told you and Regina the minute I found out. I've only known for a few months after all the trouble with Terrence and Seth's death. There was so much going on, and I just never made the time. It was never my intention to wait this long, and I apologize to you and Silk."

Garrett relaxed a bit and sat back down. He said nothing, only nodded his acceptance of her apology.

"You know," Ty jumped in, "it was fortunate that we were the only ones who did know."

Their eyes fell on him, curious about his statement. He looked at them expectantly. "Had this been common knowledge, I seriously doubt Silk would have escaped with her life or she might have been taken as well."

Garrett exhaled a deep breath, reluctantly admitting it was true. "You're right." He calmed even more and his voice returned to its normal pitch. "She probably wouldn't be here now if it were known, but you still shouldn't have kept this from us."

Sigrid looked directly into his eyes. "I know and I'm sorry." She looked at Ty and winked her thanks to him. "There is a positive side to all this, though. I have a blood sibling, something I've always wanted and now we have an ace in the hole."

Silk, who had remained quiet while the debate had raged now spoke up, her face crinkling with confusion. "I'm an ace in the hole?"

Ty piped in, "Terrence fathered two children. One he knows about and one he doesn't. I'd say that could be a definite advantage somewhere down the line."

Garrett and Silk instantaneously realized he was right, and their faces lightened as he continued. "And Sigrid has something she always wanted, a sister, family, and I for one am glad that she has gained that instead of lost someone. I think you're past due for some good news, babe."

Sigrid and Silk smiled their thanks at his statement and chuckled when he added. "But don't you dare be discussing me behind my back. I know how sisters are."

Before they could address his statement, the phone began buzzing, causing all of them to fall silent and serious.

Knowing that the call had already been cleared and deemed important through his secretary, Garrett picked up the receiver. "Fabrick Industries, Garrett speaking." He listened for a moment and then handed the phone to Sigrid. "It's for you."

She quickly took the phone. "Hello." After a few seconds, she said, "Wait a minute. I want to put you on speaker." She reached over Garrett's desk and hit the speaker button before returning the phone to his desk. "Okay, Cam, you're on."

His voice was loud and firm as he began. "I did some checking among the network, and I came across one odd bit of information. I don't know if it's what you're looking for or not, but I thought I'd let you know."

"Anything you have might help, Cam," she responded hopefully.

"All right," he said and continued. "One of our guys in Huntsville, Alabama, came across a flyer for one of those traveling carnivals. You know the type, the ones that are more rip off than anything else, and travels to the smaller towns across the South. Well, anyway, this flyer advertised a freak show that claimed to boast a wild vampire woman. He didn't bother to check it out because he figured it was a hoax. Some woman with fake fangs and a cape trying to scare the kids. As I said, I don't know if it's anything you can use but I wanted to pass it on."

"Can you get a copy of the flyer?" Ty questioned.

"Oh, hello, Ty," Cameron greeted, "Yeah, as a matter of fact, I had Jake fax one to me. I can fax it or scan it to you if you like."

Garrett quickly called out the fax number and within minutes he was holding a copy of it as well. It was a rough copy because of the cheapness of the flyer and the number of times it had been faxed, but the name of the carnival was clear.

"Thanks, Cam. I really appreciate your help," Sigrid responded as she glanced at the flyer in Garrett's hand.

"I just hope it helps," he answered. "I hope you find her soon, and I'll keep checking to see what else I can find."

"Love you, big brother," she smiled. "Tell Katie I said 'hi' and give my niece a kiss for me."

She could hear his smile through the phone lines. "Back at you, sis, and will do. Just keep me posted and I'll call if I get anything else."

Loudly, she blew him a kiss. "Will do," she mimicked. "Thanks again."

"Bye," he replied, and the line went dead.

Ty shut off the speaker and saw Garrett looking at Sigrid.

"I decided to try some outside sources," she answered his unasked question. "Our forces were at a standstill. I thought outside the box."

Deciding against raising her wrath again, he nodded and went back to studying the flyer. "The last date on this thing was two weeks ago in Albertville, Alabama. I'll make some calls and have our people pick up the trail and check it out."

"I'll make the travel arrangements," Sigrid volunteered and headed for the door.

"Wait," Garrett called to stop her. "This may turn out to be a wild-goose chase. Cameron was probably right about it being a hoax."

"That's what he wants us to think," Sigrid countered. "That's why it would be the perfect place to hide her. Not even the hunters were interested in checking it out."

Exhaustion was wearing on Garrett's nerves. "Good point. If it is something, we cannot go swooping down on these people. Terrence may be keeping an eye on them, and if he thinks for a second we've found her, we could lose her. Please, Sigrid," he begged firmly, "I know what I'm doing. Trust me."

She exhaled deeply and stared at the burgundy carpeting. "All right," she conceded. "You get things rolling and then I want you and Ty to get some rest. We need everyone on their toes, just in case."

Garrett smiled his thanks and agreement, then watched her leave the office. When she closed the door and he sensed she was moving away, he looked at Ty and Silk. "I need one of you to help me here and one of you to keep a rein on her."

Silk was in no hurry to spark her sister's temper. "I'll stay here and help," she spoke first.

Ty lowered his eyes, letting her know that he was in no hurry to face off with Sigrid either. "Fine," he sighed deeply and went after her.

They received confirmation twenty-four hours later. Garrett had managed to track down LePope's Traveling Carnival to a small town in Alabama called Fort Payne. It was scheduled to next move to a little town in Georgia called Trenton.

Allen Davies, a family member and an Alabama attorney, had investigated the tip and reported that he was almost certain the wild vampire woman was Regina, but not the Regina they knew. His description of her had frozen the blood in Garrett's veins.

The plan of action was an offer to buy the carnival from its owner, Frank "Bubba" LePope. Allen's inquires had proven that LePope was receptive and was not likely in with Terrence. His lack of intelligence and greed had simply made him a suitable outlet for Terrence's plans. Now the parties Allen represented were going to come down and look over the carnival. If they liked what they saw, the contracts would be signed, and a deal made.

Garrett had been beaten to the punch by Silk, who set up all the travel arrangements, and Sigrid personally picked who would accompany them. He decided not to argue with the older woman. Her mood as of late had not been the best and for the first time, Garrett began to understand what Regina had meant by being slightly frightened of the power emanating from the young heiress.

Sigrid remained eerily silent during the plane trip and car ride to the open field where the carnival had slung its tents. The group could feel her power encompassing them as they reached their destination and climbed out of the rented Mercury Sable van.

The carnival had been shut down for over an hour and the grounds were rapidly emptying. Townsfolk had gone home, their pockets and spirits lighter, gorged on popcorn, corn dogs, cotton candy, and watered-down beer. A few hang abouts still roamed the darkened grounds, but as Sigrid and her group walked by, they seemed to sense a storm coming and left the area. The midway was deserted as the carnies adjourned to their trailers and the local hotels for the night.

The carnival was set up in a large flat field that was several miles from what passed as the center of town. As they walked through the trampled grass, they were bombarded with the smells of grease, burnt food, sweat, urine, and cow dung.

The tents along the way were faded and tattered and smelled of mold. The only sounds this later were distant tree frogs and an occasional moo from the nearby cattle. Finally making their way to the small trailer placed off to the side of the main tent, they found their contact waiting. Allen stood still, hands firmly holding his briefcase and scanning the area as he waited. He stopped his look-see when he felt the power approaching him.

He stared down the midway and with his keen eyesight saw the approaching party. Garrett was leading the way followed closely by Sigrid, Ty, Silk, Martha, Billy, and two other men from the family.

"Allen," Garrett greeted as they met and shook hands.

He smiled at all of them and nodded his respect to Sigrid. "Good to see you again, Garrett," he replied warmly.

"Everything set up?" Garrett questioned, feeling Sigrid's impatience just as everyone else in the group did.

"Yes," Allen responded, and he sidestepped, motioning down the midway. "We're supposed to meet LePope outside the Freak tent, per your instructions."

Garrett held his ground but mimicked the motioning gesture. "Lead the way, counselor."

Bubba LePope was seething with anger. He didn't like to have his fun and pleasure interrupted and that's exactly what was happening.

LePope was a big man, easily almost three hundred pounds lined his five-foot-nine-inch frame. His bald head had a slight patch of greasy black hair around the rim, and his face was jowled and covered with beard stubble. His eyes were black and ratlike, and he had the annoying habit of sucking his teeth. The odor of sweat and cheap booze surrounded him, and he fancied bright polyester clothes. Because of his abundant girth, he had problems walking and always carried a cane to aid him, a cane that served many purposes including beating and teasing anyone who could amuse him. His new object of pleasure was the wild vampire woman.

"Come on, sweetheart, show me your fangs," he taunted as he jabbed the cane through the cage bars, laughing when he managed a hit that caused a whimper or growl.

The small ragged figure cowered against the far side of the bars, hugging the cage wall in an effort to escape the offending pain giver.

Tiny Tony, the freak show dwarf, had taken all he could. "Please, Mr. LePope. She's not feeling well and you're hurting her."

LePope stopped his poking and withdrew the cane, leaving the cowering woman to her misery. He turned around and slowly looked at the source of interruption.

Tony was a middle-aged man just under four feet tall. He was perfectly formed, except for a shorter, slightly deformed left arm. His face was lined and reflected the hard life he had led, but a closer look revealed that a current of kindness and gentleness flowed through the little man.

"Hurting her?" LePope repeated, sucking his teeth for emphasis. He took a wobbly step toward Tony, drumming his fingers on the cane handle. "Little man, you have a big mouth."

Tony backed away, knowing he was asking for trouble by interfering one of LePope's play sessions, but he also knew he couldn't let it continue. "Please sir, I don't want any trouble."

LePope grinned, sweat dripping from his thick lips as he raised the cane above his head. "I'll give you trouble," he responded as he brought the cane down on Tony's shoulder.

With his weight behind the hit, Tony was knocked to the ground, his shoulder sending out flares of pain. Gritting his teeth in an effort to block out the throbbing shoulder, he started scooting away from the big man.

"Look at the scampering little crab man." LePope laughed and brought the cane down again, this time tearing a gash across Tony's forehead and drawing blood. "What a great idea. Tony the Crab Man," he smirked and continued after the escaping man.

Stars dotted Tony's vision as he finally reached the side of the tent and wasted no time scooting under the flap. He quickly glanced around for help or another way of escape on the deserted midway but saw only darkness.

"Where you going, little man?" LePope's voice thundered as he came through the tent flap into the night air. "We're just getting started."

Tony flinched when he saw the cane rise into the air again. With nowhere else to go, he simply closed his eyes and braced for the next hit.

A hand shot out of the darkness and seized LePope's meaty wrist in midair. His thick wrist felt like it had been put into a vice and he whirled around, aching for a fight with anyone that would dare interrupt his pleasure again.

His ire vanished and his face fell when he saw the woman restraining his arm. She was a small figure, but stronger than she looked. Dressed in a black jumpsuit with curly brown hair lining her face, he unconsciously licked his lips as he leered at her.

"Mr. LePope," Allen interjected as Bubba continued to ogle Sigrid and feel the beginning of activity in his pants. "This is Beverly Tapps, the party I represent," Allen finished, his tone bordering on anger and disgust.

Sigrid released his arm and stepped back, her face cold and empty and eerily resembling Terrence even more.

LePope's greasy demeanor slipped into gear. He laughed nervously and rubbed the top of his bald head. "Sorry you had to see that. You know how employees can be."

Ty had moved over to Tony and was helping him to his feet. LePope shot Tony a warning glance and then resumed smiling. "It's nice to meet you, Ms. Tapps," he greeted and extended a beefy hand.

Garrett quickly intercepted it. "I'm Mr. Hodges, Ms. Tapps's business manager. If there's somewhere we can go, Mr. Allen, you and I can discuss our business arrangement."

"Yeah, sure." LePope grinned, already thinking of ways to spend the amount these suckers were offering. "We can go to my office. Right this way." He threw his head in the direction of the trailer and began shuffling toward it.

"I'd like to look around, while you discuss business," Sigrid said flatly.

Uncertainty crossed LePope's face, but he didn't want to risk offending the money people. "Sure, ain't much to see in the dark though. You should see this place when it's up and running. She's a moneymaker, I tell you."

Sigrid tried to offer a polite smile, but it looked more like a sneer. "I'm sure."

LePope cast a final wary glance at Tony and then led the way to the trailer. Garrett and Allen smiled broadly and followed him down the darkened midway.

Sigrid watched the fat man disappear and then turned her attention to Tony. Her face softened instantly as she neared the man. She produced a handkerchief from her jacket and offered it to him.

He waved it away and smiled shyly. "No, thank you, ma'am. I wouldn't want to ruin your hanky."

Sigrid smiled warmly and kneeled down beside the man. Gently she began dabbing at the cut on his head, her touch as soft as a feather. "You're more important than a piece of cloth. Are you all right?"

Tony shifted uncomfortably. He was not used to being treated so nicely, especially by a stranger or townie. The usual reaction he got were laughs, jokes, and disgust. "I'm fine, ma'am," he said unsurely.

Sigrid picked up on his unease and ceased her ministrations. She handed him the hanky and introduced herself. "My name is Sigrid."

Despite his initial hesitation, he got the feeling that she was a sincere person and now returned her smile more fully. "My name is Tony Duescht. They call me Tiny Tony and I'm at your service."

Her attention focused on him, she extended her hand and gave his hand a squeeze as they shook. "It's a pleasure to meet you, Tony. Would you do us the honor of a tour?"

"Sure," he answered and began scanning the area. "Where would you like to begin?"

Sigrid shrugged and looked at the other family members. "How about where you work?"

Tony laughed, surprised. "You mean the Freak tent?"

Sigrid became serious and for a moment Tony thought he had insulted the woman. Her returning smile put him at ease as she answered, "I don't like that term. Let's call it the *unique* tent."

Tony liked her statement and considered it a compliment. His chest swelled up with pride, the throbbing of his shoulder and forehead forgotten as he pulled the tent flap back and motioned for her and the others to enter. "After you, my lady."

The two men with them took up positions outside as they filed into the tent. Greeted by a large banner across the entrance that read: 'FREAKS OF NATURE AND MANKIND', her first instinct was to rip the sign down and tear it to shreds, but she swallowed the urge. The group spread out once they were inside the medium-sized tent and looked around, their eyes falling on six separate sections. Each section had a chair and platform and old faded banners announced the occupants of the roped off square. An old tattered piece of rope was strung in front of the exhibits to keep marks away from the occupants.

Tony led them to the left, where a sign announced this was the home of Tiny Tony, World's smallest man. The other signs boasted similar claims. Stanley, the snake man; Big Bertha, the world's fattest woman; Howie, the human pinhead and Gordon, the glass eater. In the far right corner, they saw a curtained off section with a sign bearing "Wild Vampire Woman in captivity."

Sigrid moved toward that section, half hearing what Tony was saying as he tried to intercept her. "The others have gone to sleep," he tried to dissuade her and finally got bold enough to grasp her hand. Sigrid stopped and looked down at him as he lightly tugged her hand. "There are other tents that are really more interesting."

She turned her gaze back to the blocking curtain. "What's back there?" she questioned.

Tony was clearly nervous now, as his voice began to rise and fall, "Uh . . . well . . . it's just Maggie, but she's not well and we really shouldn't bother her," he almost begged.

Sigrid frowned, "Maggie?"

Tony shrugged. "Well, that's what I call her. Mr. LePope got her about a month ago from a real seedy character. She's mute and I don't think quite right, you know, mentally. She was kinda sick when she got here, and she's getting worse."

Silk and Ty exchanged worried glances and for the first time, Martha spoke up. "Has LePope tried to get her a doctor or some help?"

Tony's face reddened, embarrassed. "No, ma'am." He looked back at Sigrid. "You see how he is with his employees. I've been trying to look out for her, and since she didn't have a name when she got here, I've been calling her Maggie."

Sigrid picked up on the images of what had happened before their arrival. "Is that why LePope was after you when we came? You were trying to protect her?"

His silence was the only answer they needed. The others watched as she squatted down to face Tony. "You've been looking out for her?"

Looking into those blue eyes calmed his nerves, and he knew he had nothing to fear from this woman. "Well, I bring her food, although she doesn't eat much. I got her some clothes when she first got here. The things she was wearing were filthy and if LePope had his way, she'd be nude. I can tell she's not feeling well, so I try to talk to her, sometimes just a kind voice will calm her down. She lets me closer than anybody else so I do all that I can. We uniques have to look out for one another."

"I want to see her," Sigrid stated as she stood up, her face tight and edged with anger. Before he could speak another word, she walked to the curtain and disappeared behind it.

Tony's face wrinkled with worry, and he took a few steps to follow, unwilling to let anyone hurt his friend Maggie. He watched as the older woman with them followed Sigrid, and now he did walk toward the curtain.

Ty intercepted him and patted his uninjured shoulder. "Don't worry, Tony. She won't hurt her. If she's sick, Sigrid will get her the help she needs," he reassured.

The area behind the curtain was small and dark. A soft light from above cast the room in shadows, but that made no matter to Sigrid and Martha. At the center of the area was a large cage, the same old wooden kind used in the old days of circuses for animals to travel in. Huge wooden wheels were mounted on each corner, and thick newer metal bars lined the cage completely.

The lodgings were cramped, only a little over eight feet by five feet by five feet high. As she neared, Sigrid winced at the smell emanating from the cage. Although the light was dim, she could clearly make out a small shape cowering in the back of the cage.

Martha stayed right behind her as she approached the cage and firmly grasped the bars, peering in at the occupant.

The woman was small, almost childlike, and so skinny that her bones were visible. Her black hair was matted and filthy, concealing the face from view.

"Regina?" she called in a soft voice, hands shaking on the bars.

She received only a grunt as an answer.

Clenching her teeth, Sigrid concentrated her thoughts toward the trembling figure. Without warning, the woman leapt at the bars. Fangs bared and growling.

Martha and Sigrid gasped in unison when they got a clear view of Regina's once beautiful face. She had been beaten often, that much was clear, but her eyes were wild and feral, showing not a glimmer of humanity.

Her face was dirty and hollow, spittle running down her snarling mouth and gleaming on her chin. Her beautiful brown eyes were glowing red and bloodshot and confused. They reflected no sign of recognition of the two women before her. With a final threatening grunt, she withdrew to the farthest corner of the cage, sniffing at them and then curling into a ball.

Both women were silent and stunned. Martha moved up to Sigrid and placed her hands on the woman's shoulders. "Follow the plan, Sigrid."

But Sigrid held tight, her anger radiating off her until the bars of the cage became warm with heat. The woman in the cage, reacting to the change, drew into a tighter ball.

Martha moved in even closer, feeling the heat emanating from the young woman. "Honey, you're frightening her."

That snapped Sigrid out of her trance and she reluctantly let go of the bars, bars that were now bent and red-hot to the touch. Martha pulled her a few steps back and forced her to meet her own eyes. "We have to keep our heads and tempers," she instructed, battling to control her own raging emotions.

Sigrid nodded. "Keep the others out of here. I don't want them to see her like this."

Martha moved to keep watch on the curtained doorway. Turning, she watched silently as Sigrid found the cage door and crushed the lock into metal powder.

As the door creaked open, Regina assumed a crouching position and bared her fangs. Ever so slowly, Sigrid eased into the cage, stifling the urge to cough as the smell of urine, feces, and filth assaulted her heightened senses. She held her place at the entrance, giving Regina a chance to calm down from the intrusion.

Regina continued a weakened growl as Sigrid inched farther into the cage, hunching down to fit in and seem smaller to the threatened woman. "Regina?" she called soothingly. "It's me, Sigrid. You're safe now. I won't let anyone hurt you."

Regina cocked her head slightly sideways at the sound of Sigrid's voice but still maintained her defensive posture. Her weakened state didn't make her seem very threatening, and Sigrid felt her heart begin to crumble.

"I'm going to take you home," she continued as she stopped a few feet away from Regina's quivering figure. She moved her head, trying to lock her eyes onto Regina's, when suddenly Regina lashed out, dragging ragged sharp nails across Sigrid's face. Leaving four bloody trails across the side of her face.

Sigrid never faltered. She remained still, even as Regina retreated to her corner and sucked the blood-covered fingers like a starving animal.

Martha took a few steps forward, but Sigrid raised her hand in a halting motion. The older woman stared as Sigrid bared her own fangs and closely watched Regina's reaction.

Regina stopped her sucking motions, slowly pulling her fingers from her mouth.

"Sigrid," Sigrid growled her own name, trying to elicit something, anything familiar in Regina's eyes.

For the first time, Regina showed a small glimmer of recognition, then it was gone.

"Sleep," Sigrid ordered in whisper, as she hypnotized the small battered woman. "Rest."

Regina's eyes began to droop and with a final flex of her power, Regina collapsed unconscious.

Sigrid leaned forward and gently brushed the wild, dirty hair from Regina's sleeping face. "You're safe now," she soothed, tears welling in her eyes as her heart broke.

Martha called for Billy and Ty as Sigrid carefully scooped Regina's form into her arms and eased out of the cage.

Martha was waiting with a blanket and was in process of wrapping her up, when the two men appeared, and both clenched their teeth when they saw the form in Sigrid's arms. Quickly they made sure the blanket was tucked in and with some force, took her from Sigrid's shaking arms.

With pure love, Sigrid looked at Regina's still face and caressed her cheek. "Take her to the van. Martha and Billy, please stay with her. Ty, I need you here."

Martha looked at her, knowing and sensing the turmoil that raged in Sigrid. She craved to hold the young woman and comfort her, but she knew this was the final straw, and Sigrid was no longer the little girl and innocent one she once was. Silently she recited an old English prayer, asking that the change work out for the better and that Sigrid would not completely become her father's daughter.

With that, Billy and Martha left through the back-tent flap, Sigrid watching them carry her beloved Regina into the darkness. After they were gone, she took a few deep breaths, trying to regain her composure. Ty hovered nearby and as she met his eyes, she felt a calming breeze try to brush her soul. She allowed a bit of it in but then pushed the rest aside, the pain settling in like a comforting friend. She nodded at him and headed back into the main tent, Ty close behind.

Silk's face registered shock and concern when she saw her sister emerge, bloody scratches down her face and a look of anguish covering her features. She took a step forward and saw Ty nod "no." Then she felt the vibes coming off Sigrid and decided to hold her place and tongue.

Sigrid walked straight to Tony and kneeled down in front of him. He looked at her with piercing green eyes that were wide with surprise. Weakly, he handed her the hanky she had given him. "I think you need this now. Don't be angry with Maggie, she's sick."

"Do you believe what that sign says?" she asked, gesturing to the Wild Vampire Woman sign.

Tony took a deep breath and thought for a moment. He met her eyes and shrugged. "I've seen a lot of unusual things and unique people in my life. I have no reason to doubt vampires exist."

Sigrid exhaled deeply and smiled. "I don't have much time, Tony, but I do owe you an explanation."

"Explanation for what?" he asked.

"Three months ago," she began, "My aunt was abducted by a very evil man. She is the head of our family, and we have been looking for her all this time. Tonight, in this place, we found her. The woman that you've been caring for and calling Maggie, is my aunt Regina. The man that took her has hurt her terribly, and we are going to take her home now."

"Are you a vampire too?" he asked bravely, but involuntarily took a step back.

"You have nothing to fear from us, Tony," she replied, her voice tight with anguish. "We are like you, unique. People make up stories to cover their fear and ignorance, but as you said, we uniques look out for one another. You cared for my aunt and tried to protect her from LePope. You took good care of her and I am forever in your debt. Your service will not go unrewarded."

Tony shook his head. "I don't need no reward. I did what any decent person would. I only wish I could have helped her more."

"How long have you been with the carnival, Tony?"

He was caught off guard by the question and did a double take before stammering an answer. "Uh, well . . . about thirty years. My parents came to the States from Germany when I was about thirteen. They got a job here in the sideshow. It was Granger's Traveling Carnival of Wonders then, and Mr. Granger was the greatest. He treated us like normal people and family. He died about five years ago. And that's when LePope took over."

Sigrid dabbed at the slits in her cheek and then tucked the hanky in her pocket. "I have every intention of buying this carnival, Tony, and I'd like you to help run it. I'm sure you know more about the business than any of us."

Tony was smiling broadly; it was a dream come true for him. "What about LePope?"

Her eyes took on a slight reddish tint. "Don't worry about him. I'll take care of him." Sensing Ty moving behind her, she pulled back her "change" and continued. "One of the men with us will stay here with you and explain in greater detail, but as of this moment, you are considered a member of our family."

Tony blushed from the attention and the action. He extended his hand and nodded as Sigrid accepted it. "I'm honored and will do my best to make this carnival a success for you."

"I don't doubt it for a minute, my friend," she replied and stood up. Ty leaned in and whispered something to her.

"We have to go now, but I'll be seeing you again," she remarked after she received the message.

He walked them to the entrance of the tent. "I hope Maggie . . . I mean your aunt is okay. I look forward to seeing you again and thank you."

She patted his shoulder, "No, thank you." She corrected and led the remaining entourage outside.

The two guards waiting outside fell in behind them as they proceeded to the trailer LePope used as an office.

Allen and Garrett were waiting outside and moved to intercept them as they approached. "Did you find her? Is she okay?"

Sigrid nodded. "She's safe. Martha and Billy took her to the van. Garrett, you should be with her."

Without argument or hesitation, he flew down the midway. She looked at Allen expectantly and he complied. "LePope was easy to play. He signed the papers and the carnival now belongs to Tapps Enterprises. He's a big, nasty man."

"We'll take care of that," she grinned sinisterly. "Allen, I want to keep the carnival. I want Tony, the little man we met to become a partner, and I'd appreciate it if you could stay here and help him get all the details rolling."

"Done," he replied.

Now she directed her look to the two muscle men with them. "Please keep watch outside. When I'm done, you can begin your cleanup."

"I'm coming with you," Ty stated, not bothering to ask her consent.

"Me too," Silk piped in.

Sigrid raised an eyebrow and watched them for a second. Nodding, she led the way to LePope's office.

The sales agreement had been dated a week earlier than its actual date and Frank "Bubba" LePope had, according to the police reports, been on his way to Florida to start a new life with his profits.

Unfortunately, his celebration consisted of drinking and driving, and when the police found the wrecked car that had exploded on impact, the only thing left of Bubba LePope was a pile of ashes.

The cleaners had been hard pressed to come up with even that much by the time Sigrid was done with LePope. Even Ty and Silk, as angry as they were, were startled at the ferocity Sigrid had released on the fat man. True, he had deserved what he got, but not only had her attack been brutal, she had laughed with glee as she ripped him to shreds and stomped on the pieces. Ty and Silk had started out helping, but when the attack became more violent and frenzied, they had stepped back, wary of their leader.

As the police wrapped up the incident, they ruled it a DUI fatal car accident. The family ruled it justice, and it was a conclusion with which Sigrid happily agreed.

Allen had secured a large house on thirty secluded acres of Lookout Mountain as a temporary sanctuary. Before they arrived, Ty and Garrett had made sure that there was plenty of security, and they were double checking it the minute they reached the house.

Billy and George prepared Regina's room, while Silk, Martha, and Sigrid bathed and cleaned up the injured woman.

As they tenderly scrubbed her delicate flesh, they noticed how dangerously thin she was. Patches of bruises and scratches covered her from head to toe, the sight causing Martha and Silk to weep silent tears as they cleaned the dirt and filth from her translucent skin.

Sigrid showed no emotion as she helped them. Other than the anger and pleasure she had openly displayed while dealing with LePope, she seemed to cut off all other emotional signs.

Don and another family doctor arrived a short time later, just as they were tucking the unconscious woman into bed. The doctors immediately ordered the women out so they could examine their patient and, reluctantly, they complied.

The house was a large two-story A-frame with minimal but comfortable furnishings. Thick, lush forest surrounded them on all sides but one, and it revealed a large lake complete with ducks and fish. The living room walls were clear glass and gave the room a bright airy feel as if being out in the woods, amongst nature.

Ty and Garrett had set out drinks for everyone on the oak coffee table and were sitting on the large beige sectional sofa, waiting for news of Regina's condition.

"You need to take care of those scratches," Garrett replied offhandedly as the three banished women joined them in the living room.

Automatically, Sigrid stopped, turned and headed to the bathroom, leaving Silk and Martha as they took their seats on the couch.

"I'm worried about her," Silk spoke aloud the thought they had all mulled over.

"Me too," Martha and Ty replied in unison.

"Give her time," Garrett suggested and then fell silent as Sigrid came back into the living room.

With the dried blood and the remainder of LePope's blood gone, the already healing scratches were barely noticeable. She bent down and picked up a glass, downed the contents, and then plopped down on the couch beside Ty.

He casually put his arm around her shoulder and smiled when she ever so slightly rested against him.

Garrett, ever the diplomat, sat up and looked at each of them, their faces and body language a range of emotions, except for Sigrid. "I know she looks bad," he began softly, "but we do have her back. I want you all to keep that in mind. She's home again."

"What did he do to her to make her like that?" Martha asked aloud.

Garrett sighed, trying to keep his imagination and pain at bay. "I don't want to think about what he did to break her spirit."

"Her spirit is not broken," Sigrid corrected firmly and in a tone that warned off disagreement. "Her body is injured, but her spirit is intact. Wandering and lost but still intact."

"Sigrid," Garrett began, trying his best not to sound condescending. "With all due respect, you are still a babe among immortals. Martha and I have been around long enough to recognize when someone has reverted and that's exactly what's happened to Regina."

"What do you mean reverted?" she asked, leaning forward.

Martha took over. "We are strong, but even we have our limits. I know you've heard stories about children who endure such horror and pain that they develop other personalities to deal with those traumas. Reversion is similar to that. We are stronger than mortals, but even we can be subjected to things beyond our limits."

"Even you," Garrett again spoke, "experienced reversion. The night Terrence almost killed you, you transformed into . . . well . . . pardon my bluntness, an animal."

"So she'll recover in time?" Silk asked hopefully.

Garrett and Martha remained silent.

Sigrid cocked her head sideways. "I did, so why won't she?"

Garrett glanced at Martha and she motioned for him to continue. "Reversion is an extremely rare occurrence among immortals. When it happens, as in your case, a response to pain, it is sudden and fast. The stimuli occurred and when it was gone, you returned to normal. But imagine if those feelings were continuous. Every minute of every day for weeks. Seeing and feeling such horror, that you would do anything to be free of it. For immortals, they resort to their base nature, a wild animalistic state."

Ty's voice was clear and firm as he spoke for the first time. "Can it be reversed? Now that she's home and safe, can we bring her out of it?"

Garrett's head dropped and Martha simply nodded, "No."

Sigrid jumped off the couch, emotion returning with gusto. "I do not accept that!" Her voice and face were indignant. "I may be a 'babe' among immortals, but I'm willing to try anything, whereas, everyone else seems to just want to sit on their asses and take this."

"Well, you're going to have to take this," Don's familiar voice rang out as he joined them, "Reversion is not the problem. Regina has also been poisoned and she's dying."

"Poisoned?" Silk almost shouted. "How the hell do you poison a vampire?"

Don put his hands on his hips, his eyes reflecting the sorrow and helplessness he felt. "By giving them blood that's been tainted with silver and dead blood. Just mix a single drop of either one, and *poof*, you have a poison for immortals." He took a few steps closer, lowering his voice. "It's slow, painful, and deadly. There's nothing we can do to stop it. I don't think she has more than a few days left, at most. I'm sorry."

Martha and Silk began crying. Then Garrett's strong, controlled façade crumbled, and he too wept.

Sigrid stared at him, Ty keeping his place behind her, but making no move toward her. Don stepped over to her, but she moved away and bared her fangs in warning.

He stopped and cast a surprised look at Ty.

Abruptly, she turned and ran out of the living room, smashing through the glass door and vanishing into the thick forest.

"Should we—" Don started, but Martha cut him off.

"No. She's dangerous right now, to anyone. I think she's about ready to blow, and it could be fatal to anyone that's near her at this time."

Don sighed and went back to the bedroom to keep an eye on his patient. Silk moved to Ty and he wrapped his arms around her in comfort. "I can't lose both of them," Silk whimpered as she clung to his strong body.

"You won't. We won't. I'll give her some time alone and then I'll go find her," he promised.

"Martha's right, son," Garrett replied, gaining control once again.

Staring at the broken glass that littered the floor, he simply said, "We'll see."

She tore through the forest, her anger propelling her deeper and deeper into the woods. When she began stumbling as rage overtook her, she stopped and discharged her fury on the trees, rocks, and anything that offered release to the fire within her.

Her beloved aunt, her family, was being taken away from her; only this time she wasn't helpless as she had been in her mortal days. This time she would be sure to do all that she could to prevent this and take anyone that got in her way with her, straight to hell. She snarled and gnashed her teeth as she continued to plan the downfall of the source of her torment.

Twenty minutes later, Ty went searching for her. Her trail was easy to follow—all he had to do was keep to the path of destruction. Broken limbs, trampled underbrush, and trees knocked askew resembled a tornado's path, a tornado called Sigrid.

He finally found her in a small clearing, kneeling on the ground, her shoulders heaving as she tried to catch her breath from the exertion. He heard a low growling from her as he approached, and he stopped. "Who the hell do you think you're growling at?" he asked pointedly.

She turned, surprised at his strength. He felt as if he had been staked when he saw she was crying hopelessly. Moving closer, he kneeled behind her and wrapped his arms tightly around her, pulling her close.

"I . . . can't do this," she cried. "I can't lose her, not to Terrence, not to anyone. He will not win this."

Without warning, he yanked her around to face him. Firmly he grasped her face in his hands. "I love you with all my being, Sigrid, and I will not sit by any longer and watch you destroy yourself. I don't know what's worse, the anger that is eating you alive or the self-pity that's creeping in. You're changing Sigrid, and it's not for the better. You're sealing yourself off from everyone and taking everything personally. You won't let anyone near you, and you've begun feeding off the hate that's taking control of you."

She scowled at him and tried to push his arms away, but he held firm and continued. "You've lost a lot and endured more than you should have, but you are not the only one who's lost someone. We all have lost family and friends and we keep going. We do not treat it as if it is a personal attack or war. We all love Regina and are dying inside because of what's happening, but we will go on. You are content to let your anger take control and destroy you, and if Regina saw the way you're acting now, she'd be ashamed of you."

With more force than before, Sigrid tried to jerk away from his hold, but he only tightened his grip. "Don't fight me, Sigrid. You're the one that's going to listen for a change." He looked her in the eyes and moved closer, their faces only inches apart. "You are not the same woman I met four years ago. You're an imposter, filled with hate and rage and everything this family stands against. You are so worried about being Terrence's daughter. Well, honey, you're letting it happen right before my eyes."

"Bastard," she snarled and threw her body backward, trying to escape his hold. She succeeded in tumbling backward, dragging him on top of her. He quickly righted himself and straddled her, knowing she could easily toss him off and break him like a twig if she truly wanted to. He was so incensed at what she was becoming that he no longer cared how strong she was.

"I'm not done," he snapped, his fangs gleaming in the moonlight. "I want my Sigrid back, the woman with a heart of gold, filled with the pure love that her mother Valonia bestowed on her. I know she's still in there because I've seen glimpses of her. Just a few hours ago I saw her speaking to a man named Tony. I know she's close and I want her back. Terrence be damned, give me my love back."

She ceased struggling and relaxed against the cool soft earth. Her eyes were closed, but the tears were openly streaming down her cheeks. Ty stayed in place, his chest heaving with exhaustion, feeling lighter after confessing his true thoughts and feelings.

They stayed in their positions for a long while, until her tears finally stopped, and she opened her glistening eyes. Ty watched her and noticed that her face seemed to glow. Slowly he climbed off her and leaned against the nearest tree.

She sat up carefully and he worried that he might have unwillingly hurt her. She kept her head down, afraid to meet his gaze, her voice like a whispered child's. "What do I do now, Ty?"

Rising to his feet, he walked over and looked down at her. "Your aunt, our Queen is dying. Pull yourself together, get off your ass and go to her." He kneeled down and gently grasped her chin, lifting her face to his. "Honey, she needs you and loves you. If anyone can get through to her, it is you."

He stood back up and held out his hand to her. She reached out and latched onto it is as he pulled her to her feet. She almost leapt into his arms and hugged him tightly. "I am so sorry."

He pulled her closer and kissed the top of her head. "Don't be sorry; be Sigrid."

All the rage and anger that had been building the last few months, had almost drawn her into the darkness that Terrence so relished. She shivered against him as she accepted how powerful a pull it was and how close she had come to going over the edge. "Thank you, my love," she whispered against his chest.

He smiled, knowing that she was home as well.

". . . So all I can do is make her comfortable," Don finished as they stood outside the bedroom.

"I'd also advise you to strap her down and keep your distance. She's not responsible for her actions and could hurt someone," he added.

Sigrid and Ty had stayed back, listening, and now she edged her way to the door, facing the kindly doctor. "That won't be necessary, Don. Martha and I will be staying with her for a while. Once we go in, we are not to be disturbed by anyone. Our food and anything else we may need will be left outside the door at eight-hour intervals."

Martha inched closer, probing Sigrid's thoughts. She held her head to the side as she understood the plan and smiled her agreement. "We're going to bring Regina back. If she has to die, she will recognize the family that surrounds and loves her."

The stance that the two women took offered no room for argument, and the others silently backed away from the door.

When Regina woke up, she was immediately startled by her new surroundings. Struggling to get into a crouching position, she winced in pain as she finally reached it. Her nose crinkled as she sniffed the clean mountain air and other fresh smells in the room. Her eyes roamed around her new surroundings. She was in a large room made larger by the fact that except for the bed, it was empty of furniture. The walls were a relaxing blue and she smiled ever so slightly when she glimpsed up and saw the skylight above the bed.

As her eyes dropped, she noticed herself. Her eyes widened as she looked at the clean clothes and skin, bringing her arm up to her nose and smelling the material of her gown. Cautiously, she rubbed the malleable material and admired the feel beneath her fingers and against her sensitive flesh.

She snapped her head to the right when she heard the soft sound of breathing. Her eyes continued down until they settled on someone lying on a pad a few feet away from her bed.

She resumed her defensive posture and growled at the figure.

When this elicited no reaction, she eased in for a closer look, sniffing and trying to pick up on the invader. She recognized the smell. It was the woman from the carnival, the one with fangs like her.

She edged closer but was seized by another spasm of pain. Gasping, she fell back onto the bed, curling into a ball.

Sigrid used all her strength to keep from leaping up and trying to help her aunt. The plan was to gain Regina's trust and confidence and then work from there. With her eyes barely open a slit, she saw Martha was also fighting to keep from going to their pain-ridden queen.

After a moment, Sigrid rolled over on her side and fell still.

When Regina recovered from the pain, she inched forward again to observe the intruder. She was startled to find the intruder awake and watching her. Neither of them moved a muscle, only continued looking at each other.

"Good morning, Regina," Sigrid smiled, her voice soft and calming.

Regina stayed her ground. It wasn't until Sigrid began to sit up, that she retreated up the bed and cowered against the headboard.

Sigrid slowed her motions even more. Once she was in a stooping position, she began easing away from the bed and to the bedroom door.

Opening the door, she found that her instructions had been followed and there were two warm bottles of blood, two glasses, and a small bowl awaiting her just at the entrance of the door.

She retrieved the items, her movements still at a snail's pace, closed the door, and eased back to her place by Martha. She handed one bottle and glass to her and then crept closer to Regina's bedside.

The instant she opened the bottle, Regina's nose went into the air, sniffing the wafting scent. Licking her lips, she inched closer to the intruder, still presenting a defensive manner.

Sigrid filled the bowl with the rich red liquid and held it out to Regina as an offering. The bed springs creaked softly as she moved closer to Sigrid, sniffing the contents more deeply. She stopped, staring at the bowl but refusing to come any closer or take the offering.

"It's all right, Regina," Sigrid assured her and then brought the bowl to her own mouth and sipped loudly. She lowered the bowl and licked her lips, then again held out the bowl to Regina.

Regina began rocking slightly. Torn between hunger and fear, she frowned and looked from Sigrid to the bowl. Hunger won and she timidly reached out for the bowl.

Sigrid again felt a stab of anger when she saw the stub of Regina's right ring finger. One of the first things she had done when they were cleaning the woman was check for the ring. She really hadn't expected to find it, but she had expected to find all of Regina's fingers intact. The finger wasn't a major loss; it could have been much worse. It was the brutality of the act that infuriated her.

Regina's shaky hands shot out and plucked the bowl from Sigrid's still hands. Cradling the bowl close, she returned to her safe corner, where she downed the contents of the bowl with loud slurping sounds.

Sigrid looked at Martha and smiled. The first obstacle had been overcome and, although it was a small victory, it was a victory all the same.

Hearing a grunt, Sigrid turned back to Regina, who was pushing the empty bowl back to her. Masking her enthusiasm, Sigrid refilled the bowl and again, this time more bravely Regina retrieved it from her hands. She didn't bother returning to her corner as she drank the contents more slowly. Once finished, she sighed and wiped the dribble of red off her mouth with the sleeve of her new gown.

They spent the rest of the day getting used to one another. Regina remained skittish around them, but their slow movements and calming voices helped put her at ease. If she had to share a cage, at least these two wouldn't hurt her like the fat man or the man in black. Growing bolder as the day wore on, she began edging closer to them, at one point so daring as to reach out and mildly brush her hand against Sigrid's arm.

With all the excitement and a full stomach, she finally retreated to her bed of safety and dozed off. Once she was asleep, Sigrid adjourned to the corner and sat down beside Martha.

"You doing okay?" she questioned as she settled against the older woman.

Glad to have the old Sigrid back, Martha patted her knee and smiled. "Fine, just a bit tired and stiff. I do think we're making progress though."

"Yeah," Sigrid inhaled deeply. "I hate to say it, but I think her being sick is helping. She's in too much pain and too worn out to fight much."

"That may be a part of it, but I think the major contributing factor is your bond with her. No matter what Terrence did, he couldn't take that from her. Terrence and probably others have hurt her and done who-knows-what to her, but she knows how much you love her and that you would never hurt her. Somewhere deep inside her is that bond, and that's why she instinctively trusts you so quickly."

"But is it quick enough?" Sigrid asked, her face sad as she watched the sleeping woman.

Martha remained silent. She draped her arm around Sigrid and held her close. Within minutes, both were sound asleep.

As Sigrid awoke the next morning, she felt Martha's arm holding her tightly. Puzzled for a second, as she came fully awake, she understood. Sometime during the night, Regina had left the comfort of her bed, tore her covers free and gone to sleep on the floor a few feet from them.

"We have company," Martha told Sigrid telepathically.

Without making a sound, Sigrid sat up. Regina remained still, as Sigrid inched closer to the sleeping woman.

Regina's sleep was fitful, and she was startled awake just as Sigrid got within reaching distance. Still in the throes of the nightmare, Regina didn't realize where she was or who was approaching her, but she knew she had to protect herself.

Sigrid was just as startled to see the wild fear in Regina's eyes as she jumped up and prepared for attack.

Regina seemed to bounce as she leapt at Sigrid and brought the woman crashing to the floor. For a second, Sigrid was so unprepared for the action that Regina managed to get in a few good blows. By the time she regained her senses, she had a black eye, bruised ribs, and more scratches and tears on her face and arms.

Martha moved to her aid, but Sigrid was already taking action to stop the attack. "Regina, stop! It's Sigrid!" she yelled as she shoved Regina just hard enough to lose her balance and tumble off her.

Regina rolled a few feet and stopped on her side, wincing in pain as her eyes darted around the room and came to alite on Sigrid.

Sigrid froze as their eyes met. As she stared into those wild, brown orbs, she became seized with fear, her mind beginning to lose its clear focus. Pain shot through her and threatened to take her breath away. "Martha . . ." She wheezed and reached back, her hand outstretched and shaking.

Martha's quick response betrayed her elderly looks as she flew to Sigrid and firmly grasped her shoulders, "What is it? What's happening?"

Sigrid's breath was rapid and labored as she struggled to speak. "Confusion . . . pain . . . fear. So much fear. Overpowering . . . too much . . . help me . . . Martha."

Unsure of that was transpiring, she looked at Regina. The smaller woman was still lying on her side, staring intently into Sigrid's eyes. Her rapid breathing was in sync with Sigrid's and Martha realized what was happening. "Telepathy," Martha replied as she gathered her thoughts.

"The two of you are locked in thought. What you're feeling is what she's feeling. Use this Sigrid, project your thoughts to her, calm her. This could be the breakthrough we need."

"Too . . . much . . . afraid," Sigrid whispered, her face contorting to reflect her statement.

Martha moved closer, bracing herself against Sigrid and leaned over her shoulder, her mouth right beside her ear. Softly she began to hum an old lullaby. It was a song that Sigrid had heard her hum on several occasions, and it always brought a smile to her face.

Sigrid's breathing slowed slightly and Regina's as well. "More . . . please," Sigrid begged.

"Think of pleasant things, things familiar to you. The horses running through the pasture as the two of you raced that day. The birthday party she threw for you after your first year with us. Your skiing trip, anything the two of you enjoyed together. Show her your love," Martha finished.

Sigrid focused on Martha's voice and her breathing slowed even more. Her rigid body relaxed as she regained control of her thoughts and mind and began projecting images of memories at Regina. Regina too had calmed, and her mouth gaped open as the flurry of images washed over her.

Once she had more control, Sigrid maintained her hold on the eyes of the sick woman and scooted closer until she was kneeling right beside Regina. Regina rolled on her back and offered no resistance as Sigrid lifted her almost weightless body into her arms.

Martha guided them over to the bed and helped Sigrid sit down, constantly aware of the eye contact. When they were situated comfortably on the bed, Martha pulled back and decided to give them some privacy. With a final look, she exited the bedroom for a much-needed stretch.

She was back and waiting patiently when the bond was broken four hours later, and Sigrid slumped against the headboard. Gently, she lifted Regina up, and Sigrid rolled off the bed and slid down to the floor.

Martha tucked Regina in, unable to resist planting a soft kiss on her forehead as the woman dove deeper into sleep.

Sigrid tried to pull herself up to a sitting position but found herself too weak and exhausted. Martha was by her side having pulled her across the room to rest on their makeshift bed in the blink of an eye. "You okay?" she asked with concern.

"Do immortals get headaches?" Sigrid grinned weakly.

Martha smiled and went to get them some nourishment she had brought in with her earlier. Pouring two glasses, she rejoined Sigrid and handed her a full glass. "Try this. It should help."

Shaky at first, Sigrid quickly regrouped and emptied the glass. Setting it down beside her, she leaned against the wall. "I feel like I'm drained, mentally and physically."

"Did you get through to her?" Martha asked as she wiped Sigrid's face with a cool cloth.

Shrugging, she answered, "I think so. I don't know." She rubbed her head as if her brain was bouncing against her skull. "It was like swapping stories or watching a movie. Pictures, descriptions, feelings. We shared all of that. I tried to think of every single good moment we've had together and with the family, but I don't know if it was enough."

"I told you the bond would help. You've done all you can, honey. Now it's up to Regina."

Sigrid looked down at her feet, head hanging low. "It's too bad the bond can't stop the poison. It's burning her up inside." Sigrid brought her hand to her chest and half hugged herself, "I felt it. Felt what it's doing to her."

Martha knew the next question was obvious and silently debated whether to ask it or not. Sigrid settled the debate as she responded. "Yes. I . . . felt . . . and saw some of what . . . he . . . did. Most of it was blocked out by fear, such overpowering fear."

Wishing she could retract her thoughts, Martha leaned against the wall and decided to change the subject. "Why don't you go out and let Don take a look at that eye and those scratches. You need to get some fresh air and move around a bit. I'll stay with Regina."

To Martha's surprise, Sigrid agreed and very slowly pushed herself up. With a warm, tired smile directed at Martha, she left the bedroom.

While Martha had been on her break, she had filled in the others on the details of the plan and its progress so far. When Sigrid appeared, she only added a few whispered details as Don checked her out. Telling her that she was healthy and healing, but that she needed about twenty-four hours of sleep, Don gave her the "all clear" and left to finish up on his research.

Ty took her hand and led her across the room. Opening the now repaired glass door she had broken the day before, he suggested they take a walk around the lake. Once they were alone, she confided in him more details about what had happened in the room.

He put his arm around her waist and kept her close to him as he listened and agreed with Martha's observations. He offered up his own thoughts and suggestions, and she eagerly considered them.

They finally settled under a shade tree at the lake's edge and watched the ducks play across the water. They leaned against the tree and Sigrid reclined, using his lap as a pillow. Their conversation waned and between the restful quiet and Ty's relaxing stroking of her hair, she drifted off to sleep.

The quiet was interrupted by Silk's voice calling them frantically. Sigrid instantly snapped awake and jumped to her feet, Ty right beside her.

"Here," Sigrid answered and led the way back toward the house.

They met halfway, Silk clearly in an agitated state and for a minute, Sigrid's heart dropped. "What's wrong? Has something happened to Regina?"

Silk grabbed her sister's hand, struggling to catch her breath. "She's . . . she's awake. You did it, Sig. You brought her back."

Sigrid stared at her for a moment, unsure that she had heard correctly. When she saw Silk's smile, she knew she had and took off running for the house. She moved so fast that to normal eyes she was only a blur. Two more blurs followed in her wake.

Sigrid stopped at the bedroom door, torn between rushing in and the fear that Regina would not recognize her.

Garrett and Martha were kneeling by her bedside, while Don kept a close watch on his patient.

"Go on," Silk urged from behind and nudged her forward.

Slowly she stepped into the bedroom, Martha looked up at her and smiled broadly, her eyes and cheeks damp with tears. She raised her hand and motioned the hesitant woman closer.

As she reached the bed, the wave of family parted and left her a clear view. She looked down at Regina, who smiled weakly, her eyes glistening with tears.

Her voice was raspy as she held her hand up to Sigrid. "Dear heart."

Sigrid fell to her knees, crying and grasped Regina's hand, gently kissing it. "My Queen."

Don shook his head in disbelief. "I don't know how, but you did it Sigrid. You brought her back from reversion."

"She knows all of us," Silk added moving in behind Sigrid.

"Of course I do," Regina interrupted. "Never thought I'd see any of you again." Her look warmed as she looked at Silk. "Especially you."

Silk blushed and blew her a kiss. Martha patted Regina's arm. "Well, you are seeing us and you're home safe. I know you're tired and I think you and Sigrid need a few minutes alone, so we're outta here, but we will be back."

Garrett took Martha's hand and helped her to her feet. "We'll be right outside, my love," he assured her and then began ushering everyone out of the room.

Sigrid rose and walked them to the door. Garrett was the last to leave and before he got clear of the door, she pulled him close. "Is LePope taken care of?"

He nodded. "Yes. Lenny and Ed should be here late tonight."

"I want more security up here ASAP. We got caught with our guard down once, and it won't happen again. The only way anyone gets to her is through us."

"You want our people to begin the search for Terrence and his coven?"

"No," she answered. "He's not important right now. Later, yes we will find him, but not now."

Garrett had expected her to launch a full-out search and was surprised at her attitude and calmness. Ty, hovering close by to his mate, simply smiled at the exchange.

Garrett exited the room to take care of her instructions and she closed the door behind him. Once alone, she rushed back to Regina's side.

Regina patted the bed beside her and Sigrid took a seat. Regina sought out the young woman's hands and latched onto them like a safety line.

She released one hand and reaching up, tenderly touched the scratches on Sigrid's face. "Sorry."

Sigrid leaned on to the feathery touch, closing her eyes and relishing the feel of her hand. "I probably deserved that and much more."

A tear escaped Regina's eye and rolled down her face to dampen the pillow. "You never gave up on me."

"I never will. I love you."

More tears joined the others. "I'm dying, dear heart. I can feel it."

Sigrid clenched her jaw, trying to keep her own tears at bay. "I know. He poisoned you. Don is trying to find a way to stop it but . . ."

Regina's hand fell to Sigrid's lips and she nodded with understanding. "At least I'm in my right mind, thanks to you."

The battle was lost as Sigrid began crying. "I wish I could do more."

"You can," Regina responded and squeezed her hand. "I don't want to die because Terrence decided I should. If I must die, it will be my decision."

Sigrid looked at her, realization taking a few seconds to sink in. As she understood what Regina was saying, fear gripped her soul. "No, Regina!"

"Sigrid," she said patiently. "You know the pain, you've felt it. I refuse to lie here and fade away because Terrence thought it would be amusing. You know me well enough to know that I would never want to give in to his will. Please help me."

Sigrid was silent, trying to comprehend the request. She understood and agreed with Regina to a point, but she knew she couldn't destroy her beloved aunt. She would rather die now than live without her. Yet the thought of sitting in this room and watching her die in such a painful way was just as unbearable.

"Don't answer now," Regina added, knowing the magnitude of what she was asking. "For now, just stay with me."

Sigrid leaned against the headboard and pulled Regina's small frame into her arms. Cradling her as Regina had done for her on several occasions, Sigrid embraced her, trying to relay all her love for the woman in a single touch. They did not speak, only savored the closeness and let their thoughts roam freely.

"That's the most ridiculous thing I've ever heard," Garrett argued as he paced angrily across the living room.

Sigrid had stayed with Regina until she drifted off to sleep, then left the room and joined the others in the living room. What Regina was asking of her had proven too big to handle alone, and she had told the inner sanctum, hoping they could help her.

As Garrett continued to rant and rave, she sat quietly next to Ty, looking much smaller and older.

"You expect us to let you go in there and stake her or something?" he asked as he stopped in front of her. "She is our Queen, our life. You say you love her? Well that's a hell of a way to show it."

Don stepped into the living room and joined the conversation. "She's dying, Garrett," he stated bluntly, "a very painful death."

Garrett whirled around and glared at him, pointing his finger. "You are not a part of this."

Don continued, undaunted. "Why? Because I'm not a vampire like all of you? That's true, but I've administered medical treatment to everyone in this room. I have been there for the family and always will be. I am the family doctor, and Regina is my patient and friend, therefore, I am a part of this."

Martha stood up and joined Don. "He is a part of this family, Garrett, and he's right. Like it or not, want it or not, she's dying, and there doesn't seem to be a whole hell of a lot we can do to stop it."

"And she's in pain," Silk offered softly. "I don't want to see her in pain."

Garrett clenched his teeth and resumed pacing.

"The conversation is moot anyway," Sigrid said, not leaving the security of Ty. "I can't do it. As much as I love her, I can't take her life. I can't."

Garrett stopped suddenly and punched a hole in the wall, his frustrations getting the better of him. "I want Terrence. I want to make him feel the same thing she's going through. I want his blood running down my throat so I can spit it back in his dying face." He moved to retrieve his phone from his pocket. "I'm going to have our forces find him."

Sigrid shook her head and sat up straighter. "No!"

Turning, he looked at her like she was a misbehaving child. "Excuse me?"

Her voice never rose above its normal tone. "You run the company in Regina's absence. I run the family."

He threw the phone across the room and turned to face her fully, hands clenched at his sides. She stood up and took a few steps toward him. "I understand your frustration and anger, Garrett. I want vengeance just as much as you do, but right now Regina needs us more."

The older man's features softened slightly, but his face still beamed red.

"I want to spend every moment I can with Regina. Terrence will wait for now, but rest assured that his time will come, and it will be just as painful as what she's enduring now. I promise."

"She's right," Ty replied and looked at Don. "How much time?"

"Two, three days at most," he admitted with defeat. "I've tried everything. I even thought of trying a transfusion or some sort of serum."

"Nothing worked?" Martha asked, grasping at straws.

"Only to slow it down," he answered.

Sigrid's head flew up and she seized the statement. "What slowed it down?"

"A blood serum mixture," he dismissed with hesitation.

"If it slowed the poison, then give her more of it," Garrett interceded. "Meanwhile, you can try to find a cure."

"It slowed down the poison, but it also caused some internal damage. It may slow it down, but in her weakened state, it could also kill her."

Sigrid's voice was little more than a whisper as she ambled over to the doctor. "Whose blood was it?"

He knew what was on her mind and mulled over telling her the truth. He jumped when she asked louder, "Whose?"

"Yours," he answered.

Garrett smacked his forehead and laughed, his voice rising with each word. "Of course it's yours, Sigrid. It's always the two of you and your bond. You know, since she found you, the rest of the family has taken a back seat to you because Regina's world revolves around you. I, for one, am quite sick of it. I have been with her and loved her since before you were born. I think I'm beginning to understand how Ward felt."

Martha slapped him so hard he stumbled backward, his face glowing with a red imprint. Her grandmotherly demeanor was gone and in its place was that of a wildcat. "That was uncalled for, you pompous ass. You are not the only one hurting and frustrated here, and you can just stop using Sigrid as the scapegoat for all our problems."

He brought his hand up and rubbed his throbbing cheek, staring at her in astonishment as she spoke again.

"Need I remind you that it was she who got the lead to find Regina? That it was she who brought Regina back from reversion and it was she who saved Regina's life ten years ago. You and I both know how Regina was before she found Sigrid. Ten years ago, Regina would have welcomed this from Terrence." She cut her eyes at Sigrid. "Granted, Sigrid has not been the easiest person to live with of late but what you said was just plain mean. I think you owe her and us an apology. We are all worn out and grieving, and I'm tired of all the asses that seem to keep appearing in this group."

Garrett hung his head, chastised and ashamed. Sigrid too let her head lower slightly, casting her eyes at the older woman in silent apology.

He knew she was right and took a few deep breaths to calm himself and let her words soak in. When he finally looked at Sigrid, his posture reflected his mood. "I didn't mean that, Sigrid. I'm scared and I feel so helpless and took it out on you. I'm sorry."

Sigrid waved her hand, not completely innocent herself. "I'm sorry too." He nodded his acceptance of her apology and she, his. Then she directed her attention back to Don. "If my blood will help her, I'll let you have every drop in my body."

Don walked over to the couch and sat down. She took a seat on the opposite couch across from him. "Sigrid, you and I have discussed this. We don't know what effect your blood will have on anyone, much less someone in her condition. Yes, the serum slowed down the poison, but given pure and in large dose, it could kill her."

Martha came over and took a seat beside him. "But it could help her."

Don shrugged and threw his hands up in surrender and aggravation.

"It's a chance to save her. She's dying already, so this could either help or fulfill her request," Martha reasoned to them all.

The room fell silent as they contemplated the situation.

Sigrid stood up and walked over to the glass doors and stared out into the forest. She blocked out their whispered conversations and pictured herself flying high above all the sorrow in this house. She was soaring above the mountains, dodging treetops and heading for the farthest star. She could feel the wind curling around her and carrying her higher and higher, until she could feel nothing except the blood flowing through her veins. Suddenly gravity latched into her and she was being pulled back. The trees and mountains turned into a blur as she was yanked back to the room by Garrett's voice.

"Sigrid? Sigrid?"

She returned to her body and sighed deeply before turning around. They were all seated around the coffee table, their faces long and weary. She looked at each of them, the people she loved most in the world, and her heart tightened as she saw the look in their eyes.

"It's your choice," Garrett stated, when he knew he had her attention. "We will support your decision."

Looking at Silk, she shook her head. "No, it's not just my choice." She held her hand out to Silk.

With only a second's hesitation, Silk rose and walked over to the door to join her. "Silk is my sister and Regina's niece as well."

Silk took her hand and the two of them went outside onto the deck.

"I know it hurt you that I didn't take you in with me when we brought her back," Sigrid said as she set down on the deck steps. "I wanted to explain—"

"No need," Silk smiled, taking a seat beside her on the steps. "You needed Martha then. Now you need me. You have got to stop worrying about always offending somebody by your actions. We know that you have a reason for everything you do. Yes, I was hurt, but I understood why."

Sigrid looked at her. She had only grown more beautiful as each day went by, and she felt a pang of sisterly love as she watched her. Silk drew into an Indian sitting position, her legs crossed and her hands nervously fidgeting in her lap.

A gust of wind swept across the porch, and Sigrid held up her face, letting the wind caress her. The smell of pine wafted along the breeze, and the final song of summer, the chorus of katydid and tree frogs, picked up in intensity.

"What do I do, Silk?" Sigrid finally asked lowly.

Silk stared ahead. "I know part of what you're feeling, I feel it too. But the largest part of this falls on you, and I can't begin to imagine how that feels." She craned her neck to meet Sigrid's gaze. "I have loved Regina as my Queen. Then we . . . and I loved her as my partner. Now I find that she is my aunt and a new level of love has been added. I love her in all those ways, but it's different from your love for her."

Sigrid's look became intense as she waited for Silk to continue.

"Garrett was right about your bond. It does encompass both of you, but that is not a bad thing. Each of you found one another when you thought that you would be alone for the rest of your lives." Silk laughed slightly. "It sounds corny, but your love for one another is eternal. It's deeper and stronger than what we have, what you and Ty have, what Regina and Garrett have. That's why this decision is so hard for you. Regina is your life and you are hers." She laid her hand on Sigrid's. "I love you. I love her, and I support you no matter what you decide."

Her shoulders slumped. "And if this kills her, I mean sooner than the poison, how can I look at any of you in the face knowing that I'm responsible for her death."

Scooting closer, Silk's voice became firm. "Terrence is responsible. What you are doing is trying to give back that control to Regina. To give her back her dignity."

Sigrid stared into the darkness, her eyes glistening. Silk watched her for a moment before she added, "The biggest problem for you other than grief is this misplaced blame you are assuming. Terrence is the guilty one. He's the one that's done this to her. He's the one that took her and hurt her and left her to die. Not you, not me, none of u. It's Terrence."

"So," she finally spoke. "You think I should do this?"

Silk took Sigrid's hands. "Don't you? We all love Regina and none of us wants to lose her, but if we must, let it be her way, her choice. That's the greatest gift we could grant her, a choice."

Slowly Sigrid nodded and wrapped her hands over Silk's.

The decision made, they each took turns spending time and saying final goodbyes to a much weaker Regina. They left Sigrid alone, and she spent the time meditating the way Shadow had taught her when she needed to focus.

Each family member hoped theirs would not be the final farewell to their beloved queen, but they all knew the risks in the avenue of action.

After several hours, Sigrid went to her aunt as the others disappeared from the room. Don had explained their plan and Regina readily agreed. Her only hesitation was the guilt she knew Sigrid would carry despite the family's efforts to convince her that she was not responsible.

She and Sigrid held hands and spent the time in silence. Sigrid could feel the life force ebbing away and licking her lips she said, "I love you, Reg. Always."

Regina mustered her strength and flashed a brilliant smile. "I know, dear heart. And I, you."

Taking a deep breath, Regina indicated it was time, and Sigrid gently helped her sit up. Once she was comfortable, Sigrid made a cut along her wrist, the deep red flow appearing to be fluorescent as it escaped the vein.

Her energy almost gone, Regina accepted the wrist and began suckling the blood that gushed down her throat. Sigrid used her hand to brace Regina's head and never took her eyes off the older woman.

Regina suddenly began to seize. Throwing her head back, blood spattered across the room and Sigrid. Spitting the remnants of the blood out, Regina began to scream. A pattern of blood coated the walls, ceiling, and both women.

Sigrid held tightly to her convulsing body, trying to prevent her from hurting herself. Don rushed in and flew to her aid, but the seizure was proving too strong for them.

Regina's strength magnified, and her thrashing along with the slippery blood speckling everything made it difficult for them to keep their grip.

Ty and Garrett ran into the room and immediately jumped in, firmly latching on and pinning her to the bed. Sigrid's face was red with anguish, and her tears were flowing freely leaving tracks down her blood-covered face. They finally managed to restrain Regina as her movements began to ease.

Martha and Silk rushed in and grabbed the stricken Sigrid and began dragging her away from the scene. "Regina!" she wailed in a voice that caused their hearts to break. She continued to struggle away from them, trying to retain her place at Regina's side, her power almost too much for the women. Blood still flowed from her wrist, and their grip was tenuous at best.

Now Billy joined in the fracas and firmly wrapped his muscular arm around Sigrid's waist. Martha shifted around trying to lock on Sigrid's eyes, but the woman would not take her eyes off Regina's shaking form. "Forgive meee!" Sigrid cried out as Martha forcibly held her face still and caught the girl's gaze in hers. With every ounce of power she possessed, she focused her mind at Sigrid.

It took an instant for the power to break through the anguish, but Sigrid stopped fighting them, startled at what they were doing, and then fell into a deep sleep. Taking the sleeping Sigrid into her arms, Martha carried her out of the room as the men continued to deal with their dying queen.

Regina's seizure stopped as suddenly as it had begun, and she fell deathly silent. Ty and Garrett, both tired and spattered with blood, cautiously stepped away, ready to restrain her again if necessary. Ty looked at the closed bedroom door, his heart aching for his mate and his queen.

Don had set up a mini lab in the bedroom next door, but when Regina had returned to her senses, he had moved most of the equipment into the far corner of her room. This way, he reasoned, he could keep an eye on her and continue to search for a cure.

Moving past Garrett and Ty, he gave her a quick check over, extracted a blood sample, and rushed to his lab.

Ty longed to be with his mate, but he knew she was in good hands and that he was needed here more. He took up a position at the foot of the bed, ready to help Don if and when he needed it.

Garrett stared down at the woman's pale face and then kneeled, taking her hand into his, all the while whispering to her in soothing, loving tones. Her hair was rumpled and wild from the thrashing, and he patiently smoothed it and straightened it. He savored the feel of her hair against his hand and continued to stroke it gently.

As his hand brushed away a stray wisp from her forehead, he stopped suddenly, laying his palm on her brow. "Don, why is she so warm?"

Don walked back over to the bed, preparing for another sample. He rested his hand on her face and then the bend of her arm. His eyebrows shot up at the unexpected heat he felt. It was unusual for immortals to radiate this kind of body heat, and he had only seen it one other time. A light went off in his head. "I'm not sure, just give me a few minutes."

He took the sample and sped back to his microscopes and machinery. With great skill and care, he dropped the new specimen on a glass slide and began analyzing.

For thirty minutes, Don repeated the procedure four more times. Regina remained unconscious, no better but no worse, and Garrett felt his impatience growing.

Almost an hour had passed since Regina had drunk Sigrid's blood. Don put his hands in his pockets, stepping away from the lab. "This is incredible!"

Garrett's head shot up. "What?"

He stepped forward, looking at the microscope again to prove to himself that he was not seeing things, and then chuckled softly.

"What is it, Don?" Garrett asked again, this time with anger in his tone.

Don rubbed his eyes and looked at Garrett, smiling. "She's not dying. The silver content and dead blood are slowly disappearing. I need to run one more test to check my theory, and then I think I can explain."

Before they could ask him anything, he bolted from the room with this sample equipment in search of Sigrid.

After Don had his sample, he told Martha the news and asked that she wake Sigrid. The girl was distraught when she first opened her eyes, the memory of Regina, tearing into her soul. But as Martha repeated what Don had just told her, she fell silent and stared in disbelief.

Ten minutes later, Don called all of them into the bedroom. They filed in slowly, their attention divided between Don and Regina's prone figure. The mood was sedate and apprehensive as he began to explain his theory.

"It appears Regina is getting better. The silver and blood poisoning is getting weaker with every sample I take. We knew Sigrid's blood had been altered and we assumed, I assumed, that it would be toxic to other vampires. And it may be, given other circumstances. In this case, I think it saved her life."

They were all struck by the news, unsure of what to say or do, afraid to believe it was true.

"If you'll step over here, I'll show you what's happening."

As one they moved toward the lab table and gathered around Don. He poured a vial of blood into a small copper bowl and then held up a tiny piece of silver. "This is Sigrid's blood." He informed them, motioning at the bowl, then releasing the silver piece into it.

There was no plop as the silver hit the red fluid only a loud sizzling sound. Instantaneously, the silver dissolved, turning the blood a deeper red.

The looks in their faces were a mixture of surprise and confusion.

"What we have here," he said gesturing to Sigrid, "Is the first vampire impervious to silver."

"H-how?" Garrett stumbled.

"My theory is that when Terrence stabbed Sigrid several years ago, her already strong blood chemistry mutated to adapt to the silver deposits that were left by the weapon. That's what triggered what she called the transformation. I call it a metamorphosis. Her innate powers and skills were lying in wait and the stabbing brought them to life. Her blood simply attacks the silver and, if I'm right, any foreign body that possesses a threat, and destroys it."

Silk was staring at Regina's still figure. "What's it doing to Regina?"

"When you bring someone over, your blood overtakes theirs and they adjust and convert. Basically, that's what's happened here. Sigrid letting Regina drink her blood is like Sigrid converting her. Sigrid's blood chemistry attacked the poisoning because it was preventing the conversion and wiped it out of Regina's system. The only question now is what else has it done, and we won't know that until she wakes up."

14

The stone walls stank of mildew and decay. A particularly ugly fungus grew from the aged cracks and spread along the walls and dark corners of the floor.

The stone floor was cooler than the already damp air of the small cell, and as she sat there, knees drawn to her chest, she shivered, the cold penetrating her nude body and settling into her bones.

The walls were solid and thick with no windows, and the only light came from a small oil lamp that hung from the ceiling above. The light was so dim that it only threw a few shadows across the cell, but with her keen eyesight she didn't really need any illumination to see how bare and filthy the room was.

A pile of mildewed, dirty hay that lay in the corner was expected to be used as a bed, but she wouldn't give him the satisfaction. She could smell the undercurrent of sex and violence in the room and tried to shut down her imagination at what atrocities had been committed here.

The lack of a window and information had caused her to lose track of time. She felt as if she had been here for a year when in reality it had only been two months. The first two weeks after her abduction had been spent in a pitch-black room barely bigger than a closet.

She had yelled and demanded an explanation or to see Terrence, but she was simply ignored. She had resigned herself then to keep quiet and not show any of the fear or anger this little experiment was supposed to elicit. The only feeling she allowed herself was grief over Paul and Silk.

Before she had lost consciousness, she had seen Paul on the ground and three going after Silk. She again cursed herself for not being more aware of their danger. Her lack of caution had caused the death of two of her most loved companions. She felt tears swelling in her eyes but denied them in case she was being watched.

After two weeks of darkness, she had been blindfolded and escorted to Terrence's chambers. He never said a word, only smiled as he watched his servants throw her to the ground and rape her repeatedly.

When they were finished, she was bruised and battered, her body dirty and her clothes torn to shreds. Still she showed no emotion, not trying to cower to hide her nudity or shame. He kneeled down beside her, his eyes glittering with pleasure. "Welcome to my world, dear sister."

He had laughed and motioned for his servants. "Take this piece of filth to the cellar," he instructed and then turned his back on her.

Four men had manhandled her and proceeded to drag her out of the room, her feet banging against the stone floor and sending shards of pain up her legs.

Gazing around as she was dragged through the cavernous place, she guessed that they must be in a ruined castle somewhere. The information did her little good now, her hopes of being rescued falling as each day passed.

Once they arrived at the cell, she was tossed down the steps and came to a rolling stop. Her body ached from its earlier violation and from new bruises she gathered as she was bounced off the steps. Opening her eyes, she found more of his people standing around her in the cell and again she was raped and beaten.

It became the routine as did the starving games and their little torture play. She would lie still. Never giving them the satisfaction of showing her pain or shame as they pierced her skin with silver needles and sprinkled holy water on her dirt-ridden flesh.

Twice a week she would be taken to Terrence, where he would taunt her with tales of his renewed battle on the family. He bragged about how they had fallen apart without her and delighted in giving her the gory details of their slaughter and growing numbers of the dead. She blanked out all he was saying and then he switched tactics. Her hunger would almost overtake her when he teased her with a fresh kill of blood. Clenching her teeth against the hunger gnawing at her very being, she ignored him until he tired of his games and threw the blood at her.

Her ears picked up footsteps outside and when she heard the scrapping of the door, she knew it was time for another visit with Terrence and play session with his minions.

Weakened, she stood up, refusing to allow them the satisfaction of hauling her up and dragging her to him. She stood at the foot of the steps waiting, making no effort to cover her nudity and held herself regally as they descended to collect her.

Terrence was waiting for her in a different room this time. This one was large, but not as bare as her cell. A chair and table were stationed to the left of the room next to a large grate in the floor. A warm, welcoming fire was stoked in the stone fireplace, and he leaned against it, holding a cigarette, smiling at her.

The guards shoved her with such force that she flew across the room and landed on her knees, scraping them on the rough stone floor.

"Now, now boys," he said sternly and took a few steps toward her. "Must be careful, my sister has an appointment with some very important people."

The guards laughed and walked into the room, slamming the large wooden door behind them.

"Clean her up," he said offhandedly and went to sit in the chair.

Again she was seized by the guards and taken into a small room off to the side, where a large tub of water awaited.

She closed her eyes and clenched her teeth as they dunked her in and unmercifully scrubbed the dirt from her skin. While they cleaned, they also took the opportunity to poke and prod her body with great relish. When they finished with their cleaning and groping session, she was yanked out of the tub, roughly dried off, and still nude shoved back into the room where Terrence waited.

He stood up, clapping his hands together. "Much better. I wouldn't want to get dirty."

The guards pushed her down to the floor and each caught a wrist and ankle until she lay spread eagle against the stone floor.

Like the predator he was, he stalked closer, walking around her vulnerable body and leering with great pleasure. He came to a stop at her feet and kneeled down, scooting into place between her spread legs and unbuckling his belt.

She knew what he had on his mind and began struggling against her captors. In her weakened state and being outnumbered, she couldn't break free and looked him directly in the eye. "Terrence, don't do this. Haven't you already shamed our family enough?"

He leaned down, his breath reeking of blood and tobacco. "So you do have a voice. I was beginning to wonder." With that, he plunged into her.

She gasped as he slammed into her, feeling like she was being ripped apart as he continued to work himself deeper into her.

"The question is . . .," he grunted as he began to pump harder and faster, "who is the best of the Cadmus sisters? You or Thea?"

His eyes rolled back as he growled with pleasure, and she turned her head to the side trying to suppress the bile that was threatening to erupt from her throat. He continued to pump against her with such force that several times her head bounced off the floor beneath her. She closed her eyes, trying to blank out what was happening and the feeling of him inside her.

The guards laughed and cheered him on as they watched their master work himself into a frenzy. Baring his fangs, he leaned down and clamped onto her breast, suckling the blood until his breathing picked up speed.

To her it seemed to go on forever. Just when she thought he could go no harder or deeper he would do both and finally, his body shaking, he reached climax, howling in the air like the animal he was.

A single tear streamed down her face as he pulled out of her and fastened his pants, still panting from the exercise.

"Thea was better," he acknowledged and stood up. "At least she fought me and that only heightened the pleasure."

Her legs were shaky as the guards hauled her to her feet. She felt dirty and violated in a way she never thought possible. Lifting her head, she saw him standing back by the fireplace, like a king dressed all in black. She wanted to lunge at him and tear his scarred face open, but all her strength was suddenly gone, sapped away to nothing.

He lit another cigarette and blew the smoke in her direction. He began pacing in the front of the grating on the floor, and now she became aware of sounds coming from below the floor. "Since you don't seem to like my company, I've found someone more suitable."

Her first thought was that in all his bragging, he had managed to capture one of the family. The image of Sigrid or Garrett popped into her head, but as the guards pushed her closer to the grating, the snarls and growling coming from there ruled that out.

The grating began to retract into the floor, leaving a black gaping hole. As the thing retracted, the air was filled with the scrapping and screeching of age and weight, and it bore a spike of fear through her.

He eased over to the pit and looked down, then smiled. "Those below are going to love you."

The closer she got to the edge, the more she began to fight against the guards. Their hold remained strong and she found herself teetering at the edge. When she looked down and saw what awaited her in the darkness of the pit, all her remaining strength and self-restraint vanished, and for the first time, she screamed. A scream of terror that echoed off the wall of the castle and brought a grin to Terrence's face.

She jerked up from sleep, still screaming, her eyes wild and full of fear. Silk was sitting by her side on watch and leapt to her feet, flopping on the bed beside Regina and wrapping her shivering form in strong protective arms.

"It's all right, Cherie," she assured and rocked slightly. "You're safe now. It was only a nightmare, you're home now."

She calmed and gulped in air, snuggling closer to Silk and still shaking. Silk lightly kissed the top of her head. "No one will ever hurt you again, Cherie. I promise you that."

Regina lifted her eyes and looked at Silk. "Silk? It's really you?"

Smiling, Silk nodded. "Of course, babe. It's me."

Regina calmed more but her eyes were still confused. "I-I'm not dead?"

"No," she replied. "The poison is gone. You're going to be fine."

"How?"

Silk pulled her closer, angry that the strong woman she loved had been reduced to a shivering mass by Terrence. Swallowing her hate, she mustered warmth into her voice. "We'll tell you all about it later. Right now, just rest and relax. I need to call Don in to check you over."

Regina's breathing had slowed, but she still held a tight grip on Silk's arm and wrist. When Silk started to pull away to get Don, Regina refused to release her hold.

Deciding to continue to calm the woman, Silk stayed in place. "You're safe and alive," she stated again with conviction.

Regina had calmed considerably by the time Don finished his exam. Silk continued to hold her, moving only when Don needed access.

"How do you feel?" he asked.

"Tired, scared, but stronger," she admitted and sighed.

Don stood up, smiling broadly. "You, my dear, are out of danger. The poisoning is gone from your bloodstream and, although there was some internal damage, it's minimal and seems to be healing. It will probably take you a bit longer to recover all your strength because of the severity of your injuries, but you will recover with time."

"Sigrid's blood did all that? I thought it was lethal," she questioned.

"Yes, it did all that and so did I. With that niece of yours and the changes in vampire chemistry through the years, my medical books are becoming obsolete. At this rate, Sigrid will know more about vampire medicine than I ever will."

Regina reached out and he took her hand. "Thank you, Don, for everything."

He smiled at both of them and picked up his bag. "I'll be outside if you need me. There are a lot of anxious people out there to see you, but please take it easy. You need time to heal."

"She will, Don," Silk spoke for her and watched him leave the room.

She turned her attention back to Regina. "You want me to leave so you can rest?"

Regina smiled and pulled her close, hugging her as tightly as her weakened limbs allowed. "No, sweetie. I thought you were dead, until I saw you here, and I don't ever want to feel that way again. I love you and need you with me."

Silk kissed her lips softly. "I love you too."

"Paul didn't make it, did he?"

"No," Silk answered, her voice dropping a bit. "I tried to get to him but . . .," she took a breath, "when I saw them throw you in that van, I didn't want to live either. Up until a week ago, I continued to feel that way, trying to will myself to die."

"What changed?" Regina asked, watching her closely.

Silk hesitated. She wanted Regina much stronger before she told her the truth about her parentage, and scrambling for an answer, she said the only thing she could think of. "Sigrid."

Regina kept staring at her and she continued. "After they took you and killed Paul, I . . . I couldn't seem to function. Thinking about what they might do to you . . . it left me empty inside, and I didn't want to go on." She stopped, an ironic smile coming to her face. "Sigrid forced me to realize that I was needed and to get off my ass and help get you back."

Regina finally released her hold on Silk and leaned back against the headboard. She folded her hands across her lap and looked directly at Silk. "Will you be honest with me, love?"

Silk felt her heart skip a beat, thinking Regina had seen through her hesitation, "Of course."

"How did she do in my absence, honestly?"

Masking her sigh of relief that her secret was still safe, she relaxed a little. "She spent every waking moment looking for you and still managed to keep her end of the company running smoothly. When every avenue we had explored to find you bottomed out, she tried a new one, Cameron."

Regina smiled. "The hunters' network helped find me?"

"Yeah," she laughed. "They gave us the lead and we followed it to you."

The smile disappeared from Regina's lips. "There's more though. I sense a tension amongst you. Sigrid even said something about deserving to be slapped or worse. Tell me the truth, Silk."

Silk chewed her lip for a moment but realized that her lover wouldn't be put off. "She's been a little overbearing," she admitted, "but that's because she was so worried about you. She was so focused that she blocked everyone out and tried to do it all alone. After our talk, she lightened up some."

"Some?"

Silk shifted uncomfortably and Regina rested her hand on her arm. "There's been some animosity over the bond you share. Everyone was so worried about you, and I think nerves got a bit frayed."

Regina knew that nerves had not been the only problem. There had been a shift in power and Garrett, along with other family members, would never accept anyone other than herself as head of the family. As much as Sigrid was liked and loved, some of the family would never accept her as the head of the family, especially Garrett. "Thank you," she smiled.

Returning the smile, Silk took Regina's hand into her own and brought it to her lips, brushing tender kisses across the scarred knuckles and fingers.

Regina closed her eyes. "I've missed your touch."

Scooting up beside Regina, Silk settled in and enveloped her in her arms until they were face-to-face. "Never again. I love you, Regina."

Timidly, Regina leaned over and looked at Silk's face. "I love you, Cherie." She then completed the statement with a warm kiss. In the safety of those arms, Regina drifted back to sleep, Silk watching her with love.

On the next occasion she woke up, she found herself wrapped snuggly in Garrett's arms and after they exchanged kisses, she addressed the things Silk had mentioned.

Sigrid has spent the last twenty-four hours making necessary calls and regaining her strength. One of the others from the inner sanctum stayed with Regina constantly, who was gradually growing stronger, but Sigrid had not been able to get in to see her.

Finally getting family business taken care of, she decided to put in her appearance. Walking softly to the bedroom, she stopped short of knocking when she overheard Martha and Regina's hushed conversation.

Regina's voice was shaky and low as she spoke. "I was doing okay, despite the rapes and tortures, I was holding on to my sanity. It was when I saw what . . . was in that pit and they threw me in there with them . . . I . . . just . . . couldn't . . ."

The bed springs creaked as Martha moved and, by the sound, was hugging Regina. "Don't think about it. You survived and you're home. All that's in the past."

"But I became one of them."

"You survived," Martha reassured. "You survived the only way you could. You have no burden of shame here and I don't want to even see a glimmer of it in your eyes. We found you, brought you home and the effects were reversed. That's all that matters, got it?"

"But the nightmares—"

"Will pass in time," Martha soothed. "You have been through hell and back, but you will be all right. You're a survivor and you have all of us to support you and love you."

Now Sigrid did step forward and knock softly on the door. Despite what she'd heard, she mustered a warm smile and eased her head into the room. "Good morning."

"Good morning," Martha returned and slowly stood up.

Sigrid stuck her hands into her jeans' pockets and ambled in, shuffling over to the bed. "How's the patient?"

Martha patted her shoulder, a frown crossing her face when she saw that Sigrid was wearing a shoulder holster and gun. "Fine, getting stronger and better by the minute."

Sigrid bent down and kissed Regina's cheek, then sat down on the edge of the chair that was stationed by the bed.

"I'll see you later," Martha said as she headed out of the room. Her face radiated a newfound concern that Sigrid was now going around armed.

Regina was dressed in sweat pants and a cotton T-shirt and was reclining against a pillow, her legs draped on top of the bed covers. She crossed her arms across her chest and gave Sigrid a disapproving look. "And just where have you been all this time?"

Sigrid hung her head a bit, her shoulders hunching up. "Taking care of company business and letting the family know that you're okay."

Still maintaining the stern pose, she nodded, "Uh-huh. I guess that took up all your time, so that you couldn't even poke your head in and say hi?"

"Well, I had some sleep to catch up on too, and the one time I did come by, you were out like a light," she defended.

Regina laughed and sat up. "I guess you have been busy the last few months."

Sigrid shrugged and leaned back in the chair. Regina, too, had noticed the firearm at Sigrid's side, but said nothing. "It's becoming a habit for me to thank you for saving my life. This time I really do owe you my life."

"You owe me nothing, Reg," Sigrid stated firmly. "We're family and family helps one another out, especially when one of them falls in with a bad crowd," she finished with her familiar side grin.

Seeing that grin brought a warm feeling rushing over Regina, and she chuckled as she ran a hand through her hair. "I have missed that sense of humor. If you won't accept my thanks, will you please extend it to Cameron for all his help."

Sigrid shifted in her seat and crossed her legs. "Well . . . now that you mention him, I was . . . well . . . thinking about paying him a visit. I mean, I'm so close and I haven't seen my niece in four months."

Before Sigrid could continue, Regina held out her hand, which Sigrid latched on to. "Of course, honey. It would do you a world of good. And after the last few months, I think you need and deserve a break."

Sigrid was hesitant and Regina recognized it. She had known Sigrid long enough to see the doubt. The young woman was always trying to help others but felt that her own needs and wants could wait, despite how much she needed her own time and pleasures. "I don't . . . I think I need to stay with you for now. Maybe when you're stronger—"

"Hold it!" Regina called and sat up straight, leaning toward her. "I'm fine. This place is more heavily guarded than the White House, and Don says that the poison is gone from my bloodstream. I can spare you for a few days or weeks, so go see your brother. You and I have a lifetime together, several lifetimes. Go see your brother."

Sigrid met her eyes, uncertainty still evident. "Are you sure? I don't mind waiting for a while."

"Go!" she ordered firmly, then smiled. "Tell him I said thank you."

Sigrid's face lit up, and she moved over to the bed wrapping her arms around her aunt. "If it's okay, I'll leave in the morning. The quicker I go, the quicker I get back."

Regina brushed her hand down Sigrid's curly hair. "That's fine, honey."

"Thanks," she finished, a shadow crossing over her features.

After several hours of heated lovemaking, Ty and Sigrid lay in one another's arms, pleasantly exhausted and savoring the closeness that had been absent between them the last few months.

The quarter moon cast a dim light across the landscape, but they had settled a considerable distance from the cabin, out of sight of those in the house and the twenty unseen guards that were posted around the property. Silk's sensor devices also surrounded the area and with all the precautions taken, the house and its occupant could be no safer.

Ty had spread out a blanket on the grassy hill, and they both lay nude, the feeling of the soft cool breeze making their senses and skin sing. He propped up on his elbow and lightly traced patterns on her smooth flesh with his index finger.

She closed her eyes, relishing his touch and its effect on her. Occasionally, a soft moan or gasp escaped her lips as he used his mastery and experienced touch. She reached up to caress his face and was startled to feel him frowning. Her eyes flew open and she met his. They were bright and caring, but troubled, and she realized that he knew what she was up to.

During the last few days, she had made several trips to the little town of Trenton at the foot of the mountain. Her pretense was to secure supplies, which she did, but at the same time she was also gathering supplies for her own trip. She contacted Patrick and gave him a very detailed list of the things she needed and where to send them once they were gathered. Now she had a package waiting for her at the post office in town.

"You're going after him, aren't you?"

She remained quiet, pained that she couldn't retain the feelings they had shared only moments ago.

"Answer me," he demanded.

"I have to. I'm the only one who can stop him, once and for all."

His pattern tracing stopped, and he sat up. "I'm going with you."

She too sat up and took his hand into her own. "No. I am his progeny and it has to be this way."

"You need someone to watch your back," he protested.

"No."

He decided to try another tact. "I could tell the others. Tell Regina. They'd stop you."

She leaned forward and brushed a kiss on his lips, then sat back. "But you won't. You said you wanted the old Sigrid back, and this is the only way to accomplish that. I have to face him and destroy him. Until I do this, I can never be at rest or complete."

"Fine," he argued, "but why go alone? You need some help."

"I will not be responsible for more lives lost to him. You know I have the power to defeat him, but I need to concentrate all my energy on him. I can't spare any worrying about anyone that might be with me."

He lay back down, staring at the sky. "What if it's you that's destroyed?"

She looked down at him and rested her hands on his muscular chest. "If it comes to that, and it won't, then know that I didn't die without taking him with me. If I have to die to take his life, then so be it."

He turned his eyes on her, tears beginning to glimmer in them. "I don't want to lose you."

"Nor I, you." Sigrid assured. "But if we don't stop him now, he will continue to gnaw at us until there's nothing left of the family. If I do . . . die, then know this: I love you with all that I am. All my heart and soul." She lay back beside him and rested her head on his shoulder. "I am going to see Cameron before I start my journey. Tonight, I want to be with you and be loved by you."

"Cutting your ties?" he questioned.

She propped her chin on his chest and stared hard at him. "Hardly. I don't plan on being destroyed. I just want you to realize how much you'll miss me while I'm gone."

He stroked her back and kissed her forehead. "I'm not complete without you." She snuggled closer, knowing that she had his silence, if not his blessing.

"You better come back to me, Sigrid Derrick," he said after a few moments.

She ran her hand up his thigh and raised an eyebrow. "Care to show me what I'll be missing?"

She'd said her goodbyes the next morning, remaining casual and nonchalant. The mood of the household and its residents was jovial and light as she departed. Only Ty remained quiet and solemn and stayed close to his mate.

He loaded her empty suitcases into the car then drove her down the mountain to the post office to pick up her package. Then he drove her to the local airport that was forty-five minutes away in Chattanooga, Tennessee. They spoke very little on the drive, mainly to iron out any details that might have been overlooked. He knew by speaking with her that she had been planning this since they found Regina and was impressed at all the plans she had made without anyone being the wiser.

Once they reached the airport, he checked her in and waited with her; again the silence weighing heavily. She watched him, knowing how difficult this was on him and loved him all the more for not interfering. She promised to call before she left Cameron's and to keep in touch while she was on her mission, but he knew the last promise would be broken. Once she dived into her search, she would remain submerged until Terrence was dead.

When at last her plane was to leave, he walked her to the gate and held her tightly, his body shaking with fear and grief. She clung to him, trying to soak up his love and strength, knowing she could use all the help she could get on this trip.

The boarding passengers smiled to see a couple so much in love that they didn't want to part. They kissed—a long passion-filled kiss—and with nothing left to say, she pulled away and began down the boarding ramp.

She had one stop to make before flying into Miami and had made sure to get a ticket with a layover of a few hours in Atlanta. Renting a car, she drove out of the city and headed for the country. It was a little town outside of Atlanta that she sought, and when she found it, she quickly parked the car in the grassy field. She crossed the pasture and smiled as she approached the sign flying above.

"Tony's Traveling Wonder Show" was painted in bright letters and surrounded by cheery drawings. She walked past the ticket booth into the city of new, brightly colored tents.

It had hardly been two weeks since she had last seen the traveling carnival, but already the improvements were apparent. The ragged tents and signs had been replaced with more colorful and bigger ones. The games and booths gleamed with newness, and the cheap tattered stuffed animal prizes had been replaced with better quality animals and prizes. The food booths were clean and up to code and the welcoming smells of popcorn and cotton candy soaked the breeze.

It was past noon and many of the Carnies were just getting started as they set up their booths for the night business. The fall season was going to be over in a few more weeks and with it went the show, at least until spring. With the new owners making all the improvements, the workers and booth operators wanted to make sure they would have spots for the next year.

She found several men picking up trash and discarded candy wrappers from the previous night's visitors, and she stopped one to ask for directions.

The freak show tent was larger now and much more comfortable than the old one. She had insisted that it no longer be called the Freak tent, so now a sign proclaiming it the "Unique Tent" hung over the door flaps.

She eased in and glanced around. The tent was divided into sections as before, but now each section was much more comfortable and spacious for its inhabitants. Her eyes fell on Tony at the far side of the tent.

He was dressed in black pants and a black T-shirt and was absorbed in checking all the stalls before the nightly clients showed up. She watched him a moment, her heart warmed by the energy and obvious love the man put into his job. Allen had told her that the little man was tireless and knew the business inside and out. He had been awed at how quickly, with Tony's help and connections, the carnival had actually turned into a moneymaker.

She took a few tentative steps, not really wanting to bother him when he was so busy, but her time was of the essence, and she cleared her throat.

He instantly turned around and a smile covered his face that was so genuine and warm, she thought she might cry. "Sigrid! You're back," he greeted with excitement and rushed over to her.

He wanted to hug her but feared that she might be insulted, so instead he extended his hand. She looked at the proffered hand, took it and then pulled him into a hug. He relaxed into the hug and gave her a squeeze. "I'm so glad to see you. How's your aunt?"

They parted, but both still wore their smiles. "Much, much better, thank you. I wanted to stop by and thank you again for helping her and see how you and the show are doing."

His face fell slightly. "You are staying for the show tonight, aren't you? I want you to see how much better the carnival is now."

Sigrid kneeled down. "I can't stay, Tony, I'm sorry. I have to go to Florida on some business, and my plane leaves in a few hours."

He took her hand and led her over to his cubicle and they sat down, side by side on the wooden steps. Although he was only forty years old, his eyes were those of an old man. "This business is the trouble kind, isn't it?"

She smiled and patted his knee. "Nothing I can't handle."

His gaze unnerved her, and she decided to change the subject. "The place looks great. Allen says you are a man that knows what he's doing. You can feel that it's a better atmosphere now. You're doing a wonderful job, Tony."

Hesitantly, he dropped the earlier topic. "Thank you. Between Allen's business sense and my carnival know-how, I think we can make this show a real success. Allen's even managed to get some bookings up North next spring and that is an impressive feat."

"I have complete confidence in both of you. I'm glad you're getting along so well. I want you to be happy, Tony."

"I'll never be able to repay you for all the happiness I have now." He blushed sincerely.

"No need," she returned.

Tony fell silent for a moment, glancing around the tent. "You know," he replied solemnly, "if there's ever anything I can do to help you with this business you're taking care of, you have but to ask."

Sigrid kissed his cheek. "Thank you, Tony, but unless you know anyone in Europe, I'm afraid I have to do this alone."

A broad smile covered his face. "What part of Europe?"

She looked at him, unsure of his sincerity and then remembered that he was from Germany and was bound to still have family and connections there. "I need to find the man that brought my aunt here, and I believe he's hiding in Europe."

"The seedy character with the scarred face and cane?"

"That's the one and he's a very dangerous person, Tony. I don't want you to get involved in this. You saw what he did—"

His face hardened. "Hey, danger is nothing new to circus folks and we uniques look out for one another, remember? Tell me what you got and what you need."

She left Tony an hour later in a much better mood than when she'd arrived. He understood the need for secrecy and swore to tell no one of her visit or what information he had given her. When she arrived back in Atlanta, she made arrangements for a universal cell phone to be registered and delivered directly to Tony. After making two more stops, she headed back to the airport with ten minutes to spare to catch her flight to Florida.

Cameron was anxiously awaiting her arrival at the airport gate, shuffling from one foot to the other as he took advantage of his height and searched over the heads of the other people awaiting disembarking passengers.

He stopped in mid shuffle when he spotted her. Smiling proudly, he watched some of the other men turn their attention to the beauty he once considered his runty little sister as she strode down the tunnel.

Every time he saw her, he was awed by her glowing beauty and strength. When they were together, they were teenagers again, but he could never fully ignore the power he felt that bubbled underneath her surface.

Her face lit up when she saw him waiting, and she moved more quickly through the crowd. When she reached him, he swept her up in his arms and held her so tightly that she lost her breath for a second. When they parted, she softly kissed his cheek and then clasped his hand. He started to head for the luggage carousel but felt her restrain his arm, and she explained that all she had was her carryon bag. Confused by her lack of bags, she shrugged and led the way to his car.

The Florida heat was still present as they walked across the asphalt, but the sweltering humidity was absent and signaled the fall season. Once in his Astro van, Cameron began asking her a flurry of questions about Regina and her abduction. She relayed Regina's thanks to him and began recounting the details of the last few weeks in a much less exciting and gruesome fashion. She told him how his clue had led them to Regina and of her rescue and subsequent fight for survival. He drove in silence, listening to every word and knowing she was watering down the truth, but accepting her version, understanding that she tried to shelter him from the more frightening aspects of her life.

As they neared the beach house, he filled her in on how everyone in the Reynard household was doing. Up until Regina's abduction, Sigrid had visited and called often, but that had stopped when all her efforts were focused on finding her aunt. Before that, she had even toyed with the idea of buying a house in the area, wanting to spend as much time with them as she could. She had been present at Cameron and Katie's wedding, standing as matron of honor for Katie, and she had paced the waiting room like a panther when Cheryl Ann had made her appearance in the world. While holding her hour-old niece, they had asked her to be the child's godmother, a task she happily accepted.

Cameron had barely stopped the van before Sigrid was out and jogging up the sidewalk to the house. Katie met her at the door with a smile and a hug and then moved aside for the object of Sigrid's desire.

The baby was two months shy of her first birthday and was rapidly crawling across the carpet to greet the visitor. A tuft of white hair bounced as she covered the area, and her blue eyes were wide and sparkling. She wore a huge grin that revealed four new teeth and cooed excitedly.

"Hello, my angel!" Sigrid greeted warmly, dropped her bag by the door and fell to her knees, arms open in welcome.

Cheryl Ann crawled into her arms and giggled as she was swept up into her aunt's embrace. Cameron joined Katie at the door, sliding his arm arounds his wife's waist as they watched the scene.

"Good," Katie sighed, "now Cheryl Ann has a playmate."

Sigrid held the baby close and talked in soft tones, her face glowing and the baby obviously enjoying the fuss over her.

Cameron shook his head slightly. "I swear, you could be gone a year and she would light up like a star the minute you come in. Other than us, you're the only person she takes to like that." He dropped to his knees and joined them on the carpeted floor.

"Cameron, don't you know that one child always recognizes another," Katie replied seriously as she too kneeled on the floor.

Sigrid made a face that Cheryl Ann laughed at and then set her down on the carpet. "I only pray that she doesn't get her mother's poor sense of humor."

Cheryl Ann crawled to her father and Katie stuck her tongue out at Sigrid. "Go drain a turnip."

Sigrid laughed and winked at her sister-in-law, then turned her attention back to the baby. Katie and Sigrid had a wonderful relationship that included jokes and insults that were thrown with love.

Before the wedding, Sigrid and Cameron had discussed and decided that Katie should know the truth about Sigrid. During one of her visits, they had set her down and told her about Sigrid's vampirism and immortality. To their surprise, Katie was open-minded and a fan of the supernatural. She had been a little afraid at first, but Sigrid had quickly put her at ease and happily answered all of her questions.

Katie rose to feet. "Well, I can't babysit all day with you, children. I have to fix dinner. Cam, be a gentleman and bring in your sister's bags."

"That's all I brought, Katie," she replied and motioned to the carry all.

"All you brought?" she repeated. "I thought you'd be staying a while."

Cameron gently put the baby down on the floor and looked at his sister, curious about the length of her stay as well.

"I have to leave day after tomorrow," she sighed.

"Why so soon? I thought you be here at least a week or two," Cameron asked.

Sigrid kept her eyes low and voice casual. "I have some important business to take care of. I may be out of the country for a while, and I wanted to see you before I left."

An uncomfortable silence fell over the room and even the baby frowned as she looked at the adults to be reassured. Sigrid saw the look in her brother's eyes and picked up the baby, immediately changing the subject. "You have an anniversary coming up and my angel has a birthday, so I thought we might do some shopping tomorrow. I hope to be back before then. Is shopping okay with you guys?"

Katie's eyes lit up. "Shopping? Shopping? That's the magic word favorite sister-in-law of mine. I think we can accommodate you. Now, if you'll excuse me, I need to get dinner started."

"Business trip, huh?" Cameron said skeptically.

Sigrid leaned over and hugged him. "Yes. Business trip. I need to go upstairs and call Ty, let him know I arrived safely."

"Sure," he answered and watched her climb up the stairs to her room.

Shopping was an understatement once they got going. The four of them hit every mall, specialty shop, and outlet strip within a twenty-five-mile radius. She bought Cameron several sweaters and pairs of pants, Katie some business suits for work, and Cheryl Ann got whatever caught her fancy. Sigrid bought herself some business suits saying she needed them for her trip, but she also managed to slip a few other items among her purchases.

By four o'clock that afternoon, Cameron's Astro van was packed with clothes, toys, and four very pleasantly tired people. Cheryl Ann insisted on staying close to her aunt and she was now napping as Sigrid gently strapped her into the car seat.

Knowing how tired they were, Sigrid offered to treat them to dinner, an offer that was quickly accepted. Cameron drove to a small, quiet restaurant not far from the beach house, and they had a good hearty meal.

Once home, Cameron put Cheryl Ann to bed and then joined the two women downstairs for drinks and adult conversation. "I wish you could stay longer," Katie smiled as she settled next to Cameron beside the fireplace.

Sigrid took a sip of her special brandy mixture and leaned against the chair across from them. "Hopefully this trip won't take long, and I'll be back in no time."

Cameron sat up straighter and looked at Sigrid sternly. "Why do I get the feeling that if I picked up the phone and called Regina, she wouldn't be too happy about this trip?"

Sigrid met his eyes, then looked away, saying nothing.

"Do you think I didn't notice the armory you were slipping in amongst all those purchases today? You're going after Terry on you own, aren't you?"

"Cameron, don't," Sigrid said softly.

Katie put her hand on Cameron's shoulder. "Honey, this is something that Justine obviously doesn't want to discuss."

Cameron's voice and posture mirrored his father and Sigrid felt a chill go down her spine. "That's right. She just wanted to say her goodbyes and disappear into oblivion."

"You don't understand, Cam," Sigrid stated, shifting uncomfortably on the floor.

"Revenge! It's not that hard to understand. Terry had been messing with you for years and when he hurt Regina he went too far."

Cameron and Sigrid both tensed and Katie realized that they were getting ready to face off. She started to leave them alone when Cameron grabbed her hand. "Sweetheart, please stay. If she won't listen to me, maybe you can talk some sense into her before she goes off and gets herself killed."

Katie hesitated. She and Sigrid's relationship had been great since day one, and she loved her sister-in-law, but she also respected the power the woman held. "I don't know all the details of what's happened between you and this Terry Baker, but I do know he is dangerous, and I want my daughter to know her aunt, not just a memory of her."

Sigrid's defenses dropped some. "Low tactic, Kat."

"Good!" Cameron jumped in. "Vampire or not, I will not stand by and let you just go off and get yourself killed."

Sigrid rose up to a crouch. "Why are you so sure I'll be the one killed?" she shot back.

"He's older, more experienced. I am not a complete novice on these things. Hell, look at what he did to Regina. I don't want that to happen to you."

"It won't," she replied softly.

"You can't be sure of that," Katie added with concern.

"Tine," Cameron said, his voice calmer, "I know you have reason to hate him and want him dead. He killed your mother and has tried repeatedly to kill you and Regina. The only reason he hasn't come after me is because he thinks I'm dead. Please, honey, don't do this."

"And what about if he does find out about you? You have a family now and I won't let anyone destroy that. His reign of terror is going to end now. I will not allow him to hurt anyone else that I love. I have to do this."

They remained silent for several minutes. Cameron and Katie soaking in what she had said and trying to come up with a convincing argument. Sigrid sat patiently, waiting on the next barrage.

"I appreciate you wanting to protect us, but not at the expense of your life. There's more going on here than you're saying. Why now?"

She took a deep breath and decided to finally be honest with him. "Cam, he's my father."

Cameron's brow furrowed and then his eyes widened, his face draining of color. "I . . . I thought he was your uncle."

"That too."

Now he was puzzled. "Huh?"

Katie's understanding clicked in and she looked at Sigrid with sympathy. "He raped his sister, your mother."

Cameron's face fell as she saw Sigrid nod yes. "Oh, honey," he said and leaned forward resting a hand on her arm. Before she could say anything else, his hunter instincts kicked in. "But vampires can't reproduce. That's what all the literature says."

"You should know by now how misleading that is. It's very rare, but not unheard of. Ty's parents were vampires as well. Regina said that normally the children die." She left out the rest as it was too much information to share with a mortal, even her brother.

"One of them was Terrence's other child," he said with worry.

Sigrid smiled. "That mystery's been solved."

"You know who and were they are?"

"Silk," she answered softly.

Cameron cocked his head to the side. "Silk?" he repeated, thinking of the redheaded French girl that was one of Sigrid's closest friends.

Sigrid nodded. "Yes, I have a sister."

"We have a sister," he corrected.

"We," she agreed.

Katie interrupted them. "I understand your reasons for hating this guy, and I don't blame you, but the point is he's stronger and probably more powerful than you."

"Unless . . ." Cameron pondered aloud as he stood up. He began pacing around the room as his instincts and knowledge kicked in full throttle. "If two of the oldest, most powerful immortals were able to conceive, chances are the child could equal, maybe even surpass the parents." He stopped suddenly and looked at Sigrid, realization dawning on his face. "That's why he wanted you, the child, killed. The only question is, were his fears realized? Are you more powerful?"

"Yes," she stated simply without a hint of conceit. "And I'm the only one who can stop him once and for all."

The next question she expected. "How powerful are you and who was you Sire?"

She simply smiled and shook her finger at him. "Now, Cam, you know I can't tell you that. I know what you're thinking, so suffice it to say that old Terrence is in for a few surprises."

Katie scooted off the ledge of the fireplace and kneeled in front of Sigrid, taking her hands in her own. "I've always joked with you about your . . . life and maybe . . . to be honest, I was a bit afraid when I first found out, but I thought it was cool and admired your conviction, loyalty, and strength. You are part of my family and I love you. I know you well enough to know that you have to do this, so go and please be careful. Come back to us in one piece, because I want my daughter to have you in her life. I count on you to watch over her when we're gone and when she's a grandmother. You're the only one who can." With that Katie kissed her cheek, stood up, kissed her husband, and disappeared upstairs.

Brother and sister watched her leave and exchanged smiles. "I'm glad you found her, Cam. She reminds me of Mom."

Cameron sat down beside her and put his arm around her shoulder. "Yeah, she's something special."

They sat in silence, side by side, watching the crackling fire for a long while. Finally, he spoke up. "Okay, you have to go, but I have one condition."

"Name it."

"You call me every two days between 8:00 and 9:00 p.m. my time. If you call one minute past nine, the line will be busy because I will be alerting Regina and the whole damned family. In the meantime, I'll stall Regina and give you as much time as I can. Is it a deal?"

Sigrid kissed his cheek. "Yes. As a matter of fact, it's a good idea."

"I do have them occasionally."

"Well, I'm exhausted and I need to check in with Ty. I want to be on the road in the morning."

Cameron remained seated as she stood up. "Good night, Tine. I'll see you in the morning."

"Good night, big brother," she answered and went upstairs.

The mood that morning was quiet and sedate. Katie had fixed a light breakfast, and she and Cameron watched as Sigrid played with the baby. Even the little girl, usually so happy and energetic, seemed to pick up on the mood and was whining and clinging to Sigrid.

By eight o'clock, Sigrid was packed and ready to leave. She kissed Katie, the woman hugging her tighter than usual and gave Cheryl Ann a hug and kiss, then promised to be back as soon as she could.

Cameron walked outside and watched as she made sure her bag was tied to the Harley Heritage. As he observed her, he couldn't help but snicker. She was dressed in black jeans and boots, a purple shirt and a long black coat, similar to the ones worn by gunslingers of old. A fitting analogy since the coat harbored at least ten different weapons, each one deadly and in perfect working condition. She put on her sunglasses and turned to face him.

"You look like the Terminator in drag," he grinned.

"Just the look I was going for."

He grabbed her and hugged her fiercely. For a moment she felt like a little girl again and longed for the innocence that accompanied childhood.

"You do what you have to," he whispered in her ear. "Kick his ass and then come home."

"I will," she sighed, not wanting to release her brother.

Laughing self-consciously, they parted and she took a few steps to the bike. She climbed astride the Harley and pulled on her helmet.

"Day after tomorrow," he called as she primed the engine.

She tapped her watch and replied, "Day after tomorrow." Then the engine roared to life.

He was reminded of the sound of a hungry lion as the bike growled down the street and vanished.

With Cameron's help, Ty managed to keep Sigrid's whereabouts a secret from Regina for a full week, which was longer than he expected. Now, having told her, he was prepared for her wrath.

Her health had improved rapidly over the last few days, and physically, she was as good as new, according to Don. Psychologically, she would need some time and support to heal fully, and it would not be an overnight process.

Her eyes sparkled as she stood up and faced Ty, a cynical smile playing on her lips. "I couldn't have heard you correctly. She went where?"

Martha and Garrett silently entered the living room, ready to take action if need be.

"She's gone after Terrence. She's going to finish this, once and for all," he repeated unwaveringly.

Regina laughed, her eyes glowing red. "Finish Terrence! She's a child! And you let her go on a suicide mission, you bastard!" Regina leapt at him and landed firmly against his chest, knocking him backward, and they both crashed into the coffee table. The force and weight fractured the table and sent shards of wood and glass across the living room.

Not wasting a second, Regina straddled him, her strength and speed catching him off guard as he lay on the floor in the ruins of the furniture. He offered no resistance as she leaned into his face. "How much of a head start does she have on us?"

When he didn't answer, she bared her fangs, spittle dripping into his face. "You tell me everything, you bastard, or I'll rip your throat out."

"That's enough!" Garrett stated firmly as he and Martha moved in and secured a restraining hold on Regina, lifting the tiny woman off her much larger opponent.

"Let go of me!" She growled and fought against them. "If I find out the two of you had a hand in this, I'll tear you to ribbons."

Ty stood up and dusted himself off as Regina was dragged over to the couch and shoved into a sitting position. Taking deep breaths, her fangs began retracting and her struggles subsided slightly. "You were all in on this, weren't you? Her visiting Cameron was just a ruse."

"No," Ty answered but kept his distance. He was still aching from her attack and was in no hurry to have her attempt it again. "She did go visit him. She left his place five days ago."

"Did he know where she was going? What she was facing?"

"Only the two of us knew."

"We've got to get moving and find her." She looked at Garrett and Martha. "And you two can let go of me now."

Martha and Garrett exchanged looks and loosened their grip, backing away from her, but still within reach.

Ty sighed, "You won't find her."

The two restrainers stepped forward, and their grip tightened again as she leaned forward. "Why not?"

"Because she doesn't want to be found or followed," Martha spoke softly. "You know as well as I do that this isn't Ty's fault. This was her decision. He loves her and that's why he helped her." With that, she released her hold on Regina and stood up.

Martha ambled over to Ty and put a reassuring hand on his arm. "You knew it would eventually come to this, Regina."

"I'm sorry, Regina," Ty replied. "I tried to talk her out of it, offered arguments, but you know how she is when she's determined. She was going after him one way or another, and I thought at least this way we would have contact occasionally."

"Terrence has been around for hundreds of years. Sigrid has been immortal for eleven years. I know firsthand what he's capable of. Sigrid is not ready for this." She shivered as she remembered what she had just been through in his hands.

For the first time, Garrett jumped into the conversation. "She's a grown woman, Regina. I think you're underestimating her powers." His thoughts began to echo Cameron's. "Logically speaking, she could destroy him."

"You never liked her," Regina shot back. "You think she is a challenger to my throne."

Garrett's face reddened as he bit his lip to keep from telling her his exact thoughts. "Stop and think for a minute, Your Highness. Remember what she's done in the past and her powers. Perhaps she is the one to destroy him."

It was Regina's turn to blush as she lowered her head, regretting her words to her lover. Sighing, she flopped down on the couch and cradled her head in her hands. "But not alone, Gar. She will surely need help."

Ty smiled and stooped in front of his queen. "I never said she was alone. She just thinks she is."

Shades of Gray

15

Finding one of Terrence's stateside bases had been easier than Sigrid had expected. Riding among the biker groups, especially the ones that rode only at night, she had easily locked up with some of his soldiers. For all the effort he put into secrecy and keeping a low profile, Terrence's soldiers liked to talk and brag, and it wasn't long before she found out that his main hub of operations was in California. Hollywood Boulevard was no stranger to unusual people, so Terrence's agents had fit right in. One of the things Sigrid learned in the business world was how to listen and find information, and she employed all her skills as she shadowed his safe houses and bases. To her surprise and pleasure, she found out that three of the people responsible for Regina's abduction and Paul's death were stationed in Los Angeles, including the Amazon.

The Amazon was apparently one of Terrence's new breed of soldiers and had pleased her master with her role in the kidnapping. As a reward she had been put in charge of the California operation. It was she who helped coordinate Regina's return to the States and residence at the LePope carnival, or so the gossip went.

The base was run out of a night club called Night Shadows, located on the seedier part of the boulevard. It was housed in an old warehouse and catered to the young street people and party crowd. The customers weren't even aware that they were serving two purposes, recruiting soldiers and feeding the troops that passed through the club. It was not at all unusual for one or more people to vanish per week, and because most of them were runaways or throwaways, nobody ever missed them and investigated. This was Los Angeles and it had almost become the norm.

Once she had found them, she spent a few more days observing the club and the coven members. She spotted various immortals coming and going through the club, and judging by the brutality and senseless violence they displayed during their nocturnal hunts and feeding, the new soldiers were much more dangerous than his previous coven.

While she followed them, using her powers to get closer without being detected, she was disgusted by their acts of terrorism, but couldn't help admire the grace of their speed and skills. They moved like shadows, a dark deadly beauty swirling through the night.

When she felt like she had learned all she could and knew their routines, she decided to make an appearance at the Night Shadows club.

When she walked into the dark, smoky club, she was dressed completely in black. Her hair, cut short and spiky, had been bleached sun-blonde and her attitude was one of superiority and menace. It was a look that was prevalent to the denizens of the club, and one that she felt surprisingly comfortable wearing.

New wave punk music throbbed from the speakers, and various colored lights flashed to the beat. The bouncer, a large bear of a black man, sat by the doorway and she knew instantly that he was one of Terrence's.

Sensing her presence, he turned and stared at her wearily. They weren't expecting any new visitors, and he always got tense when unexpected guests showed up. He sat up straighter and flexed his massive biceps. The mortal girl who had been flirting with him noticed the exchange and leaned in closer to him.

Sigrid's eyes never left his as she walked into the club's interior doors. She stopped when she came up beside him and he rose to his feet like a giant. His voice was deep and hostile as he asked, "You need some help?"

Sigrid cocked her head sideways and looked him over. Her look unnerved him and he could sense the power radiating from those blue eyes. Her voice was strong and dismissive as she replied, "Not from you."

Continuing into the crowd of dancing teens, she left him watching her suspiciously. He sat back down and when the girl resumed her flirting, he pushed her aside and picked up the house phone, never letting the newcomer out of his sight.

Feeling no threat from the bouncer, Sigrid moved among the dancers, enthralled by the energy and frenzy of the young mortals. Her club was geared to the upper class, but this place was so basic. No fancy clothes or light shows. The patrons were dressed in jeans, mini-skirts, T-shirts, just ordinary streetwear. The dance floor was concrete, littered with cigarette butts and dirt; the theme was to be yourself, no one to impress or buy. She watched the gyrating couples for a few minutes, completely mesmerized.

For ten years she had been so sheltered in Regina's world that she had lost touch with the real mortal world. The sights, sounds, and smells of it brought her senses to an ecstatic frenzy, and she began to understand the draw of Terrence's lifestyle.

She started moving through the crowd again, savoring the life energy and the feeling of freedom it brought. Finally reaching the bar, she pushed aside a young mortal boy with bright orange hair and took his place at the bar. He turned, anger coloring his face, but with one look at her, it faded. He simply nodded and stepped aside, freely offering her his space.

The bartender, another immortal, moved to take her order. He was short, a slender Chicano with piercing brown eyes. "What'll it be?" he questioned, trying to get a reading on her.

"House wine," she answered simply. Her time spent observing and listening had prepared her for the right code words and attitudes.

He nodded and vanished to an area behind the bar wall, leaving her to gaze around the room, people watching. She felt her hunger beginning to stir. Unconsciously, she licked her lips as she spotted a young fast dancing man nearby.

"Your drink," the bartender replied and set a wine glass filled with a thick sparkling red liquid in front of her. She turned back to face him, picked up the glass and sniffed it. Satisfied, she took a small sip. Her body sang as the red fluid coursed down her throat and, without hesitation, she downed the glass in one gulp. Setting the empty down, she looked at him. "Another."

The bartender smiled and went to get her a refill. He was back in no time and placed another glass in front of her.

Reaching for the glass, she felt the Amazon's presence approaching from behind. She did not move as a hand came to rest on her shoulder. "You're new around here," Amazon stated in a voice as smooth as honey and slid next to the bar beside her.

As Sigrid turned around for her first close-up look, she was astounded at the woman's beauty. She was almost six feet tall, slender, muscular, and well proportioned. Her long, sandy brown hair was draped over her shoulders and framed a slender, smooth, high cheek-boned face with glowing brown eyes.

Sigrid reined in her power, not wanting to tip her hand, and replied coolly, "Haven't been here before." Then she downed the second glass of house wine.

The Amazon smiled, her teeth perfect and pearly white. She motioned for the bartender and leaned against the railing. "My, my. You're either very thirsty or like the wine."

Sigrid licked the last few drops from her lips. "It's been a long trip. As for the wine, I've had fresher."

Amazon laughed. "Well, I'm sure we can find a vintage more to your liking." She turned and made a sweeping gesture toward the dance floor and its patrons.

Sigrid let her eyes follow and forced a smile, remaining quiet.

The silence made the Amazon shift uncomfortably. "Long trip, huh?" she repeated, changing the subject. "Where are you from?"

"Europe," Sigrid answered simply as she took out a pack of cigarettes and slid one between her lips.

Amazon immediately perked up, knowing this wasn't just their normal visitor. She reached into her pocket, retrieved her lighter, and offered the flame to Sigrid. "That's interesting." She smiled as Sigrid leaned in and accepted the light. "I have a few friends in Europe."

Sigrid exhaled a plume of smoke and looked directly into the woman's brown eyes, moving close. "I know."

Amazon took a half step back, still maintaining her smile, but faltering slightly. "My name is Keeran and I own this place. And you are?"

"Paula," Sigrid supplied and extended her hand. "Nice to finally meet you, Keeran."

Keeran stood up straight and nodded across the room. "It's too noisy out here. Why don't we go somewhere where we can talk?"

Sigrid dropped the cigarette onto the floor and smashed it out with the toe of her boot. "Lead the way."

Nervously, Keeran began moving through the crowd, constantly looking over her shoulder to ensure that her guest was close behind. She led them across the room and to a steel door behind the sound booth. She punched in a code on the pad by the door and then holding the door open for her guest, Sigrid walked in and found a long hallway; stopping just inside the door as Keeran locked it behind them. The hallway was empty save for seven doors stationed at intervals along the way. Keeran offered her a smile and continued down the hallway stopping at the first door they came to. Unlocking it, she again held the door open, and Sigrid was escorted into a lavishly furnished living room.

The far wall was all two-way glass that presented a panoramic view of the dance floor and the club. Four small steps led to a platform with a row of chairs set up to observe the dancers. The room was done in black and soft blues, and the furniture was all leather and brass. Slowly climbing the steps and looking through the glass, Sigrid felt like she was looking into a human lobster tank. It had only taken her an instant to realize this was the way their guests chose their meal for the evening. The immortal could pick and choose their dinner or playmate from the dancing patrons, and then have them delivered.

Keeran watched Sigrid closely, trying to gauge her reaction to the room. "Amazing, isn't it?" she suggested. "It beats hunting on the streets."

Sigrid felt her stomach turn, but smiled. "Remarkable, but I prefer the hunt."

Keeran nodded in understanding. "Well, you can't beat the taste of fear, that's why we have the playroom."

Sigrid turned her head, looking at the woman curiously.

"Don't worry, Paula," Keeran replied as she moved up the steps and sat down in one of the chairs. "I'll give you a tour later. For now, let's talk."

Sigrid looked at the woman, knowing everything was riding on this. If she ever had any hope of finding Terrence, she would have to be successful with this bluff. She had done her homework and prepared for this, now if she could only keep her cool and play along she would find the information she needed and settle all debts. Jumping in with both feet, she took a seat beside Keeran.

"How are things in Europe?" Keeran began.

"Progressing nicely."

"How is our Master?"

"Fine, last I heard. I don't see him often."

Keeran's brow furrowed. The short answers she was receiving and the attitude of this visitor unnerved her. "Just what is it you do, Paula?"

Sigrid allowed her power to increase and noticed Keeran shift in her seat as she felt it too. "I take care of loose ends."

Keeran's face fell slightly and Sigrid was surprised at the wave of pure fear that engulfed the Amazon. "Loose ends?"

Smiling, Sigrid patted Keeran's shoulder. "Don't worry. You're in no danger from me," she lied. "The loose ends I refer to concern a certain group that has lost their Queen."

Keeran sighed and relaxed, but the fear was replaced by sorrow as her thoughts drifted to Regina. "Oh. I thought that was taken care of. She should be dead by now."

Sigrid was thrown off by the woman's emotions. Pushing it aside, she nodded and leaned back in the chair. "True, but her niece is still alive and well and will undoubtedly seek a reprisal. I'm here to take care of that."

"How can I help?" Keeran questioned more out of obligation than enthusiasm. Sigrid knew that she was trying to score a few points with her and used it.

"Only to provide me a safe haven for a few days. I'm exhausted from my trip and need to do some recon before I move against them."

Keeran smiled in agreement and patted Sigrid's hand, surprised at the shot of electricity she felt at the touch. "Of course. My place is at your disposal. Anything you want or need, just ask."

Sigrid smiled, picking up on Keeran's thoughts and feelings. The Amazon was anxious to help her accomplish her mission, but there was an underlying sense of dread and mistrust. The woman held a secret and was terrified that Sigrid would learn it and report it to the master. Deeper down, Sigrid picked up on the sexual stirring of interest. It was a yearning that she decided could prove advantageous later on down the line.

Keeran blushed when she realized that her thoughts were being probed. "I apologize. I didn't mean to insult or embarrass you."

Sigrid swallowed her disgust and hatred as she moved closer to Keeran and firmly grasped her face. The fear that again swept through the woman pleased Sigrid. "I'm not either, only flattered and interested in possibly pursing this when my job is over." With that, she lightly brushed her lips across Keeran's. After a second, another kiss followed, this one more passionate and longer. Keeran responded immediately, wrapping her arms around Sigrid. Sigrid struggled to keep from giving her own response. Masking her surprise at the sparks the kiss lit in her was no easy task, and she ended the kiss quickly, just as there was a knock at the door.

Keeran pulled away, flushed and irritated at the interruption, an interruption Sigrid was pleased had come along. Sigrid sat back in the chair, resuming her cool, calm exterior as Keeran rose up and walked down the steps.

"Who is it?" she yelled and tried to slow her breathing and arousal.

The door opened and two young men came in. One was tall and muscular with wavy long blond hair, dressed in jeans and a black dress shirt. For a split second, Sigrid thought she was looking at Ward or at least a very close facsimile, then she realized that there was no connection and so kept her face emotionless.

The other man was short, skinny, and dressed from head to toe in brown leather. His hair sported a crew cut with a green streak down the side and a large gold hoop earring in his right ear and another in his left nostril.

"What do you want?" Keeran asked as she regained her composure.

"Raven said we had company," Crewcut answered and looked at Sigrid.

Keeran nodded. "This is Paula, a guest from Europe. She'll be staying here a few days and is to receive every courtesy."

Sigrid looked at them and gave a nod of introduction. Keeran turned and offered her a bright smile. "Paula, this is Razor," she said gesturing to Crewcut. "And the strong, silent one is Max. These are my associates."

Sigrid eased down the steps settling beside Keeran. She looked at the two men and feigned recognition. "Oh. The two that helped you nab the bitch."

Razor stepped forward and extended his hand. "You bet we are. I'm the one that tore the little mortal to pieces," he bragged.

Keeran jumped in before Sigrid could take his hand or answer him. "Razor, don't bore her with details she already knows."

Sigrid smiled and stepped back, using every ounce of her control to prevent the change from coming on and tearing these three to ribbons. *Soon*, she promised herself and inhaled deeply.

Max remained silent and watched her intently, making no attempt to hide his distrust. She could feel his hatred, and it made her smile more sincerely.

"You and Max have something in common," Keeran stated as she moved beside him. "He ties up my loose ends." Then she turned and faced him. "Paula is here to take care of a few loose ends for Terrence regarding the Queen."

"She's dead," he stated flatly, insulted at her presence.

Sigrid decided that he would be the most dangerous and slipped into bitch mode. "I wasn't aware that it had been confirmed. Is this something that I should relate to Terrence? You do have confirmation, correct?"

Razor grinned, revealing stained teeth. "Of course, she's dead. Terrence fixed her real good. That's the only reason he turned her loose."

Keeran picked up Sigrid's mood, but could do nothing as her guest's anger surfaced. "He didn't turn her loose, as you put it, he simply changed cages." Then she turned her ire on Max. "And until I see a body or the remains of such, I don't assume anything. Assuming can get you killed. If you are in charge of loose ends around here, I think Keeran needs a new fixer, one that doesn't openly show incompetence."

Those words went deeper than Sigrid would have guessed as Blondie took a few steps forward, his fangs bared. Sigrid's smile only infuriated him more, as did her taunt of, "Come on, little man."

"That's enough!" Keeran barked and moved between them. Sigrid held her ground, ready to rip the little grunt to pieces, but Keeran shoved him backward. "Max! Paula's right!"

He turned his glare on her, amazed that she had the gall to side against him. "Excuse me?"

Keeran tried to maintain her strong front, but when Max challenged, it crumbled slightly. "Max, until we know for sure about her, we assume that she is still a threat. Don't you remember what our Master said about her or more importantly, her niece?"

At the mention of the master, he calmed but still showed signs of anger bubbling below the surface. Grudgingly, he backed down and moved off a few steps.

"At least I know why Terrence values you and left you in charge, Keeran." Sigrid growled, wanting to get in one final jab. She turned abruptly and walked over to the bar to fix herself a drink.

Keeran's eyes flashed red at her associates for upsetting their guest, especially one this important. "What do you want?"

Razor knew her mood was bad, so he spoke quickly and to the point. "We wondered if we were going out or staying in tonight. Plus we wanted to meet our company."

Keeran sighed and glided over to the bar. Sigrid leaned against the bar, body tense, her back to them and sipped the whiskey as Keeran sat beside her. "I'm sorry, Paula. They get over anxious. They're new to the life and still have a lot to learn."

"Stupidity is no excuse. In fact, it can cost you your life," Sigrid said softly but with conviction. She noticed Keeran was fidgeting and unable to cover her unease at having her guest so upset. The ruse was working well and she had no desire to overplay and put her hostess in distress. "I'm sorry for getting so upset," she sighed. "This mission is top priority. If I should fail . . ." she hesitated, emptied the glass of its amber contents, and leaned over to Keeran. "Our Master's temper can be very destructive."

The woman's face softened and she nodded sympathetically. "I know . . .," she responded with certainty, "but don't worry. He wouldn't have sent you if he hadn't thought you could handle it."

Razor shifted from foot to foot, so full of energy he couldn't stand still. Max, on the other hand, stood unmoving, his back to the wall, watching the quiet conversation between the two women. With each second that passed, his anger grew brighter and more dangerous.

Razor's hunger was rising and he was anxious to get an answer to his question. His main concerns in life were food and sex, and he was so focused on them that he was sometimes sloppy. His talent for ruthless, violent acts earned him his life around the others. Max was the thinker. The brain. He still felt distrust for this visitor, but didn't want to take the chance of offending the master. Of course, if his guard dog were to fail and be staked, then Max could carry out her mission and move up in the master's hierarchy.

He studied her closely. He had met a lot of immortals in the last two years of his new life, but this one was different. She was no doubt older than them with more experience, and she seemed to have the ruthless quality that Terrence sought out, but there was something underneath it that bothered him. He tried repeatedly to get a telepathic link to her, but was blocked at each try. Never had anyone been able to block him out, but when he tried to probe her, he was met with a cool, silent wall. She was completely closed off to him and that angered him even more. The topper was that Keeran was obviously attracted to the powerful visitor and that could topple his setup here. His mind clicked again, and he realized she could use that attraction as a distraction for the guest and now a slight smile appeared on his lips. His job was to listen, watch, and act—and that was exactly his plan concerning this Paula person.

"Why don't we go hunting tonight? It will help alleviate the tension," Keeran suggested, trying to dispel the mood that was settling over the room.

Sigrid smiled, knowing that the strong but slightly insecure ploy had worked, yet she was still troubled by the mixed emotions radiating from Keeran. The Amazon was strong, intelligent, and faithful, but there was an underlying fear and sympathy with what Sigrid said. The most disturbing thing was the regret that was at the woman's core, something she felt compelled to investigate. "That sounds good," she finally confirmed.

"All right!" Razor squealed, "We be hunting tonight!"

Keeran shrugged, embarrassed. "Kids."

Setting the glass on the bar, she followed her new crew out.

It was the custom, Sigrid had discovered, to feed one at a time when they had a guest along. It was like a competition, showing off who had the quickest, best, or most brutal hunting skills. The four of them rode their motorcycles through the streets as if they were part of a gang or more accurately, a pack of wolves.

When they finally settled in a hunting area, the rest of the pack stayed undercover but within range to watch the activities as the hunter of the hour began their stalking.

They watched from a burned-out storefront as Razor propositioned a hooker on her way home. Tired, but in need of a quick buck, the skinny brunette accepted, and Razor led her way into the alley. Once settled in the darkness, he quickly copulated with her and then bared his fangs. The woman screamed, trying to get away as Razor tormented her like a cat with a mouse. When she tried to run past him, he reached out and seized her shoulder and threw her to the ground. Leaping on top of her, he ripped her skin-tight dress off and buried his fangs into the veins just above her breast and raped her as he drank his fill. Her screams and struggling stopped, and he finished his business by slashing her throat with an old straight razor that he carried in his boot.

Sigrid now knew how he came by his nickname as he ran across the street, giggling like a child, a smear of blood on his chin, and joined them. "I've always been a breast man," he laughed as a trail of blood dribbled down his fuzz-covered chin.

They nodded their approval of his hunt, Sigrid biting her tongue to keep the bile from rising and left the building. Climbing astride the bikes, they moved a few blocks down the street. Max was up next and his hunt was the quickest and most violent of all.

This time the pack watched from the shadows underneath a railway track as Max lured a little boy, no more than twelve, into an alley and picking the child up, bit into the soft flesh of his neck. Sigrid started to rise, ready to stop the insanity now, when she felt a hand on her arm, restraining her. Looking down, she saw Keeran's hand and jerked her head up to look into the woman's eyes. To her surprise, there was a tear in the Amazon's brown eye and a look of profound sorrow and fear on her face. Clenching her teeth, Sigrid stayed in place, her emotions jumbled. Razor was intent on the show and never noticed the exchange as Max drained the life force from the child and snapped the boy's neck. He tossed the lifeless body aside like a rag doll and licked his fingers in salute to them. The entire act had only lasted five minutes, but it was enough to let Sigrid know how dangerous this man was. He would be the first one she dealt with when the time came, and she tried to picture the act of retribution to keep from being sick at his calculated murder of an innocent child.

The pack moved on in silence, Keeran's hunt up next. They took position on the roof of a building, and Sigrid focused on the woman and her hunt. The whole evening so far had been disturbing. But even more so was the stirrings she was feeling. She couldn't take her eyes off the Amazon.

Keeran's tall, lithe frame was covered in a skin-tight, black mini-dress, the material hugging her shape and highlighting every generous curve. As she moved slowly and deliberately up the street, she made sure to tease the men loitering outside the adult theater and liquor store. After only a few minutes, she had a bite and clinging to the short, overweight businessman, she led him into the darkened parking lot of the adult theater.

The couple came to a stop in the shadowy corner, and Sigrid felt uncomfortable as the man began to paw Keeran. Amazon only tolerated the treatment for a moment before pushing the man away. Angry at the rebuff, he became forceful and shoved her against the wall, trying to take her forcefully. Releasing her fury, Keeran leapt on the man, forcing him to the ground as she buried her fangs into his thick neck.

Sigrid was surprised at the rage she witnessed and even more so because she recognized it. It was the pent-up aggression of a woman who had been on the receiving end of abuse and misuse at someone's hands. Even in her agitation, Keeran made the kill quickly and satiated her hunger, an act that Sigrid found alluring and seductive. She admired the woman's style and actions and let out a soft sigh of want.

Cutting her eyes to the side, she saw Razor and Max eagerly watching the kill, and she silently scolded herself for the lapse. Her plan had been to come here, infiltrate Terrence's group, learn his location, and then destroy his coven, particularly these three.

As she researched and watched them, knowing that they were responsible for Regina's abduction and Paul's death, her only thoughts had been of hate and retribution. With her two rooftop companions, killing them was no problem. It was the Amazon that was the problem. She found her thoughts seemed to linger on the woman, the way Keeran looked and moved brought a new wave of thoughts and feelings that completely threw her off kilter.

She was intrigued by the woman and the mixed feelings she was picking up from her. At first she had seemed like just another of Terrence's soldiers.

But Sigrid was realizing that she was not like his typical soldier. The young woman carried off the tough, seductive outer shell, but certain phrases and the persona Sigrid had employed had drawn the real Keeran close to the surface—a very frightened Keeran. Sigrid thought back to the look on her face when she restrained her from stopping Max. She wanted him stopped, was just as sickened by his actions, and instinctively tried to protect Sigrid from exposing those same feelings. Then the fear of being exposed had terrified her. Her secret that she had buried—that she wasn't an animal like the rest—had been outed in one simple movement.

Shaking off the thoughts, Sigrid smiled as Keeran joined them on the roof of the adult bookstore. "Very nice," she complimented as she helped Keeran slip into her jacket. Keeran was still unsure about Sigrid's keeping her secret quiet, but she shivered with delight as the older woman's hand brushed her skin.

"Your turn," Max interrupted, his face radiating jealously.

They started to stand but Sigrid stopped them. "No need. I've already spotted my dinner."

Sitting back down, Sigrid now arose, took off her leather jacket and cover shirt and leapt off the building, handling the three stories as if it were only a jump off a step ladder. Once on the ground, she was wearing only her jeans, boots, and a tank top. She began primping, fluffing her hair, and making sure that a generous amount of cleavage was showing. With a sigh of satisfaction, she strolled out onto the street.

Her mark was still in the same place he had been when they first rode down the street for Keeran's hunt. He was a common-street thug and a quick probe of his mind revealed that he had killed at least two people, raped several women, robbed stores, and mugged little old ladies and kids for their lunch money. He was just the type that needed a good dose of his own medicine, and Sigrid was in the mood to play doctor.

He was leaning against the front of the liquor store, scanning the street with beady green eyes in search of his next target. He spotted her an instant later and couldn't suppress his smile.

As she got closer, she picked up his scent, detecting no odor of alcohol or drugs in his bloodstream. Which meant his acts of violence were simply because he got off on them. She eyed him inconspicuously as she drew near. He was tall and lanky, his brown hair dangled from a ponytail, wearing torn jeans, black sneakers, and a Mega Death T-shirt and fatigue jacket.

Her boot heels clicked as she made her way up the street, and she could feel his eyes checking out the merchandise. She swallowed her laughter as he broadcast his thoughts and intentions and struggled to keep her face neutral.

He straightened up and took a cigarette from his jacket pocket, flicking open the lighter just as she walked by. "Evening, good looking."

She came to a stop and faced him, slipping into her comfortable Southern accent. "Well, good evening to you."

He took her response and the sound of the Southern accent as a cue of her interest and forged ahead. "You look lost. Could I be of some assistance?"

Smiling brightly, she put her hands on her hips and thrust her chest out. "That's mighty kind of you. I just got into town yesterday and decided to do some sightseeing, then my scuzzy cab driver left me down here. I'm a wee bit nervous about being alone in this part of town."

He smiled back sweetly. "Never fear, pretty lady. I'll be happy to escort you to the cab stand a few blocks over, if you like."

"Why, thank you. I feel safer already."

Raising an eyebrow, he snickered and held his hand out to her. She wrapped her arm around his and they began walking down the street chitchatting. As they approached an alley, she was seized by the hair, a hand clamped over her mouth and was dragged, kicking and fighting into the darkened passageway.

He stopped midway down the alley and shoved her against the cool brick wall. Pressing up against her, he whispered in her ear. "I'll take my hand away if you promise not to scream."

She nodded yes, crocodile tears streaming down her face.

Slowly, he took his hand from her mouth. "I'm not going to hurt you, I just want to taste your Southern comfort," he soothed and grinned at his own joke. He began rubbing his hands down her shoulders, across her breast, and down her waist. "They do grow them beautiful in the backwoods." Licking his lips, he began kissing her neck and chest.

"Please, don't," Sigrid whimpered, but with a smile on her face.

"Oh, I promise you'll like it," he answered as he thrust his hands down the front of her top and harshly grabbed her breast, fondling it roughly.

Sexually, she wasn't at all aroused, but the smell of his heated blood made her breathing increase. He heard her breath become uneven and attributed it to her pleasure, deciding to attack with more gusto. He nuzzled her breast and fumbled with her jeans as she turned her gaze to the rooftop across the street.

Keeran felt a chill as their eyes met and Sigrid smiled. She leaned forward, propping her elbows on the rim and cradling her face in her hands. Razor was as enthralled as she was, but Sigrid's look had told her this show was just for her.

Max too watched with interest, but not for the same reason as the others. He wanted to know his opponent, so as to be able to construct her downfall and his ascension.

The thug continued fumbling with her jeans, when suddenly he felt hands on his upper arms. Without warning, he was spun around, slammed into the wall and found his small, Southern Belle in the aggressor position. His face registered surprise at the action and his eyes widened as Sigrid slid her hands under his shirt and began rubbing his chest.

"Where I come from," she cooed, "we give what we get."

He slumped against the wall as her hands ventured into his pants. He groaned at the contact enjoying how this little scene was playing out, but stopped in mid grunt, snapping his head forward to look at her. Pain coursed through him as her grip tightened on his swollen manhood. His pain mixed with fear as she smiled and revealed her long incisors. "What are you?" he wheezed as she applied more pressure.

"An avenger," she growled and brought him to his knees.

He reached up toward her and she squeezed harder. "Don't touch me, you piece of garbage." Her instincts, long denied, came to full bloom, and she clamped down on his throat.

She easily supported his weight as he weakened and leaned against the wall, her body tingling as his life force raced through her. The only time she had anything but bottled blood had been when she was brought over and when she had been hurt. This was the first time she had hunted and fed, and his fear had made him all the sweeter. Her eyes rolled back as the flame of his heat encompassed her, making every nerve in her being scream in delight. Draining him dry, she let his body slump to the ground. Slowly she stood up, her heightened senses making her dizzy and giddy. She refastened her jeans and smoothed her shirt, licked her lips, then vaporized and drifted out of the alley.

Her body sang as she floated on the night air, and she savored the feeling that was engulfing her. Never had she felt so powerful, so energized; and she was anxious to explore all these new feelings.

The pack was waiting in the alley beside the bikes when she took form. Max was sitting on his bike, quiet and staring.

"Fan-fucking-tastic!" Razor glowed as he patted her back. "That was the coolest! I like your style."

Sigrid took her shirt and jacket from Keeran and slipped them on. "Thanks, Razor. A good hunt is nothing without the proper level of want and fear." She climbed astride the bike, then turned to Keeran, her eyes no longer hiding her desire. "Ride with me?"

Keeran smiled and quickly jumped on the back of the bike, wrapping her arms around Sigrid's waist. "Razor, make sure my bike gets back to the club," she instructed as the bike came to life.

With that, Sigrid revved the bike and tore down the alley, tires squealing in protest as she exited the hunting grounds.

Sigrid maneuvered the bike up and down the streets of Los Angeles, ignoring the speed limits and traffic signals. Keeran hung on tightly behind her and more than once urged caution, but her warnings were wasted as Sigrid continued at breakneck speed. Giving up, Keeran snuggled against her back, enjoying the ride and the company.

For the first time, Sigrid really understood what it was to be immortal. At the moment, riding the bike at eighty-five miles per hour and jumping parked cars and other stationary objects, the feeling was fostered. In her heightened state, she was also aware of another feeling. One that she couldn't explain or understand, but that she wouldn't refuse.

Tiring of dare-deviling and becoming more aware of Keeran pressed against her, she headed back to the club.

They still had several hours before dawn, and Sigrid followed Keeran through the club's back door and into the observation room. Once inside, Keeran locked the door and turned to face Sigrid. Neither woman could mask their want, but Keeran did pick up on her companion's hesitance. Stepping forward, she met Sigrid's eyes and seeing no reluctance, leaned in and softly kissed her.

She lingered when she felt Sigrid returning the kiss and resting a shaky hand on her hip. Parting, she leaned back and looked at Sigrid, not expecting to find her looking so childlike. "What's wrong, Paula?" she asked softly.

When Sigrid spoke, her voice was husky with passion, but her face radiated embarrassment. "I'm sorry . . ."

Keeran stepped back. "There's nothing to be sorry for. We don't have to—"

Sigrid tightened her grip on Keeran's waist, her eye's widening. "No," she protested. "I want to . . . it's just . . . that I've never . . . been with . . ." her features flushed red.

"You've never been with another woman?"

Sigrid's head fell slightly and she sighed.

Keeran found herself in an odd situation. She was not accustomed to being the aggressor or instigator. With Max or their visitors, she had always been a passive participant; her time with Terrence teaching her that the path of least resistance was also less painful. She was no novice when it came to sex. Max let her know that one of her main duties was to please their guests any way they required. Only twice during her lifetime had she been with someone she truly cared about and she had lost them both early. The woman before her had stirred something she thought had long been dead. Her desire for Paula was not in question, but whereas she expected to be taken by the strong visitor, she now found she would be the strong partner, and it was a very pleasant feeling. "I've got news for you, Paula," she smiled. "Most of my experiences have been with men. I have been with a couple of women, but I'm no expert."

Sigrid was uncomfortable showing this much vulnerability and allowing someone else to be in control, but her sixth sense told her the gamble was worthwhile and her aching for the Amazon continued to grow. She didn't understand how she could be attracted to a woman in that way, but she knew she had to be with this woman, touch her and savor her. Tentatively, she stepped forward meeting her eyes. "Please . . ."

One simple word. Its effect washed over her and Keeran wanted nothing more than to take this woman in her arms and shower her with love she no longer thought she possessed. Opening her arms in welcome, she quickly received Sigrid as she walked into the embrace.

As one, they moved toward the door off to the side of the room. Keeran reached out, twisted the door knob, and pushed it open, revealing a small but luxurious room with a king-sized bed, adorned with black silk sheets.

The room was painted dark blue and lit only by candlelight. Over a hundred candles threw light across the room, more than enough to see by, but not too bright. Again, Keeran shut the door and locked it once they were over the threshold. Their eyes never leaving one another, Keeran led her to the center of the room, stopping at the foot of the bed. Keeran would have preferred to go to her own room for this, but desire was almost to the breaking point, and there was no time to waste, so the guest room would do for now.

She felt hands brushing through her hair and leaned into the touch. Their lips came together, soft and questioning at first, then becoming more hungry. Regretfully, Keeran pulled away, looking at her student. "If you want to stop or have any questions just say the word. I want to know what pleases you."

For the first time, Sigrid's voice and posture showed strength as she ran her hands across Keeran's body. "Show me how to please you."

Slowly and deliberately, Keeran began to undress, taking pleasure in Sigrid's reaction to each new piece of exposed flesh. Dropping her last piece of clothing to the floor, she held herself proudly, letting Sigrid see her fully.

Sigrid's breath caught in her throat as her eyes drank in the beauty before her. She had already seen that Keeran had a fit and muscular body but now she was being treated to every peak and valley that the bothersome clothes had covered. With her eyes roaming and the flickering candlelight dancing around the room, she was awestruck at the marvelous body being offered her. As she took in more of the new territory, her eyes came to rest on the full, firm breast, and she unconsciously licked her lips. "Beautiful," she whispered, causing Keeran to blush at the open admiration. Sigrid started to take a step forward, tentatively reaching out. She ached to feel the soft skin against her and taste the saltiness of her body, but inexperience kept her at bay.

Keeran smiled, sensing the trepidation. She reached out, taking Sigrid's hand into her own. Sigrid trembled at the contact but quickly clasped the hand tightly and brought it to her chest. Keeran leaned in and softly delivered kisses on the smaller woman's neck and face. "I want to touch you and I want you to touch me. Show me and tell me what feels good and what you like and I'll do the same. That way we can learn together."

Sigrid moved into the hungry lips and began their own exploration of Keeran. She offered no resistance as she felt cool hands removing her clothing, only shifting when urged to free her from the fabric restraints. Her skin prickled as the last thread was discarded, and she wasn't sure if it was from the cool air or the feel of Keeran's skin against her own.

Their bodies came together, fitting like two pieces of a puzzle, and Sigrid was amazed at the bolt of electricity that shot through her as she felt hardened nipples press against her chest.

Wrapping her arms around Keeran's waist, she pulled her closer and began running her hands across the woman's shoulders, back and progressed farther south. Keeran brought her knee up and nestled it between Sigrid's legs, delighting in the dampness she felt. Sigrid's thighs gripped the brace and she pressed herself against it, smiling at the feeling of friction. She started planting light teasing kisses and bites on her tall companion and was so enraptured by the taste and sounds issuing from her that she never noticed they were moving across the room.

Keeran guided them to the bed and eased her partner down on the silk sheets. Sigrid stretched out as Keeran sat beside her, taking in the smaller woman's beauty and admiring her comely figure. Sigrid's skin was translucent gold and smooth save for a savage scar on her shoulder just above her breast. Her eyes held on the firm breast and she reached out, gently caressing and kneading it, smiling as the nipple puckered and rose in salute to her touch.

No longer able to resist, she bent down and ran her tongue across the rising skin, the action bringing a soft moan from Sigrid. Liking the sound, she proceeded to softly grasp the nipple between her teeth, twirling her tongue around it. Sigrid's hand flew up and grasped Keeran's hair, urging her to take more. With her free hand, she began rubbing the other hardened bud, lightly flicking her nails across it and drawing an even deeper moan from the woman beneath her.

Suddenly she felt two heated hands exploring her aching breast and groaned at the contact. As the hands became more insistent, she ceased her feast and lifted her head to meet Sigrid's eyes. Lovingly she removed the exploring hands and pinned them down by Sigrid's sides.

Sigrid eyes glowed with desire, her eyelids drooping in hunger and reflecting confusion at the interruption.

"No," Keeran corrected in a husky voice. "I need to concentrate on you and please you. I want to feel your hands all over me but for now . . . be patient."

Sigrid's only response was to run her tongue over her lips seductively, an action that held Keeran mesmerized as she felt her own desire rising. Taking that as a yes, she bent down and met Sigrid's parted lips, their tongues beginning a slow dance that picked up speed and intensity as the minutes ticked by. Both women felt the growing tension but neither was in a rush to end the feeling.

Keeran felt hands brush against her read-end and squeeze slightly, then a firm thigh settled in between her legs and began a steady rubbing, the touch sent tingles through her that landed in her core. Moaning into Sigrid's mouth, she rapidly struggled to regain control, seizing the hands and again putting them down at Sigrid's sides. "You're distracting me."

"I want to touch you," Sigrid whispered, the sound of hunger in her voice sending chills down Keeran's spine. "I want to taste you, touch you, and make you scream with pleasure."

Keeran's arousal stepped up with those words and the images they brought to mind. She felt her own nipples becoming painfully hard and taking advantage of the situation, Sigrid scooted down, reaching a dangling breast and latched onto it, gently grazing it with her teeth. Her tongue danced over the nub and she sucked with vigor, trying to pull as much of Keeran into her mouth as she could.

The sensation of Sigrid's teeth and tongue caused Keeran to gasp and her eyes rolled back in her head. She arched herself forward, pushing more weight and more flesh against Sigrid. She felt herself floating and a warm wet sensation settling in her lower regions.

Sigrid got greedy and decided she wanted to taste more. Releasing her treat, she moved slightly, preparing to service the other awaiting nipple, Keeran realized that she had a respite and pulled herself out of reach as Sigrid tried to seek purchase.

Sliding down, she met the frowning face of her student. "You're misbehaving again." She fussed and then stopped as she looked into those blue eyes that held no deception or reluctance in showing their desire. There had been others, too many to count. Most were men but there had been a couple of women and she had never felt this way with any of them. Her past was jaded and she was no novice at sex. It was an action, plain and simple. A part to be played and then it was over, each person going on with their business.

In her mortal days, she had found love. Both times she thought it was true love like in the fairy tales and for a while it had been. But then the sparks died and with it the romance, and they had ended leaving her doubting that real love did exist. Knowing that Paula was one of Terrence's soldiers, Keeran had expected the usual cold abusive type that served him. On the surface, this woman met that criteria but when they were alone, she sensed and caught a glimpse that there was more than that. She wanted this woman, wanted to be with her like the fairy tales from her childhood. As she gazed into those blue pools of light, she saw that this was more than just an act to her as well. In those hungry eyes, she caught a glimpse of the real Keeran, someone that had been gone for a long time.

"What's wrong?" Sigrid asked as a tear escaped Keeran's eye. Reaching up, her face full of concern, she tenderly wiped the tear away. "What did I do wrong?"

Keeran sniffed the rest of the tears back and smiled, touched by the action. "Nothing. You've done nothing wrong. I just want it to be perfect for you. I want to please you."

Sigrid clasped her hands around the face hovering above her. "That goes both ways, Keeran. You are not some hooker that's here to service me. This has to be for both of us. This has to be mutual or it doesn't mean a thing."

"A dream." Keeran told herself and she didn't want to wake up without experiencing every sensation this woman was pulling from her. Before the dream was over, she wanted to be with this woman intimately and love her with all she was. "It is for both of us," she replied and turning her face, kissed the hands that held her. She took one of the fingers into her mouth and began sucking.

The heat that had ebbed was again sparked and burning. Their lips met in a renewed passion, converging on one another with intensity. This time Sigrid complied and kept her hands to herself, lying back and soaking up all the loving attention Keeran showered on her. Keeran's hands and mouth were blazing trails across her skin, and as she worked her way down with brushing kisses, Sigrid wrapped her hands into the silky brown hair and guided her to the right avenues.

Groaning loudly, Sigrid threw her head back as Keeran reached her target. Her tongue darted and lapped at the treasure she found, taking her time to explore every crevice and fold with skill and care. She relished tasting and feeling the textures and especially the sounds she was drawing from the woman as her tongue caressed the small hardness she found. She eagerly complied when Sigrid asked for more and smiled against the tasty treat when she inserted two fingers into the awaiting woman. She felt the muscles tightening and she knew that she was running out of time, so she picked up speed. Sigrid's hips took on a life of their own as she felt the heat from Keeran's mouth continue its stroking, matching the rhythm of the long slender digits inside her.

"Harder," Sigrid begged raggedly, her body shaking with the sensations Keeran was causing, and she felt every nerve tingling with life, experiencing a pleasure like no other she had ever felt before.

Keeran did as asked, the moaning from her partner spurring her on and causing her own senses to sing with arousal. She felt Sigrid tense as the muscles tightened around her fingers. Focusing all her willpower on the task at hand, she continued, knowing that her lover was close to exploding.

Sigrid's hips arched and her grip tightened on Keeran's hair as her body released. Keeran smiled as she felt and saw the release, her smile broadening as the deep happy groan escaped Sigrid's lips accompanying the waves of pleasure that were engulfing her. Slowing her movements to a stop, she waited until Sigrid had relaxed before firmly thrusting her hand and tongue into the treasure chest again. The sudden action brought Sigrid over again, just as intensely as the first time. She finally had to stop after the third time when she heard Sigrid gasping for air.

Sliding up her still buzzing body, she settled next to Sigrid, taking the sweating woman into her arms and kissing the top of her head lightly. Despite herself, she cared about this woman and even though she knew Paula would leave soon, she wanted to spend every free moment of their time together relaying that love and pleasing her.

They lay in silence for several minutes, then Sigrid looked up at her, face brimming with new found energy. "Your turn." She grinned and let her hands resumed their interrupted explorations.

Rolling onto her back, Keeran granted her student the access she so craved and within moments was being kissed, nibbled, and fondled to new heights.

Leaving a trail of fiery kisses across Keeran's body, she repeated the actions of her teacher and integrated a few of her own. With gentle, loving touches and mouth actions, she was brought to a crashing orgasm in a matter of minutes. Unready to stop her explorations she continued, bringing Keeran's nerves to the surface. She was a very patient student and took great delight in torturing Keeran by bringing her to the edge of release and then stopping. She had Keeran whipped into such a frenzy that when she did finally bring her over a second time, it was even more fierce and intense. The older woman showed true talent with her tongue and mouth exploring Keeran's folds with the tenderest touch she had ever felt. What she didn't have in experience, she made up for in effort and ingenuity. True to her word, she succeeded in making Keeran scream out in pleasure and was able to bring her to orgasm multiple times, learning more from each round.

When Keeran begged her to stop for a moment, she eagerly slid up the Amazon's body and kissed her. Tasting herself on Sigrid's lips, made Keeran tingle again, and she let her hands start a journey down Sigrid's back, resting them on the firm rear end. They just held each other, inhaling deeply one another's scent and savoring the feelings that engulfed them. After a few minutes, Keeran took the lead and proceeded with the next lesson. A lesson that Sigrid learned just as rapidly and eagerly as she was introduced to all the modes of pleasure, and this time it was Keeran that made her scream out in pleasure.

Drowsy, Sigrid lay still, watching the dancing shadows that the candlelight threw across the room. Keeran was curled up beside her, her head resting on Sigrid's chest as she dozed. Sigrid ran her hand down the woman's hair, over her shoulders, and across her back, coming to rest on the thin scars that covered Keeran's back.

Just the feel of her lover's skin excited her, her own body still humming from the sensations that Keeran had introduced. The thought of their heated explorations made her senses tingle, and she longed to continue the lessons, but both were nearly exhausted.

Her mind drifted to Ty and a wall of guilt came crashing down on her. She loved him and when they were together their passion could light the night sky. He was a part of her and she knew that without him, she didn't want to live. However, now there was Keeran. She still loved Ty, but she also felt something for Keeran. The Amazon had made her aware of sensations and feelings she had never experienced before. She shuddered slightly just remembering the way her body responded under Keeran's gentle, loving touch. She had learned quickly and was able to return the attention much to her lover's delight and pleasure.

Keeran's stirring brought her out of her replay. The woman brushed a kiss on Sigrid's stomach and lifted her head, offering a dreamy smile. "You sure you've never been with a woman before?"

The compliment brought a blush and grin to Sigrid's face. "Positive. You're an excellent teacher."

Keeran slowly drew her fingers along Sigrid's jaw. "It helps to have a very attentive student."

They fell silent for a moment before Keeran asked, "Do they bother you?"

Puzzled, Sigrid stared at her, then realized that she was fingering the scars on Keeran's back. She stopped instantly, blushing brighter. "I'm sorry."

"Don't be," Keeran assured. "I love the way you touch me. It's been a long time since someone has touched me that way."

Sigrid moved her hand to Keeran's shoulder. "I was only curious."

Gaining some bravery, Keeran moved up Sigrid's body, planting kisses along the way before she stopped at her shoulder and tongued the scar there. "Me too."

Sigrid held the woman tighter. "You are beautiful and nothing could take away from that."

"They're whip marks," Keeran answered the unasked question. "I displeased the Master."

She was caught off guard by the anger that swelled up in Sigrid. Meeting her eyes she saw the red glint that quickly disappeared. She felt Sigrid's arms grip her tighter, trying to protect her from a beating that had happened long ago.

"Same thing," Sigrid finally admitted. "Silver sword. Almost killed me." With that she pulled Keeran closer and positioned herself so that they were spooned together.

Keeran shivered when she felt Sigrid's lips feathering over the scars on her back. Although a novice, Sigrid knew exactly how to make her body come alive, and Keeran longed to stay like this forever. Their lovemaking had been passionate, intimate, and both had screamed with the intensity their partner had sparked. Now Keeran could feel an exhaustion approaching that had nothing to do with their activities. "Dawn's coming."

"I know. We still have a little time and I want to give you something to sleep on," Sigrid purred as she rolled over Keeran so that they were face-to-face. Keeran's smile signaled agreement and Sigrid's mouth began its exploration that earlier had driven Keeran into a frenzy.

Thirty minutes later, as was the custom with Terrence's people, dawn lulled the Amazon into a deep sleep. Smiling and happy, Keeran fell still, Sigrid watching her as dawn broke. Tired from the heated encounters, she too drifted off to sleep. She only needed a few hours to replenish her strength and when she awoke, long before sunset, she eased out of bed. With her new lover and most of Terrence's people asleep, she was left to her own devices.

Ty hung up the phone and slumped on the couch. He sighed deeply and rubbed his hands against his beard-stubbled chin.

He had remained quiet and aloof during the last two weeks, only showing sparks of life when Sigrid had called to check in a few days earlier. He had talked to her for about five minutes before Regina commandeered the phone.

Keeping the call short, she told them that she had a lead and was following, that she was fine and loved them all and would call when she could. When she hung up, he had called Cameron and found out that he had received a similar call only his told him that her next call would be delayed two or three days as she was going undercover. Cameron had protested, but knew that her mind was made up, and it was useless to argue so he grudgingly agreed.

With his phone call, Ty felt his level of worry go off the scale and the regret at allowing her to go on this mission overpowered him.

"What's wrong?" Regina questioned as she entered the living room, where he sat brooding.

They had decided to stay on in the mountaintop house, and with all the precautions taken, all knew it was possibly the safest place they could be.

Ty leaned back deeper into the couch and shook his head. "I think you were right."

Her eyes widened, her mind thinking the worst as her heart sank. "About what, Ty?

"That she's not ready for this."

Regina sat down beside him, her worry dissipating slightly at the present tense of words. "Who called?"

"She infiltrated his coven last night."

Regina's tension and impatience were rising as he kept his answers short and irritatingly slow. "Ty, what's the problem? If she infiltrated his coven that means she's on Terrence's trail. Has she been hurt? Just spit it out, Ty."

"She killed someone last night. A guy off the street in a very brutal manner. Then she went dare-deviling around town and finally ended the evening by sleeping with the Amazon. The enemy and a woman. Her appearance has changed and she's not acting like herself. What is happening to her, Regina? What have I done?"

"Ty . . .," Regina soothed as Garrett came in and joined them, remembering how he had felt in a similar situation many years ago.

"Where is she?" the older man asked.

Ty shrugged, "She won't tell me—that was part of the agreement. All I know is that she is still in the States. That and she killed someone and went to bed with a . . . woman." He stopped there and cast a look at Regina remembering her relationship with Silk. "No offense meant."

Regina ignored his jab as Garrett continued, "And she's safe. It sounds like she was successful getting into his coven, and that probably required a change in appearance and attitude."

Ty shook his head. "Yeah, right Garrett. She killed an innocent mortal for sport."

"No," Regina disagreed. "Mortal, yes. Innocent, I doubt it. You know Sigrid as well as I do. If part of her cover included feeding on a mortal, you can be sure that she chose him carefully. He was most likely a criminal and, knowing Sigrid, someone that had it coming."

"Okay," Ty replied through clenched teeth. "Those you can explain. But can you explain her sleeping with the Amazon? Not only someone else, but with a woman!"

Regina nodded sympathetically and grasped his hand. "I can give you a whole list of explanations on that, but not one of them will ease your pain or help your ego get over it."

"Part of her cover, right?" he snapped as he stood up and walked to the glass doors leading outside. He shoved his hands into his pockets and glared at them, pain radiating from his eyes and voice. "Dammit, she's my wife. I love her and thought she loved me. It's bad enough that she had to sleep around on me but—" he stopped there not wanting to repeat it again.

Garrett leaned forward, clasping his hands together. "Son, I know what you're going through and how you feel." He glanced at Regina and she quietly left the room.

Ty watched and waited until she was out of the room. "It's not the same between us, Garrett," he continued.

"Oh, but it is," Garrett corrected. "Regina and I were the two of you many years ago. I loved her with all my heart, and it just about killed me when she took another lover."

"What did you do?"

Garrett laughed. "I brooded around. Had a chip on my shoulder and was mad at the world. I wondered what was wrong with me that I couldn't make her love me as much as I loved her. I wanted to find the other man and kill him. Hell, I even decided at one point that if I couldn't have her no one would."

Ty was completely involved now. "So what happened?"

"Martha's husband, George, sat me down and had a long talk with me, just like the one we're about to have."

"Garrett . . .," he sighed, "it wasn't just another man; it was another woman. It's not the same."

"Sit down and listen, Ty," Garrett instructed firmly.

Sulking like a little boy about to be lectured by a parent, he slumped onto the couch.

"What I'm about to say," he began slowly and deliberately, "is not an excuse but an explanation. All I ask is that you consider what I'm saying."

Ty nodded and sunk farther into the couch.

"I had to deal with this problem twice. The first time Regina took a lover and then when she took a female lover. It was a huge blow to my ego that she sought out a woman. I learned to deal with it, but it wasn't easy. Vampires are a highly sensitive breed. You know yourself how the senses are heightened and the desires are stronger. When you kill and feed, those feelings explode and . . . there is no way to describe how you feel. We are also an interesting breed, Ty. We are like mortals in that some of us, a lucky few, find one mate to spend their lives with, like Martha and George. Then there are those that go from one relationship to another, never finding or wanting to find that special bond. Mortal life spans about eighty years. Ours can last hundreds. It is logical that during those hundreds of years, we will meet and fall in love with more than one."

"Sigrid and Regina are very special women. Because of who they are, their needs and desires are doubled. Regina has had several lovers over the years, and she's loved each and every one of them, but none like she loves me. It is I who is still with her and will be until my death. That is my choice. I know she loves me and that my place in her heart is secure, despite the fact that she has other lovers, no one can touch my part of her. If I wanted to be with someone else, she wouldn't say a word because there is no jealousy between us. There doesn't have to be. No one could ever replace what we've been through together."

Ty looked up at the older man, his eyes watery. "But it happened so soon, Garrett."

"I know, son," he sympathized. "But answer me this. Have you been with someone before Sigrid?"

Ty shifted uncomfortably against the couch and his eyes dropped a bit. "Well, yes, but I was young and thought I was in love. This is different."

"Why? If you had been with someone when Sigrid came along, could you have just turned it off, your feelings for her? I don't know about you, but the first time I saw Regina, she had my heart. We can't help who we fall in love with or when. If we are lucky, we can go against the norm and have our cake and eat it too." Garrett leaned forward again. "You were Sigrid's first. She was infatuated with Ward, but you were her first love, the one she gave herself to. You don't realize how special that is in this day and age. If both of you live for hundreds of years, no one can ever replace those feelings for each other. Maybe because she's never been with anyone else, she was curious or maybe this was part of her plan. Then again maybe she does love another, but

I promise you, it isn't the same love she has for you, and she does love you, son. Don't ever doubt that."

"What if I lose her?"

"That . . .," Garrett smiled, "is up to you." He stood up and stretched his back. "If she does love another, when she gets back, you could demand that she give up this new lover. And knowing Sigrid, she would for you, but she would also resent you. Maybe not outwardly, but as time went by, it would eat at her and you too. This won't be an easy decision, but I'll tell you this much. I wouldn't trade my life with Regina for anything. I'm with the woman I love, and although I have to share her occasionally, we're together."

With that said, he left Ty alone to do some thinking. Regina was waiting for him in the hallway.

She grabbed his collar and pulled him close. "That was very nice."

"Thank you," he blushed. "How about we go upstairs and I remind you why I'm your favorite."

Regina took his hand and led him up the stairs. Once upstairs, as their passion grew, Regina discovered that her experience at Terrence's hands had scarred her more than she thought. They instead just lay together in each other's arms.

"I'm sorry," Regina whispered.

Garrett leaned down and kissed her forehead. "No need, my love. You've been through a terrible ordeal. I'm content to hold you. Things will get better and you know I have infinite patience."

She snuggled against his chest and remained silent.

"You're worried about her."

"Uh-huh," she said into his chest. "Do you remember your first kill?"

"Yes," Garrett admitted, thinking back to the pure ecstasy of the hunt and kill. The almost uncontrollable feelings of desire and lust to kill again just to feel that euphoria. "You're afraid she'll be tempted by the lifestyle."

"One of the most difficult things I ever did was convince the family that senseless killing was wrong. The taking of the blood of donors was just as good and would prevent needless deaths as well as keeping the hunters at bay. The hardest part was giving up the hunt and taste of fear." She rolled over and propped her chin on his chest. "This is her first kill. With her already heightened senses, what can it be doing to her? I didn't prepare her for the hunt and kill. Maybe that's why she slept with that woman, her entire chemistry was thrown for a loop. I know my niece and she would not willingly sleep with that . . . animal. Not knowing that she was one of the ones that took me to Terrence. And to be honest, I never thought Sigrid would sleep with anyone other than Ty, especially a woman."

"Bigot," Garrett chided. "Look who's calling the kettle black."

Regina didn't laugh. "I'm serious, Garrett."

"So am I. You sound like Ty. Did you not listen to what I told him?" When she fell into silence, he pushed on. "You have taught her well, my love. It will take more than one kill to sway her to Terrence's ways."

"True," she conceded, "But she could be caught in the middle." Slowly she sat up, drawing the sheet close to her. "You joined us as we were smoothing out the old way of life. Yes, you've killed in order to feed, but you quickly assimilated to the new way. I know what it's like to be caught between civilization and Terrence's ways. I'll be honest with you, Gar. I regret the lives that I took, well most of them. But the thrill and rapture of it? Oh Garrett, I long to feel that vibrant again."

Garrett rolled on to his side and looked into her eyes. "She is an adult, Regina. Yes, you love her and I know you consider her your child, but children do grow up. For all the love and guidance we give them, they have to choose their own way. You let her stretch her wings four years ago when she and Ty went to New York and she soared. She is no longer a child, and you must trust that she will make the right choices. And you must live with those choices no matter how much you disagree."

"I've been kind of obsessive about her, haven't I?"

Garrett held up his hand, fingers suggesting a bit. Then he looked at his watch. "Gee, it only took you eleven years to realize that."

Her head snapped up. "Garrett, I searched for years for her. Her life was anything but pleasant growing up, and she has saved not only my life, but Martha's, Silk's, and yours."

"And she's the child you lost, Regina," he blurted out.

Regina pulled away from him, curling into a ball and hugging the covers tightly against a nonexistent chill.

Garrett sat up and turned to face her, choosing his words carefully. "We have never discussed our son, or the pain we both felt losing him. Your despair was so deep, I thought I might lose you as well. The only thing that could reach you, that saved you, was the search for your sister's child. You took everything you had for our son and put it into Sigrid, that's why you never gave up. I shudder to think what would have happened if Sigrid had been dead when you found her. You don't know how happy I am that you found her because she saved your life twenty years before you found her."

"Is that wrong?" she questioned.

Garrett took her into his arms and held her tightly. "No, dearest. You're probably the closest thing to a mother she's ever known. Valonia died when she was three; then her adoptive mother when she was eleven. She's had you longer than either of them, and she loves you like her own mother. But it's time to let her go. She's a grown woman who has her own life to lead. Let her go, my love."

She kissed him softly, snuggling against his strength. "It won't be easy. Bear with me?"

"Always," he assured.

Sigrid stood on the roof of the night club, soaking in the last few hours of sunlight. Normally it was one of the most relaxing, mind easing things she could do, but not this day. She planned to be back downstairs with Keeran, feigning sleep when she awoke, but she needed to get some air and try to deal with her raging thoughts and emotions.

Her betrayal was foremost on her mind. By falling for Keeran she had betrayed Ty, Regina, and the family as a whole. She had never considered being unfaithful to Ty, especially with a woman, but Keeran drew something out of her she never knew existed. She loved Ty, now and forever, and the last thing she wanted to do was lose him or hurt him, but her actions last night had probably done both.

As much as she tried to blame her first kill for her emotions and loss of control, she knew it was just an excuse. True, the elation of the event had given her enough courage to act on instinct, becoming more primal, but she knew the truth of the matter. She was drawn to Keeran, wanted to be with her, hold her, and love her. Terrence had scarred the woman horribly, mentally, and physically, and Sigrid wanted to take her out of his world and show her what a real life was like.

Realizing that she was pacing across the roof, she skidded to a stop, stray gravels crackling across the roof. A decision had to be made, and it was a simple question of following her heart or her eyes. Taking a deep breath, she went back downstairs, anxious for Keeran to awaken so they could talk.

Sliding under the covers beside Keeran, Sigrid propped on her side and watched her companion sleep. She had always enjoyed watching Ty sleep, the peaceful reflection of his soul etched on his features soothed and fascinated her. She discovered it was the same as she let her eyes roam over her new lover.

As Keeran awoke, she was startled and pleased to find she had a rapt observer. She yawned and stretched seductively, her eyes never leaving Sigrid's as she rolled over and settled face-to-face with her. "Good evening."

Sigrid smiled and caressed her face. "Sleep well?"

"I thought it was just a very vivid and wonderful dream, until I woke up and saw you still here. No one has ever made me feel like you did. Fantastic, incredible, wild—no word is strong enough."

Sigrid's features softened and she brought the woman into her arms, kissing her. "Thanks for being such a patient and attentive teacher. The feelings are very mutual. I wasn't sure that I did everything—"

Keeran placed her finger across Sigrid's lips. "You were perfect. I give you an A plus." Then she snuggled closer, draping her leg over Sigrid's hip. "Ready to pick up where we left off?"

The heat and want pouring off Keeran were distracting, and it only became worse when Keeran's hand found its way to her breast. Quickly, she intercepted the hand and brought it to her lips, gently kissing each finger and then the palm. "I would love nothing better than to stay here with you indefinitely. However, I've got a mission to get started."

Disappointment covered Keeran's soft features and Sigrid felt her heart sink, not wanting to hurt her new lover this soon. "I promise I'll be back in time for a replay."

Keeran accepted the compromise and sighed, "Okay." She kissed Sigrid's cheek and disentangled from their embrace. "You stay here and I'll get some drinks."

Sigrid lay back and watched Keeran. "Breakfast in bed sounds good."

Knowing that she had an audience, Keeran took pleasure in teasing her partner as she got out of bed and stretched her nude body suggestively. "Too bad you chose door number 2," she scolded as Sigrid's breathing increased and her lips parted. Deciding to end the torture, she grabbed her robe and blew her companion a kiss. "Be back in a flash."

The club wouldn't be open for another two hours, but some of the staff had already arrived or risen. Breezing into the kitchen, Keeran fetched the freshest bottle and two wine glasses. A broad smile covered her face and her soft humming drew stares from the others, but she was in too much of a hurry to notice. Once everything was loaded into a wooden tray, she made her way back to the observation room, not noticing the silent figure waiting behind the door. "Aren't we just so happy."

She whirled around, almost dropping the tray, save for her quick reflex, it would have crashed to the floor. Max stepped forward and snatched the tray from her shaky hands, then placed it on the nearby bar.

He blocked the way to the guest room as Keeran glanced over his shoulder at the closed bedroom door. She started to send out a message when Max seized her and slammed her into the wall. She kicked out her legs in an effort to get free and then added her long nails to the struggle, clawing at his hands as they tightened around her throat. He ignored her blows and leaned in. "Stop fighting me, slut, or I will hurt you."

He had shown his ability to make good on that promise in the past, a skill he seemed quite good at. She ceased her fighting, hoping Paula had heard the commotion and would appear at any moment. For a split second, she feared for her if she did show up, but then something about Paula told her the smaller woman could teach Max a few things about pain.

Reading her thoughts, Max chuckled. "Give it up babe. The room is soundproof and even if she wanted to, she couldn't stop me."

Said with such conviction, her shoulders slumped and his smile reappeared. He brought his left hand down from her throat and it disappeared under her robe, his right hand holding her in place against the wall. Not wanting his touch, she tried to fight again, squirming to move away from his probing hand and then he made good on his promise of pain.

She gasped, almost crying out and stilled against his infliction. Satisfied that he'd made his point, he released his grip and grinned as she sucked in air. A bolt of pain still radiated in her genitals from his touch, but she would not let him see her cry, not ever again.

"Did you have fun last night," he whispered against her ear. "The two of you going at it like bitches in heat? I know you're supposed to service our guests, Keeran, but I thought you only like men. The way you were humming and smiling, like a schoolgirl in love, it was sickening. Now that I know what a slut you are, things are going to change around here."

"Bastard," she growled and instantly regretted it as his grip tightened on her throat.

"Your job is to please our guests and pick their brains for useful information," he reminded her. "Terrence may think you're bright enough to run things around here, but we both know better. You look good and you fuck good and that's it."

"Please . . .," she wheezed, struggling to get air into her lungs.

"Good," he oozed sweetly, "you remember your place now."

She stifled the cough that threatened to erupt as he released his hold, fearful that he would interpret it as an attempt to signal Paula and set him off again.

"Did you find out anything useful, while you whores were probing one another?"

Keeran tried to maintain her calm, "Like what, Max? She already told you who sent her and her mission."

"You'll excuse me if I don't buy her story," he shot back. "I want to know who she really is."

Unable to hide her disbelief, she starred at him. "You're paranoid." His harsh look couldn't still her tongue as she added. "And jealous."

"Jealous?" he repeated with surprise. "Jealous of that pit-bull bitch. Like she could actually compete with me."

Keeran smiled, no longer fearing his actions. "She wiped the floor with you. She made me scream so loud I'm surprised the whole club didn't hear it. After her, I won't let another man touch me."

His smile faltered and he used his body to keep her pinned to the wall as his hands went to his belt. "We'll see about that. When I'm done with you, even the memories will be painful."

Keeran steeled herself for the infliction of pain, but suddenly felt a presence in the room. Max felt it as well and stopped his actions, holding her in place and scanning the room.

The room was empty, but both felt the power emanating from behind the bedroom door. Only once before had they felt anything like it and that had been with their master. Both realized now that the visitor was stronger than either one of them had first thought.

"I'm being paged," Keeran sighed with relief.

Snorting with anger, Max released his hold and stepped back. Keeran rubbed her throat and watched him.

"She won't protect you forever and when she's gone, we'll continue your lesson." Seething with fury, he stomped out of the room leaving Keeran dazed and fearful.

Sigrid had sensed Max even before he entered the observation room. He thought himself of superior intellect and powers, but Sigrid easily read the man and his thoughts. He thrived on cruelty and was nothing more than a bully and thug.

With her age and powers, it was no problem observing their discussion. The challenge had been biting back her rage as Max manhandled Keeran. When she'd had enough, she released her power mixed with her anger and brought an end to the intimidation.

Once Max was gone, she slipped back into the bedroom and used her martial arts exercises to calm herself.

Keeran was still shaken and never noticed that the bedroom door was open a crack as she approached. Walking into the room, she found Sigrid lounging on the bed, smiling in welcome. "I was beginning to worry about you."

Offering a weak smile, Keeran carried the tray to the bed, desperately trying to hide her shaking hands. "I'm sorry. There was a problem at the bar that needed my attention."

Sigrid sat up and accepted the glass from Keeran, making sure to maintain their hand contact for a few seconds. "Anything I can help with?"

Keeran felt some of her fear dissipate with that touch, and she quickly climbed back into bed. "No, thanks. Just everyday stuff. Besides, you have a mission, remember?"

Sigrid emptied the glass of its red fluid, feeling her energy level rising rapidly as the nourishment took hold. She noticed that Keeran's glass remained half full, her appetite gone. "Yeah, mission," she said half-heartedly and scooted closer to Keeran.

The flinch was so subtle that Keeran didn't even realize she had done it, but Sigrid did. The woman brought the covers up to her chest and curled her knees in tight. Sigrid cocked her head to the side and looked at the woman. "Have I done something wrong?"

Fear blazed in Keeran's eyes. She turned to her lover and rested a hand on her arm. "No, Paula. You haven't done anything wrong."

"What is it then?"

Not willing to give an honest answer, Keeran simply asked, "Is there something I can do to help you with your mission? Can I go with you?"

Sigrid grasped the woman's chin and brushed her lips with a kiss. "I wish you could come with me. You, however, would be such a distraction, that I'd never get my mission done. Besides, I don't really want you to get involved in this; it could be dangerous." With that she eased out of the bed and slowly began to dress. She decided that the time had come to see whose side Keeran was truly on. "To be honest, I want to get this job over with. I don't like feeling like Terrence's attack dog. I'd like to be able to do what I want, not what the Master desires."

Keeran's already confused state tripled with those words. She felt safe with this woman and wanted to trust her, to be honest with her, but Terrence was not above testing the loyalty of his followers. "I'm sure he values you and your skills very highly. He even allows you to go anywhere you like and move around."

Sigrid laughed softly. "As long as it relates to the job, sure I can go anywhere. As long as I do my job correctly. I'm on a longer leash than the rest. But if I screw up . . . I'll be in the pit too quickly to talk about it."

Keeran curled into a tighter ball, the statement shaking her so badly that Sigrid instantly picked up on it. "Is that what happens, when you try to leave?" she questioned softly. "They catch you and give you to those below. Is that what causes them?"

Keeran's true thoughts slammed into Sigrid with such force that she unconsciously took a step back. *She wants out! She wants to escape from him.* Her instincts had been right; this woman was not like Terrence's other soldiers, that's why she had been drawn to her. This frightened woman before her had a conscience and could be saved.

Taking a few steps forward, she smiled. "Not all." She had been surprised to learn that some family members had indeed been part of Terrence's coven at one time, but they sought a refuge and different way of life. That life was available through Regina and the family. "Some make it to safety," she answered honestly.

Keeran leaned forward, trying not to seem too interested. "But he sends people like you after them, right? You capture them and bring them back to him?"

Sighing, Sigrid sat down beside her. "Sometimes he sends people after them it just depends who it is that ran. I personally have never been sent after anyone." She stopped and cast a wary look around the room as if to make sure they were alone. "Just between us, I wouldn't take the assignment. I think we should be allowed to leave if we want and to live like we want. We are not children to be ordered around by a temperamental parent. If I wanted to leave this place and you wanted to come with me, I think we should be able to."

Keeran lay her head on Sigrid's shoulder. "You would take me with you?"

Sigrid brushed a loose hair from Keeran's brow. "Yes. That is if you wanted to be with me."

Snuggling closer, Keeran smiled into Sigrid's shoulder. "Of course I do. If only it were that easy."

Sigrid rested her head against Keeran's. "It's obvious you're unhappy here, and you are not like Terrence's other soldiers, so how did you hook up with him?"

Keeran sat up and pulled away from Sigrid, keeping her eyes downward. "He bought me," she admitted with shame.

Jolted, Sigrid sat up straighter. "What?"

Keeran's voice was small and weak. "About four years ago, while I was in college, I got in with a bad crowd. We went to a party one night and the next day I woke up in a cage and was told my life as I knew it was over. Terrence bought me from a white slaver as a mortal plaything. I somehow survived his affections and play sessions and showed what he called "fire," and he made me a vampire as a reward—or curse—depending on how you look at it. I was a good soldier, obeyed orders, and moved up. When the inner circle was wiped out, he put me in charge here. End of story."

Sigrid wrapped her arms around Keeran and pulled her into a tight embrace, like a mother comforting a child. "Oh sweetie, I'm sorry I asked. I didn't mean to upset or hurt you."

"I never told anyone how I got here," Keeran wept as she sat up. "I don't know why I told you. Now I know you don't want me, but I had to be honest with you."

"What you told me doesn't change anything. I still want to be with you."

Disbelief covered the Amazon's features, but was edged with hope. "I don't know who you are, Paula, but I know that I've never met anyone like you or felt this way before. You say I'm not like the Master's other soldiers, but neither are you. Can I trust you or is this one of the Master's famous loyalty tests. I don't know if I even care anymore."

Sigrid took a deep breath and slowly exhaled. "Isn't it funny how sticky he is about loyalty, and yet he keeps us so screwed up we don't know who to trust anymore."

"So you think I may be testing you too?"

Sigrid simply shrugged.

Keeran scooted closer and pointed at her chest. "Look in here and find out. I know you're older and more powerful, you can look and tell me what you see."

Sigrid already knew the answer. She cared for this woman and could see the feeling was mutual. To Keeran, Sigrid was a life preserver and until she had come along, Keeran had been slowly sinking. She could be salvaged and saved. "I don't have to." She leaned forward and their lips met, lingering for several minutes before they parted.

Standing up, Sigrid met Keeran's eyes. "I won't betray you, that's not my style. Right now I have got to go out and take care of a few things, but when I get back we will continue this conversation. And I will be back, okay?"

Still unsure, Keeran nodded and lay back down.

Sigrid secured her weapons, pulled on her coat and headed out to finish the job she came for.

As she rode the streets of LA, she had to slow down several times to give Max a chance to catch up. He had been following her since she left the club, and he was not very good at it or keeping up. She led him across the city and finally ended up in the warehouse district, easily finding an empty building amidst the shipping containers and warehouses.

Parking the bike inside the building, she dismounted, removed her helmet, and walked to the center of the room, waiting.

"You care to tell me what you think you're doing, Max?" she called, after allowing him enough time to enter and find a hiding place.

Shaking her head, she stifled the smile she felt coming. He was so obvious as she walked in a tight little circle, so easy to read as he watched her and let his evil little mind work away.

"Come on, Max. I'm not very patient. Especially when I have someone like Keeran waiting on me."

"Bitch." She heard him growl from the rafters above. His next comment was louder. "Who are you really?"

Sigrid smiled and looked at the shadows surrounding her. "What's wrong, Max? Not man enough to face little old me. You like to hurt women so come on down and show me what you got. I thought you wanted to take me down and score some points with Terrence, yet you hide from me. That just about cements my suspicions about your manhood, especially after what Keeran told me about you."

The comment scored a direct hit and she felt his anger skyrocket. She could smell his rage and knew that the change had already overtook him. Her ears picked up on his increased heartbeat and with that pounding, she knew that he was positioned fifteen feet up and to her left.

"Don't believe everything that overgrown slut says. I'm smart enough to know that you are not who you say you are." His voice boomed from the darkness, echoing off the long empty walls of the warehouse. "You fooled the blonde nymph and Razor, but that's not hard to do. You can't fool me."

Placing her hands on her hips, she sighed. "Well, smart guy, who am I then?"

"One of the Bitch Queen's people. I figure you either found her or found out what happened to her and now you want the Master."

Laughing, Sigrid shook her head harder. "You're good, Max. Unfortunately, that idiot gene just outweighs everything else."

Temper flaring, his words became garbled as his fangs elongated. "Oh yeah! Well I pegged you, didn't I?" The grunt of the wood was soft as he prepared to leap on her from his perch above.

Her laughing stopped. "I'm not one of the Queen's people." She looked up directly at him, eyes glowing red. "I'm Sigrid, her niece."

Her admission surprised him and he hesitated. Sigrid took advantage of it and leapt up, seized him by the throat and brought him back down to the floor. He struggled to get away, fighting with all his might. She allowed him to get a few hits in to go with her plan, but now her anger had surfaced as well. With her other hand, she grabbed his crotch and squeezed harshly. "Doesn't feel good does it, you piece of shit."

He continued struggling but the pain in his throat and crotch was causing him to weaken with each passing second. "You hurt her for the last time. You killed my friend and hurt my aunt." Sigrid informed him. "Do you have any last words?"

A flash appeared to her left, and she released his crotch and shot out her hand, seizing his wrist and the silver spike in his grasp. The warehouse was dark, but a stream of light poured through a rooftop window, and it cast a gleam on the sharp weapon. "Poor last words, Max," she stated and twisted his arm, and with a strong shove, forced the spike into his heart.

Releasing him, she stepped back, letting him look down at the spike that now protruded from his chest. Blood poured from the wound and he coughed, shooting out another spray that speckled Sigrid. "I wanted to take my time with you but you opted for suicide. Suicide was not the answer, Max." She chuckled as he fell to his knees, the blood flow increasing.

He looked up at her, eyes wide and tried to speak, but no longer possessed a voice. He gasped for breath, a vain attempt and then fell forward, smacking the ground with a satisfying thud.

"Goodbye, Max," the darkness called.

Razor was hunting alone this night and was in his favorite hunting grounds, Hookers' row. The pickings were slim on this night, but he had found a prime piece of meat and was about to make his move when he heard a faint call for help. Tuning his hearing, he located the voice in a nearby alley.

"Dinnertime," he mumbled, licked his lips and strolled across the street to the beckoning passage. He walked slowly down the alley, scanning the shadows for his main course. Sometimes the hookers got hold of a bad John or ticked off their pimp and ended up beaten and hurt. Most times they were dumped in an alley and either die or crawl for help. Twice before he had found these, what he called ready-made meals, and fed without the effort of capturing them. "Don't be afraid," he called with a giggle. "I won't hurt you."

"Here," a woman's voice called almost inaudibly from farther back in the alley.

He picked up speed and rushed down the way, anxious to feed on a live hooker, rather than a newly dead one. Suddenly he hit a brick wall—the end of the road, so to speak.

"What the hell . . .," he growled as he ran his hands over the cool bricks.

From behind him he heard. "Tsk, tsk." He whirled around, ready to attack, when he saw the unimposing figure of Paula. Breathing a sigh of relief he grinned. "Shit, Paula, what's going on?"

"Razor," she scolded mildly, "Don't you know that the wounded bird is one of the oldest tricks a hunter uses? I'm disappointed. And this from the man that helped in the Queen's abduction and even killed one of her inner sanctum."

"I'm . . . I'm . . . sorry Paula," he stammered, rocking from side to side. "I didn't know you were here to test us. Please don't tell the Master or Max. I'll do better, I promise."

"Max?" she repeated,

Razor's many faults included talking too much and supplying information even when it wasn't requested. "Yeah, listen, I know Terrence thinks that Keeran's running the show, but that's because Max has been covering for her. She doesn't have the killer instinct anymore, so Max has been screwing her while calling the shots. That's why he doesn't like you. He's afraid you'll take over our operation. He likes being in charge here."

"Max is not in charge any longer."

"Oh, uh, well, okay." Razor smiled. "Then I guess he was right about you taking over. No matter, I'm flexible. I'll do better, Paula. Please give me another chance."

Sigrid smiled and extended her hand. "Of course, Razor."

He took her hand and shook it fiercely, laughing nervously. "Thanks, boss."

Continuing to keep a firm grip on his hand, Sigrid asked, "By the way, do you remember the mortal man you killed when you took the Queen?"

Eyes lighting up, he nodded strongly. "Yeah, I tore him to pieces."

Sigrid's face fell and without warning, she yanked his arm out of its socket, spraying the alley with blood.

Razor looked down at the bleeding stump, not fully comprehending what had just happened. Confused, he looked back at Sigrid, just as she was tossing something that looked like an arm down the passageway. The limb thumped against the wall and landed in a pile of week-old garbage.

"His name was Paul. He was family and I loved him," she growled.

It was over in a matter of minutes. When Sigrid left the darkened alley, it was littered with little pieces of Razor along with the usual garbage.

Keeran jumped out of her seat when Sigrid came into the observation room and slammed the door. She gasped when she saw the blood splattered all over her lover and rushed over. "Paula, what happened? Are you all right?"

"We have problems," she answered, walking past her and over to the sink. She filled the sink with water and started undressing. "I was out scouting and came across Razor and a group of vampires. I thought they were some of Terrence's until they attacked him. There were too many and they tore him to pieces. I did get close enough to see them and it was the Queen's people. They have LePope's carnival and have declared full-scale war."

Keeran stared in disbelief, trying to process the information. "But you're okay?"

Sigrid nodded as she finished wiping the blood from her face, arms, and chest.

"What can I do?"

Tugging clean clothes from her nearby saddle bag, she began ticking off instructions. "Get in touch with Terrence; tell him what I've said. Tell him we are bugging out now and will be in touch when we get settled, then get your things together."

Keeran couldn't move. Shock kept her frozen in place until Sigrid ordered, "Now!" Then she dashed for the phone.

Pulling on a clean shirt and her armaments, she listened carefully as Keeran called a telegraph office. The message she gave them was that the carnival had been put out of business by the competition and that they were being forced out of town. Keeran was so intent on the call that she never noticed Sigrid moving up behind her. Once the message had been repeated back to her she gave them a credit card number to pay for the telegram and then the address in Switzerland. Sigrid smiled and committed the address to memory as Keeran hung up the phone.

When she turned around, she ran into and felt the point of a kingi sword at her heart. Sigrid stood firm, her eyes or arm not wavering.

Keeran didn't seem surprised. "You are a test from Terrence."

"I'm his daughter."

This did draw a look of mild surprise from Keeran, and then she started laughing. That action caught Sigrid off guard as did Keeran grabbing the point of the sword and pulling it closer to her chest. The silver point broke the skin over Keeran's heart, and Sigrid tightened her grip to keep it from going any deeper until she was ready.

"Go ahead, Terrence's daughter. I'm tired of being his plaything and slut. I want out of this world and this is a good a way as any. Please don't try the torture thing, though. Your father has pretty much been there and done that, and I think you'd be disappointed. I've built up a strong resistance after all these years."

Reading her thoughts, Sigrid faltered slightly. Keeran did want to die. She saw Sigrid's betrayal as the final straw as her heart shattered and was ready to end everything. Sigrid released her full power and Keeran shifted as the strength surrounded her. "Answer a question for me."

Keeran nodded.

"Why didn't you kill the woman that was with Regina the night you abducted her? You remember the redhead, don't you? You only injured her when you had the advantage and could have staked her. Why?"

Keeran sighed. "I had no reason to kill her. I had no reason to abduct the Queen, other than I wanted to live. We are vampires and although some call us a noble race, I haven't seen anything noble about it. We kill one another for insane reasons, like different beliefs or being on the wrong side. It's genocide, no matter how you look at it. The redhead was my way of trying to fight back."

"Your noble act?"

Keeran glared at her. "You got a problem with that? I didn't ask for this curse, but if I had I would have prayed it be on the other side."

Both remained silent and stared at each other. Sigrid was the one to finally break the silence. "Do you want away from him, Keeran? Out of his coven?"

"Yes."

"Where is he?"

Doing a double take, Keeran answered quickly. "A castle in the Swiss Alps. I'm not sure of the exact location, only where to send his messages."

"That was the address you gave to the telegraph office just now?"

Puzzled, Keeran nodded. "Yes, but don't you know that already? Who are you?"

Sigrid pulled the sword away and lowered it, "Sigrid Derrick, the Queen's niece. The redhead you saved was my sister."

Keeran leaned against the counter, this whole thing taking too many turns to make sense anymore. "So you're here to avenge the Queen, your aunt?"

Consciously, Sigrid lay the sword down within Keeran's grasp and turned her back on the woman, walking slowly to the bar.

Keeran looked at the sword and then let her eyes drift up and watch Sigrid as she poured out two whiskeys. "Sit down Keeran," Sigrid instructed, recapping the bottle.

Sigrid listened as Keeran walked to the observation deck, climbed the steps and took a seat, watching the rapidly filling club through the window.

Joining her, Sigrid handed her a glass of whiskey. "Max and Razor are dead."

"And I'm next."

She exhaled deeply and turned to face her. "I'm going to give you a choice. I did come here to kill all of you for what you'd done to my family and through you find Terrence. The last thing I planned on was meeting someone, especially one of Terrence's soldiers, that I care for."

Keeran looked up, hope flickering in her brown eyes and heart.

"I know what you've told me so far is the truth. You were brought into this life without a choice and forced to choose a side. Now I offer you a chance to decide for yourself." Keeran nodded understanding, so Sigrid continued. "I can end your life now, make it painless and quick, an option your two comrades didn't get. Or I can offer you a chance to be a part of a family. One where we work together, have no doubts about loyalty, and are free to live our lives as we choose."

Keeran shook her head. "Now I know you're toying with me. The Queen could never take me in. Not after being with Terrence, being his slut, and helping put her in his hands. She could never trust me."

Sigrid looked at her sternly. "I trust you. That will be enough for her. As long as you're under my protection, you will be safe and accepted." Leaning forward, she took Keeran's chin in her hand and held her gaze. "Don't you see the chance I'm taking here? I care for you and am willing to accept you. If you are a really good actress, I could be exposing my family, my life to danger. If you were to betray me, you could take everything that I love away. Keeran, I don't make this offer lightly. I've been wrestling with it ever since I met you, trying to tell myself that this is just wrong, but I keep coming back to one point."

"What?"

"I care for you and want you to have a better, real life. If I can help you get away from him, then I will, and you are under no obligation to me whatsoever. I don't want you with me out of gratitude or as payment. I want you with me because it is your choice."

Keeran could no longer keep her emotions bottled up. "I'm a whore!" she shot back, struggling to pull away from Sigrid. "I'm used, dirty merchandize. You deserve better."

"Oh yeah?" Sigrid answered, latching a firm grasp on Keeran's arms to hold her in place.

"I'm the product of an incestuous rape." Releasing her hold, Sigrid stood up, her anger flaring. "You told me your story, let me tell you mine. Terrence raped his sister, my mother. She got away from him and went into hiding, but unfortunately he found her, us. At three years of age, I watched as the hunters Terrence led to us, stake my mother. They captured me and I spent two years in an orphanage where I was beaten, molested, and starved. Then the hunter that killed my mother decided to adopt me so he could study a vampire up close. I became a living experiment to him." She had begun pacing now, Keeran never taking her eyes off the angry woman. "For twenty-eight years I lived that life, not knowing the truth. Then I met Regina, my aunt. Against many family members' wishes, she brought me in, gave me my true life, and my birthright."

Her anger was subsiding as she stopped in front of Keeran and kneeled. Resting her hands on Keeran's legs, she looked at her pleadingly. "You are not a whore, Keeran. You're like me, a victim of circumstance. I love you and want to be with you. I can be no more honest with you than that. I will go one step farther and tell you that there is another in my life that I love as well, but believe me when I say I have enough love for both of you. We are running out of time and you have to decide now."

"If you're going after him, I'm coming with you." Keeran gave her answer, "I won't lose you this quickly."

"Quicker than you think," a new voice stated.

Both women turned and rose to their feet, finding Raven, the doorman, standing in the doorway, a loaded crossbow aimed and ready to fire.

He stepped in and shut the door. "Max warned me to keep an eye on you."

Sigrid rolled her eyes, taking a few steps forward. "Do you mind? This is a private conversation."

"Yeah, I do mind," he snarled.

Keeran heard a buzz and then saw Raven fall to the floor, a huge red stain spreading across the front of his yellow T-shirt. She snatched her head to the side and looked at Sigrid, seeing the gun in her hand.

"I told you this was private," Sigrid repeated and slid the gun back into her jacket.

Keeran looked back at Raven and then again at Sigrid. She had never even seen the woman reach for the gun and she had only looked away for a second. "Then again," Keeran grinned weakly, "I may have underestimated you."

Sigrid smoothed out her coat. "Don't worry, everyone has." Then she turned back to her. "You're certain about this?"

Keeran reached out and took Sigrid's smaller hand into her own. "I do want to be with you, more than I could ever say. I will never betray you because I could never hurt you. I'd rather die first. I'm afraid to stay here while you're gone. I don't know any of the others in your family and they probably won't trust me. How long will you be gone?"

"Now that I know where he is, maybe three weeks to a month," she answered. "I've already made arrangements with friends for you. They used to be part of Terrence's coven and defected about ninety years ago. They are very nice and they know the situation; I think you'll like them. Now we have got to get a move on, so if you're going, get packed and let's go."

Keeran planted a gentle kiss on her cheek. "Thank you Pau . . . Sigrid."

Sigrid blushed. "Thank you for not killing Silk. My sister means a lot to me and that showed me your true side. Now get packed, I'll be back in five minutes."

"Where are you going?"

Sigrid smiled her side grin. "To take care of the bartender and clear the way."

Fifteen minutes later, they were on Sigrid's bike heading east; and the fire that claimed the club was just starting to burn well.

They arrived on the outskirts of Las Vegas a few hours before dawn. The ride had been quiet, and with each mile Keeran felt that this was really happening and not a dream.

Donna and Lance Freeman owned a small diner and gift store only ten miles from Las Vegas and had been with the family for ninety-four years. They had been inducted by Terrence and according to Lance, they were just his type to recruit, until they met one another. Like lightning from above, they had fallen in love, but Terrence had his eye on Donna; and when she rebuffed him, he had ordered his competition removed. Fearing for their lives and tired of the waste that their life had become, they ran. It had not been an easy adjustment to Regina's way, but once they saw how much things were different, they had become model family members. Sigrid had spent time with them during a jaunt to Vegas and had liked them instantly, and she knew she could trust them.

They were welcomed warmly when the Harley carrying the two women pulled up in front of their two-story house, several hundred yards away from their business. During her thinking time the previous day, she had called the Freemans and explained the situation to them. Because they had once been with Terrence, they understood what Keeran would need in the way of support and training; and within an hour of meeting her new host, Keeran felt more at ease than she had in years.

During a late dinner, the three of them explained their way of life to her including the difficulty of refraining from the hunt. It would not be an easy adjustment, but they would do all they could to help and encourage her. The young couple couldn't help but notice the way Keeran kept throwing looks at Sigrid and almost constantly maintained some kind of touch with the older woman. They were reminded of a frightened child seeking the reassurance of a parent, and their hearts went out to the newest family member.

They left their guest an hour before dawn to get ready for the morning-trucker crowd, and the two women decided to take a walk in the desert before sunrise. The walk turned into a lovemaking session a few hundred yards from the house and afterward they lay together, watching the darkened sky. Sigrid had promised to wait until the next morning before leaving, and she really wanted to spend that time reassuring Keeran that she was truly safe now. On the ride there, she had decided to share a gift with Keeran, and as the woman sat up and began pulling her clothes from the sandy pile, Sigrid sat up and placed a restraining hand on hers.

"It's almost dawn, we need to get in," Keeran reminded. When Sigrid didn't move her hand, Keeran opened her eyes wider. "Sigrid, sunlight. Burn to death, turn to ashes, anything ring a bell?"

"Do you trust me?"

Keeran looked into those blue pools that she had lost her soul to. She never believed she could love someone again, but this woman had broken through the barriers and ignited a spark within her heart. Her heart had been cold for so long that she wasn't even aware of the missing heat until it returned and set every part of her on fire. Sigrid was so strong and fierce, yet she never had a more gentle, generous lover. The only time she had ever been with a woman was during her slavery period and of the three, not one had interested her in that way. Her two loves had been men and that had been before Terrence's world. The woman before her asked if she trusted her. The answer was yes, so much so that it hurt. When she had been at the club and found out the truth, she felt like her heart had been yanked out. Against everything she was, she had fallen for the mysterious stranger; and then to find out it was just another test of loyalty had been too much. When she saw the sword at her heart she almost leapt on it. Thankfully, Sigrid had managed the situation and now she had just been intimate with the person that she planned on being with until she died.

"Of course I do," she finally answered. "I love you."

Sigrid leaned down and kissed the healing scratch on Keeran's chest. Keeran rested her head against Sigrid's shoulder. "If you want me to sit out in the sun and burn to death I will. I would jump in a vat of holy water for you. Just tell me what you require and I will do it."

Sigrid smiled, the smile inflaming Keeran's desire again. "Nothing that drastic," she promised. "I just want to be with you the first time you experience something. If you want to wait, we will."

"No. Terrence told us that he had the power to allow a chosen few to experience the sun's rays, but it was a very select group. I used to pray that I would earn his favor and be so blessed. In my mortal days, I loved the beach and the sun."

Sigrid began pulling on her clothes as she felt the sun's power beginning to grow. Once dressed, she pulled Keeran in front of her, wrapping her body protectively around her frightened lover. "He had no special power, only his manipulation."

The sky began to lighten and Keeran tensed with fear. Sigrid held her tighter, leaning against her ear. "I promise I won't let anything hurt you. If you want to go in . . ."

Clutching on to Sigrid's arms, Keeran shook her head. "Show me . . ."

Sigrid held her close, feeling her trembling increase as the sun licked at the sky and eased over the distant mountains. They remained silent, Keeran holding her breath as the morning sun spread across the desert floor. She jumped when the first streaks played across her skin and Sigrid began to whisper words of comfort and love in her ear, trying to relax the terrified woman.

As more sunlight cascaded onto Keeran and she didn't explode into flames, she began to weep, the feeling of warmth against her skin robbing her of words. She tentatively held her hands up in front of her, trying to touch the light. Sitting forward so that she was no longer reclining against Sigrid, she whispered, "I'd forgotten . . . how it felt."

Sigrid's heart and soul were warmed by the reaction just as Keeran's flesh was. "We have to build up a resistance, but you can go into the sunlight. That's one more thing that Terrence has no control over. When we get your resistance up, I'll take you to the beach myself."

"Promise?" Keeran cried as her feelings raged with the new sensation.

"On my life."

Keeran turned around until she was facing Sigrid. "Come back to me, Sigrid," she said, echoing Ty's words from a month earlier.

"That's the plan," she laughed and brushed her fingers over Keeran's jaw.

Keeran wanted to stay longer in the new light, but afraid for her safety. Sigrid led her back to the house ten minutes later. They both fell asleep wonderfully exhausted.

Sigrid was up a few hours later and giving the Freemans last-minute instructions. Once everything was ironed out, she entrusted them with several letters, the names of the recipients written on the front of the envelopes. In the event of her death, she asked that they forward the letters. Reluctantly, they agreed; then she went back to the house to spend the rest of her time in the States with Keeran.

16

It took less than three days for Sigrid to travel to Switzerland and only two days to find his lair. As Keeran said, it was a castle in the Swiss Oftorn mountains, constructed of mountain stone and by the looks, at least three hundred years old. It was similar in style to the old castles of medieval England, located on the highest snow-covered peak of the local mountain range. It sat overlooking the land like a silent protector and had she not known who its occupants were, she would have fallen in love with the winter wonderland. The nearest neighbor was fifty miles away, and the mountains surrounded three sides of the castle, making it perfect for indefinite defense against enemies that might attack.

The silence of the area seeped into her and helped her focus as she spent a week observing the stronghold. The frigid temperatures had no effect on her, and other than a few hours of sleep each morning in a nearby cave, she never left the castle unwatched. As the days passed, she learned the comings and goings of Terrence's people, mentally locking away every piece of information. Regina had told her that her stealth would come in handy and indeed it did. She was able to get within feet of the castle without anyone sensing her. Using a snow tarp, she spent most of her time a few yards out, in plain view but fully camouflaged.

On the day of her arrival, she had seen the messenger arrive and deliver Keeran's telegram. As expected, she watched as Terrence sent a large number of his troops to the States to pick up the fight. During her observation, she had counted at least twenty occupants left in the castle and on three occasions had glimpsed the master himself. The sight of him had at first brought a sting of fear to her belly, but then it was joined by something else. Something stronger. The power of justice and retribution. The feeling began to grow each day until she no longer thought of those she loved, only the evil within the stone walls. It was when that feeling reached a crescendo that she knew it was time.

She drifted to the castle as the morning sun peeked over the snowcaps. Her form as a cloud of smoke floated silently to the watchtower and slowly encompassed the sneering guard. Without a sound she appeared and drove a silver shaft into his heart. With her hand firmly over his mouth, he struggled to fight her, but the attack was so quick and unexpected that he had no advantage to use. She held firmly to him and after a few more seconds, he fell still and slumped against her.

When she was certain he was dead and began smoldering, she dropped the body and covertly entered the castle, descending the steps.

As she climbed down the darkened stairway, her senses were sharply heightened. Every musty, dank odor, every scurrying rat, every stone shifting. Every time Terrence walked across the stone floor, she heard and felt all of it inside the bowels of hell. She stopped suddenly when she felt Terrence tense and hold his place. They sensed one another, and she could feel his mixture of pleasure and fear at her arrival. He only felt a radiating heat like nothing he had ever felt before.

As she exited the stairwell, she found two guards waiting for her. Sighing, she only smiled as they approached. Before they could get within five feet of her, she had pulled out a silenced .44 and fired two wooden bullets into their hearts. Both dropped to the ground like rag dolls and she simply stepped over them, heading for the center of the castle where she knew he was waiting.

Every corridor and chamber of the castle consisted of the same stone walls and designs. There was no electricity; the only light were those coming from oil lamps and torches positioned along the walls. For a split second, she felt as if she had gone back in time to the days of King Arthur and the dragons, but the thought was quickly pushed away, her only focus was on the dragon ahead.

The hallways curved, climbed, and descended. A mortal would easily become lost within the maze and that had no doubt been the builder's intention. The design was meant to prevent enemy troops from gaining easy access to the castle and its occupants. Bud Sigrid was not a mortal any longer, and she knew exactly where she was going and where his people lay in wait.

Two more of his coven were waiting as she turned one corner, but she quickly fired the mini wooded stakes and dispatched them. She would allow no barriers or obstacles to get in the way of finding him. She had waited too long for this confrontation, and as she rounded another corner, she felt him close.

At the end of the passageway was a large drawing room, sparsely but comfortably furnished. She couldn't see the occupant, but she knew he was in there waiting. Her eyes scanned the room, and she recognized it from her exchange with Regina, although the metal grating in the floor was now covered with a huge rug. Her senses told her what his plans were, and she took a second to prepare and hide that knowledge from him.

"You might as well come in," his voice called from deep within the room.

Boldly, she stepped into the room and turned to the left, where he was standing by a window. Dressed in his typical black ensemble, minus the cane, but still carrying the visible scars from their last meeting, he kept his hands at his sides, loose and dangling, indicating an absence of malice. Cocking an eyebrow at her, he sneered, "You should have knocked. I assume you have some manners."

"Like father like daughter."

"Ah," he nodded, "so you do know the truth."

"Everything."

Slowly, without threat, he walked across the room and took a seat next to the fireplace. She never took her eyes off him, watching his every move and holding her ground.

They exchanged looks, sizing up one another in silence. As she stood before him, dressed in black leather pants and matching flowing coat, he could see himself in that face. At first glance, she looked like her mother, but her mannerisms and expressions were his. Their kind could not procreate, yet he had been the exception. He had created another life, one in his image. He couldn't help but admire the part of him that was standing in front of him. For the first time, he felt a pang of regret. Had he known that Valonia was carrying his child, he would have never let the hunters have her. He would have taken the child and raised her as his own successor, and he would have had a powerful ally. Now he was facing a strong enemy, someone possibly endowed with more powers than he.

"You're late," he smiled, breaking the silence. "I expected you at least three months ago. I'm afraid you've missed Regina."

Sigrid took a breath, crossing her arms across her chest, the leather of her coat crackling. "Don't be coy, Terrence. You know we found her."

He laughed softly. "What was left of her anyway?" Sitting up straighter in his chair, he became more animated. "How long did she last? Was it extremely painful? Please tell me, I'm just breathless with anticipation." He sat back waiting for his taunts to set her off.

Instead of the expected reaction, Sigrid laughed and glanced down at his hands and spotted Regina's ring glittering on his left pinky. When she looked back at him, she stifled the rage and instead mustered a face that radiated a mixture of amusement and condescension. "You fucked up, old boy. Regina is still alive and in power. You failed."

His face fell slightly, his lip curling in anger. "You're lying. She could not possibly be alive, not after ingesting silver and dead blood. Impossible!"

Resting her hands on her hips, she looked directly into his black eyes. She felt his inquiring probe and allowed him to scan her thoughts and see the answer to his question. He sat up straighter as he got the information, his casual demeanor replaced by a more serious one.

Lowering her head, she narrowed her eyes and became the very image of her father. "With me, anything is possible."

He rose to his feet and took a step toward her. "You know this will only be over when one of us is destroyed."

She matched his step and raised him a sneer. "That's what I'm counting on. I'm here to tie up loose ends."

"Is that what you did in LA?" he asked switching tactics. "Max had a lot of promise and Keeran was . . . well . . . very enjoyable." He got no rise out of her. "You, young lady, have a nasty habit of interrupting my plans and fun."

She had already sensed the movement around her and knew that his coven was moving in closer, awaiting the word from their master. "You have a nasty habit of running away when you get in trouble," she countered, her body tensing for action. "How many of your loyal coven has died for your cowardice? At least that's one of your traits I didn't inherit."

"Let the games begin!" he barked in response and backed away from her. Five men and a woman moved in and began encircling her, just out of reaching distance. Their minds were so open and controlled that she knew exactly what the plan of action was, and she prepared to cooperate.

One of the men leapt at her and she turned, seized him in midleap and threw him into the far wall. A crushing sound filled the air as his head met the stone wall, and he crumpled to the floor, dazed.

One at a time they came at her, trying to tire her and wear her down. She was kept busy fending off punches, kicks, and lunges with silver spikes and swords. They presented no challenge as she rebuffed their attacks, staking one on occasion when she got too bored. She knew the instant the grating in the floor was uncovered and opened even though her four sparring partners did their best to distract her.

She allowed their volleys to move her across the room, making sure she kept her back to the waiting trap. Tiring of the play, she drew her gun and fired off two shots, taking out two more henchmen in one fluid movement.

"Finish her!" Terrence ordered and then dashed out of the room.

She sighed and smiled as she heard his footfalls disappear down the hallway. Turning her attention back to the last two playmates, she motioned them closer. "You heard him, finish me!"

Like mindless robots, they charged her. She took a few steps back and then vanished down into the waiting hole. A second later, the grating was closed, and the two thugs eased away, proud that they had accomplished their master's instructions.

Sigrid slightly miscalculated the drop and landed not on her feet but on her knees. She shook off the surprise and stayed in attack position. Letting her eyes grow accustomed to the darkness and trying to assimilate her new surroundings.

The stench was almost overpowering as it wafted over her nose. It was a smell she recognized from the first time they had found Regina at the carnival. But it was much stronger and potent here, and she felt her eyes water as she struggled to keep her stomach down. The hole wasn't completely black as a small bit of light came through the grating above, but she didn't even need that much light to see the outline of five figures crouched nearby.

As bad as Regina had been when they found her, she had been the picture of health compared to the occupants of the pit. Their bodies were little more than bones, hair long and matted, eyes wide and red. They were hunched over, no longer able to stand upright, almost to the point of being down on all fours. There was no spark of humanity left in their red eyes, and she knew that for them reversion was permanent.

Despite their appearance, they were quick and fierce, and in the blink of an eye they were on her. She was so surprised by the ferocity and speed of the attack that it wasn't until the biting and clawing sent waves of pain over her that she was brought back to her senses.

With all the power she could muster, her mind reached out and called them to stop. She sent a wall of heat against them to emphasize the point.

The attack stopped as suddenly as it had begun. Staring at her and snarling, they eased back, watching her every move.

She sat up, gritting her teeth against the pain that coursed through her body. When she was in a comfortable position, she looked at each of them, probing their minds and trying to find some vestige of humanity. Their pain, anger, and fear gripped her as she linked with them, but she wouldn't give up and finally managed to lock on to the last shreds of humanity in each of them. Her eyes glowing red, she focused her thoughts and told them, "I am one of you and I will not hurt you. I only want to help and give you peace."

Amid the chaos of their thoughts, she received one unanimous answer. "Peace. Give peace."

Giving them her answer, she watched as they gathered in a tight group, nestling together and staring at her with pleading eyes.

She moved closer, slowly crawling to them and reaching out to tentatively and lovingly touch each of their faces. With each touch she focused her mind. "Sleep, children. A deep peaceful, infinite sleep where there is no pain and no fear. Your pain is over and no one will ever disturb you again. Sleep until you reach your final resting place and then be free."

Her breath hitched in her chest as she watched them drift away. With a single thought flames began licking at their peaceful, sleeping forms. A lone tear ran down her face as she mourned them, and she stayed until she was certain that the suggestion had been taken. Backing away from the fire, she dropped her head and tried to choke back more tears. People pushed beyond their normal limits just because of one man's evil, one man who was more of an animal than anything she had ever seen in a zoo. "Coward," she muttered under her breath.

Anger and hatred welled in her again and she stood up. "It stops here, you manipulating, murdering bastard." It was her final promise to those below as she changed into smoke and drifted up through the grating.

Sigrid moved like a bulldozer through the halls, shooting various coven members as she went. There was no need to take aim or waste time fighting. No. All her energy was reserved for Daddy dear. As a coven member moved against her, she simply fired point-blank, her boots' heels clicking loudly with menace as she moved more deeply into the heart of the castle. Another man jumped out at her and she fired two shots, the first doing its job and the second empty click signaling her. She popped the clip out of the gun and slammed another full one home, never missing a step.

"Come on out, Theo. The game is getting dull," she called, closing in. She had kept a mental tally of how many of his people she had erased and knew that he was down to about ten or less, and they would be little more than shields to allow him time to escape. That thought jolted her and she picked up speed.

Only one thing occupied her thoughts now. This was no longer about the family or Seth or even Regina. This went back to a spring day in Austria when a three-year-old girl had watched her mother murdered as Terrence watched the specially arranged private show. Her mother's face and all the memories she had repressed or lost were surfacing and driving her forward with unstoppable force.

At long last she reached a large wooden door at the end of the main hallway. Without missing a beat, she approached the door and kicked it open. The wood splintered and impaled the thug that was waiting behind it as she passed through the doorway and stopped at the top of the ancient stone steps. She gazed around the room, taking in the sight of the old torture chamber.

The room was as large as her nightclub in Atlanta, but nowhere near as welcoming. A large fireplace was situated in the center of room and a bright fire blazed within. There was a faint undercurrent of blood and pain in the room, and she wondered if it was from Terrence's occupation or the previous tenants. Two small jail cells were built into the far wall. A fully functional rack and Iron Maiden were across the way, and a row of manacles lined the nearest wall. A large table with restraints held court in a corner and beside it was another table with a potpourri of pain-inflicting devices, including a black leather whip with silver beads woven into the lashes, the kind that could leave small scars across a victim's back.

Her eyes finally fell on the object of her desire. Terrence was waiting in the farthest corner of the room, two of his followers waiting along the downward spiral of the steps and the remaining coven placed at various points across the room between her and Terrence.

"You look surprising well after your time with those below," he greeted, his tone nonchalant. But the look on his face showed a sign of worry.

Gingerly, she began down the steps. "Our talk went well. They are at peace now. I knew you were evil, but I didn't realize how despicable until I saw them. How could you do that to another being, to your sister?"

As she reached the seventh step, a woman lunged at her with a silver sword. Sigrid's hand shot out, her own spike in hand and drove it into the woman's heart. She released the spike as the woman plunged over the steps and crashed to the floor below.

"Why, Terrence?" she asked as she continued her descent. "They were your sisters. Why rape them? Why kill them?"

"Because I could," he answered, shocked that she didn't understand his reasoning. He leaned against the wall and put his hands in his pockets. "They were weak. They were always weak. Your mother was the worst, always believing in art, peace, and literature. We rule this world! Mortals are our food, our prey, yet they believed it was wrong to kill. Everything has to give up its life so that others may live. Mortals are our cattle." He shook his head slightly. "Oh sure, for the first few hundred years, my sisters lived up to their potential and used their superior abilities, but then they got civilized. That's the worst thing that can happen to a predator, when they get spayed or neutered. They decided they were better than their kind, and that if they had to kill it would be those below them, like criminals and social rejects. Personally, I'm not that discriminating—a meal's a meal. But they thought they were too good for that."

As she reached the fifteenth step, a man moved forward. Before he could take two steps, a silver arrow shot out of her coat sleeve and slammed into his chest, and she continued downward. "You haven't answered my question."

"We were given this power," he emphasized. "Not using it to its fullest would be a sin. My sisters didn't deserve the power. They didn't know how to properly wield it. I am the rightful ruler. The only one with the true power!"

"Yeah," she smiled as she reached the end of the steps. "That's why you were on your knees begging Erasmus for it. He came to bring over Regina and my mother. You were an unexpected drawback."

Terrence's eyes flashed red as he stood up straight. "So Regina has told you the family history. Too bad none of you knew what was going on."

The seven remaining coven members held their ground, unsure of the exchange between the two, but noticing a distinct change in the room and unwilling to rush into sure death.

"The only thing I don't understand is how you convinced him to turn you. He had to sense the evil within you."

Terrence took a few steps forward and draped his arm around the rock steady man in front of him. His demeanor was cocky and confident. "He was as weak as they were. I told him if he didn't give me the power, I'd tell the entire village the truth. The remaining family would have become outcasts, disgraced, and the village would have hunted them down and staked each and every one of the Cadmus clan, vampire or not. You should know how deep ties are in Greek families. I was his brother, he couldn't kill me, so he had no choice."

Realization hit her. "You killed Erasmus! Then you made it look like the hunters! You are so self-absorbed and power hungry that you won't let anyone in your way, even if it means killing your own siblings."

He laughed brightly. "Your intelligence was obviously inherited from me. However, you still haven't fully grasped what we are, what our purpose is."

Sigrid was tiring of his maniacal ravings. "So enlighten me, Pop."

He patted his props cheek and moved over to the next living pillar of protection. "We are the ultimate evolution of power. Ageless, tireless, boundless beings with the world at our feet, at our control. The strong mortals join us and serve us as followers and servants. The weak ones are our prey whose lifeless bodies we crush beneath our feet. I have seen many mortals who aspire to our greatness. Hitler, Napoleon, Kahn, Manson, all had promise, but no power."

Sigrid's mouth gaped in disbelief. "Forget it. You can't answer my questions, I see that now. You are as mad as a hatter, a curse on the Cadmus family."

He moved back to the wall and leaned. "A curse that has procreated, dear daughter."

It was all the motivation she needed. With a scream of rage she rushed toward him, knowing that she would have to clear a path first.

Four of his coven met her in the center of the room. As she fought them, she never heard his bellowing as two of his dedicated soldiers dashed up the stairs, fleeing the madman they had so blindly followed. His anger dulled her agility and caused her to lose ground in the fight as she tumbled to the cold stone floor, the coven landing on top of her. They landed a few good hits before she used all the techniques one Sensai Shadow had taught her to squelch the anger and dispatch her attackers.

As the last one was tossed to the side, dying, she rose to her feet, showing slight signs of wear. The attack had netted her two stab wounds from silver spikes, her left shoulder and lower back oozing blood from jagged wounds. Although not life threatening, Terrence's new metal did cause a nasty sting. Ignoring the pain, she met his eyes. Never taking her eyes off him, she fired her gun in first one direction then in another and took out two more soldiers. "One left, Pop, and then it's you and me."

With no warning, he grabbed the remaining man's throat and rammed a dagger through his back into his heart. The protector turned his head, looking over his shoulder at his master with surprise. Then he dropped to the floor, twitching a few times before falling still and starting to smolder.

Terrence looked at his progeny, his eyes glowing red as he bared his fangs. "You want me, you runt bitch, then come and get me."

Throwing off her cumbersome jacket, she made sure to keep a tight hold on the samurai sword made of purest silver. Holding it firmly by her side, she moved closer, and they began circling one another, looking for an advantage.

Terrence focused his mind and she was hit with images of her mother's and Regina's rape. Another flash and she saw her mother's death from Terrence's vantage point. Yet another showed her the horrors he had visited upon Regina.

The images were fast and furious and more than a little vivid. The volley left her slightly dazed, and she staggered back a step.

"What's the matter, daughter? Don't like Daddy's home movies?" he taunted.

Shaking the images from her mind, her own eyes took on a red glow and now she brought her own fangs to the party. She felt the reversion trying to kick in, but she stalled it and launched herself at him. Soaring at him with unexpected speed and power, she delivered a staggering punch that drove him to his knees.

Landing a few feet away, she twirled around, crouched, and launched upward again. This time her strike landed on his already scarred face and opened new gashes to join the old.

He screamed in anger, the sound echoing off the walls, as his hands flew up and grabbed his mangled face. Thinking he was distracted by the damage, she tried a third pass, but this time he was ready. Waiting until the last instant, he raised his dagger and caught her in midair, slicing through her shirt and deep across the soft skin of her belly.

Thrown off balance by the movement and pain, she landed with a thud, knocking the air from her lungs as she rolled across the floor, leaving a red smear as she went.

Smiling and pleased with himself, he jumped to his feet and rushed toward her, dagger raised above his head. "Time to die, little bitch."

When she sat up, he saw that she was still holding the sword and now it was out and waiting to greet him. He tried to stop but his boots slid on the bloody floor, and he skidded straight to her. She leaned in, driving the sword through his stomach.

He gasped, clutching the protruding handle and reeled backward, wrenching the sword from her grip. He stumbled and finally fell beside the smoking body of one of his followers.

With a satisfied grunt, Sigrid rose to her feet, grimacing and clutching her bleeding stomach. She took a few steps and watched as he clumsily grabbed the handle of the sword and began easing it out of his midsection. He groaned as the tip cleared, dripping blood, and he collapsed across the body lying beside him.

"Hurts like hell, don't it," she called, fatigued but still ready for action. "Come on, Pop. We're just getting started."

He sat up swiftly, aiming the gun he had lifted off his dead soldier. "No, daughter, it's over!" A shot rang out and then another.

Sigrid dodged and moved but staggered backward when one of the bullets tore a bloody trail through the side of her throat. Eye's wide, this time the pain did bring her down. She slid to the floor, trying to pool her reserves and get back to her feet. She managed to pull a gun from her boot and fired off three shots, two hitting his torso and leg.

Both stayed on the floor for a few seconds before trying to stand up. Sigrid had no luck but Terrence rose to his feet and went over to her, a gun aimed at her heart and a proud grin on his face. "Oh well. I was hoping you would be more of a challenge, being my daughter and all, but then I never really wanted kids anyway. They're annoying little creatures."

"Then you should have stopped after the first one." A new voice rang out.

Startled, both turned and looked up the staircase to the descending figure. Only Sigrid wore a smile of greeting.

Silk seemed to float down the steps, her hair bouncing and swaying with each step. She was dressed in a black jumpsuit and held a loaded crossbow aimed directly at Terrence's heart. At that moment Sigrid was certain that this woman, her sister, was the most beautiful sight she had ever seen.

Terrence cut his eyes at her and then let them fall to the crossbow in her hand. "Who the hell are you?"

Reaching the bottom of the steps, she continued toward him, the weapon in her hand held steady. "A young French girl, twenty-something years ago. You came to her as an angel and took her as a lover. When she had served her purpose and found out how evil you really were, you tried to kill her. But she managed to get away, taking with her your unborn child."

The story seemed to recall a distant memory and his face relaxed some. He did recognize the finely chiseled features and flaming auburn hair. "Giezel?" he mumbled and looked deeply into her brown eyes. His features softened and he forgot the woman at his feet, taking a step toward Silk. "You're Giezel's daughter? I fathered another child?"

"My mother went mad and died in an asylum because of you. Then you try to take my beloved Regina and my sister."

He read her thoughts and smiled. "You and Regina are lovers? That's my girl," he said proudly.

Her brow creased in fury, but she didn't acknowledge it. "You procreated twice, you asshole, and now it's come back to settle the score."

Hurt, Terrence stepped back from the menacing weapon. "I loved you mother," he replied and dropped the gun. "Giezel was my world. I wanted her to be with me forever and be my mate. She made me feel things that I never felt before. Had she loved me as much as I loved her, I might be a different man now. When she found out what I truly was, she was frightened and ran from me. I loved her and didn't want to lose her so I pursued her, rabidly. But my intention was never to hurt her. Had I known she was carrying our child, I would have waited until she was ready. I could never hurt her. If I'd wanted to, I could have killed her before she took her own life."

Silk listened as she eased over to Sigrid. Sigrid quickly accepted Silk offered hand and pulled herself up to her feet. She took a few deep breaths and seemed to be energized. "Nice of you to join us," she smiled to her sister, her voice rough and grave from the bullet wound.

"It's not too late," Terrence pushed on. "I am your father. Give me the chance to make it up to you, to your mother."

"At least he wants you. Me, he just wants wiped out of existence," Sigrid commented.

Terrence turned and glared at her. "You are hell spawn!" Turning back to Silk, with love in his eyes, he said, "You were conceived in love."

It was time for Silk's eyes to take on the red glow that seemed to dominate the room as she held the crossbow closer to him with menace. "You stand before me and speak of love, an emotion you obviously know nothing about."

"You don't believe me?" he questioned.

"Not for a second."

Sighing, he shrugged, the usual condescending features returning. "Well, it was worth a try," he said offhandedly.

Silk couldn't hide the hurt of his words from Sigrid and she felt her sister's hand tighten on her waist in support. Focusing a hated look at Terrence, she responded, "This is your fight, Sigrid. I am only here as moral support, and I wanted to meet Dad before he's wiped out." With that she stepped away and took a seat on the stairs.

"Thank you," Sigrid mouthed silently and attacked Terrence with everything she had.

With perfect aim, she hit him squarely in the chest, propelling both of them into the far wall. Gaining the upper hand, he grabbed her shirt collar and twirling her around, slammed her into the wall. A bloody gash was torn across her head, but she ignored the injury and seeking purchase, snagged his collar and returned the favor.

Terrence leaned against the wall, shaking off the dizziness the hit had caused. Sigrid had taken a few steps back and was staring at him. Once his head was clear, he spun around ready to launch at her, but stopped when he saw the concentration on her face. Suddenly he felt searing pain in his arm and looking down, saw his arm was now on fire.

Sigrid never moved. Holding her head slightly to the side, she watched as he quickly brushed out the flames, a lazy trail of smoke steaming from his arm.

Terrence looked back at his firstborn, truly frightened. "How did you do that?"

She said nothing, only bared her fangs and emitting a guttural growl, flung herself at him. With only a second to prepare and still in shock, he managed to intercept the attack, and they locked together. Like wild animals, they bit and slashed at one another, leaving splatters of blood and pieces of flesh scattered along the way.

Terrence was visibly shaken as Sigrid gained the upper hand and with a back leg sweep, brought him to the ground. She straddled him, pinning him to the floor and began the wailing that had been started so long ago at the quarry. As she inflicted more punishment to his already battered and bloody body, she followed each pass with a name. "Valonia! Regina! Seth! Erasmus! Silk! Paul! Garrett! Keeran!" and so on.

Silk was shocked when she heard Ward's name mentioned among the others.

Terrence managed to land a few more blows, only one causing any real damage as her chest was slashed, but as she tired, he simply lay exhausted in his own blood, broken and gasping. His face and body were little more than a bloody mass now. Only his eyes still burned with anger, anger that his body was unable to act upon.

Sigrid stopped her assault, her breath labored and heavy. Turning over to the right, her eyes landed on Silk and she held out her hand to her.

Silk was immediately by her side and more than a little concerned as she saw the full extent of Sigrid's injuries. "What can I do?"

Sigrid reached into her boot and withdrew a sturdy handmade silver shaft. She held it in her bloody hand, taking comfort in the weight of it. Then she held it out to Silk. "Together?"

Silk smiled, tears stinging her eyes. She lay the crossbow down and grasped Sigrid's hand. "Together."

Silk steadied Sigrid's hand as they placed the sharpened point against Terrence's chest.

His eyes fluttered open and he looked at each of them. He smiled and whispered, a trickle of blood oozing from his mouth. "My girls. You're just like your mothers, vindictive bitches."

Together they shoved the silver through his heart. Neither of them moved as he weakly thrashed about trying to dislodge them and the stake. Blood poured from the wound and stained them both, but still they didn't move. As he finally fell quiet, they continued to hold their position, both of them trying to accept the fact that he was really dead.

Silk came to her senses first and urged Sigrid up, offering her shoulder to her unsteady sister. Sigrid stopped midway and seized his dead hand. With a firm yank, she retrieved Regina's ring and tightly grasped it. That done, they stepped clear of Terrence and with a final look from Sigrid, his body burst into flames.

"How'd you find me?" Sigrid questioned as they stood hand in hand watching the fire, her voice raspy.

"I've been with you since you left Florida—your guardian angel of sorts."

Realizing that she had seen everything that had happened the last two months, including her time with Keeran, Sigrid blushed and her voice became edgy. "From Regina, no doubt. I guess you saw a lot that surprised you."

Silk tightened her grip on Sigrid's waist. "I've been on my own on this. Regina doesn't even know where we are. As for surprising things, every day is a surprise and you're my sister, so I expect it of you."

Sigrid laughed at Silk's easy acceptance and blessing, then the laugh turned into a hacking cough, and Sigrid spat out a glob of blood. Silk locked her jaw, concern consuming her, but knowing that Sigrid would not leave or accept help until she was ready.

Sigrid turned and looked at her. "You saved my life. Thank you. I guess everybody was right—I wasn't ready for this."

"Bullshit!" Silk answered firmly. "We both know you were playing possum. I only let you know that you weren't alone here. As I said, moral support."

Tears began streaming down Sigrid's face and mixed with the blood that was drying there. "I love you, Silk. More than I can ever put into words."

Silk squeezed her hand softly. "I love you too, big sister."

They returned to watching the flames and within minutes, the blaze began to die away, leaving only a pile of charred bones and ashes.

Sigrid released Silk's hand and staggered over to where her coat lay in a pile. Silk was worried as she watched the slow, unsteady movements and started to go to her aid, but Sigrid waved her away. All she could do was stand there and watch the battered, bloody body that was her sister as she fumbled through the coat pockets.

Her black shirt was ripped and saturated with blood. Her pale skin, visible through the tears, was littered with bite marks, gashes, chunks of missing tissue, and bloody smears. Blood still dripped from the bullet wound in her neck and now Silk understood why her voice sounded so rough.

Sigrid found what she was looking for in the jacket and tried to stand up. Her equilibrium gave her a spin and she almost toppled over, but her hand shot out and she steadied herself against the wall. When the room quit spinning, she eased to her feet. "I'm okay," she stated as she heard Silk move to help her.

She ambled back to where Terrence had died and dropped to her knees, clutching the retrieved items close to her mangled chest. One item was a large plastic bottle full of water. The other was a very small glass vial. She set the larger bottle beside her and leaned forward over his remains with the smaller vial.

The silver spike was charred black but still at the center of a blackened pile of ashes. She took the cap off the vial and dipped it into the ashes around the spike. With deft skill, she filled the bottle three-quarters full and then recapped it, tightly sealing the lid and sliding it into the pocket of her tattered shirt. She grasped the other bottle and then began sprinkling the water over the rest of Terrence's ashes.

Silk could tell by the way it sizzled on contact that the bottle was full of holy water. She watched impatiently as Sigrid emptied the last few drops out of the bottle onto the muddy remains at her knees. "Hell will be an interesting place now," she offered as final words.

Steeling herself against the pain that was swimming over her, she willed herself to her feet and took a couple of unsteady, wobbly steps. The world went black and Silk was there to catch her as she collapsed. "It's okay, Sig. You'll be all right, you hear me? Just hang on!" Silk soothed as she scooped her up in her arms and quickly moved to vacate the castle.

Sigrid faded in and out of consciousness, at one point opening her eyes and seeing the small face of Tony beside Silk. His voice was slow and dreamlike as he slurred, "I told you, my friend, we look out for one another."

She tried to speak or offer a smile, but couldn't find her voice or energy. She shivered as she felt the Swiss cold settle in her bones, and an instant later a blanket was draped over her. Silk stroked her hair, trying to hide the worry and fear from her. "Rest, sweetheart," she said and focused her mind.

Sigrid offered no resistance and drifted off.

17

For two days Sigrid floated between worlds and times. In her fevered dreams, she saw ancient Greece and the Cadmus clan; she saw images of wars and peace times. When she became frightened, she found herself in Seth's arms, where she felt safe and protected, a feeling that she enjoyed. Then she felt a force pulling on her, and Seth released her with a smile and a wave. Suddenly she was being drawn to a cold surface of alertness and jerked awake, sitting up in bed and struggling to breathe the cool air.

In her dreams the pain had been but a distant tugging, one that was easy to ignore. But here it crashed down on her like a wall, and she slumped back onto the bed, aware of strong hands helping to guide her down.

"Relax, baby. You've got to stay still," a familiar man's voice comforted.

She longed for the warmth and safety of the dreams, but forced her eyes open, desperately wanting to see the owner of the voice. At first blurry, Ty's face soon became clear as did the worry and concern that covered it. His eyes were red rimmed and he had a good growth of beard on his face. Leaning over, he lightly brushed her lips with his own.

Mustering her strength, she reached up and stroked his face. "I'm glad to see you, but you look tired."

Ty kissed her hand as it neared his mouth. "Haven't been sleeping too well the last couple of months. Bed's been too empty. When Silk called, I commandeered the company plane and have been on the move ever since. I got here late yesterday."

Glancing over his shoulder, she caught a glimpse of Don moving around the small room. "Where am I? Where's Silk?" she asked as grogginess edged back into her voice.

Ty smiled and it warmed her heart. "Just so happened that Tony's cousin had a circus in the area, and they let us hitch a ride. Silk is fine. She hasn't left your side since you got hurt. I made her get some rest when I got here," he supplied and watched as her eyes dropped and then closed. He lay his head beside her and inhaled deeply her scent.

"I love you, Ty," she responded as she drifted back to dreamscape.

"I know," was his reply.

Tony had located his cousin easily when he learned of Sigrid's destination. Telling his cousin the highlights of their meeting and explaining that he needed their help, the traveling circus decided to take a short detour to help one of their own. Luckily, they had hooked up with Silk on the outskirts of a small Swiss town.

She had been surprised and a bit angry at first, but he had explained that Sigrid had come to him for help and after a brief argument, he finally convinced her that his traveling caravan could be of some help and at the very least provide adequate cover if they needed a quick escape. Reluctantly she had agreed and was glad she did when she found Sigrid so seriously wounded.

She carried Sigrid from the castle, not encountering a single one of Terrence's remaining coven, and found Tony waiting nearby with a covered wagon and healer. Once they were loaded and the wagon on the move, they hurriedly accessed her injuries. Silk regretted that she didn't bring Don along, but was pleasantly surprised at the deft skill of the old woman who treated the wounds. They cleaned Sigrid up and bandaged the injuries, the healer using several combinations of roots and herbs as medicinal treatments. Once they had done all they could, they began feeding her.

The wagon and caravan stayed on the move, never slowing a step for fear that once the coven sensed Terrence's death, they would swarm back and seek revenge. When they did reach a small village in the Swiss border, Silk called Ty and Regina. She only told them that Terrence had been destroyed, and Sigrid was badly hurt, but alive.

Ty had relayed the information to a frantic Regina and, despite her protest, went to Sigrid without her.

After his talk with Garrett, he had thought long and hard about their relationship. It wasn't a hard decision to reach because he did love her. He wanted to be with her for as long as he lived or for as long as she would have him and want him. When he entered the wagon the night before and saw the extent of her injuries, he thought that he wouldn't have much longer time with her. That changed just now when she awoke and spoke to him. In his heart he knew that she would be all right and that they would be too.

Later, when Silk came in to check on them, she began to fill him in on the battle and Terrence's death. As she told the story, neither of them let their eyes stray very long from the sleeping, recuperating figure beside them.

Four days later Sigrid was up and moving around, recovering nicely, if a bit slowly. Don had arrived at Ty's request and been impressed with the treatment that she had received from the healer. Other than checking a few things, he could do nothing to improve on the woman's prescription. He did explain to them that the reason she was healing so slowly was that she had an enormous amount of silver in her body; and although she was immune, it took her body some time to get rid of it. He had been so taken with the healer's skills that when they weren't watching their patient, he was conferring with the healer on treatments.

Sigrid had been uncharacteristically quiet and introspective since she'd been up and around. Silk and Ty allowed her plenty of space, but both were relieved when she asked them to take a walk with her one day.

The air was brisk and refreshing as they walked, talking about various things as they wove through the circus setup. Johann, Tony's cousin, generously gave them sanctuary and a wagon to use as they traveled. They always set up a good distance away from the other wagons but were still sociable with their host, joining them for meals and evenings around the fire. After several minutes, they left the shouts of workers and laughter of children and found themselves in a secluded grove of larch trees. A soft breeze wafted through the trees and emitted a whispering whoosh.

"I sense your concern. It radiates like heat from an oven," she stated in a voice that sounded older and more mature now. The bullet that tore through her throat had done some damage and now her voice was softer, but just as strong.

Silk and Ty remained silent as they came to a stop in a secluded grove. This was her time and her meeting, and they were in no hurry to rush her.

"I have no regrets about the last few months, except for hurting Ty," she replied as she gazed at the cloudless deep-blue sky. "I honestly believe that the past twelve years of my life have been in preparation for my meeting and face off with Terrence. My purpose for being was to put an end to his reign of terror." She brought her gaze back earthward and looked at Silk, then Ty. "I've also come to realize that each of us was born for a purpose. Our kind does not procreate, yet for a five-year span, eight children were born and four survived. Three of them came together."

She reached out and took Silk's hand. "Two are sisters." With her other hand she stroked Ty's cheek. "Two are husband and wife. I think my reason for birth has been fulfilled. I feel wonderfully empty and light." She grinned, her eyes sparkling. Although Ty and Silk said nothing, they could both detect almost a luminescent glow surrounding her.

"Now I can deal with some things I need to and really start to live my life. With Terrence gone, we all can," she finished.

"You're leaving the family," Ty said bluntly.

Inhaling deeply, she nodded. "In a way, yes. I want to see and experience everything. I can't do that and retain my position with Regina." She saw the hurt in Silk's face and explained further. "Honey, I am not abandoning Regina, you, or the family. I just need and want some time for me, away from worry and responsibility. I need some time to get myself together and maybe be a jobless bum for a while."

Silk understood, knowing her sister needed some time away from all the turmoil and as much as she would miss her, she couldn't deny her any happiness. "So it will be like an extended vacation, right?"

Sigrid smiled. "Exactly. I'll still be around, especially if you or the family needs me."

Ty cleared his throat and looked at the ground. "What about us?"

Silk picked up the cue and turned, walking back toward the encampment, allowing them some privacy.

"I love you, Ty. That has not changed," Sigrid answered and tightly clasped his hand, "I know you know about Keeran."

He remained silent and she pushed on, hanging her head and digging her toe into the earth. "I didn't mean for it to happen. I never planned on being with anyone else. I didn't know I could love two people at the same time, not that way. But it has happened. I love you, Ty, and I can't fully explain it, but I care deeply for Keeran too. The last thing I ever want to do is to hurt you, and I have done just that. The thought of you suffering because of me breaks my heart, and I would rather die than watch you in pain. If you want to leave, I'll understand. But please know that I will never stop loving you or caring about you."

"Do you want me to leave?"

Her head snapped up, tears welling up in her eyes. "No! My feelings for you haven't changed."

"Do you feel the same way about her?"

"Not the same, no, but I do care about her, and I want to be with her too," she struggled to explain the feelings, but the words eluded her.

"Would you leave her if I asked you to?"

She met his eyes. "I could tell you yes, and I think a large part of me would believe it, and do it just to make you happy, but I can't honestly say. If Keeran asked me to leave you, I could honestly tell her no, but I would like to see where this goes."

He had spent a lot of time soul searching after his talk with Garrett. It hurt him to think that she could love someone else, even have another lover. But her absence during the last few months had been even worse. When he saw the extent of her injuries, he knew that if she died he would be right with her. To share her would take some getting used to, but to lose her completely? The more he thought about it, the lower his heart sank. He saw how happy Garrett and Regina were and decided that it was a situation he could live with.

He smiled warmly and grasped her shoulder. "That's all I need to hear. I do love you and will stay by your side as long as you want me. I'm already a bit jealous and you know how fragile the male ego is. Bear with me, my love?"

Two days later, Don gave Sigrid the okay to travel and they were on a plane bound for the States. The day before they left, Sigrid and Tony had vanished for a few hours for a private talk, and when they returned both were in jovial moods. Neither Ty nor Silk questioned her about the meeting, and she volunteered no information, so they waited in silence, the curiosity almost overwhelming. Both knew that when and if she needed to discuss or tell them something, she would in her own time. Sigrid also made sure that a nice donation was waiting in Johann's circus bank account for the next season.

Once on board the luxurious company plane, Sigrid reminded them that they had to stop over in Nevada to pick up Keeran. Silk hesitated, then told her that the stop over wasn't necessary. Keeran had been with Regina for the last three weeks.

Sigrid's eyes flared with anger, her motions becoming agitated. Silk assured her that Regina only wanted to help Keeran assimilate and posed no threat to her new friend. Don had scolded her for getting so upset in her current condition. Silk and Ty both managed to calm Sigrid down, convincing her that Keeran was in no danger and the flight proceeded.

As the plane prepared for takeoff, all four took their seats and belted in. Silk noticed Sigrid grimace as she fastened the seat belt and again when the jet lifted off. Don had told them that although she was healing, she would most likely have pain for some time. Her injuries had been life threatening and once again, he was amazed that the young woman had beaten death. Silk continued to worry even though her sister's outward appearance seemed better. The grimace showed that she was still in pain.

Sigrid caught her staring and blushed like a guilty child. "I'm all right," Sigrid assured her once they were in the air. "Just a little sore."

Don cast a side look at her and again she held her head down, uncomfortable at their scrutiny.

When they had been in the air awhile, the pilot told them it was all right to move around the cabin and, as they did, Sigrid began to lay out her plans. The occupants of the cabin remained silent, taking in her revelations and decisions and when she was done, she and Ty adjourned to the back cabin for a much-needed reconciliation. Silk and Don watched them disappear. "I guess she is feeling better," Don mumbled and went back to his paper.

Martha had been so taken with the mountain scenery that she and George bought a house and eighty acres on Lookout Mountain. It was a few miles down the road from where they had brought Regina, and it was here that they had Sigrid's welcome home party.

Martha had been cooking and making Sigrid's favorite dishes. They limited the attendees to the inner sanctum due to Don's advice that the young woman needed to be in a quiet, secure environment. Regina had been in regular contact with Cameron, and knowing that she was home and okay, he decided to wait until Sigrid could come to Florida for their reunion.

Regina paced, going to the door every few minutes to look for the SUV carrying her family. Garrett, Keeran, Martha, and George were all anxious—Martha cooking, Keeran helping in the kitchen, and the men playing chess to occupy their time.

Hopping around like a rabbit, Regina froze when she heard the crackle of gravels on the driveway. Rushing to the door, she saw the black SUV pull up to the front porch. The doors opened slowly and she watched as Ty, Silk, and Don exited the vehicle.

Sigrid eased out and Regina could no longer contain herself and rushed out to the porch. When she laid eyes on the girl, she was excited but also had to mask her surprise at the young woman's appearance.

The short, spiky blonde hair was shocking enough, but she had lost at least twenty pounds and looked lean and weak. Although not obvious, Regina could tell that Sigrid was moving slower and a little gingerly, and she could feel the pain gnawing at the girl's body.

Unable to stand it any longer, Regina ran down the steps and met Sigrid at the foot and embraced her. Conscious of the still painful wounds, she held the woman, never wanting to release her hold.

Sigrid welcomed the embrace, wishing she could put all the love she felt into the action. Both women were weeping as Sigrid whispered in her ear, "I'm sorry. I had to do it this way."

Regina kissed her bruised cheek. "Dear heart, you're home now. That's all that matters."

Silk and Ty moved up behind them, and Don moved around them and made his way into the house. The women finally and hesitantly parted, and Regina took her hand and led the group into the house.

Keeran was waiting nearby, unsure of her approach. Sigrid released Regina's hand and held out her hand to her lover. As she approached, Sigrid smiled seeing how relaxed the young woman was with the other family members and how she had blossomed away from Terrence's influence.

They hugged, exchanged a kiss, and Keeran's face faltered at the pain she could feel within Sigrid. She received a reassuring smile and kiss on the cheek from the smaller woman. "We'll talk tonight," Sigrid whispered.

Martha, George, and Garrett were next, and after a lot of hugs and a few tears, they began celebrating.

Ty had told Sigrid that he would make himself scarce the first night so that she and Keeran could have some time together. She learned that he had spent a few days with Keeran before he flew to Switzerland and, despite his anger, had come to like her and could see what had drawn Sigrid to her. At that moment, she loved Ty even more than she thought possible and had shown him, as best her injuries had allowed.

Sigrid got a short tour of the house and then they adjourned to the dining room. Sigrid was thrilled to see the food Martha had cooked, and her stomach gave an encouraging growl. Terrence's people didn't eat food, their only nourishment coming from their victims. Although vampires didn't need regular food, they had an enjoyment of it, and Sigrid had missed real food and adored Martha's cooking. They sat around the table, watching Sigrid eat her fill and were encouraged by her appetite.

Sigrid wasn't up to discussing what had happened in the castle, so they kept the conversation light. Catching her up on their activities, talking about Tony, the cross-country bike ride, and Sigrid's new look.

As dinner wound down, Martha asked Sigrid if she was up to a full tour of the house. Knowing she was probably exhausted and in pain, she was not surprised when the young woman asked for a rain check.

Noticing that Sigrid was pale, Ty suggested that Keeran take her to their room to rest and catch up on her sleep. So after a round of hugs, kisses, and promises to make good on the rain checks, Keeran took her hand and led her through the house.

They exited the house and Keeran led her across the yard to a small guesthouse several yards away from the main house. It was a single-story, two-bedroom ranch style that had been added on as a house for guests by the previous owners.

The furnishings were old country modern, and Keeran gave her a brief tour, but she could see and sense how tired Sigrid was. When Martha had told Ty and her that this would be their guesthouse, they tried to make it more comfortable for Sigrid when she came home. The master bedroom had been refurnished to their taste.

A king-sized bed with cotton sheets was against the far wall, a table and dresser were on the opposite wall, and the door leading to the master bathroom with Jacuzzi was opposite the main door.

The curtains were drawn and Keeran turned on a small lamp to give them some light. When she turned back around, Sigrid was waiting with her arms open. The two women embraced, both needing and craving the contact.

There was no need for words, just the feel of one another's bodies, the loving touches and sounds. Keeran scooped Sigrid up and carried her to the bed, planting feathery kisses on her face.

"Let me start the Jacuzzi to help you relax and ease your pain."

Sigrid's eyes sparkled as she thought of soaking in a hot tub. "That sounds wonderful, sweetheart."

Keeran placed her delicately on the bed. "I'll be back in a few minutes. Do you need or want help undressing?"

"No," Sigrid assured her. "You get the tub started and I'll meet you in there."

Keeran started to leave but Sigrid held onto her hand. She hesitated unsure of how to say what was on her mind. "What is it, honey?" Keeran questioned.

"My . . . body . . .," Sigrid said softly, "my injuries . . . there are marks." She cleared her throat trying to find the words. "I have some ugly scars."

Keeran put a finger across her lips and she fell silent. "I love you scars and all. Do you not know that in these eyes you are perfect? My desire for you now is the same as before. It's taking all my self-restraint not to strip you down and make love to you for the next twenty-four hours."

"You haven't seen them," Sigrid said flatly.

Keeran tugged her hand, pulling her to her feet. "You come with me, while I start the tub. I'll help you get undressed, and I promise, nothing I see will change how I feel."

Sigrid nodded in agreement and let Keeran lead the way. The bathroom was almost as large as the bedroom and done in cool beiges and blues. The Jacuzzi was off to the far side of the room.

After starting the hot water in the tub, Keeran lit some candles and turned on some relaxing music and then returned to Sigrid who had begun undressing.

Keeran didn't rush or push, she let Sigrid take off the clothes at her own pace. She had expected to see a few marks but Sigrid was covered with healing wounds. She still had a bandage on her stomach and back. The bite marks and stab marks were healing, but there would be some scars. Keeran helped her slip out of her shirt and steadied her as she took off her jeans. Then came the time to take off the bandages. With a quick yank, Sigrid tore the one off her stomach and revealed a jagged seven inch tear that was healing but still an angry red and barely starting to scab. Sigrid held her head down as it was revealed, and Keeran said nothing, just turned her around and helped removed the other bandage that revealed a deep puncture mark.

She could tell Sigrid was embarrassed and ashamed as she stood before her completely revealed. She took a step forward and wrapped her arms around the small frame. "You're beautiful," she whispered in Sigrid's ear. "I see the woman I fell in love with. Yes, you have some scars but as long as I have you, scars mean nothing."

Sigrid let go of the pent-up tears she had been holding. A similar exchange had occurred between her and Ty on the plane. He had been just as understanding and loving with her, but there was a nurturing that Keeran had that Sigrid didn't realize she needed. She held tightly to Keeran and they swayed to the music, Sigrid regaining control after a few minutes. Keeran then helped her into the large deep tub.

The hot water enveloped her like a warm glove, and she sighed with pleasure. Keeran got a towel and washcloth from the cabinet and laid them on the table by the tub. "I'll wash your back if you like."

The familiar sparkle was in Sigrid's eye. "Only if you do it from in here with me."

A bright smile lit up her face and Keeran undressed, putting on a little show for her rapt audience. Her body shivered as she finished undressing not from the room temperature but from the look in Sigrid's eyes.

She stepped into the tub and settled across from Sigrid, rolling her eyes at the sensation of the jets and heat. "This is a great house," Sigrid said and moved beside her.

"Martha said it was ours, so we would have some privacy whenever we were here for a visit," Keeran supplied and draped her arm over Sigrid's shoulder.

Sigrid settled in against her. "Are you sure, the scars—"

"Don't exist in my eyes," Keeran promised.

"Can you just hold me for a while? There are some things I want to talk over with you, and I really need to feel you right now."

Keeran unexpectedly swept her up and set her down in her lap, then wrapped her arms around the woman and held her close. "This is OK?"

Sigrid lay her head on the woman's shoulder, "Oh I missed you, Keeran." She could tell that her words had made Keeran a little anxious so she sought to ease her fears.

"My feelings for you haven't changed. I love you, Keeran, and I still want to be with you for as long as you want to be with me. There are some things I'm going to change, and I want you and Ty both to be aware of them so you can make any decisions you need to."

Keeran kissed her forehead. "As long as I can be with you, that's my decision."

"And that makes me happy," Sigrid said, relieved. "I have some healing to do other than my body." Sigrid tapped her head with her finger. "I have to deal with what happened with Terrence, so I may need some alone time, but it is never because I want to be away from you."

Keeran pulled her even closer. "I understand, Sig. You've got to get your head on straight. I'm working on that myself."

Sigrid hadn't realized that Keeran was going through an adjustment time as well. "How are things with you? Any problems settling in?"

"No, not now." Keeran answered. "It's still taking some getting used too. This life is so different from what I've known for the last six years. Everyone has gone out of their way to make me feel comfortable, even Regina. I was terrified when I first saw her."

"You are part of our family now, and it will take some getting used to, but we'll always be here for you. I'll always be here for you."

Sigrid lifted her head and the two women kissed, softly at first and then more urgently. Sigrid slid around on Keeran's lap until she was straddling her. Their hands explored and touched, their tongues dancing as the steam surrounded them.

Keeran broke the kiss reluctantly. "Honey, are you sure you're up to this?"

Sigrid looked at her with heavily lidded eyes. "Just go slow and easy."

"Not a problem, my love."

Two days later, things around the house had settled down. Sigrid's healing had picked up some speed, and there was still a jubilance in the air. Martha, Regina, and Garrett stood outside the pasture fence and watched Sigrid ride and coach the horsing skills of Silk, Ty, and Keeran.

George had picked out two calm mares for Silk and Keeran, one black and the other cocoa brown. Both were a bit nervous and timid around the horses at first, but George and Sigrid had made sure they spent time with them before trying to ride them. After an hour of getting to know the horses and some coaching, the two women were astride the horses and trotted in small circles. Like Regina and Ty, Silk had grown to like Keeran too, and they were becoming fast friends.

Ty had taken to horses like a pro and was now galloping around on a large black quarter horse, occasionally laughing out loud, a rare action for the stoic young man.

Sigrid sat astride Thunder and observed their escapades with the expression of a mother watching her children, the same expression Regina was watching her with.

"She looks so different," Martha observed from the sidelines. "Not just her appearance either. It's something I can't put my finger on."

"She reminds me of my father," Regina replied, smiling at the warm memories of her youth. "He always seemed so at peace, so content. I swear I can see him in her face."

"Has she talked about what happened yet?"

Regina shook her head no. "We haven't really had any time alone."

Garrett took over the conversation. "Silk only filled us in on a few details. We know that he has definitely been destroyed and that the majority of his coven is dead. But other than that, they've been pretty tight lipped."

"How is she healing?"

When Regina didn't answer, Garrett continued. "There were some very serious injuries, but she is recovering. She will have some reminder scars of their fight, mentally and physically, but Don thinks she will be all right given time. She is a little bit undernourished, but he says that despite everything, she's in a remarkably good shape."

"She's remarkable, period." Martha grinned as Sigrid urged the mare to gallop across the pasture. Ty reined in his horse after her, but a few minutes later, it was apparent that his skills were no match for hers.

"She's an odd combination of her parents," Regina finally spoke up. "She has Val's compassion, grace, and tranquility, and Terrence's single-mindedness and ferocity when provoked. I hate to admit it, but the things that made me despise him, she's integrated quite well."

"She also has her aunt's love of family and determination," Martha added. "All in all, I think it's a nice combination."

Regina leaned against Martha, smiling and about to respond, when Sigrid reined in the horse to a stop in front of them. Her blue eyes twinkled as she leaned over and extended her hand to Regina. "Ride with me?"

Her voice was calm and soothing, yet so filled with power that Regina almost took a step back. The bullet injury had seemed to only make her voice softer, but nothing could hide the power that flowed there. Regina regained her composure and clasped Sigrid's offered hand.

Sigrid lifted her up with no effort, and once she was settled behind her, they rode off, disappearing deep into the pasture.

They rode around the land, galloping and trotting at various intervals. Sigrid took great delight in sharing the skills and talents of her and Thunder with Regina. Regina wrapped her arms around Sigrid's waist and leaned against her back, resting her head on the girl's shoulder, smiling.

They rode in silence, happy to be spending time together, words unnecessary at the moment. Both women knew the time had come, so as they crested the next hill, Sigrid brought the mare to a halt.

She helped Regina down, then dismounted herself. Regina strolled over to a large oak tree that covered the hill with shade and watched Sigrid. The young woman removed the saddle from the horse and with a loving pat on the rear, sent the mare off to the nearby pond for a well-deserved drink.

Sigrid was slightly out of breath as she joined Regina. "The only thing better than riding a motorcycle is riding that mare."

"It shows," Regina replied with a soft smile as she sat down on the soft grass under the tree's shade and leaned against the trunk.

Sigrid slowly sat down beside her. "I'm fine," she stated before Regina could even ask or comment.

"I'm sorry, honey. I don't mean to be a mother hen."

Sigrid cut her eyes at her. "Yes, you do." Then her own smile appeared. "And it's nothing to be sorry for. Without you, I'd probably be dead by now."

Regina snapped her head up in surprise. "How do you figure that? I always thought it was the other way around."

Sigrid snatched a blade of grass and toyed with it. "You trained me, nurtured and cared for me. Technically, I had three mothers, Valonia, Cheryl, and you. It was you that I learned the most from."

Regina's face radiated more surprise and confusion, so Sigrid scooted around to face her and continued. "You taught me what it is to be a part of a real family. You gave me my true identity, even when others begged you not to. You showed confidence in me and my skills and gave me opportunities to grow. More importantly, you gave me a purpose. Without all of that, I would have died in that castle."

Regina shrugged. "I may have helped with the foundation, but you did all the work and building . . ."

Sigrid reached out and touched her hand. "Don't you see, Reg? You were the cement that held me together."

A tear escaped her eye. "Honey, I think that's the nicest thing anyone has ever, in four hundred years, said to me."

Now Sigrid blushed and her head dropped slightly. Regina patted the hand on hers. "Everything you've done has brought you here. You know that now I am just filling in—"

Sigrid looked up and held her hand up to halt her aunt and interrupted. "Whoa! Don't even say it! I don't want that position."

"But you've earned it."

"That's not true, Reg. My powers may be unequaled and that allowed me to destroy Terrence, but it doesn't make me Queen. This is our life not a contest. You are our Queen! Our only Queen! Period."

Regina leaned her head against the tree and sighed. "I disagree, but I don't want to argue with you. Just answer me this. If and when the time comes, will you acknowledge it then?"

"I'm not the only heir."

"Silk," Regina nodded. "Yes and I'm still a little ticked off at you for not telling me the truth about her. I didn't find out the truth until the two of you were gone. What I can't believe is you kept it from me, that she was Terrence's daughter also, and even after you knew we were lovers."

Sigrid sheepishly sulked. "Sorry. What difference would it have made then anyway? The two of you were already a . . . couple."

Regina sighed, "Well I'm dealing with that. I love her and she loves me. It's just something we'll have to work out. In answer to your point, yes, she is an heir but you are the oldest and, no offense to her, the best qualified."

Sigrid smiled and shook her head. "I don't know about that, Reg. She stuck with me for over two months and I didn't even suspect it. That was not an easy feat, both skills wise and emotionally. Some of the things that happened had to be upsetting for her to watch. Hell, they were difficult for me and I was the one doing them. She was also the one that kept her cool in the castle. I may have had the power, but she had the restraint. With the proper training, she could really surprise you."

"You certainly did," she conceded. "But will she stay with me or go with you?"

With those words, Sigrid knew that Regina was aware of her plans to leave. That had been one of the main reasons for the ride, so they could discuss her decisions. Sigrid clasped her hands together. "She'll stay with you. We're sisters and we love each other, but not the way you two do. You're better for her than I am right now because I'm not sure what I want to do or where to go." Sigrid stopped and reached into the pocket of her denim jacket and pulled out something. She held out her hand to Regina and opened it, revealing her ring that she had taken back from Terrence. "I thought you might want this back."

Almost afraid it wasn't real, Regina slowly reached out and plucked it from Sigrid's palm. She stared at it, her eyes filling with tears. "Thank you, honey. I never thought I'd see this again."

Wanting to keep from discussing any of the events in the castle, Sigrid changed the subject. "I do know that I want to go to Florida in a week or so for a nice long vacation. I've got a lot of catching up to do with Cameron and his family. Then I think I'll join the circus, see the country, worry about mundane and ordinary things for a while."

Regina sniffled her tears back and slipped the ring on her remaining pinky finger. "That, you've earned. You have your own niece now and you must spend as much time with her as possible. What about Ty and Keeran?"

Even the sound of their names brought a grin to her face. "They'll stay with me. They were a bit uneasy around each other at first but are warming up to one another quickly. They're going out of their way to make it comfortable for me, and I'm the one that started the trouble. I guess that's why I'm the one that's uneasy now. How did you adjust?"

Regina leaned against Sigrid and nudged her arm. "Who says I did?" Both laughed and she pressed on. "It will take awhile, but it helps if you have patient and tolerant lovers and by the sound of it, you do. Garrett was wonderful after the initial shock wore off. But you must be careful and don't become jealous, or let them play you against one another. Later on, Ty or Keeran or both may take another lover or even leave you. Are you prepared for that?"

Sigrid snickered softly. "I guess I'll have to be. I only want them to be happy. I love both of them and sometimes I feel—"

"I know," Regina sympathized. "This is a partnership and all partnerships take work. I know and love Ty and despite my initial trepidation toward Keeran, I've grown to like her. When I first found out the situation, I was shocked and hurt. Ty and I had to know what kind of witch she was to turn your head so rapidly. I know I overstepped my bounds and I apologize."

Sigrid shifted slightly and leaned back, still facing Regina. "Did you not trust my judgment?"

Regina replied thoughtfully, "Yes and no. It was just . . . well . . . I know the effect of your first kill, and I was worried the bloodlust might have thrown you off just long enough to make a mistake. But when it comes down to it, the main reason was curiosity." Now Regina leaned forward, her face serious. "Keep in mind that the last time I saw this woman was when they attacked us and took me to Terrence. I had to see her and face her before you could coach her. I had to see for myself."

Sigrid nodded and Regina continued, "When I first walked into the Freemans and saw her, she was petrified. She reminded me of a deer caught in headlights and, for a split second, I wanted to leap on her and tear her throat open. She was frightened, but she didn't run and tried to keep it hidden. Only one thing was on her mind and it wasn't escape of defense, it was you. Her main thought at the time was that she would never be with you again and how much she loved you. That is what brought me out of my rage. To see the pure love in her heart for you, made me realize that maybe you were right. I calmed her down and explained that I only wanted to bring her home and help her adjust to her new life. Over the last few weeks, I have come to genuinely like and care about her."

Sigrid beamed proudly, her cheeks flushed that Regina had seen Keeran's love so openly and that, by her own reaction, confirmed the mutual feelings to her aunt.

"I would have acted on instinct," Regina continued. "I would have destroyed her without a second thought, but you went beyond your instinct. You saw something that none of us did or even considered seeing, that some of Terrence's people were not with him willingly."

"Has she told you how she came to be with him?"

"No," Regina admitted, "but I gather from our talks it wasn't pleasant. She's strong though and I admire her for that. As I think back now, I remember one small act of kindness that she did when they abducted me. Two of the men were hitting me and about to beat me senseless, and she stopped them by reminding them that Terrence wanted me unharmed. Then she came over and helped me up. At the time I thought she was doing her Master's bidding, but now I realize there was more to it than that. I was certain of it when she refrained from killing Silk."

"She's stronger than you think. She endured some of his torture as a mortal."

Regina patted her leg in support. "You made a wise choice with her, Sigrid. You trusted your heart."

Sigrid's face turned solemn. "That reminds me," she stated and reached over to the saddle nearby. She fumbled in the saddlebag for a moment, then came out with a necklace, clasped in her hand. Once free of the bag, she held it up, revealing a long gold chain with a gold-capped glass vial dangling from the end. She turned back to Regina and handed her the necklace.

Regina accepted it and closely inspected the contents of the vial. After a few minutes she looked up at Sigrid. "It's beautiful, sweetheart, but what is in the vial?"

"Despite our suspicions, he did have a heart."

For a moment she was puzzled by the statement and again gazed at the vial, shaking the powdery substance inside. Her eyes widened as the truth dawned on her. Sigrid remained silent, letting the information fully soak in for a minute.

"I know it's morbid," Sigrid replied as Regina stared at her. "But I wanted you to know that he is truly gone and will never hurt you again."

Regina tightened her grip on the necklace as tears began streaming down her face. Sigrid felt her own tears welling up. Gently she reached out and wiped away Regina's tears. "The only thing remaining of him, other than what's in that vial, are Silk and me. There are also a few of his coven that are still roaming around, but without him I don't think they're too much of a threat."

Regina pressed Sigrid's hand against her cheek and lightly kissed it. "Garrett is working on that now. I think Silk would be great at helping him coordinate. As for what's left of Terrence, the only thing I see is the one good legacy he ever created and that's my beautiful girls."

Regina sensed a turmoil within Sigrid and frowned. "What is it, honey? What's bothering you?"

Sigrid frowned as well and then spoke aloud the thought that had been gnawing at her for a week. "Yes, he was evil and had no redeeming qualities, but he was my father. I killed my father. I hated him and wanted him dead, but for some reason I can't get the thought out of my head that I killed my father."

Regina mulled over the admission and chose her words carefully. "I think that's normal. But keep telling yourself that he was evil and hurt a lot of good people. He tried to kill you and me and every other member of this family. He was the seed, but he was not your father."

"I just don't understand how I can feel this way."

Regina leaned forward, "Because you have a soul and a loving heart. You need to grieve and come to terms with everything you've been through. I have to do the same thing after what he did to me. We take it one day at a time and look at all the gifts we have. It will get better."

"He's been our main concern for so long. It's going to be awfully quiet around here from now on."

"Without you, it will be awfully lonely," Regina replied sullenly.

"Hey," Sigrid replied, "I'll still be around. We'll visit and if you ever need me, you know I'll be here. I just need some time to get my head on straight. I explained that to Ty and Keeran, and they understand that I may be out of sorts for a while but having them will help me."

"This conversation sounds awfully familiar," Regina said remembering their conversation in the airport several years before. "You have accomplished more in the last few years than I thought possible, and I am so very proud of you, honey."

Rising to her knees, Sigrid leaned over and hugged her tightly. "You don't know how much that means to me. I love you with all my heart, Regina. I always will."

They clung together, savoring the feeling and knowing that their relationship had taken another step in its progressing journey. The tortured child-woman that Regina had found was gone now. In her place was a confident, seasoned, loving woman with a heart full of warmth. Regina herself had relaxed, mellowed, and relearned what it was to have a true family, the change making her a better person and queen.

In their own way, each longed for those first few months of their relationship, even as tumultuous as they had been. Regina longed to return to the mother figure she had become for Sigrid when she first joined the family, and Sigrid wished she could recapture some of the lost innocence of her mortal life.

They parted from the embrace and slowly rose to their feet. Joining hands, Sigrid grabbed the saddle in her free hand, and they casually strolled over to the lake where Thunder drank her fill of the cool, clear water. When she saw them approach, she began to romp and play near the water's edge.

"When do you have to leave?" Regina questioned.

Sigrid clicked her tongue for Thunder who promptly came up to her. She slung the saddle over the horse's back and began tightening the straps. "I'd like to stay here for a couple more weeks. I like it here and there are still some details we're working on. If that's okay?"

Regina rolled her eyes. "Of course it is. You know this is your home too. Martha and George even gave you their guesthouse. I didn't even rate that."

The familiar side grin appeared, and Regina laughed. "You know that you have been accruing a salary all these years, so you and Ty have a nice little nest egg to start you out."

Sigrid stopped working on the saddle and stood up straight. "Excuse me?"

Regina nodded. "You and Ty have been getting weekly paychecks from the company. Before you . . . turned, you used your check for everyday living but as all this other mess started up, your paychecks were just being direct deposited into your account."

"Regina, you don't have to—"

"I didn't," she corrected. "You have been on the payroll and have earned those paychecks many times over. Of course I did deduct the vacation time when we went skiing."

Now it was Sigrid's turn to laugh. "I don't remember the account number or the bank."

"Garrett has all the information and will go over it with you and Ty whenever you want. I just wanted you to know that you weren't going to be starting out broke and looking for work. I want you to be able to enjoy your . . . retirement. You also have stocks in the company and some of the subsidiaries. This is your money, sweetheart. You earned it. I've just been socking it away for you until you were ready."

Sigrid was speechless. Her mind was going in a dozen different directions. She hadn't even thought about money or stocks. After she turned, those things were not important with all the turmoil with Terrence. Anything they needed had always been there. "Yeah, Ty and I need to have a sit down with Garrett. I'm just . . . surprised."

A gust of wind came over the hill, and both women and the horse could sense the coming storm. "Let's head back," Regina suggested.

Sigrid nodded and gave the saddle a final tug to secure it, then she climbed onto the horse, holding out her hand and pulling Regina on behind her.

There was no need for any further words. Their feelings and plans were known, and they were as prepared as they could be for the paths that would lead them into the unknown future.

The End